Stalked by Death

Riley Malloy Mystery, Book 4

Judith A. Barrett

Wobbly Creek LLC

Dedication

Stalked by Death is dedicated to white trucks and to farm dogs and barn cats.

Stalked by Death

Riley Malloy Mystery, Book 4

Published in the United States of America by Wobbly Creek, LLC

2022 Georgia

wobblycreek.com

Cover by Wobbly Creek, LLC

ISBN 978-1-953-87025-4 eBook

ISBN 978-1-953870-26-1 Paperback

Previously. . .

RILEY

My name is Riley Malloy. I'm a vet tech, and I understand animals, which must be why people call me a "dog whisperer." Toby is my five-year-old black and brown German Shepherd-Labrador Retriever mix. He was abandoned at the veterinarian clinic where I worked. After the clinic closed, Toby and I moved to Barton, a small Georgia town where I spent my summers as a young girl with my Grandma. I found a new job at a fantastic animal hospital with wonderful people.

Ben Carter is a lanky deputy with greenish hazel eyes and the love of my life. Not only is he a stellar law enforcement officer, but Ben has extensive knowledge about caring for animals from the summers he worked with his uncle, a veterinarian, but more about that later.

After the finance manager of the local distribution company suddenly disappeared, a friend gave me a copy of the manager's partially completed Western novel. The novel featured a main character who discovered evidence of fraud. When I read the story, I understood how the storyline matched the circumstances at the local company.

The mastermind of the fraud at the distribution center was a cold-blooded criminal who realized I could expose him and tried to kill me on three separate occasions; fortunately, he was unsuccessful.

BEN

Riley is brilliant, has a remarkable talent for communicating with animals, has fiery red hair, and is the prettiest girl I've ever seen. Still, I'll never adjust to her being the target of murderers.

Both of us applied and were accepted by the University of Georgia veterinary program. Still, I realized that wasn't where my heart was, so I applied to the Georgia Bureau of Investigation and was accepted. The GBI training center isn't that far from UGA; Riley will become a veterinarian, and I'll be a GBI field agent.

Riley let me save the best for last: we were married in Barton and had two wedding receptions: one in Barton with our friends and a second one at my folks' house with family. Some people might say we rushed into marriage too quickly, but I doubt they'd say it in front of Riley.

Chapter One

"What do you think Mom and Dad will say when we tell them I'm not going to veterinary school after all?" Riley asked as Ben drove to his parents' home.

"I have a more important question. Do you think your crime-fighting days are over?" Ben peered at her over his sunglasses.

"Absolutely. I'm a vet tech, so what would I be? A bounty hunter? No, that's not right. A hapless victim?" Riley giggled.

Ben chuckled. "My damsel in distress, but don't tell Mom because she'll find you a long, flowing princess gown for you to wear in your castle tower, which Dad will build you in the barn loft."

Riley laughed, then feigned a growl, "You changed the subject."

"Pretty slick of me, wasn't it? They love you, Riley; they'll be briefly disappointed because they know what a successful veterinarian you would have been, but they want what's best for you, and so do I." Ben smiled as he glanced at Riley. "You already knew that."

"I did intellectually, but I like hearing it."

When Riley's phone rang, she raised her eyebrows. "It's our real estate agent, Helen."

After Riley answered, Helen said, "Let me know if this is a bad time to chat. I have a few interesting tidbits for you."

"Now is fine; Ben and I are on the way to his folks' house."

"Ben asked me to find you all a place that was close to Macon; I'm not having much luck because everything is so expensive, but that's not my interesting news. One of your mother's old friends called me. She wanted to know whether we had heard anything from your mother or your Aunt Millie. I don't remember her, and I don't even think she told me her name, but I thought that was curious coming out of the blue like that. She said she had some of your mother's jewelry and wanted to send it to Millie if I had her address or yours since she can't seem to find your mother."

Riley snorted. *It's not likely that I'll ever see Mother again. She left Dad and me years ago.*

"I don't remember any of Mother's friends; it's been a long time since I've seen or heard from her."

"That was what I thought, but this friend was adamant that she had to get in touch with you, your mother, or Millie. I told her to send the jewelry to me, and I'd make sure you got it."

Riley frowned. *I'm not interested in anything that belongs to Mother.*

"Thank you," Riley said.

Helen chuckled. "That's not what your mother's friend said. She told me she knew other people that would be nice enough to help her out, then she hung up on me. I thought my offer was perfectly reasonable. She didn't even give me a chance to explain that Millie travels and you're in the process of moving to Macon. Tell Ben I'll keep looking."

After Riley hung up, Ben asked, "What did Helen have to say?"

"Not much; I think she just wanted to check up on us."

"She hovers almost as much as Mom does." Ben smiled.

Riley returned his smile. "Grandma used to worry about me, too."

Ben exhaled. "Babe, I might not have realized how completely you were burned out by the four solid years of college coursework you did while you were working before we met, but it was brutal to watch you suffer through that first class and then slug it out with the second class to get your prerequisites for the veterinary college behind you. The material wasn't hard for you, but you were miserable every minute you worked on an online project or tackled the next section of assigned reading. When you told me you couldn't continue after you completed your second class this week, I was relieved because you've been so down and not yourself all summer."

"I had hoped it didn't show."

Ben grinned. "You saved me from playing my husband card and demanding that you withdraw from the veterinary college."

Riley giggled. "I can only imagine what your version of demanding I do anything would be; I'm so sorry I missed it."

Riley leaned back and gazed out the window at the passing fields of corn. "The corn's already tasseled here."

"The rain we've had this past week helped." Ben smiled. "Isn't it nice to have a normal conversation without anyone shooting at you?"

When they turned at the Carters' driveway, Toby woke and panted in excitement as Ben parked close to the house.

While the Labrador retriever puppies, Duffy and Finn, scrambled to the truck, Ben opened the door for Toby. Then, Toby and the puppies raced to the field behind the house and back as Riley climbed out of the truck. After Ben lifted out the duffel bag with their clothes, they all headed to the house with Toby in the lead.

Jake met them at the back door with a scowl and his arms crossed.

"Your mom is thrilled you're coming to visit for the weekend. What's wrong?"

Riley's eyes widened when Ben laughed. "Riley, he's fishing for a confession. You first."

"Your son just threw me under the bus again," Riley growled as she pushed her way past Ben into the house.

"I noticed she still didn't answer my question," Jake said as he followed Ben inside.

"She's good," Ben said.

Riley put her nose in the air as the two tall men strode past her, then she rushed to hug Melissa, who was a few inches taller than she was but curvy like Riley. Melissa's halo of curly gray hair in her short, dark brown hair sparkled when she was in the sunlight.

"Are they badgering you, honey?" Melissa asked.

"Don't answer until I get back," Ben called out as he carried their duffel bag upstairs. "If you hold out, you'll be bribed with cookies."

"I thought we could have a lovely chat after dinner with wine, beer, snacks, and cookies in front of a roaring fire in the fireplace," Riley said.

"Roaring fire? It's the middle of July; are you suffering from heatstroke? I'll get you a cool cloth to put on your forehead," Melissa said.

"I think I went a little overboard," Riley said.

Melissa snorted. "You can have wine or beer and snacks in this overheated kitchen, and we'll have that little chat; you can have cookies as soon as you tell me what's going on."

Ben raced down the stairs and joined them. "Did I miss anything?"

"Mom's holding out on the cookies," Riley said.

Jake opened two beers and handed one to Ben before he poured two glasses of wine for Melissa and Riley, then pulled out their snack from the refrigerator. He set a platter of cheese, crackers, and smoked venison summer sausage on the table along with a jar of hot mustard and a spoon. "Your mom isn't all that into intrigue; have you noticed?"

Melissa gave everyone a small plate and a napkin before returning to the stove and stirring the simmering chili pot. "I'm listening."

Riley tasted a tiny nibble of summer sausage and then created a sandwich by putting it between two squares of cheese before she sipped her wine.

"I finished my last online class and realized I can't continue."

"Riley spent the past four years studying for her bachelor's degree while working full-time before she moved to Barton," Ben added.

Melissa joined them at the table and peered at Riley. "You're totally burned out as far as any more classes are concerned, aren't you?"

Tears slipped down Riley's cheeks. "I really am, but it's more than that; I don't want to run a business by myself or be less mobile as far as going where Ben goes, but Doc Julie Rae, Ms. Lindsey, and their friends went to great lengths for me to take away any obstacles when Ben and I were going to attend together; I hate to let them down."

"What do you want to do?" Jake asked.

"I want Ben to complete his training, and I want to work as a vet tech," Riley said.

"Ben?" Jake asked.

"I want what makes Riley happy."

"I raised him right, didn't I?" Jake winked at Melissa.

She rolled her eyes. "Yes, honey, you did. So, how do we make that work?"

"Doc Julie Rae has excellent contacts. She could find me a vet tech position in Macon, but I'm not sure I'm prepared mentally to work somewhere for four months then move on quite yet." Riley sighed. "I sound like a diva, don't I?"

"Your Uncle Seth is drowning in work and is desperate for a good vet tech or a willing eight-year-old," Jake said.

Melissa tapped his arm. "Jake!"

He shrugged. "Blame Seth: that's what he told me."

Ben grinned. "I started going on farm visits with Uncle Seth when I was eight, but how would that work? The training center is two hours from here."

"What do you think, Riley?" Melissa asked.

"We need to understand the logistics before I talk to Uncle Seth," she said. "I talked to him at the wedding reception; I think he'd be amenable, but we need to iron out the details."

"What about farm visits? That's where Seth needs the help," Jake said.

Riley smiled. "Uncle Seth knows I have very limited farm experience; he told me he enjoys teaching, and I love learning, although it might not look like it right now, but using my skills to learn is different."

Jake rose and carried his beer to the back door. "I've got some work to do in the barn; are you coming, Ben?"

Riley side-glanced at Melissa, who smiled.

Ben frowned and then glanced at Riley, who nodded.

"Sure, Dad." Ben carried his beer to the door; the two men left.

"Ben's going to get a Dad talk, isn't he?" Riley asked.

"Sure is. Princess is out there; maybe we can get the details from her later." Melissa's eyes twinkled as she smiled. "While I'm thinking of it, Mugsy called me yesterday. She wants you to be sure to drop by to see her at the coffee shop when you go into town. Give her a call; we could probably drop by in the morning if you like."

When Riley called, Mugsy answered, "Big Mug Coffee Shop; it's about time you called, Short-stuff. Cookie and I thought you'd gone all high-falutin' and had forgotten about us."

Riley giggled. "Want some company tomorrow morning? Mom and I thought we'd come to see you."

"Cookie and I found an envelope that may or may not be important. I'll have a fresh pot of coffee waiting for you." Mugsy hung up.

"She'll have a fresh pot for us," Riley said.

"I need to do a little grocery shopping too, so if you and Mugsy want to catch up on news, you can have all the time you need," Melissa said.

When they strolled into the barn, Ben said, "I know you're in here, Princess; we're planning on having a private discussion, so you're on notice that you can't tell Riley or Mom any details."

Princess leaped down from the hayloft and rubbed against Ben's legs.

Jake stared at Princess as she flipped her tail before she left the barn. "I keep forgetting how much Princess understands you." Jake took a drink of beer and then sat on his bench. "I had an idea, but I didn't want to bring it up until you and I had a chance to talk it over."

"I might know what it is. Riley could stay with you and Mom while she works with Uncle Seth. She'd love to have more hands-on experience with large animals; she told me she was the only vet tech who would go with Dr. Truman on the occasional farm visits outside of the town of Pomeroy, and I know how much she loved going to Lindsey's farm with Doc Julie Rae. The problem is mine, though; Macon is two hours from here, and I need to be available from early morning until late at night for four months until I complete the certification. I'd have weekends off, but I don't want to see Riley only on weekends."

"So, what are you thinking?" Jake asked.

"I'm not excited about Riley being alone late at night, so even if we find a place that's closer to Macon, I'd be leaving before daylight and getting home long after dark." Ben sighed. "I was worried about that when Helen and I talked about finding a short-term rental for us that would allow a big dog, although Helen told me Toby was the least of her worries; she was more concerned about finding an affordable short-term rental that wasn't more than an hour away. She's been working on it since the beginning of summer but hasn't found anything yet."

"Does Riley know this?"

Ben shook his head. "I didn't want to add to her stress."

"So, what do you think?"

"Riley spent twelve weeks in agony so she could complete those courses. She was on the computer when I woke up and stayed on until she went to work, which was after I did. She cooked, and we ate supper. She was on her computer when I went to bed, so I didn't know how many hours of sleep she got each night. Seems like with a strong model like that, I could certainly spend sixteen weeks learning and enjoying what I was doing."

As the two men strolled to the house, Jake asked, "What do you think Riley's going to say?"

Ben snorted. "Something unpredictable."

Riley smiled when Ben and Jake came inside. "Toby, Duffy, Finn, and I were on our way out to tell you that supper will be on the table after you wash your hands."

Riley opened the door, and the three dogs rushed out. Princess sat near the stove and meowed.

"Princess said to hurry up." Melissa chuckled.

"Traitor," Ben muttered as he washed his hands at the sink.

Princess licked her paw and preened, and Riley giggled as she poured four glasses of sweet tea.

After Ben dried his hands, he stepped behind Riley as she set the glasses on the table. He wrapped his arms around her and whispered, "Princess makes up stories."

Riley turned around and held his face with her hands. "You poor thing."

Ben grumbled, "Don't you dare say, 'Bless your heart.'"

Riley kissed his grumpy face on the mouth, and then she and Melissa laughed.

"What's going on?" Jake asked as he sat at the table.

Ben scowled. "Ask Princess."

"Ouch," Jake said, and Ben nodded.

After they ate, Melissa said, "I made a cheesecake with peach topping. Who's game?"

Ben cleared the table while Jake sliced the cheesecake, and Riley put the dessert plates and forks in front of Jake.

While they ate, Ben asked, "What did Princess say?"

"She told me that you came up with a solution that did not involve a bath for her." Riley placed her last forkful of cheesecake into her mouth. "This is so good, Mom."

Princess meowed as she leaped onto Ben's lap, and he stroked her back. "Well played, Princess; you got me good."

After Ben explained his idea, Riley said, "It's not the perfect solution, but it's doable for sixteen weeks. We'll need to use the downstairs bedroom so Mom won't hear you sneaking up the stairs to my bedroom on Friday nights. What do you think, Mom?"

"I think you should take the upstairs bedroom, so I can wake up Jake to tell him Ben is trying to sneak into your bedroom."

Jake rose and put his plate in the sink. "You two are a mess. Ben, you're on your own from here." He chuckled as he went outside.

"What do we need to do?" Riley asked.

"I'll need to sign up for the onsite lodging and dining, and I can do that online if we're sure this is what we want to do. Dad probably is calling Uncle Seth right now," Ben said.

"I'll find out if Seth is coming here for lunch or supper tomorrow; we'll all help you with your interview, Riley." Melissa snickered as she wiggled her eyebrows, and Riley rolled her eyes.

After Ben and Riley went upstairs to unpack, Riley asked, "Are you sure about this?"

Ben sat on the bed, and Riley sat next to him. "It's really the best solution, babe. If you were living an hour or so from the training center, I'd worry about you during the day because you and Toby were alone, and I'd want to rush home at the end of the day to be home to eat supper with you, but that would rarely be possible, from what the guys say. I think you'll love working with Uncle Seth, and you and Toby are comfortable with Mom and Dad, which takes a huge burden off my mind. What about you?"

"I'm looking forward to farm visits; I'm not sure I could tolerate not working. If I were somewhere else and was working at a vet clinic, either the staff would be nothing like Doc Julie Rae's team, which would be horrible, or they would be as good, and I'd be miserable again because I'd have to leave them after four months."

"I don't suppose I could convince you to avoid anyone who might shoot at you." Ben hugged Riley.

"You say that like I had a choice." Riley rolled her eyes.

On their way downstairs, Ben said, "We can move next weekend; I'll get on the computer now to sign up for housing and food. Want to watch me?"

Riley snickered. "As entertaining as that sounds, I've put in my computer time for this month, so I'll see what Mom's doing."

When Riley went into the kitchen, Melissa wore her sunhat. "I'm going to check the garden and maybe weed or pick what's ready. Do you want to go along?" Melissa asked. "I have work gloves for both of us."

Riley removed her ballcap from her backpack, and the two of them strolled together to the garden.

"Everything settled?" Melissa asked.

"Yes, and next week is my last week at Doc Julie Rae's, so we'll move out of Helen's house next Saturday. My goal for today and tomorrow is to practice relaxing because I'm not sure I remember how anymore."

"A long, soaking bath will help," Melissa said as they pulled weeds, "especially after you finish a row or two of weeding."

When Ben and Jake roared past them in the farm utility vehicle with Duffy and Finn trotting along behind them, Ben waved.

"Where are they going?" Riley asked as she returned the wave, and Toby joined them in the garden.

"They'll check the trail for any downed trees. A clear trail has become important to Jake now that he has the puppies to go with him; they love it, and so does he."

After they finished weeding the bean patch, Melissa rose and picked up her basket. "We have enough green beans for supper tomorrow night. I'd planned a chicken and rice casserole, and a generous serving of fresh green beans makes a perfect side dish."

On their way to the house, Melissa said, "We need to get you a sunhat like mine to work in the garden, and you might want to consider wearing it when you go to farms with Seth. Your face is beet red. I'm not sure if you're overheated, sunburned, or both. You'll want sunscreen and bug spray too."

"Grandma and I always slathered on sunscreen when I visited her because she said we had pale Irish skin that had never seen anything like the Georgia sun, and even if we were just checking her deer stand, we always took water; I'd forgotten about that."

"We'll start a list," Melissa said as they went inside. "I expect Jake and Ben won't be coming in until after dark, so I'm going to put up my feet and read."

"Sounds like a perfect time for my long, soaking bath." Riley smiled.

After her bath, Riley shampooed her hair then dressed in soft pants and a T-shirt under a long-sleeved flannel shirt. When she and Toby went into the living room to join Melissa, Ben and Jake came inside with Duffy and Finn bounding in and dashing straight to the water bowl.

"Honey, we're home," Jake called out.

Melissa smiled. "He loves saying that. I'm sure they'll have all kinds of stories. I'll pull out the snacks, and we can sit at the kitchen table."

"I'm glad I hadn't gotten comfortable on the sofa yet because I'm not sure I could have gotten back up."

Melissa chuckled. "It is comfortable, isn't it?"

When they went into the kitchen, Jake had already pulled out two beers and handed one to Ben.

"It's not that often my son isn't on duty," Jake said as he lifted his beer to Ben.

Ben nodded. "All it took was two large trees across the trail to adjust to an actual weekend off."

"We've got snacks and more cheesecake if you want it," Melissa said as she put a large bowl of tortilla chips and a bowl of salsa on the table. She pulled out small bowls, spoons, and small plates from the cupboard while Riley put a stack of napkins in the middle of the table.

"I'd like a sliver of that cheesecake too," Jake said.

"So would I," Ben added.

Melissa winked at Riley as she plated two slices of cheesecake. After she set down the plates, Melissa asked, "What would you like to drink, Riley? Beer, wine, sweet tea, or hot tea?"

"I'd like a cup of hot tea," Riley said.

"I think I will too. What about cheesecake?"

"Not quite as big as their slivers." Riley snickered.

While Jake told Melissa and Riley about the biggest tree he'd ever seen in his life that had fallen across the trail, his phone rang.

"That's strange." Jake rose and stepped away from the table as he answered.

He listened to the caller then said, "Just a second, and I'll ask her. Riley, Seth has a new mama cow that is struggling to deliver her first calf. He wants to know if you'd like to ride along."

Riley glanced at Ben, who grinned. "I sure would. How much time do I have to be ready?" she asked.

"Ten minutes," Jake said.

Riley dashed upstairs, and Ben followed her.

"Dress in layers, babe," he said as she put on her jeans.

"Do I take my concealed piece?"

"Always," he growled.

Riley slipped into her oldest pair of boots then put on a long-sleeved shirt under her flannel shirt.

"Pull back your hair into a ponytail and wear your ballcap, but you may need to turn it around backward," Ben said. "Ask Mom for some exam gloves that are closer to your size; stick a pair in your pocket and add the extras and some water to your backpack in case it's a long night. I'll check your flashlight to see if it needs fresh batteries, and my headlamp is around here somewhere; I'll ask Mom."

Riley smiled as he dashed out of their room and down the stairs. *Why do I feel like he's sending me off to my first day of school? I wonder if he's going to tell me not to eat the crayons.*

After Riley put her hair into a ponytail, she hurried downstairs.

"Here are several pairs of my gloves, and Ben went to the barn to look for his headlamp after he checked your backpack," Melissa said. "He is very excited for you."

Ben returned. "I found the headlamp, but the mice got to the strap ages ago; we'll get you one later."

When Seth stopped at the end of the driveway, he lowered his window. "Let's go catch us a calf, Riley."

Riley grinned as she hurried to the truck with Ben and Toby alongside her. Ben kissed her before she climbed in.

As he drove up the driveway, Seth glanced in the rearview mirror. "Your two fellas are still watching. I've got a feeling that both of them wish they were going along."

Riley smiled. "Toby usually does. The only farm he and I have visited is a horse farm, but he went with me and loved seeing the horses."

"We'll have to take him along on some of our visits to see how he likes the farm animals around here. I very rarely go into the office; I'm on the road from Monday through Friday and make emergency visits only on Saturdays. I don't see any patients or even answer my phone on Sunday unless it's Jake or Ben. I'll add you to my exception list. I made that rule long ago, and it saved me from burning out. The farm isn't that far away from here, which made me think of you in the first place."

As Seth drove on the dark country road, Riley glanced in the side mirror. *Is that a car following us?*

After Seth turned onto a dirt road, Riley turned to glance at the road, and the car continued past the dirt road.

Seth said, "This is a first-time mother, so she's scared, and our farmer is relatively new at farming. He has adjusted to the challenging work and is eager to learn, but this is his first newborn, too, so he's just as scared as the new mama. Not to be too dramatic, but we'll be walking into a barn with fear dripping from the walls."

"So, our first task is to calm everybody down," Riley said.

"You got it; I'm letting you take the lead on that." Seth smiled.

Riley returned his smile. "It's my specialty."

Seth parked near the barn. "That's what I hear. Let's settle 'em down, so I can tell what's wrong with that reluctant newborn that has probably picked up on his mama's fear."

Seth removed his medical bag and a butcher apron from the backseat of his truck.

As they strolled toward the anxiously awaiting farmer, Seth said, "I brought a second apron with me for you, but we'll have to get you some of your own; you'd trip over one of mine if you put it on."

The farmer's eyes were as wide as the heifer's eyes. *I'm not surprised.* Riley began humming a tune, and the farmer walked alongside her as she approached the heifer.

"She doesn't look so scared," he whispered. "You must be Doc Seth's new assistant; my wife heard you had a talent with animals."

"Tell me how she's been acting," Doc Seth said.

"She was pretty restless all day yesterday, and my wife or I checked her every hour, including overnight, because I was getting nervous. My wife's napping now; we're taking turns. Should I wake her?"

"Let me check this little lady first. How has she been today?" Doc Seth asked.

"Early this morning, she was arching her back and raising her tail, then not long after lunch, my wife told me she saw a gush of brownish-yellow fluid, just like the document from our class at the ag school described."

While the farmer described the heifer's day in great detail, Riley asked, "How are you doing, sweet girl?"

The heifer switched her tail and moaned.

"Let me take a peek." Riley went into the stall and checked the heifer, then calmly interrupted the farmer. "Excuse me, Doc. You may want to check her."

Doc Seth had pulled on his exam gloves while the farmer talked. As Doc Seth moved to examine the young cow, the farmer asked, "Is everything okay?"

"Just a little work to do here; the calf has an anterior presentation, which we like, but one leg is in flexion; I'll give the calf a little push to bring that leg in line with the other one. Come watch, Riley."

"I gotta get my wife." The farmer ran to his house.

Riley moved close to Doc Seth.

"Calf moved when I touched its hoof," Doc Seth murmured.

Riley nodded. *Calf is alive; good news.*

The farmer and his wife rushed into the barn, and Riley strolled to meet them.

"Doc Seth will get that one leg in line like it should be." Riley walked back to her position next to Doc. He glanced at her and smiled.

"I brought our folder from the ag school; here's a diagram of the anterior presentation with one leg in flexion." The wife handed the page to her husband, who read it and nodded. The two of them strolled to the heifer at the same pace that Riley used when she joined Doc Seth.

After Doc Seth assisted the delivery, Riley checked the calf's breathing and airway.

"Breathing rate is normal, and the airway is clear," Riley said.

Doc Seth smiled at the farmer. "Can you take it from here?"

"Oh my goodness, what a sweet calf; we certainly can," the wife said.

When they were back on the road, Doc Seth said, "You were a huge help to me; I'm sorry I didn't believe how useful your skills could be and was shocked at how quickly the farmer and the cow calmed down when you walked into the barn. Did the heifer talk to you when you asked her how she was doing?"

"She told me something wasn't right, so that's why I asked you to check her. Is there something I should have been able to see with an external observation?"

"Maybe some very subtle changes, which is why I thought it was curious that you checked then asked me to check because I wondered what you saw." Seth smiled. "You didn't want to tell me what the cow said in front of the farmer. He might have gotten all huffy and told me that's why he called: something wasn't right. What did you think about the farm visit?"

"I've got a lot to learn."

"Yes, you do, and so do I. When can we start?"

"Next week is my last week with Doc Julie, then Ben and I will move to Mom and Dad's on Saturday." Riley bit her lip. "Ben will be in Macon in class Monday through Friday and will come home Friday evening, then leave again Sunday evening every week. I don't want to be working weekends when he's home because that's the only time I'll be able to see him."

Doc Seth nodded. "Jake mentioned something like that to me; what if I don't call you on weekends unless I really need help, then you bring Ben and Toby too. Actually, bring Toby on any night calls. I don't know the new people all that well; I wouldn't mind having Toby with us to watch our backs."

"I'd enjoy having Ben along because he could coach me, but I'll check first to be sure he agrees, and Toby's definitely the right dog for the job." Riley smiled then texted Ben, "Coming home."

When they reached Jake's farm, Ben and Toby were waiting at the driveway; Seth stopped but left the engine running.

"Aren't you coming in?" Riley asked.

"I've had my excitement for the weekend; there's a beer in the fridge with my name on it. I'll give you a call next Saturday to let you know what time our first appointment on Monday will be, but I may be here tomorrow if my sister-in-law has already planned for me to eat with the family. I'm smart enough to never turn down one of Melissa's homecooked meals."

Seth pulled out a business card from his console. "My cell number's on this card. Send me a text, and I'll have your number. I'm excited about what lies ahead because we'll be a great team."

Ben opened the passenger's door, and Toby yipped.

"See you tomorrow." Riley climbed out of the truck, and Seth headed up the driveway.

Chapter Two

Ben took her backpack and put his arm around her as they strolled to the house with Toby at Riley's side. "Mom and Dad can't wait to hear about your farm visit, and Toby and I are excited to see you back."

"Come relax with us in the living room," Melissa called out when they went into the house.

"Riley, would you like a glass of wine or a cup of tea? Mom put out a wine glass for you, just in case." Ben smiled.

"I'd like to change back into my comfy clothes, then wine sounds good."

"I'll meet you in the living room with your glass." Ben kissed her before she dashed upstairs.

After Riley walked into the living room, Ben grinned as she sat next to him on the sofa. "I told Mom it wouldn't take you long to put on your relaxing pants." He handed her the glass of wine. "Tell us about your farm visit."

"One of the farmer's young cows was having a hard delivery because the calf had one leg tucked under its body. Doc Seth repositioned the leg; then the calf was born. Doc Seth doesn't answer his phone on Sundays, except for you all. I sent him a text before I changed clothes so he'd have my number too. He takes only emergencies on Saturdays, and Ben and Toby can go with us if he needs me. If we have an emergency at night during the week, he wants Toby to go with us."

Melissa narrowed her eyes. "Jake, make sure Seth knows I'm planning for him to join us for supper tomorrow night."

"Sheriff Murray called and told me he'd heard I'd be attending the GBI training. He's coming by tomorrow, so we can talk," Ben said.

"It'll be good to see Forrest; we haven't seen him since we had that young bear roaming in town with her cub, and he asked me to speak to the local community groups about feeding bears and to show them examples of secured garbage cans," Jake said.

"I knew the folks in town didn't realize they were teaching the young mama bear and her baby to mooch for food from people, but it still made my blood boil," Melissa said.

"What happened to the bear and her cub?" Riley asked.

"The Wildlife agents caught her early enough in her career of scrounging and relocated her to a safer place for her and her cub. The City Council passed an ordinance that made it illegal to feed wildlife or to leave garbage in an outdoor can that wasn't properly secured from wildlife that could knock over the can or remove the lid," Jake said. "The sheriff advised them to use the raccoons that were knocking over garbage cans at night, waking entire neighborhoods of dogs and babies, as their major selling point. It wasn't long until the raccoons left town for easier pickings."

"It was a brilliant marketing campaign, wasn't it?" Melissa smiled.

"Do you still have the examples you showed to the groups? I'd love to see them," Riley said.

"Do we still have the handouts, hon?" Jake asked.

"Sure do; I filed them away. I'll give you a copy in the morning, Riley; I'm off duty." Melissa sipped the rest of her wine and yawned.

Riley yawned. "I guess I am too."

"If it were only true," Ben mumbled as he took the two empty wine glasses to the kitchen.

When Ben returned, he put his arm around Riley, and they went upstairs.

After they were in bed, Riley kissed Ben and then flopped back on her pillow. "It was scary and wonderful: I loved it."

"I knew you would."

When Riley woke, Ben was still sleeping soundly. She slipped out of bed and picked up her soft pants and a clean shirt on her way out. After she tamed her wild bedhead, she tiptoed downstairs to a dim light in the kitchen. Melissa was reading a book as she sat at the table with a small lamp on the counter for light.

Melissa smiled. "Coffee's fresh; what got you up so early? Not even the dogs have stirred yet."

Riley poured herself a cup and refilled Melissa's cup. "I'm used to getting up early. I always got up early to get in an hour or two of study for my online classes before I went to work in Pomeroy, and after I graduated, I was obsessed with trying to beat Doc Julie Rae into work. What about you?"

Melissa chuckled. "I'm a combination; I'm obsessed with reading before Jake rolls out of bed."

"Doc Seth told me I needed a butcher's apron; I didn't understand why until he maneuvered the calf before it could be delivered."

"I have several that were Ben's when he was twelve or so. You can try them on to see if they would work for you. They're stained because his version of cleaning his room was to pile everything in his closet. My nose told me when it was time to have him drag everything out so I could find the most offensive clothing. According to my friends, Ben did not invent that particular cleaning strategy."

Riley giggled. "I used to hide my stash of snacks, books, and my favorite flashlight in my closet."

Melissa smiled. "I'll get you a nice box with a lid for your stash here."

Riley's eyes welled up. "Grandma did that. She called it our private, magical box and said if anyone besides the two of us touched it, the magic would burn their fingers. I believed her and even kept my diary in it for a while. I haven't thought about that in years; I wonder where it is. Ben and I can go to the cabin next week so I can look for it."

"Every time you tell me a story about your grandma, I love her even more."

"Who are we talking about?" Jake came into the kitchen and pulled out a cup from the cupboard. "Did you leave me any coffee? Ben's not already outside, is he? Why are the dogs still sleeping? Did they already go out and are taking their nap? Why did you let me sleep so late?"

Melissa chuckled as she poured the last of the first pot into a cup for Jake. "You need coffee, honey."

While Melissa started a fresh pot, Toby trotted to Riley and whined. She opened Duffy's and Finn's crates and picked up her flashlight before she took the three of them outside. While Duffy and Finn romped, Riley and Toby went into the barn.

Riley's eyes widened at the three mice lined up in the middle of the barn. "You had a good night, didn't you, Princess? Well done; Dad will be happy. Ben, too; did you hear about his favorite headlamp?"

Princess purred from the rafters, then leapt down to join Riley in admiring her overnight kill.

After Princess told Riley the story of how she tricked all three mice and caught them, Riley smiled. "I'll have to remember that."

When Riley headed toward the house, Toby yipped, and Duffy and Finn rushed to join Toby and Riley.

Ben met them before they were too far from the barn; he had a cup of steaming coffee in his hand. "I must have been more tired than I realized. I would have panicked when I woke up, and you were gone, but Mom and Dad were arguing about how many chickens were too many, and I was relieved because it meant you hadn't disappeared."

Riley giggled. "Do you think we'll have chickens soon?"

"No telling; it's sometimes hard to interpret whether Dad's annoying Mom or negotiating. If we do, Toby will have to train Duffy and Finn not to chase them."

Toby yipped, and Riley nodded. "That's doable. Let's go to the barn. Princess has something to show you."

Ben wrapped his arm around Riley's shoulders, and she put her arm around his waist as they strolled to the barn together.

Princess stood in the barn doorway and yowled as they neared the barn.

"She's singing her song of the triumphant hunter for you, Ben," Riley said.

When they went inside the barn, Ben said, "Wow, Princess. This was definitely a successful hunting night, wasn't it? Well done."

Princess purred as she rubbed Ben's legs, then jumped onto the gate of a stall and sat with her chest out as she surveyed her bounty of three mice.

Toby yipped, and Riley said, "The boys are ready for breakfast; what about you, Princess?"

Princess dashed to the back door with Toby, Duffy, and Finn following her. Before Ben and Riley reached the house, Jake opened the back door, and Princess and the boys rushed past him.

Jake smiled. "Melissa has your food ready."

When Riley and Ben went inside, Melissa said, "Our breakfast is ready too."

While she removed the egg casserole from the oven, Riley set the plates of bacon and biscuits on the table, Ben refilled coffee, and Jake pulled out the strawberry jam and butter from the refrigerator.

Before he joined the family at the table, Ben opened the back door, and Princess, Duffy, and Finn hurried out while Toby stayed near the stove.

"Toby's my kitchen guard." Melissa split open her biscuit and put butter inside it. "I think he hopes I'll drop a morsel of bacon or whatever I'm cooking on the floor."

"What's the plan for today?" Jake asked.

"We'll leave after supper for Barton," Ben said. "Until then, I'm available to help with any projects."

"I've been thinking about repairing the chicken coop," Jake said.

"That sounds like a good project," Ben said. "Are you thinking about getting chickens?"

Ben winked at Riley; she shoved a large piece of biscuit with jam into her mouth so she wouldn't smile.

"You just never know; it's always good to have options, isn't it, honey?" Jake smiled at Melissa, who returned his smile.

"Toby, could you train Duffy and Finn not to bother the chickens?" Melissa asked.

Toby growled.

Melissa said, "Thanks; I know it won't take you long at all."

"Do you have enough lumber?" Ben asked.

"I think so, but we'll have a better idea after we see what needs to be repaired. Can you check it with us to ensure we're not missing anything, Riley? You'll be seeing it with new eyes, and we lost all of our last flock to a raccoon that got into the coop one night."

"Good point, Dad. I think I would have focused on repairing the coop and not necessarily thinking about security," Ben said.

After they cleared the table and loaded the dishwasher, Jake asked, "Are you Ready to survey the coop?"

"I'm coming too," Melissa said, "I want to learn more about security for the chickens. I think they'll be fine during the day because the dogs are out, but I was worried about what could happen after we bring the puppies in at night."

While Jake took notes about the lumber they would need to repair the coop, Riley checked the fencing and the wire around the run.

After Ben and Jake finished their list, Ben asked, "What do we need to do, babe?"

"The chicken wire on the windows and around the run needs to be replaced with hardware cloth. Chicken wire keeps in chickens but doesn't keep out predators." She pointed to a section of the fencing around the run. "See how this has been pulled apart? This must be how the raccoon got in. If you cover the run, including the top, with hardware cloth, you can leave the coop door open and not worry about closing them up at night or letting them out in the morning. You may want to extend the run so that they'll have plenty of space and won't have to free range if you have somewhere to go."

"That's a timesaver," Melissa said. "Can all that be done in one day?"

"I doubt it," Ben said, "but we'll do what we can. I'll be back next weekend, and we can finish up."

When Ben and Jake headed to the barn to check the scrap lumber, Riley and Melissa went inside.

"I'll find those butcher aprons and give them a good prewash treatment," Melissa said. "They'll never look like new, but you won't look like it's your first time out into the field either."

"Thank you; if you don't have anything else you'd like me to do, I'll start our laundry and then pack."

Riley smiled when she went into their bedroom to collect their dirty clothes. *Ben made the bed; I wonder if we have a last-one-out rule?*

After she started the washer, Toby whined to go out; when they stepped outside, the sheriff was parking his cruiser. He smiled and strode to her. "Nice to see you again, Riley. Sam Dunn from Barton gave me a call yesterday, and we had a long talk. I'd heard he and your dad were old friends, but I didn't realize how close they were. Where's Ben?"

"He and Dad were in the barn earlier. They could be at the chicken coop if they aren't there." Riley squinted at the barn. "They must be in the barn because Duffy and Finn are guarding the door."

The sheriff followed her gaze. "I see those rascals; they've really grown, haven't they?" Sheriff Murray strode to the barn, and Duffy and Finn yipped their greeting.

"Let's walk to the road, Toby; I feel like stretching my legs."

Toby trotted ahead of her, and Riley picked up her walking pace. When she reached the road, she was out of breath. "This is awful, Toby; the driveway isn't even as long as the lane to the cabin. I've become really out of shape."

After her breathing rate slowed, Riley slowly jogged back to the house and muttered, "Here goes nothing."

When she reached the house, she said, "I've gotten out of shape; I need to work on my stamina."

Toby moaned.

"Yes, you too. I know Duffy and Finn run a lot, but I've also noticed you don't run with them very much anymore."

Riley and Toby went inside. Riley refreshed the dog bowl of water for Toby and then poured herself a large glass of iced tea. While Riley sipped her tea, Melissa came into the kitchen from her bedroom.

"You certainly worked up a sweat. What did you and Toby do?"

"We went up the driveway to the road and back. We're both out of shape, so we'll be doing that regularly."

Toby moaned, and Melissa chuckled. "Sorry, Toby, but I appreciate that you're taking one for the team."

"Sheriff Murray's here to see Ben. I sent him to the barn, so he must have found him."

"Forrest always told us that Ben wouldn't be a deputy for long because he was so talented. Of course, Seth always hoped Ben would become a veterinarian, but he may have realized he really wanted an outstanding vet tech like you."

"Thanks, Mom." Riley smiled and then downed her iced tea. "I'll move our clothes from the washer to the dryer. Should I put the butcher aprons in the washer?"

"I want to run the aprons on the sanitizing cycle, but I'm going to let them soak a little longer before I put them into the washer. I almost forgot to tell you that I heard your phone ding, but I didn't know where it was."

"I must have left it upstairs. I'll check it right after I get the dryer going."

Toby followed Riley up the stairs.

Riley picked up her phone and read the text from Claire, "Call me."

Riley sat on her soft chair, gazed out the window at the swaying treetops, and called.

"I hope you weren't busy," Claire said. "Someone called the office yesterday and said you had an insurance refund, but they sent it to your apartment in Pomeroy, and it was returned as undeliverable. They asked for your address, so I gave them the office address. Do you know about a refund? I thought maybe it might have been a scam, but it sounded legitimate."

"I don't know anything about an insurance refund, but I guess we'll see if it's delivered."

"That's what I thought too; by the way, Thad is driving me crazy. He wanted me to call Doc Julie Rae because he's certain she knows what you and Ben are going to do, but I told him he didn't want her to think he was worried or anything. We have three possibilities, and he wanted me to ask if any of these are right. Please don't answer me so I can tell him you wouldn't tell me."

Riley giggled. "I'd love to hear what my options are."

"First option: you're staying here and divorcing Ben. Just to let you know, Thad didn't like that one."

"Oh my gosh; I'm not sure Ben would go for it either."

Claire tittered. "Imagine that. I tossed in that one to gain your confidence in how bad our choices are, so if you accidentally cough or something, I'll know which option was right."

"Okay, so you've got my full confidence because I can count on you to make me laugh."

"Second one: Ben changed his mind and is going to veterinary school with you. Third one: You changed your mind, and you applied for the GBI and are going to school with Ben. I didn't hear you cough; I'll bet it's the third one."

"You all are remarkably astute," Riley said.

"Good, so now that we've got that out of the way and you trust me completely with your secrets, are you bringing in cinnamon rolls?"

"Oh no, I didn't even think about cinnamon rolls. We're going home tonight after supper. I suppose I could make them after I get home."

"I have a better idea: email me the recipe, and I'll make them for tomorrow, and now my secret's out: Thad wanted me to ask for your recipe, but that would have been dull."

Riley laughed. "You are so funny; I'll send it to you as soon as we get off the phone."

"Okay, thanks; bye." Claire giggled as she hung up.

Riley smiled as she turned on her laptop to send Claire the recipe. *Claire will always be my friend.*

When Riley went downstairs, Melissa was in the kitchen. "I'm making soup for lunch in the slow cooker in case Forrest decides to stay. If he doesn't, I'll freeze what we don't eat; then we'll have soup whenever we want soup and a sandwich. You were longer than I expected. Is anything wrong?"

Riley smiled. "Claire misses our pranks, and so do I, but we're usually co-conspirators, so this one definitely caught me off guard."

Riley told Melissa what Thad supposedly said and their theories.

Melissa laughed. "You certainly can't tell Ben the details about her call."

"Not at all. He'd go into a tizzy and worry about how I could possibly think that was funny. What she really called about was she wanted my cinnamon roll recipe."

"I don't think it was just the recipe: she had a chance to talk to you and make you laugh," Melissa said.

"You're probably right."

"Ready to visit Mugsy? The soup can simmer in the slow cooker," Melissa said.

When Riley and Melissa went into the coffee shop, Mugsy's black and white cocker spaniel, Cookie, met them at the door. Mugsy pushed back her black hair with streaks of silver with her forearm and then poured coffee into three cups.

Cookie yipped, and Riley laughed.

"What did Cookie tell you?" Mugsy wore her white apron with dancing coffee cups on the bib.

"I think she gave away your secret. Who is Ryan?"

"Ryan is back in town?" Melissa's eyes were wide. "Is he still single?"

Mugsy glared at Cookie, and Cookie grinned.

"I believe he may be, but that's irrelevant and not why I wanted to see you, Riley." Mugsy handed Riley a white, letter-sized envelope with 'RC' printed in block letters. "It wasn't sealed, but I didn't open it because I don't butt into other people's business, unlike some certain canines." Mugsy narrowed her eyes at Cookie.

Riley opened the envelope. "It's empty."

Melissa peered over Riley's shoulder. "No, a small piece of folded paper is in there."

Riley pulled out the slip of paper, scanned it, crumpled it, and stuffed it into her front jeans pocket. "A grocery list." She folded the envelope before she stuck it into her back pocket. "Where'd you find the envelope?"

"I found it under one of the counter stools a couple of days ago when I swept the floor before I closed up."

Riley and Cookie examined the floor around the counter stools. "We don't see anything else."

"RC doesn't necessarily mean Riley Carter," Melissa said.

"You're right, Melissa; I jumped to the most obvious conclusion, given the usual happenings when it comes to Riley," Mugsy said. "I appreciate that you came in this morning, though; I've neglected my paperwork because I couldn't stop worrying about that envelope."

"We have some shopping to do; maybe you can get your paperwork taken care of before your late-morning customers show up," Melissa said.

"I'd appreciate it. Are you going to be around a while, Riley?"

"I may; Ben and I are still discussing our options."

"Come see me when you can." Mugsy hugged Riley and Melissa before they left.

On the way to the grocery store, Melissa asked, "It was more than a grocery list, wasn't it? What did it say? All I caught before you wadded it up were the words 'not' and 'here.'"

Riley exhaled. "All it said was, 'You're not wanted here.' I didn't want to worry Mugsy."

"Well, Ben's self-proclaimed fiancée isn't around, so I can't blame Pamela Suzanne, as much as I'd love to. Did you notice Mugsy didn't say anything more about Ryan?"

"Sure did. Who is Ryan?"

"Ryan had some rough years when he was in high school; he was a heavy drinker and was arrested at least twice after starting a brawl at the diner and was kicked out of school more than once. He didn't have many friends, but Mugsy thought the world of him. I always thought he must have had a kind heart that only Mugsy could see. After high school, he quit drinking and then went into the military. After being honorably discharged, which surprised everyone, he found his calling when he attended a trade school and left Carson to work with his brother in Columbus, Georgia. His brother owns an RV repair shop, and Ryan is a very talented diesel mechanic. I'll have to find out if Ryan is just visiting or if he's returning to open his own shop," Melissa said.

When they returned from shopping, Melissa put away the groceries while Riley removed the clothes from the dryer and took them upstairs to pack.

When Ben and Jake came into the house for lunch, Jake inhaled. "Smells good in here. I told the sheriff he should stay for lunch, but he said he's got a date with a hot fishing pole."

While they ate, Melissa asked, "Did the sheriff drop by on a social visit?"

Jake downed his coffee and refilled his cup before he answered. "No, he and Ben talked. Sam, the sheriff from Barton, told Forrest to make sure Riley had his cell number and wanted to make sure Forrest wouldn't be surprised by Riley's skill with animals or her talent to take down bad guys. Forrest must have been checking Sam's story with Ben."

"Is he okay now?" Melissa asked.

"I think he's skeptical, but at least he's willing to take Sheriff Dunn's word that Riley has unusual talents that Sheriff Murray shouldn't underestimate or discount," Ben said.

"We're all packed, except I left out clean clothes for you, hon, so you can shower later. How is the chicken coop project going?" Riley asked.

"I repaired the coop and am working on extending the run. Ben has the hard part: he's doing all the wire work," Jake said.

"I'll have the wire finished by the end of the day except for the wire for the extended run," Ben said.

"We can certainly wait until the coop is ready before we get any chickens. Just think, honey, we'll have more time to discuss how many chickens we should get to start." Melissa smirked as she side-glanced Jake.

Jake rose. "Work's not getting done while we sit here talking about it. Let's go, Ben."

"I'll be out after the dishes are out of the way; I can do the lower wire work," Riley said.

"That would be a tremendous help. I could finish up installing the wire on the top of the existing run," Ben said.

By the end of the day, the coop was secure from predators and ready for chickens.

"We couldn't have finished without your help, Riley," Jake said.

"Looks good, doesn't it? I loved your idea to bury the four-foot field wire to protect the run, babe. I hadn't thought about the diggers, but foxes, in particular, are known for burrowing to get to chickens," Ben said.

"It's not really bear-proof, but Duffy and Finn would have a fit if a bear came around," Riley said.

"I'm ready for a shower," Jake said. "We can look at it again next weekend to see if we missed anything else."

As Ben and Riley climbed the stairs to their room, Riley said, "You take the first shower; you don't take as much time as I do, and I won't have to rush."

After their showers, they went downstairs; Jake joined them as they strolled to the kitchen.

Melissa said, "Y'all smell good; I may have to bow to the peer pressure and take a shower myself."

Jake wrapped his arms around her and inhaled as she stood at the stove. "You smell like roasted chicken. You've outdone all of us."

Melissa giggled. "You just earned yourself an extra helping of mashed potatoes and gravy, you smooth talker, you."

"What can I do to help?" he asked.

"After Seth's here, you can mash the potatoes while I make the gravy."

Ben opened the back door, and Toby led Duffy, Finn, and Princess into the house while Riley dished up their food.

"We were working on the chicken coop; how much time will you need with Duffy and Finn to be sure they know to guard the chickens?" Riley asked, and Toby yipped.

When Princess meowed and swatted her paw towards the puppies, Riley laughed.

"What's the verdict?" Melissa asked.

"Toby said he needs a week, and Princess said she could knock sense into their thick heads in a day. I paraphrased."

Ben smiled. "I think you could, Princess."

"I think I could give Toby a week, especially if he reminds Duffy and Finn that Princess has permission to step in if they slip," Melissa said.

Princess purred.

"Thank you, Princess," Melissa said.

Duffy and Finn scrambled to the door, and Toby followed them.

"I think my brother might be here." Jake opened the door, and the dogs rushed outside while Princess took her time.

"I want to show him the chicken coop before it gets dark," Jake said, and Ben went out with him.

"Shall I set the table?" Riley asked.

"If you don't mind going outside, you can tell Jake the potatoes are ready to be mashed. Jake is convinced no one mashes potatoes like he does. After you talk them into coming inside, we'll have plenty of time to set the table."

After Riley joined the men at the coop, Seth said, "I like the extra security you added, Riley. Where did you learn all that?"

"Grandma had chickens; bears and one pesky fox, in particular, were her biggest worry. I helped bury the field fence as a horizontal defense from digging around the coop when I was six. When a neighbor who had used chicken wire around his coop to save money came to inspect Grandma's new chicken coop that we'd built, he told Grandma he was an expert and knew that chicken wire was for chickens, and she'd spent way too much money. Grandma told him he was an idiot and wouldn't have chickens for long, and that was when I knew she was my hero."

Seth chuckled. "I knew you had a decent upbringing. That's a real teaching opportunity for some of our less experienced folks."

Riley smiled. "Dad, before I forget, Mom sent me out to tell you it's time to mash the potatoes."

Jake said, "We'll talk more later; she's a great cook, but she'd be the first to admit mashing potatoes just isn't her favorite task."

Seth followed Jake, and Ben put his arm around Riley as they walked to the house. "I love every one of your stories, but especially the ones about your grandma."

"I'm glad that you don't mind listening because she was so important in my life."

When they went inside, Seth said, "I understand you're leaving for Barton after we eat, and Melissa said you deserve a proper interview. I need to know who has the most experience in attending interviews because it isn't me."

"It's not me," Ben said, "because Sheriff Dunn didn't really interview me; he interrogated me because he was so protective of Riley."

Melissa sighed. "I tried, Riley. I didn't want you to feel like Seth is hiring you just because you're family."

"What's wrong with being family?" Seth asked. "Some of my best friends are family."

"You know what I mean." Melissa scowled as she stirred the gravy. "You have to know how highly qualified she is; she'll be a great asset."

"How is she qualified?" Seth asked as he winked at Riley.

"She's an experienced vet tech with a rare gift," Melissa said.

"Can we eat?" Seth asked. "I'll tell you about her first farm visit with me while we eat."

"Your bribes worked, hon." Jake smiled. "Potatoes are ready."

Ben and Riley filled the glasses with ice and sweet tea before everyone sat at the table.

"We're eating family style; just pass the serving bowls around," Melissa said.

Chapter Three

While they ate, Seth said, "Riley and I visited a farm that a nice family from the city bought a year ago from the longtime owners who wanted to retire. I suspect we'll be visiting their farm regularly for a while, but they are smart and willing to learn. Do you agree, Riley?"

She smiled and nodded.

"The farmer and his wife had a heifer who was having difficulty delivering her first calf and were smart enough to call me. When we walked into the barn, the farmer and the heifer were terrified, then the most astounding thing happened. Riley hummed a quiet tune and moved slowly as she headed toward the young cow, and the farmer and his heifer instantly relaxed. Riley moved into position to check the heifer then almost immediately told me to check too. When I examined the heifer, I was surprised to find the calf was in a position that required manual adjustment before I could deliver it; only a physical exam could have found the problem. It was amazing, but even more amazing is that the heifer told Riley that something was wrong; I didn't know that until Riley told me later. My people doctor friends tell me they always listen to what their patients have to say. Now, I understand why. Jake mentioned to me that Riley communicates with animals, but there's nothing more vivid to drive home a point than personal experience, is there?"

Melissa rolled her eyes. "So, why didn't you say so earlier?"

"And miss an invitation to sit down to one of your homecooked meals?" Seth widened his eyes in feigned surprise, and Melissa giggled.

Riley and Ben cleared the table while Melissa sliced the fresh strawberry pie.

"We're planning to leave after the dishes are done," Ben said.

"You can leave whenever you like, Ben, because the dishes are mine," Seth said. "I always pay for my dinner, so I'll be invited back."

"We're packed, so I guess we'll hit the road after we finish dessert," Ben said. "We'll probably be back Friday for supper, Mom."

"What about a thermos of coffee?" Melissa asked.

"It's an hour away, hon; they'll be okay." Jake patted her hand.

"I packed your lunches for tomorrow and have two casseroles that might last you until Thursday. I'll load the cooler for you," Melissa said.

While Jake cleared the table, Melissa filled the cooler with drinks and food, and Seth loaded the dishwasher. Ben brought down the duffel bag and Riley's laptop from upstairs; while he carried them to his truck, Riley took Toby, Duffy, and Finn outside   for   a break.

After Ben loaded the cooler into the bed of the truck, he joined Riley as she, Princess, and the dogs headed toward the house.

"I told Princess we'd see her on Friday," Riley said. "She's coming inside for her supper."

"I'll feed you, Princess." Jake reached down and stroked her as she rubbed against his legs and purred.

After they said their goodbyes, Riley climbed into the truck while Ben opened the door for Toby, then hopped in and started the engine.

"I've evidently been replaced by an older man." Ben headed up the driveway to the road.

Riley giggled when Toby yipped and then grinned.

Ben turned toward the highway. "You're right, Toby, women are fickle."

"He didn't say that," Riley said.

"He thought it." Ben smiled when Riley rolled her eyes.

"We got away quicker than I expected." Riley glanced toward the west. "We'll catch the last bit of sunset at home, but I'd like to go to the cabin before we leave at the end of the week."

"What do you think about staying at the cabin after we get the house packed? Your grandma's cabin feels like home; I suspect it always will." Ben accelerated onto the highway and set the cruise control. "I don't expect to be assigned to stand by duty, but if I am, we'll stay in town."

Ben pulled into their driveway and parked. After he opened the truck's back door, Toby leaped out and raced to the porch.

"I'll text Mom that we're here."

"Smart move." Ben carried the duffel bag, his backpack, and Riley's laptop to the porch and unlocked the front door. He lugged the duffel bag to their bedroom, then carried in the cooler and put away the food. Riley took in their backpacks and her laptop and put away their clothes.

"It's a good thing we're only going to be gone for five days; this poor refrigerator is busting at the seams as it is," Ben said. "You have a hankerin' for a big ole glass of sweet tea and a snack, ma'am?" Ben winked.

"You've just swept me off my feet with that fancy talk, sexy cowboy, but we don't have any snacks."

"The chuckwagon musta had extra because the head cook stuck in snacks for us, including some of that stinky cheese we like so much and hardtack that the city folks call crackers."

"I'll bet that cost you a fortune."

"Sure did; I had to give up my single room for one with a bunkmate."

"Rough life." Riley snickered.

Ben filled two glasses with ice, and Riley poured their sweet tea; Toby followed them as they took their tea to the back porch and clinked their glasses together.

"To us," Ben said.

Riley pointed as the dark night crept in, and tiny lights randomly flashed in the backyard. "Look! Lightning bugs."

Ben snorted. "When I was in the second grade, a new teacher corrected one of my friends in class and told him the actual name was firefly. In all my seven-year-old wisdom, I explained that lightning bugs were winged beetles, not flies, and the light was not a fire: it was a chemical reaction in their butts that caused the glow."

"You said, 'butts'?"

"Sure did, and my buddies in class appreciated it as much as you're probably imagining, and the teacher sent me to the principal's office. The principal called Mom to come to school, and when she arrived, she told me to wait in the hallway before we went home. After I graduated from high school, Dad told me that she scolded the principal and told him the school system needed to educate their new teachers on entomology."

Riley chuckled. "Was that the teacher's first and only year to teach?"

"Not at all; it turned out she was made of iron. After fifteen years of teaching, she retired from the school system last year, and I went to her retirement party. She's an author and writes under a pen name, but everybody knows since nobody is supposed to know what it is. She began writing during her second year of teaching; her novels are very chilling, psychological thrillers."

"I wonder if she began writing for stress relief." Riley smacked a mosquito.

"Probably." Ben picked up their glasses from the porch. "Time to go inside."

Toby hurried to join them as they went into the house.

Riley said, "I told Mom about a box I had in my closet at my Dad's house when I was a kid where I kept my stash of snacks, books, and a flashlight; then I remembered that Grandma and I had what Grandma called our 'private magical box.' She said if anyone besides us touched it, their fingers would burn. I put my favorite items in it, including my diary. I'm sure it's still at the cabin; I would like to look for it before we leave."

"Want to go now? It's not too late, and we can have our snack when we get back," Ben said.

"I'd actually like that because I'm not sure when we could work in another trip before Friday if we're going to pack to move."

When Ben parked at the cabin, he opened Toby's door, and Toby leaped out, dashed down the lane, and disappeared in the brush.

"Is he planning to clear the entire property of rabbits?" Ben asked as Riley climbed out of the truck.

"Either that or claim success when he gets tired," Riley said.

When they stepped onto the porch, Toby bounded around the corner. After Ben unlocked and opened the door, Toby dashed inside; Ben followed him and filled Toby's water bowl.

Toby drank his fill and then grinned as he flopped onto the kitchen floor and stretched out.

"I'm happy to be here too," Riley said.

"Where do we look first?" Ben asked.

"I'm certain it's on the top shelf of the bedroom closet in the far corner near the back. That corner is not lit, so a dark box would be in plain sight if you know something is there; otherwise, it would be invisible."

Ben peered at the top shelf. "I can't see in that corner; the shelf is too deep."

He went to the kitchen, returned with a kitchen chair, and stood on it. "It's too dark; I still can't see anything."

Riley handed him a flashlight, and he turned it on. "I see a box. Do I need gloves so I don't burn my fingers?"

"You count as me; it won't burn you."

Ben smiled as he reached back into the corner and then pulled out a large boot box that had been sprayed black with streaks of gray. "It blended in. Your grandma painted the back wall black and gray, but the darker wall wasn't noticeable because it's a dark corner."

"Grandma always said the best place to hide anything was where it would be overlooked. It might seem like she put in a lot of extra work, but she never did anything halfway." Riley opened the box and smiled. "The box is full. My diary's not here because I took it out years ago to write in it. Let's go back to the house; I can look through the box later."

After Ben parked in their driveway, he asked, "What do you think about a beer with our snack? Neither one of us is on duty."

"Sounds great to me, but we don't have any beer."

"Beer was one of those extras from the sous chef. Dad told me he slipped a six-pack into the box."

"I didn't know chuck wagons had sous chefs," Riley said.

"It's one of those best-kept secrets of the Old West," Ben said, and Riley giggled.

Riley poured crackers into a bowl and put the cheese and a cheese knife on a plate while Ben opened their beer and picked up two napkins, then they carried their treats to the living room.

While they sipped their beer and enjoyed the cheese and crackers, Riley asked, "Do you know what you'll be doing this week?"

Ben smiled. "Sheriff hired two new deputies and assigned me to oversee their training next week. My goal is to give them a good foundation to be successful; the sheriff and I talked about the basics and what I wish I'd been taught when I first started. We decided on shooting and tactical basics, map basics with a general knowledge of the roads, businesses, and local landmarks, traffic duty safety, reports, and community relations with a school visit on Friday morning. Sheriff will take over Friday afternoon for a debriefing before he tells them what to expect their second week."

"That sounds like a full week and a great start for them." Riley yawned. "Sorry, I'm tired, not bored."

Ben kissed her before she rose to go to bed, and then he took her empty bottle and picked up the plate and bowl. "I'll be there in a few minutes."

After Ben and Toby came into the bedroom, Ben turned off the light, climbed into bed, and wrapped Riley in a snuggly hug.

Riley listened to the tree frogs' loud, incessant songs of impending rain. *I don't remember there being so many papers in our private, magical box. What could Grandma have put into the box? Should I get up now and look? Is there an updated will?*

Ben's and Toby's soft, slow breathing broke into her swirling thoughts, and she relaxed and closed her eyes.

Riley woke to the slight creak of the back door. *She patted the empty space next to her and then hurried to the kitchen. Ben was already up.*

"You are just in time, babe." Ben smiled. "Coffee's ready. I don't have to rush into work quite so early this week, so I'm your breakfast chef. We're having shredded pork breakfast burritos, courtesy of Mom."

He poured her a cup of coffee. "I'll shower while you enjoy your first cup of the day; when you shower, I'll follow Mom's detailed instructions on putting together the burrito. She's worried that we'll starve this week, you know."

Riley kissed him good morning, picked up her cup, then carried her steaming coffee outside to sit on the porch while Toby roamed the backyard. She rocked as she waited for her hot coffee to cool. *I'm not sure it will cool; the air is already warmer than usual and sticky with humidity.*

When Riley and Toby went inside, Riley fed Toby and refilled her almost full cup.

"Your turn." Ben strode into the kitchen in his uniform.

Riley smiled. "You clean up right sexy, as usual, cowboy."

He blushed as she set her cup on the table and headed toward the shower.

"I'll warm up your coffee for you while you're getting dressed," he said.

"Don't you dare; it will be exactly the right temperature when breakfast is ready," Riley said.

"I don't understand why anyone would want to drink tepid coffee," he muttered.

"I heard that," she called out. "Don't touch my coffee."

After Riley dressed, she returned to the kitchen and giggled at the sight of a towel on top of her cup.

Ben snatched away the towel. "Pretend you didn't see that. Our breakfast burritos are ready to come out of the oven."

While they ate, Riley asked, "Was the towel supposed to keep the coffee warm or block the offending cooling coffee from your view?"

"Both." Ben took a big bite of burrito.

After they had eaten, Ben said, "Mom made our sandwiches for today."

"I'm not surprised. I'll take care of the breakfast dishes this week if you'd like to go in earlier than you'd originally planned; I have a few minutes before I usually leave for the clinic," Riley said.

"I appreciate it; I don't feel right wandering in like I have office hours. I'd rather go in early." Ben kissed her, grabbed his lunch, and left.

Riley loaded the dishwasher and picked up her lunch. "Ready to go to work, Toby?"

Toby bounded to the door, and they left.

When they went into the breakroom, Doc Julie Rae smiled. "I knew you'd be here early; coffee's ready."

Doc Julie Rae poured two cups of coffee while Riley put her lunch in the refrigerator.

"Doc, I need to talk to you," Riley said as she sat at the table. Doc Julie Rae peered at her and then joined her at the table.

"I've been miserable all summer. I was burned out after I spent four years working and going to classes to complete my bachelor's degree, and I struggled to get through the two classes this summer. I'm not ready to go back to school."

Doc Julie Rae sipped her coffee. "I noticed and was worried. Have you withdrawn?"

"I did, with Ben's blessing. I love being a vet tech and am more mobile to go wherever Ben is assigned."

"I'm sad, but I'm not. You'd be a fantastic veterinarian, but you're a fantastic vet tech and a wonderful person. I'll talk to Lindsey and your support team; I know they'll understand, too. Do you want to stay here while Ben's in training?"

Riley smiled. "Ben's uncle is a veterinarian, and his practice is farm visits. I'll work with him and stay with Ben's parents; Doc Seth doesn't mind that I'll be with him only four months."

"Wow, farm visits. Now, I'm jealous." Doc Julie Rae smiled.

"I'd like to tell the rest of the team before the day begins."

"Makes sense to me; I'll pull everyone together for a meeting. I have news for you: Doc Thad and I have reviewed vet tech candidate applications for the past few weeks; last week, he discussed our top five with Pia, Zach, and Claire. Our team selected three candidates for phone interviews, and I talked to them by phone while Doc Thad checked their references. We have two excellent vet tech candidates coming in today. The third one decided she didn't want to relocate to a 'small, sleepy town,' which were her words." Doc Julie Rae chuckled.

She opened a file and handed copies of two applications to Riley. Riley read the applications and Doc Thad's reference notes. "Whitney has two years of experience at a large clinic in Augusta; Norman is a new graduate, and his grades are great. I'm impressed."

"Whitney's family has a farm outside of Albany, Georgia, so she'll be much closer to her family; Norm's family is in Valdosta, and he'd like to be close, but not too close to them. When they get here, Pia will give them a quick tour and discuss how we operate, then we'd like each one of them to work at least one patient with you, or better yet, two if there's time. While you're working with one candidate, Claire will review our computer system with the second. Charlie told me our finances can easily handle two vet techs, and I would still like to hire a third veterinarian, so we can hire one or both depending on how well we think they will work with our team."

"Do I tell them I understand animals?" Riley asked.

"Doc Thad and I talked about it and decided you should only if they ask; we're interested to see how quickly they catch on. Our plan to end their interviews is for Claire and Doc Thad to take Whitney to lunch; Zach and I will take Norm. That leaves you and Pia here by yourselves, so text Doc Thad because Claire can certainly answer any questions Whitney might have."

"I like how you have involved the entire team in the process, but I didn't expect to be included," Riley said.

Doc Julie Rae poured herself a second cup of coffee and smiled. "Charlie wanted me to be sure to tell you that the budget always has room for you any time you want to come back to work with us."

"That is so nice to hear. You never know, right?"

Doc Julie Rae left for her office; Claire and Doc Thad arrived before Riley and Toby left the breakroom to check the day's schedule and voicemail messages from the weekend.

"I've brought cinnamon rolls for your first day of your last week here until you come back," Claire said.

"I suppose Doc Julie Rae's in her office; I'll take her one." Doc Thad put cinnamon rolls on two paper towels, poured his coffee cup, and left.

"I'll ask her later if you gave her one, so don't get sneaky, Thad," Claire said.

Riley selected a cinnamon roll. "I read the applications and references. I think Doc Julie Rae and Doc Thad found excellent candidates."

"So do I." Claire picked up a cinnamon roll and headed to her desk.

Riley poured a cup of coffee for Claire and then carried it to the receptionist's desk.

Claire waved her thanks as she listened to the messages and took notes.

"Let's check the exam rooms, Toby," Riley said.

Toby lay down at Claire's feet and peered up at Riley.

Riley shook her head and hurried to check the exam rooms. *No surprise: everything is fine.*

Riley raised her eyebrows when her phone rang. *Why is our landlord calling so early?*

"I hope I'm not calling too early," Helen said. "I wanted to catch you first thing. I'm excited for you and Ben and your new life together. You're welcome to take anything from that little house you think you could use. The bed is yours; are you interested in the sofa, the soft chair, and the dining table? I'm not being generous. I'm going to put the house on the market to sell and will want to stage it with stylish, not comfortable furniture. I'm going to replace the washer and dryer too, so take them if you can use them."

A tear ran down Riley's cheek. "You are being generous, and I appreciate it. Ben and I will discuss what we might want, and I'll let you know."

"You're going to be busy all week. Just take what you want and leave the rest; I'll figure it out."

When Riley returned to Claire's desk to review the scheduled appointments, Claire said, "Thankfully, we don't have any emergencies from this weekend, but I did get a call this morning. I'll schedule appointments for the callers from Tuesday through Thursday. We'll add Wednesday evening appointments as soon as we hire at least one new vet tech because we have enough clients who work Monday through Friday that have been waiting until Saturday. That will take pressure off our Saturdays, so we can leave on time at noon rather than slipping later and later and becoming a full day, which has been ruining everyone's Saturday plans."

Zach and Hector, his brown, two-year-old pit bull mix, came in the back door and stopped at the breakroom before they hurried to Claire's desk.

"Good, you're here, Zach. Thad told me to grab everyone and meet in the breakroom when you got here. Doc Julie Rae wants to have a quick meeting. I'll meet you two there with Thad and Doc."

Claire hurried to the offices while Riley and Zach strolled to the breakroom; Hector followed them.

"What do we have today?" Zach asked.

"So far, nothing urgent." Riley scratched Hector's ears. "You can pick."

"I'll take the first one," Zach said as Hector trotted away.

"Where's Hector going?" Riley asked as Claire joined them, followed by Thad and Julie Rae.

"He likes to inspect the kennels every morning; he wants to be sure they're ready if a patient needs them. He's a helicopter pit bull: always checking to be sure we do everything right," Claire said.

Zach nodded. "That's true."

"This will be quick," Doc Julie Rae said as she nodded at Riley.

Riley repeated what she told Doc Julie Rae about burnout, withdrawing from UGA and the veterinary school, and farm visits with Ben's uncle.

"You would be a fantastic veterinarian," Claire said, "but not at the price of hating what you're doing every day like you did this summer."

"That's the truth," Zach said, and Doc Thad nodded.

"Was I that obvious?" Riley asked.

"Yes, you were, honey." Doc Julie Rae smiled.

"I guess I was a determined diehard..." Riley frowned as she searched for the right word.

"Dolt? Drudge? Dinglebat?" Claire asked.

Riley laughed. "One of those."

Claire grinned as she hurried to her desk with her coffee. Thad and Julie Rae refilled their cups and took them to their offices, while Riley and Zach downed their coffee and went to Claire's desk.

"Our first patient's here." Claire drained her coffee cup. "I did get a call, and we'll have our second patient here soon."

Riley picked up Claire's cup and took it to the breakroom, and Doc Julie Rae joined her. "I was hoping I could catch you. We have a hiccup for today; it's two hiccups, but one's minor. Pia forgot she had a dental appointment, and Tom wouldn't let her skip it, so she'll be a little late. Doc Thad reviewed the applications we didn't select and found one with a reference who is an old friend. Doc

Thad talked to his friend and then asked me if I would consider a third candidate. Check with Doc Thad then tell me what you think. The new candidate might be available this afternoon or tomorrow morning. I'll call Charlie after I see our first patient."

Riley hurried to Doc Thad's office. "I'm really sorry I didn't pay closer attention to the references when I read the applications the first time," Doc said. "Percy's overall grades are average, but when I called my old buddy, he told me Percy is dyslexic, did great in all the labs and practical courses, and would be a phenomenal vet tech. He graduated six months ago but can't find a job because no one will consider him because of his grades. Look at his grades and my notes from the call, and tell me what you think."

Riley read over his application and then reviewed his grades and Thad's notes. "You're right; look at his grades in math. If we develop a system for him to record his findings, his dyslexia won't slow him down at all."

"Claire could do that; reading disabilities is her forte," Thad said.

"You're right. I'd say bring him in," Riley said.

"Thanks, I'll call my friend now and then be right with you and our patient."

Riley hurried to the desk.

"What did you think?" Claire asked as a woman came in with a cat carrier.

"Bring him in."

"Good."

Riley picked up the folder and smiled at the scowling black cat in the carrier. "Nice to see you, Archie."

Mrs. Hartway's daughter smiled. "I think there's something in Archie's right paw, and it might be infected. He's been licking it for a week, then I noticed last night it was red and swollen. He hasn't let me touch it, but it smelled bad yesterday. He did let me soak it in warm water with Epsom salts last night for a bit; that's when I decided I should bring him to the clinic because he is not fond of baths at all."

Archie meowed, and Riley said, "Let's go into exam room one and look at that foot. Do you suppose I could weigh you first?"

Archie growled.

"We can save it for later, but I will have to take your temperature. I'll be quick," Riley said.

Riley peered into the carrier after she set Archie's carrier on the exam table. "I'll be right back."

She returned with a capped syringe and a collar. "I need to help you out of the carrier so Doc Thad can take care of that paw for you. Shall I lift you out very carefully, or do you think you can get out on your own?"

Archie whined, and Riley positioned the carrier toward the end of the table, unzipped it, and lifted him out while he protected his paw against his chest. She lowered him to the table slowly, and he resumed licking his paw.

"I need to take your temperature. Do you suppose you could lie on your side?"

Archie growled, then Riley helped him onto his side and quickly took his temperature. "Thank you. I'm going to put on the collar because I know you're licking your paw because it hurts, but licking doesn't help, does it?"

Archie's low meow was mournful; Riley slipped on the collar as Doc Thad walked in, and Archie hissed.

"Sorry, Archie, but I think we might have some medicine that will help your foot not hurt so much when I touch it. Any temperature, Riley?"

"Elevated and the medicine is on the counter, Doc."

"I'm only going to touch your paw with the medicine, but Riley and I will need to touch your leg to hold it still."

Archie closed his eyes, and Riley firmly held Archie's leg. "I'm holding your leg, Archie. We're ready, Doc."

Archie flinched when Doc slipped the needle into his paw, then Riley said, "That's over."

She held onto his leg while Doc Thad shone a light on the swollen paw.

"I see a piece of glass embedded in his paw. Does he have any cuts on his tongue?"

"I didn't notice any," the daughter said.

"I didn't see any either. Archie, I need to see in your mouth," Riley said.

Archie opened his mouth and yowled, and Riley giggled. "I did ask, didn't I?"

"You were right: no cuts." Doc Thad asked the client. "Do you know if he was around a broken glass or vase?"

When Mrs. Hartway's daughter paled, Riley quickly moved to help her sit on the chair. "When I went to check on Mother last Monday morning, her hands were cut and severely bleeding. I asked her how she got the cuts, and she told me it was paint, and she had painted me a nice picture, but she didn't know where it was. My husband helped me take her to the emergency room, and they cleaned her cuts, removed the glass, and stitched up a few of the cuts. They called her doctor, and he called me. By the end of the day, she was placed in the senior residential home for dementia patients."

"Would you like a glass of water?" Riley asked, and the woman nodded.

"I'll get it." Doc Thad left and then quickly returned with a small cup of water.

After taking a few sips, the client continued, "I couldn't go back to her house. My husband cleaned up the glass and blood, then brought Archie to our house along with all his food, bowls, bedding, toys, and litter box."

She smiled weakly. "I've always been fond of Archie. I called professional cleaners to clean Mother's house, and they cleaned on Friday. They told me they found larger pieces of glass in the bathtub. My husband didn't go into her bathroom, which makes sense to me. I think Mother might have thought she was throwing it in the trash, but I'm not sure. I didn't even think about checking Archie, and when he started licking, I thought it was stress because Mother wasn't around."

"I would have thought the same thing," Doc Thad said.

"Really? Thank you. What do we do now for Archie?"

"We'll soak his paw, remove the pieces of glass, and start him on an antibiotic for the infection. I'd like to give the swelling time to go down a bit before we decide to put in any stitches. We'll keep him overnight. Claire will call you tomorrow to let you know how he's doing."

"I hate to leave you, but you're in good hands, Archie."

Archie purred, and the woman said, "Thank you."

While Doc Thad walked the client to the receptionist's desk, Riley said, "I'll roll you to your special kennel here, then clean your carrier so it will be ready when you go home."

Riley slid Archie from the exam table to their padded utility cart, which was their transport cart, and rolled Archie to the kennel. When they neared the cat kennel, Hector whimpered, and Archie purred.

"Thank you, Hector. I appreciate that you'll keep Archie company." Riley transferred Archie to the cat kennel, and he closed his eyes.

When Riley strolled to the receptionist's desk, the client and Doc Thad were shaking hands.

"Archie is sleeping. He must have kept you awake too with his constant licking. You should have a peaceful night," Riley said.

"Thank you." A tear slipped down the woman's cheek, and she left.

Claire exhaled. "I can't imagine the stress that poor woman has had. Riley, Zach is giving our two candidates a tour."

Jordy followed Pia as she rushed in the back door. "How can I help?"

"Zach's showing our candidates around; you can join them and ask the candidates what they've seen so far. I'm sure Zach will hand off the rest of the tour to you," Doc Thad said.

"On it."

"They're in the trauma room," Claire said. Jordy flopped down near the desk, and Pia strode to the trauma room.

"After sweet Zach, those poor candidates are going to think they've been hit by a bomber when Pia takes over," Riley said.

"It's how we roll." Doc Thad chuckled.

"Our next patient will be here in ten minutes for Zach and Doc Julie Rae," Claire said.

"Good. I'm going to eavesdrop." Doc Thad hurried to the back hallway.

"You will not," Claire said.

"Fine, then I'll do some paperwork," Doc Thad called out as he disappeared.

Zach hurried to the desk from the trauma room. "Pia said I had a patient."

"In ten minutes; here's the folder," Claire said.

Zach knit his brow, then shrugged. "I'm confused, but thanks."

Riley hurried to clean and straighten the exam room, then took Archie's carrier to the kennel to remove the pad and sanitize his carrier and the transport cart.

Riley's phone buzzed a text from Ben. "Hey, Miss Rita. Y'all having a good day?"

She snickered as she replied, "Sure 'nuff, SC."

Hector whined.

"Zach's right. Ben and I are leaving Barton because Ben has a new job. We'll visit because I have a cabin here, but we don't know where we'll be after he finishes his training."

Hector yipped.

"Thank you; I'll miss you too."

Pia led the wide-eyed applicants to the kennel. Norm had red-orange hair, freckles, and a build that reminded Riley of Hector: sturdy and low to the ground. Whitney had short-clipped, wiry hair and creamy chocolate skin very much like Doc Julie Rae's; she was slender and tall and moved with the same grace as Regina, the beautiful standard poodle who had captured Toby's heart.

"This is the kennel where we keep our guests for treatment and observation. Mr. George, a retired animal control officer, stays overnight. He used to come in only when we had a sick or injured patient, but he told Doc Julie Rae he's a night owl and would rather be here than alone at home at night, so he's our night security too. This is the end of your tour. Nice to meetcha." Pia strode away.

"I'm Riley. The plan for the rest of the morning is for you to see patients and be introduced to our computer system. One of you will go with me, while the other will work with Claire or Zach; our plans are fluid."

Riley smiled. "We'll switch in the middle of the morning. You've survived Pia. She's a good vet tech and passionate about her work. Who is first to go with me to see patients?"

Norm glanced at Whitney and then said, "I am."

I wonder if they did rock, paper, and scissors to decide?

"Let's go to Claire's desk; Whitney, you can work with Zach while Norm and I review the folder for our next patient."

Chapter Four

Mildred Malloy

Millie's phone, which she had stored in a drawer inside of a tin box lined with open cell foam, buzzed a text. She frowned as she opened the drawer, pulled out the phone, and glanced at it. *I forgot I'd left this phone on; I've been afraid to throw it away.*

She shrugged then read, "Riley and Ben were married. Lovely reception. Sorry you missed it. Helen."

Millie dropped her phone into the drawer without turning it off. *Helen still thinks I have this phone. If I don't answer, no one can trace me, but then there's spyware stuff.*

She pulled out her phone, turned it off, and returned it to the box in the drawer.

"How you doing?" the older man growled.

The younger man removed his headset and leaned back. "I thought I had something for a minute there and even saw a blip on the screen, but it must have been an anomaly. I got nothing."

"Well, stay on top of it. Which phone was it?"

"The old one that's out of date, but those are the ones most likely to throw errors."

The older man shrugged. "Whatever you say, you lost me. You're the expert; let me know if there's anything I can follow up on. We might need to shift our focus to a different target. I'll ask the boss."

The techie nodded and put his headset back on.

Chapter Five

Riley and Norm went to exam room two, and she gave him the folder. "Read it and tell me about our patient."

Norm read the folder. "We have a pug coming here for her annual checkup." He pointed to the folder. "Her name is Laverne, right? Is that why it's printed in all caps with black permanent marker?"

"Exactly. Laverne is our patient. What else?"

"She has a previous history of being overweight, but her weight's fine since Doc Julie Rae subscribed a special diet for her." He frowned. "It doesn't say what the diet was."

"Good catch. Sometimes, our clients have friends who give terrible advice. Laverne was overweight because of too many extra calories and a lack of exercise. I have another question for you. What's the client's name?"

Norm frowned as he scoured the folder and the enclosed documents. "I don't know," he said.

"It was a trick question." Riley smiled. "We don't put the client's names on the folder or our records, only the patient. Claire has records of the clients' names with the patient record, but we have no reason to know their names. Doc Julie Rae told me she learned early in her career that if she didn't try to remember the client's name, she couldn't get it wrong, but she never wanted to get her patient's name wrong."

Norm smiled. "Really? I have trouble with people's names, but I know all the dogs in my neighborhood, at my parents', and where I live now."

"Let's see if Laverne is here. Where will we start?"

"Weight then temperature."

"I'll introduce you to Laverne, then you weigh her and walk her to exam room two."

"Yes, ma'am," Norm said as they walked to Claire's desk.

Riley whispered, "Don't call Pia or me ma'am, especially Pia."

Norm gulped. "Okay, Riley."

Laverne grinned when she saw Riley, and Riley gushed, "Ooo, Laverne, don't you look good. This is Norm. He's new and very nice."

Norm grinned and waved.

"Shy too," Claire added, and Norm blushed while Laverne grinned at him.

"Would you come with me, Laverne? I'm supposed to weigh you, but you'll have to show me how," Norm said as Laverne pranced alongside him.

The client elbowed Riley and beamed. Riley blinked and then smiled. *Are we bonding too?*

Laverne stepped up on the low scale and side-glanced Norm, who peered at the scale. "Okay, got it. You are doing great, aren't you? We're going to room two; I'll show you."

Laverne followed Norm.

"I'll pick you up to put you on the exam table. I'm gentle."

Norm lifted Laverne to the table.

"I suppose you know I have to take your temperature," Norm said, and Laverne plopped down to sit on her bottom.

"Please?" Norm asked. Laverne huffed and stood up, and he quickly took her temperature.

"Thank you; it's normal. We knew it would be, but we like our records to be complete," he said. "Anything bothering you?"

Laverne scratched her ear.

"Really? Your ear?" Norm asked.

Riley raised her eyebrows. *Good hint, Laverne; good catch, Norm.*

"She has been scratching that one ear for about a week, but I didn't think anything of it. Sorry, Laverne," the client said.

"We'll ask Doc Thad to check her ears," Riley said.

Doc Thad walked in, and Norm held up the folder to face Doc; Riley's eyes widened. *Good move.*

Doc Thad smiled. "You're looking good, Laverne. Got a problem?"

Laverne scratched her ear.

"I'll check them out," Doc said, and Norm moved to the supply drawer and pulled out the otoscope for Doc Thad.

Riley smiled. *Pia must have rattled off where the equipment is stored; she'll be proud that Norm listened to her.*

"You're right, Laverne; there's a little infection in there. Let me check your other ear."

Laverne turned her head, and Doc Thad smiled. "You are one of my favorites, girlfriend, but you knew that, didn't you?"

Doc Thad checked her ear. "This one's good. We'll give you an antibiotic, and your ear will feel better in a couple of days, but you'll have to keep taking the medicine until it's all gone so the infection won't return."

Laverne yipped, and the client said, "We will."

"Norm will take you to Ms. Claire's desk while Riley gets your medicine. Nice to see you again, sweet girl. We'll want you to come back to have that ear checked. Norm will tell Ms. Claire."

Doc Thad scratched Laverne's good ear, and she went limp and grinned at him.

Doc Thad smiled as Norm lifted Laverne from the exam table. After they left, Doc Thad said, "I think you gave Norm permission to let his talents shine, Riley."

"I'm not sure it was me, but that's good." Riley hurried to pick up Laverne's antibiotic and then took it to Claire's desk.

Norm still held Laverne in his arms, snuggling her against his chest with her eyes closed. Laverne peeked at Riley.

Riley rolled her eyes. *You old faker.* "Time to go, Laverne. You'll need to walk to the car so I can see that your balance is still okay."

Laverne snorted and opened her eyes as Norm set her on the floor. She walked with carefully placed steps that resembled a sashay to the door. When she reached the door, she looked at Riley over her shoulder and smiled, and Riley snickered.

The client stared at Laverne, and Riley shook her head and opened the door.

After they left, Claire laughed. "I couldn't believe that walk; Laverne is sassy."

Riley nodded. "Let's clean our room and talk, Norm."

Riley said when they were in the exam room, "We sanitize all the surfaces and replenish any supplies. We'll wipe down the otoscope and thermometer, even though we used the disposable speculum and thermometer cover, and then put them where they belong. We don't sweep and mop after every patient unless there's a mess; we usually empty the trash unless we're really slammed and have back-to-back patients because it looks sloppy when the client comes into the room."

"Who takes the x-rays?" Norm asked.

"We all do, but if Zach is available, we have him take the x-rays, especially if it's a trauma patient because he's so fast and thorough."

"Pia told us if we're in the exam room and the doc asks for a piece of equipment, to look in the top drawer first because that's where most of the frequently used assessment equipment is. Pia's scary, but she gave us her best hints to help us."

"Claire will introduce you to our computer system. We use the same system that all other clinics do, but our processes are a little different."

Norm nodded.

When they reached Claire's desk, Whitney was waiting for Riley.

"Next patient is ours, Whitney. Have you read the file?"

"Yes, ma'am; oops, sorry. Norm warned me, but I forgot. Pia went over some of the basics about the folder with me. The next patient is a golden retriever; her name is Gracie. She's an older girl, and the client thinks Gracie's arthritis might be bothering her because she has trouble sleeping at night and has been pacing."

"What do you think?" Riley asked.

"I think the client might be right because pacing and licking at night are typical symptoms of pain, but I don't want to get too focused on Gracie's arthritis until we're sure she doesn't have a new medical problem," Whitney said.

"So, what would you do first?"

"Say hello to Gracie." Whitney smiled. "I got a little coaching from Claire while you and Norm were busy."

Riley glared at Claire.

"I'm immune." Claire giggled, then whispered to Norm, "Did you catch what Whitney said?"

"Yes, ma'am," he whispered.

When Gracie and the client came into the clinic, Whitney said, "Hello, Gracie; I'm Whitney, and Riley will be with us too. We'll need to weigh you before we go to room one."

Gracie whined, and Riley said, "I'm sorry you don't feel good. Do you want any help getting on the scale?"

Gracie shook her head as she stepped on the scale.

Whitney quickly jotted down Gracie's weight. "Got it, thanks. Your weight's up a little bit."

"My weight's up too, but I thought it was just stress because my mother came to live with us. I don't think I've been paying attention to Gracie like I usually do because I didn't realize her weight was up. We've always walked twice a day, but I've been tired and busy with Mom; I had forgotten how much we enjoyed our daily routine, and I'm sorry to say we haven't taken a walk in at least a month."

"Sometimes it's hard to do everything," Whitney said. "Has Gracie been eating okay?"

"Not really, and I thought it was the heat."

Gracie whined, and Riley said, "The new routine's hard on you, too, isn't it? Doc Thad will be here in a minute to check you, so Whitney's going to take your temperature."

Whitney hurried to pick up the thermometer and cover but opened the second drawer.

"First," Riley whispered, and Whitney bit her lip and nodded.

While Whitney took Gracie's temperature, Riley stroked Gracie and hummed, and Whitney relaxed. The client sat in a chair near the exam table.

"Gracie, does your skin itch?" Riley asked.

Gracie whimpered, and Whitney's eyes widened.

"Good news, Gracie: your temperature's normal," Whitney said as Doc Thad came into the room.

"Hi, Gracie," Doc Thad said. "How's my girl?"

Gracie grinned, and Whitney peered at Riley, who nodded.

"Gracie has been pacing and licking at night; her weight is up a little, but her temperature is normal. Riley petted Gracie and then asked her if her skin itched, and Gracie whimpered."

"I'm going to check your skin, Gracie." Doc Thad knelt next to Gracie; as he examined her skin, he asked, "Do you mind lying down so I can check your belly?"

Gracie flopped down on the floor and then rolled onto her back for Doc to rub her belly.

"There's a Little rash on your belly," he said. Okay, jump up so I can check your gums and ears."

Gracie rose without difficulty, and Whitney had the otoscope ready for Doc.

Doc checked her gums and teeth. "Gums are fine." He peered into her ears. "No sign of infection."

Doc Thad rose to his feet. "Gracie, I think you've got a little skin allergy. Your arthritis medicine is working because you are as spry as a puppy. We won't have to see you again if you're feeling better by Thursday."

"That's good news," the client said. "Gracie, I promise we'll go back to our walks starting this evening."

"I'll go with you to Claire's desk while Whitney gets your medicine," Riley said.

"We like Doc Thad, don't we, Gracie?" the client asked as Gracie walked alongside her, and Riley followed them.

Whitney joined them at Claire's desk and handed the medicine bottle to the client. "Give Gracie one pill in the morning, then one in the evening. She should feel more comfortable by Thursday, but call if she isn't available or you have any questions."

The client repeated the instructions, and Whitney nodded. Whitney knelt next to Gracie, rubbed her ear, and whispered, and Gracie grinned.

After Gracie left, Riley and Whitney went to exam room one to clean.

Whitney grabbed the sanitizer, sprayed the exam table, then scrubbed it and sprayed again.

"Slow down, Whitney," Riley said. "Let's talk."

"I'm absolutely mortified." Whitney bit her lip. "Claire told me to talk to our patient, and I didn't pay attention to Gracie. I didn't touch her and wouldn't have taken her temperature for another twenty minutes while I chatted with the client if you hadn't nudged me. The clinic where I worked was busy, but we were supposed to make the client feel good about our service. You and Doc Thad made the client feel good by the way you treated Gracie. This was an eye-opening experience for me. Am I fired?"

Whitney frowned and then giggled. "Are you going to tell Doc Julie Rae to hire me so I can be fired? I've totally lost it, haven't I?"

"Pretty much." Riley chuckled. "I was going to tell you that we didn't use the exam table, so there is no reason to clean it."

"I'm a mess right now, but I'm trainable," Whitney said. "I loved how Doc Thad checked to see if her arthritis medicine was working and how you checked her skin by stroking her back. I was in awe when you asked Gracie if her skin itched, and she responded. I'm certain she told you that it did. I've never seen anybody do that before, but I'm going to ask my patients questions from now on. I might not always understand, but it will keep me focused on my patient."

"Your skills are great, Whitney; your only disadvantage is that you worked at a clinic with a different philosophy than Doc Julie Rae's."

"Doc Julie Rae's approach makes sense to me; I like it." Whitney wiped down the otoscope and the thermometer with sanitizer, then glanced at the trash. "We empty it, right?"

"If we have time, we do; I suppose that's one concession we make for the client. If the trash can is empty, they see the rest of the room as clean."

When Whitney picked up the trash can, Riley said, "I'll take care of it. Find Norm and take a break in the breakroom. You deserve a breather."

After Whitney left, Doc Julie Rae came into the exam room. "I understand you told Whitney to take Norm to the breakroom, so I thought I'd see what you think. If I hire only one, which one should I hire?"

"They are at two distinct career stages, so I'd never try to compare them. Both are willing to learn and will bring unique talents to the clinic."

"You just said exactly what I was thinking." Doc Julie Rae sighed.

"I'm busting in." Doc Thad came into the room. "I thought I'd find you two having a private conversation, and I have something to add. My friend knew Percy preferred to find something close to his family and friends, so he told two or three people in confidence that we were interested in Percy, and word got around." Doc Thad chuckled. "Percy has offers from two clinics in his hometown that interviewed him last month. His parents are ecstatic. My friend thanked you for being a catalyst because he planned to talk to the parents this afternoon."

Doc Julie Rae smiled. "I'm glad we could help Percy, and your friend helped me. Charlie told me we can't afford more than two vet techs except for Riley. He said he's got a reserve set aside for you, Riley. Thad, we'll talk after lunch."

"Claire and I think we should hire both. What does Pia say, Riley?" Doc Thad asked.

Riley smiled and then headed to the door. "I don't know yet."

When Riley arrived at Claire's desk, she peered under the desk. "Where's Toby?"

"He and Jordy went to the kennel to check on Archie and keep Hector company. Pia took the next patient and grabbed Norm to go with her."

"Give Pia and Whitney the next patient. Doc Julie Rae asked me what Pia thought about our candidates. We couldn't have planned it any better."

Claire chuckled. "That's devious. We're taking full credit, right?"

"Yes, where's Zach? I haven't seen him since Pia got here."

"He's in Thad's office working on a marketing plan for the clinic. All I know is that Doc Julie Rae asked him to do it because Charlie said he wanted a marketing plan to go with his business plan because he wants to apply for a grant for the clinic."

Riley's phone buzzed a text. "I'll bet this is from Ben."

"Read it. I won't peek."

Riley pulled out her phone and read Ben's text.

"I meant, read it aloud," Claire said.

Riley chuckled. "Do we have plans tonight? Tom & Pia want to treat us to dinner."

"I've got dibs on tomorrow night," Claire said.

"You got it." Riley replied, "Sounds good."

"Too bad we can't give Pia the rest of the afternoon off. She's a fantastic cook, and you could ask to bring a plus one; you know, plus one for you and a plus one for Ben." Claire wiggled her eyebrows, and Riley shook her head as she replied to Ben's text.

When Pia and Norm came out of exam room three with the patient and client, Riley headed to the kennel to check on Toby, Hector, and Archie.

She washed her hands before she opened Archie's door to check on him. "Your dressing is still dry, at least on the outside. Doc Thad may want to change it before lunch, but we'll let him decide."

Riley closed the kennel door and sat on the floor next to Toby. "We'll miss our friends, won't we? The good news is that we'll be coming back to visit while we vacation at the cabin."

Riley's phone buzzed another text, and she smiled. "Ben's a little bored."

Her eyes widened as she read the text from Sheriff Dunn. "Call when you aren't busy."

She frowned and then called him.

"Brian Johnson, a coworker and old friend of your dad's, will be in town tomorrow. He'd like to see you. Do you suppose you could get away for a long lunch?"

"I'll check with Doc Julie Rae, but I suspect I can. I'll check and get back to you."

After she hung up, Riley held onto a kennel to help herself to her feet. "I was getting stiff. I'll bet I'll be more limber after working a few weeks with Doc Seth."

She stretched and then went to Doc Julie Rae's office. Doc Julie Rae glanced up from her computer when Riley tapped on her door to get her attention.

"Sam called me; enjoy your lunch tomorrow," Doc Julie Rae said.

Riley smiled. "I should have known he'd call you; thanks."

She headed back to the kennel and texted the sheriff, "Doc said okay. What time?"

"Will pick you up at eleven."

Riley raised her eyebrows. *He said long lunch, but I thought he meant an hour.*

"What are you doing back here? Hiding?" Doc Thad asked as he strolled into the kennel.

"Exactly. Whitney's up next with Pia, so I'm staying out of the way. Are you here to check Archie?"

"Archie's my excuse to be a little scarce for a couple of minutes before I join Pia and Whitney. I thought Zach and I would change Archie's bandage after lunch and again this evening before we leave."

Doc Thad peered into Archie's kennel. "I'm glad you've found a comfortable position, Archie. I'll see you after lunch." After Doc Thad left to see his patient, Riley finished sanitizing Archie's carrier and then checked and replenished the kennel supplies.

Pia joined her at the kennel. "It's nice and quiet back here; I'll have to remember that. We're supposed to see Doc Julie Rae while the rest of them are getting ready to leave for lunch."

When Riley and Pia walked into her office, Doc asked, "Which of our two candidates is the best fit for our clinic, Pia?"

"I think it would be a mistake to pass on either one of them. Both are good and will need only a little training before they can work on their own; Riley does the work of two, and it wouldn't be fair to any of us to replace her with only one person with our growing patient load," Pia said. "If either or both of them can start tomorrow, we can take advantage of having Riley here this week to oversee their training."

"Riley?" Doc Julie Rae asked.

"Unanimous, as far as I'm concerned."

"I'll tell both of them they are hired if they want the positions, so our lunch will be a celebration, not an inquisition."

Riley and Pia headed toward the door. "Bring us back dessert," Pia said.

Doc Julie Rae chuckled. "Will do."

Before the two groups left for lunch, Claire said, "There aren't any appointments until one, so I don't expect you to have any patients. I've sanitized my desk, so you can sit here and eat together. Do you have lunch, or do we need to bring something back for you?"

Pia side-glanced Riley. "Dessert would be nice."

Claire nodded. "I'll tell Thad to pick up dessert for both of you."

Riley locked the back door behind the four of them after they left, picked up her lunch, and joined Pia at the receptionist's desk.

"Ben and I had a long talk this weekend, and I've decided against four or more years of college."

"I want to hear the whole story, but I'm relieved. You were a total wreck this summer from those two classes. The only time you were your old self was the two-day break in between the classes."

"That bad? Why didn't you say anything?" Riley asked.

Pia glared. "Are you kidding me? I casually asked if you meant to wear your bedroom slippers to work three weeks ago, and you bit my head off."

"That is not what you said. You asked me if a four-year-old dressed me that morning and where was my blankie?" Riley growled.

Pia shrugged. "Same thing."

Riley rolled her eyes and told Pia what she was going to be doing while Ben was in training.

Pia chuckled. "Just remember to wear your boots when you go on your farm visits. I'm glad you finally came to your senses."

"You're lucky I'm not stressed and burned out." Riley sneered as she wrinkled her nose.

While they ate, Riley asked, "Do you think we'll each get two desserts?"

"It was a gamble; we'll see." Pia took a large bite of her sandwich as the phone rang, and Riley answered it.

Riley picked up a pen to take notes as she answered.

A man asked, "Does Riley Malloy work there? I heard she might be working in Barton."

Riley narrowed her eyes. "No, not here."

"Well, that's what I heard. You must know her. Barton can't be much of a town; I couldn't even find it on the map. I need to talk to her; just give me her number and quit wasting my time. You can tell me where she works."

"I actually can't, but if you give me your number, I can ask the sheriff to call you; he might know…"

When the man hung up on her, Riley frowned at the phone as she hung up.

"What was that?" Pia asked.

"A man said he heard Riley Malloy might be working in Barton and wanted to know if she worked here. It seemed creepy to me, so I told him she wasn't here, and that's true because I'm Riley Malloy Carter. He became agitated to the point of being a total jerk and insisted I knew where she was; I asked for his number so he could talk to the sheriff."

Pia gazed at Riley. "Did he hang up on you?"

"Sure did."

"You need to tell the sheriff or Ben, except I don't know what you'd tell them." Pia narrowed her eyes. "Are you in the middle of something you haven't told me about?"

"Not that I know of; his phone showed the words 'Private Number' and no number on our office phone. Do you suppose he was a telemarketer?"

"If you're not in the process of cracking a cold case, then that's the only thing that makes sense. What do you think we'll get for dessert? I'm hoping cheesecake."

"Cheesecake sounds great. Mom packed our lunches, and I'll bet I have cookies or pie. We could have our second dessert on Tuesday, then cookies or pie on Wednesday."

Doc Thad and Zach returned before Riley and Pia had finished half of their lunch and before Doc Julie Rae and Claire returned.

"I'll take the desk if you want to finish your break in the breakroom," Zach said.

"Thanks," Riley said.

Doc Thad met them as Riley and Pia headed to the breakroom with their half-eaten lunches.

"Your desserts are in the refrigerator. Claire told me about your brilliant double dessert scam, Pia, and we decided not to bust you because you two deserve a little extra treat for taking care of the office," he said.

Pia grinned. "Thanks, Doc."

After Doc Thad continued down the hall to his office, Pia rushed to the refrigerator and peeked into a paper sack.

"Score, girlfriend! We've got cheesecake." Pia pulled out the sack and set the two containers on the table while Riley set their napkins and plastic forks on the table.

"Dessert, first," Pia said.

After they finished their cheesecake, Riley threw away their trash and their leftover sandwiches as Doc Julie Rae and Claire came in the back door.

Doc Julie Rae came into the breakroom and set a white paper sack on the table. "I heard from Whitney and Norm, and both will be here in the morning. Here is your dessert, as promised; inside the sack is an IOU. Charlie will make you a special dessert, and I'll bring it in the morning."

"I'd say we were busted, but dessert from Charlie? That's a bonus," Pia said. "Tom told Ben to come to our house around six tonight. I didn't know if you'd gotten the message yet. Tom's being very secretive, probably because he thinks I'd tell you everything, which I would. I'm unsure if he's ordering takeout or cooking, or we'll go somewhere together from our house. Bring Toby; Jordy will enjoy seeing him."

Toward the end of the day, Riley finished cleaning exam room one when her phone buzzed with a text from Ben. "Call when you can."

"I'll be in the breakroom, Claire, if you need me," she said.

Claire nodded and picked up the ringing phone.

When Ben answered, he said, "Two of the deputies are sick, and the sheriff is shorthanded. Would you mind if I'm on call tonight? I'll ask Tom to give you a ride home if I leave."

"I can drive my car. Pia invited Toby to visit with Jordy so Toby would be with me."

"Thanks, babe. You're the best."

Riley smiled. *You keep thinking that.* "Do you know where we're going?"

"Sorry; I thought I told you: Tom and Pia's house. Gotta run."

So much for my finely honed investigative skills.

As she headed back to the receptionist's desk, Doc Thad and Zach passed her on their way to the kennel.

"How's Archie?" she asked.

"The swelling seems to be going down a bit, and the largest wound is still draining. I'll ask George to call me if he notices anything tonight," Doc Thad said.

While Riley straightened the breakroom and wiped down the counters, Zach and Hector joined her.

"Are you happy with being a vet tech? Do you think you'll ever regret not becoming a veterinarian?" Zach asked.

Riley peered at him. *He's even more serious than usual; I'm not sure I'd have thought that was possible.* "I'm a vet tech and love the contact I have with dogs, cats, and any animal daily. As far as regrets, I don't think so because I'd be giving up four to six years of freedom that I could have spent enjoying life with Ben and Toby and visiting our cabin. Why?"

Chapter Six

"My family has always assumed I'd become a doctor because I'm smart, and I kind of bought into it, even though I wasn't happy about it. You're one of the smartest people I know, and you're happy; that was such a foreign concept to me." Zach grinned. "So that leaves me smart, in a career I love, and with the bonus of taking the most loving, protective dog in the world to work with me."

Riley's eyes twinkled. "What else?"

"There is this girl..." Zach blushed.

Hector yipped, and Riley smiled. "Hector likes her too."

"We like her a lot, don't we?" Zach sighed. "Kayla and I met a few months ago and were instantly friends. She is super smart, cute, and fun. Neither one of us is that good at small talk, especially in a group, but when it's just the two of us, we talk nonstop. Kayla is a registered nurse who works in the intensive care unit at the hospital; when her day off falls on a Saturday or Sunday, the three of us go hiking. I want her to move in with Hector and me, but she insists that we need to meet each other's families first. She's already met Amanda, and Amanda loves her. Amanda has been pushing me to take Kayla to meet my parents. We're going to see them this weekend, but I want to cancel and go live in a monastery."

Riley giggled. "A monastery?"

Hector snorted, and Zach chuckled. "I think I'm rattled."

"Ya think? So, what worries you most?"

"My parents are embarrassing. Mom will stress because Kayla isn't Vietnamese, and when she mentions it in her own heavy-handed way, Dad will laugh because he isn't Vietnamese either; we'll have to endure the big chill from Mom until Dad breaks her down with his string of bad jokes." Zach rolled his eyes. "I don't know which is worse: Mom's silent freeze or Dad's terrible jokes."

"So, what are you going to do? I mean, if you don't leave for the monastery?"

Zach snickered. "I have the perfect solution, and Kayla will love it because she might be as stressed as I am. I'll let her choose: monastery or the big chill followed by Dad jokes."

"I see why you, Hector, and Amanda like Kayla; she definitely sounds like a good match for you."

"Thanks for listening, Riley." Zach whistled as he and Hector left the breakroom.

When she heard George come in the back door, Riley met him in the hallway. "Come into the breakroom; I have news for you."

"Break it now, unless you're going to start crying, then ask Zach to tell me. He's not a crier and will get right to the point," George said.

Riley giggled. "Okay, I'll hold back the tears, and here's the bottom line: I'm not going to veterinarian school, and Ben's uncle, who is a veterinarian, offered me a job making farm visits with him. I'll live with Ben's parents while Ben attends the GBI training."

"Good." George continued to the kennel.

Riley stared at him as he walked away, shook her head, and then strolled to Claire's desk.

"As soon as Doc Julie Rae and Pia finish up with our last patient of the day, we'll be closing shop. I'm looking forward to tomorrow, aren't you?" Claire asked.

"I'm excited that I can help give them a boost before I leave."

Pia and the new patient and client came to the desk, and Riley hurried to the exam room to help Pia clean.

When Pia joined Riley in the exam room, she said, "If Tom cooks his favorite, sauerkraut and sausage, take a few bites and move the food around your plate. Toward the end of the meal, I'll quickly clear our plates. Tomorrow, I'll bring arroz con gandules for our lunch with our Charlie dessert."

"Okay, but I've never had sauerkraut and sausage; I might like it. You're bringing rice with what?"

"It's rice with pigeon peas; if you've never had them, they taste similar to edamame. Trust me; you'll love the arroz con gandules, but you won't like it the way Tom cooks sauerkraut and sausage. I'll finish up cleaning here; there's not much left to do."

As Riley headed to the kennel to let Toby know she was ready to leave, Claire met her in the hallway.

"Are you going to the kennel? Tell Thad I'm ready whenever he is. Do you have any requests for our fancy dinner tomorrow?"

"I love everything you cook."

Claire smirked. "I knew you'd say that; I'll make something that's just outside your current level of cooking skills, and then you'll have to ask me for the recipe when you decide you want to tackle it."

"I didn't expect that; you're brilliant."

Riley met Thad on her way to the kennel. "I was coming to the kennel to get Toby, and Claire said she's ready when you are."

Toby trotted from the kennel.

"Let's go. You're invited to Pia's house, too," Riley said.

After Riley parked, she said, "Ben's not home yet. I'll feed you, then take a quick shower."

Riley measured Toby's food and set down his bowl. While he ate, she showered and dried off before pulling on a fresh pair of jeans and her hot pink shirt. She took her hairbrush with her to the back porch, and while Toby roamed the yard, she brushed out tangles.

Toby yipped. Riley listened. "Ben's truck."

She went to the front door while Toby stayed on the back porch.

Ben bounded to the front porch and grabbed Riley, then bent her backward and kissed her with toe-curling passion.

After he returned her to a standing position and beamed, Riley said, "Wow, Sexy Cowboy."

She peeked past him and snickered. "Everyone on our street who can see our porch is peeking through their blinds."

"Should I turn around and take a bow?" he smirked.

"Don't you dare."

After they were inside, Ben said, "I talked to Tom; he's happy to give you a ride home if I get a call. He said Pia was looking forward to having a glass of wine with you after dinner."

"Pia and I rarely have time to relax and chat; that sounds nice."

"I'll need to put on a fresh uniform. Do I have time for a shower?" Ben asked.

"Go ahead. Toby and I will be out back."

Riley rocked while Toby lay on the porch next to her.

When Ben opened the back door a few inches, Riley whistled. "I see your skivvies, Sexy Cowboy."

Ben chuckled as he stuck a bare foot outside. "This is my sexy pose. I have only one uniform here that is clean. I must have been distracted when we left for Mom and Dad's."

Riley bit her lip to keep from smirking while Ben continued, "If I start a small load of uniforms, would you put them in the dryer when you and Toby come home if I'm on a call?"

"Sure will. Do you have a uniform for tomorrow?"

"If we do laundry, I will." Ben quickly closed the door.

"Toby, he didn't give me time to think up a snappy retort, but I do wonder if he is focused only on his uniforms. I'll start another load with the rest of our dirty clothes after we put his uniforms in the dryer."

Ben swaggered outside. "Ready to go, ma'am?"

Riley rose from her chair, and Toby trotted to the back door. "We're ready; you look nice, honey."

When he leaned down to kiss her, her eyes twinkled as she met his lips with hers. After their lingering kiss, he hugged her and then gave her an extra squeeze. "You're gorgeous."

Toby nosed the door, and they hurried to the truck.

On the way, Riley asked, "Do you know what Tom's cooking?"

"Almost there," Ben said.

"Sometimes, you are just flat-out maddening," Riley grumbled.

After he parked, he grinned. "Yes."

Pia flung open the door when Ben opened his truck door, and Jackson and Jordy rushed outside. Jordy barked until Toby jumped out of the truck, then yipped, and the two of them raced toward the back of the house.

"We'll be in the backyard, Mom." Jackson ran to catch up with Toby and Jordy.

"Come on in." Pia smiled. "You'd think we never have company by the way we act, wouldn't you?"

"Hey, Ben, come join me; I'm getting ready to throw the burgers on the grill," Tom called out from the kitchen.

After Ben hurried to the kitchen, Pia said, "I can't tell you how relieved I was when I came home, and Tom told me he realized he should have started fermenting his sauerkraut six weeks ago. He and Jackson decided on cheeseburgers and just got back from shopping."

While Pia poured their sweet tea, she asked, "Are you going to be okay leaving Barton?"

"It would be hard if I didn't have Grandma's cabin." Riley sipped her tea. "It's strange because I lived in Pomeroy my entire life and don't miss it a bit; Barton's my home."

Pia nodded. "I feel the same. We haven't been here long either, but I can't imagine feeling at home anywhere else like I do here."

Ben came inside. "I'm the sous chef, and Jackson will be here in a second to set the table; y'all need to clear out of our kitchen, per the grill master."

"Yes, sir." Pia saluted. "It's too hot for the front porch," Pia said as they strolled to the living room.

"I happened to be at Claire's desk late this afternoon when she got a call to verify your employment, but she told them it was office policy not to discuss prior or current staff over the phone. Her voice was so cold it chilled my blood. That's two calls at the clinic today trying to get information about you."

"Whoever is calling must not be in town because all they'd have to do would be to watch the parking lot or come into the clinic," Riley said. "I'd really like to know what this is all about."

"If anything else comes up, I'll let you know. I'm glad you're going to be here to help train Whitney and Norm. I don't have the patience, but pushing it off onto Zach wouldn't be fair."

"I'm looking forward to it because I'll feel like I spent my last week here helping instead of moping around because I was leaving," Riley said.

"I'll mope for you; I will really miss you. Tom told me he and Jackson want to camp and hike on weekends and would like for me to go with them. I'm not the outdoors type, but I told him I'd go. I hope you know it's your fault because I'm afraid you'll lose a bunch of weight by tromping around farms all day, and I don't want to be left behind."

Riley snickered. "Our plan to start running never really worked out, did it?"

"You didn't hear me complain, but you can expect whiny emails every week and long, complaining phone calls from me once or twice a month."

Ben came into the living room. "The burgers are almost done; Tom needs to know who wants jalapeno or melted Swiss cheese on their burgers."

"Both for me," Riley said, and Pia nodded.

As Ben hurried to the kitchen, he said, "Full house for the hot mess, chef."

"Hot mess?" Riley whispered.

Pia snorted. "Must be diner lingo."

"Mom!" Jackson yelled from the kitchen.

Pia whispered, "Watch this."

Jackson trudged into the living room. "Dad said to tell you that supper was ready, but then he said you might be talking, so I should check to be sure you heard me."

"Thanks, Jackson, we'll be right there."

"She said they'll be right there," Jackson shouted on his way to the kitchen.

Pia rolled her eyes, and Riley pursed her lips to hold back a giggle.

"All the fixings are on the table," Tom said as Pia and Riley strolled into the kitchen. "Take a seat, and Ben will refresh your tea while Jackson and I bring in the burgers and fire-toasted buns."

"Sit by me, Riley." Pia pointed. "Jackson can sit next to you, and Ben can sit across from you."

While they ate, Jackson asked, "Will you and Toby visit us, Aunt Riley?"

"Sure will. My grandma has a cabin near town, and we can visit on weekends."

"That's good because Jordy will miss Toby."

"Toby will miss Jordy too."

After they finished eating, Pia pushed back her chair, and Tom motioned for her to stay seated. "We'll clear the table, load the dishwasher, and serve up dessert. You don't get many chances to relax after you get home from work, honey."

While Jackson cleared the dishes, Tom loaded the dishwasher, and Ben placed the condiments in the refrigerator.

Tom pulled out ice cream from the freezer and a cake from the refrigerator.

Pia's eyes widened. "We are having a fancy dinner: Italian cream cake is my favorite."

While Ben sliced the cake, Tom dished up the ice cream.

After Pia took her first bite of cake, she said, "Mmm. I never had Italian cream cake until we moved to Georgia. I don't know why it's called Italian cream cake, though, because it's strictly a southern cake."

"Maybe it came from southern Italy," Jackson said.

Tom nodded. "The cake was your surprise, honey; now for your surprise, Riley."

"There's more?" Riley asked.

"This surprise is for you and Ben," Tom said.

Jackson squirmed in his seat. "I know; I know what it is. It's the best ever, Aunt Riley. You'll be surprised, and I can't tell what it is." Jackson put his hands over his mouth.

Tom chuckled as he pulled out a flash drive from his pocket and set it on the table. "Guess what it is."

Riley stared at the flash drive, examined his face, and gasped. "Your book! You finished Phantom Cattle!"

"What gave it away?" Tom asked. "This version is with an editor; after the final edit, I'm going to publish it."

Riley picked up the flash drive and smiled. "Wow. I'm excited that you finished it and thrilled to have a copy."

"You might want to start from the beginning because I made quite a few changes to the earlier part of the story that you read when it was a first draft and only half completed."

"Okay, I have to go home now, and I'm only partially kidding," Riley said. "You were right, Jackson; this is the best ever surprise."

"Tom, would it be okay if I take a copy to read in the evenings while I'm in training?" Ben asked.

"I'd be honored." Tom blushed, then cleared his throat. "Pia, if you and Riley would like to make yourselves comfortable in the living room, I'll bring you after-dinner drinks so you can relax and talk. Beer or wine, Riley?"

"Wine sounds good."

"I won't bother you because us men will go to the back porch and talk man things," Jackson said.

After Tom and Ben brought the wine glasses to them, the two men high-fived as they strolled out of the room.

"It really was a fantastic surprise." Riley sipped her wine. "This is really good. Ole Jackson is growing up, isn't he?"

Pia nodded. "Close your eyes because I watched you read Tom's mind; I have another surprise for you."

I already know what it is. Riley closed her eyes. "I'm a dog whisperer, not a mind reader; I guessed 'Phantom Cattle' because it was what I hoped for the most."

"We're not telling anyone for a while, but I wanted to tell you myself before you left."

Riley kept her eyes closed and waited.

"My glass has grape juice." Pia whispered, "We're going to have a baby."

"Congratulations," Riley whispered as she kept her eyes closed. "That's really exciting news."

"You can open your eyes now," Pia said quietly. "Jackson doesn't know yet; we'll tell him before we tell our folks. We just learned last week, so it will be a while before we say anything to anyone else, and we haven't made any plans as far as what I'll do after the baby arrives. Tom wants me to be a stay-at-home mom, and I might, or I might ask Doc Julie Rae if I can work part-time."

Riley smiled. "I am so happy for you; I'll be only an hour away, so let me know if there is anything I can do to help."

Pia frowned. "Did you already know?"

"How could I know before you told me?"

Pia's eyes widened. "You just reminded me that you're a dog whisperer; Jordy told Toby, didn't he? He forgot you would understand."

Riley giggled. "He's excited."

Pia shook her head. "You are really good. If I didn't know you, I never would have guessed that you were just letting me have some privacy. Thank you."

"What about Ben?" Riley asked.

"Tom plans to tell him when Jackson comes inside; Jackson will get bored with the man talk soon enough."

The back door opened and then slammed as Jackson, Jordy, and Toby rushed into the house.

Jackson raced to the living room. "Jordy and Toby wanted a drink; can I have some electronics time in my room? All my homework's done."

"Of course; you deserve a little evening relaxation, too."

After Jackson went into his room with the dogs following him, he closed his door.

"Tell me more about your weekend," Pia said.

"Doc Seth asked me to go on a farm visit with him. A heifer was having trouble delivering her calf." Riley told Pia how Doc Seth managed the difficult birth and what she learned.

"That's amazing; it's like Doc Seth had x-ray hands that told him the calf's position and what was stopping the baby from being delivered."

"That's exactly how I felt, too," Riley said. "There's just so much to learn, and this is a wonderful opportunity for me to expand my skills."

"Will you ever want to go to veterinarian school?" Pia asked.

"Zach asked me the same thing; I've always been happy to be a vet tech. I don't see that changing, particularly since Ben is happy with his decision to stay in law enforcement."

Pia nodded and then checked her phone. "It's almost time for Jackson's shower. I need to give him a ten-minute warning."

"We need to go too. You probably guessed Ben's on call. I'd like to get home before he tears out of here." Riley picked up their glasses and smiled. "I might have a little reading time if he does."

"Give me a second so I can hug Ben before you leave. I might not have another opportunity."

When Pia returned, Riley hugged her. "That was a hug because I'm so happy for you. I can get my goodbye hug later this week."

Ben and Tom were shaking hands when Riley opened the back door.

"I'm ready to go home before you get a call. Tom, dinner was great, and so was my surprise. Thank you," Riley said.

"Take some cake home with you," Tom said. "We can't freeze it, and we certainly don't need to it all."

"Pia can bring what she wants to the clinic tomorrow. It won't go to waste," Riley said.

Pia snickered and elbowed Riley. "Good choice of words, but you know that's what cakes do."

Riley giggled. "I would have missed it."

On their way home, Riley said, "I was surprised when Pia told me they are expecting a baby."

"Tom is really happy; I would be too." Ben side-glanced Riley.

Are we about to have the baby discussion? I call first dibs on the timeline.

Riley nodded. "Pia told me they waited three years before they had Jackson. I think two years would be fine. We should be settled by then, don't you think?"

Ben smiled. "I think so."

Toby whined, then barked at a tree, and Ben chuckled. "We'll be home soon, Toby, and we have plenty of squirrels around for you to keep out of our yard."

As they went into the house, Ben's phone buzzed. "Good timing; gotta go."

He kissed her and lightly patted her bottom twice before he dashed to his truck.

After he left, Toby whined. "I know Jordy's excited about their baby, and you would like for us to have a baby too, but thanks for covering up with a bark at the tree."

Riley put Ben's uniforms in the dryer and then started a full load of dirty clothes before she went outside. She settled in her chair and rocked while Toby barked at the nearby dogs who answered his neighborhood call of the wild.

When Toby trotted to Riley and put his head on her knee, she rubbed his ears. "I can read "Phantom Cattle' or go through the private, magical box. Checking the box first would be faster, then I could read Tom's Old West novel until Ben gets home."

Toby yipped, and they went inside.

After Riley sat on the sofa, she opened the box and recognized the tight, neat handwriting. She swallowed hard, and her eyes welled up. *A letter from Grandma to me.*

Sweet Girl,

I don't know when you'll open our private, magical box, but now you have. Please wait to read the rest of the letter until you have someone you trust with you.

I regret not telling you all this in person when I could. I know this is going to be blunt, but I don't know of any way to soften the blow. Please remember that your dad and I loved you and tried to do what we thought was best for you, and please, please forgive us.

I know the truth will confuse and even hurt you, but you need to know that Vivian Echols is not your mother. Your mother's name was Erin Larson Malloy; she was the sweetest woman in the world and was wild about your dad. Sadly, she died in a tragic car crash in Naples, Italy, when you were six months old; your dad was devastated and felt guilty his entire life because she was on her way to join him on one of his extended business trips. He married Vivian a year later; theirs was a loveless marriage, but he thought he was doing the right thing for you. Vivian arranged to have your birth certificate legally updated to list her as your mother. Your original birth certificate is here. If nothing else, I owe you that.

My updated will is in here, in case I'm not around, but it is also on file with the county probate judge. Millie has a copy of the older will that only had the cabin going to you and doesn't know about this one. The cabin, of course, is yours, and Frank regularly sent me money to keep for you after he married Vivian. He emptied two of his bank accounts and then arranged the deposit of an automatic withdrawal every month into a new bank account that he set up and shared with me. I have stocks, bonds, and a bank account that a trust company is managing for you until you claim them. No one knew about the money I was putting aside for you. You'll find the trust company contact information included in our private box.

That's the business part. Now, for the personal, this is as hard for me to write as it will be for you to read. I don't think your dad's death was an industrial accident. I have no real proof except for the enclosed documents I don't understand. Maybe you will.

I feel so guilty that I didn't fight to keep you with me when I saw how Vivian mistreated you. Your dad begged me repeatedly to give her a chance because she had convinced him that you deserved a mother. I agreed to give her more chances than I should have and will forever regret that I did.

Keep dancing!

All my love now and always,

Grandma

Riley wailed, and Toby howled. She hugged him and sobbed. "I need Ben, Toby."

Toby rushed to the front door and scratched to get out.

Riley spoke in between sobs. "I know you'd get him for me, but we'll wait for him here. I'll be okay."

She slid down to sit on the floor to be closer to Toby, and he leaned against her. While Riley wrapped her arms around his neck and rocked until her sobs slowed, Toby licked the tears on her face.

Riley hiccupped as she wiped away the tears and slobber with her shirttail. "The letter was such a shock. I don't know how I could have handled it if you hadn't been here."

She inhaled deeply, then exhaled slowly. "I'll wait for Ben to go through the documents."

She leaned back against the sofa and closed her eyes as she hummed the tune of comfort that Grandma had taught her.

Chapter Seven

An hour later, she was still on the floor. Toby rushed to the door and barked, and Ben rushed inside. "What's wrong, Toby?"

When Ben saw Riley on the floor, he raced across the room and lifted her to the sofa. "Are you hurt? What's wrong?"

She handed him the letter, and he read. "What? This is unbelievable."

He tossed the letter aside and grabbed Riley. "I am so sorry I wasn't here."

"Grandma tried to warn me. You're here now. I haven't looked at any of the documents; is it okay that I don't really want to do that tonight?"

"I don't blame you; I didn't even finish the letter; I quit after I read about Vivian Echols. Is it okay if I finish reading now?"

After he finished reading, he picked up his phone. "Sheriff, could you take me off the roster tonight?"

He listened. "Thanks."

"I'm on Riley duty tonight," Ben kissed Riley's cheek. "What can I do for you?"

Riley sniffled. "Ice cream?"

Ben chuckled. "I can do that. Is it okay if I change clothes first?"

"Pull your uniforms from the dryer."

While Ben carried his uniforms to the bedroom, Riley removed the papers from the box and slipped them into a large manila envelope. Underneath the papers were pieces of jewelry. *Grandma didn't wear rings or necklaces.* She wrapped the jewelry in a clean dishcloth and then placed the wrap into a plastic bag before she put the brown envelope and plastic bag in her backpack. *I wonder if Claire knows anything about jewelry.*

Ben returned after he changed to move the wet clothes from the washer to the dryer. He dished up two bowls with large servings of ice cream and gave Riley hers.

Riley's eyes widened. "This is too much."

"Sorry, I went overboard; eat what you want."

"I want it all but can't eat it all." She took a bite. "What was your call?"

"A missing four-year-old that had crawled into the family dog's crate and fallen asleep. You should have been there because the dog thinks we're all slow learners, and he's right. He followed the girl's father around and whined. Everyone thought he was concerned about the little girl, and he was, but he was more concerned that everyone was so thick-headed. I finally asked him where she was, and he led me to his crate."

Riley smiled. "I'm glad you remembered to ask him."

"We'd still be searching the neighborhood and considering locking down the town and calling in the state police if it hadn't dawned on me: 'What would Riley do?'"

Riley shook her head. "Sounds like a tall tale to me."

"It isn't, and I have at least one reliable witness. The sheriff laughed when I asked the family dog where the little girl was. He knew where that came from. He told me later that he wished he'd thought about it before they called me in and said he wouldn't make that mistake again."

Riley giggled. "Thanks for telling me about your call. I'm glad you went."

"I'm sorry I wasn't here, but I'm grateful Toby was."

Toby leaned against Ben and whined.

"Did you want to go outside, Toby?" Ben asked.

Toby flopped on the floor.

"What is he saying, babe?" Ben asked.

"I can't say because he's wrong."

Toby grinned.

"Tell me later when you two aren't arguing," Ben said. "What do you think about going to bed? I'm exhausted, and I know you are too. It's been a long, stressful day for both of us, and we'll be getting up early."

Riley yawned. "I didn't know I was so tired, but you're right."

They strolled to the bedroom with their arms around each other.

Riley woke to the aroma of coffee that tickled her nose. She listened to the splashing water of the shower. When Ben tiptoed into the bedroom, she said, "I'm awake, honey. Is it my turn for the shower?"

"I didn't mean to wake you up; I thought I was being quiet."

"You didn't wake me up; the smell of coffee did."

She tossed her nightgown on the bed, and Ben whistled as she dashed to the bathroom.

She climbed into the shower after she had the water at the temperature she liked.

Ben tapped on the door and then opened it. "Do you suppose you could do that again, babe? I might have missed something."

Riley giggled. "You didn't miss a thing, and you know it."

"Can't blame a guy for trying. Do you want eggs and toast or a breakfast burrito?"

"One egg and one slice of toast. I'm still full from last night. I should probably jog to work because we're going to the Faradays' tonight."

When Ben rolled his eyes, Riley giggled. "But I won't. It's a good thing we're leaving at the end of this week, or I'd have to buy all new clothes, and I'm not kidding."

While they ate breakfast, Ben asked, "Are you going to be okay today?"

"I'll be fine; do you expect to be on call tonight?"

"No, the sheriff might call me in if he really needs my help, but he told me last night on the phone that he needed to break in the new guys."

"I haven't had a chance to tell you that Helen called me yesterday morning; she's planning to put this house on the market after we leave and will be redecorating and replacing all the furniture and the washer and dryer. She told me that we could take anything we could use because she wanted to start from scratch. We don't have to decide right away because she said to take what we need and leave the rest."

"That's really generous of her. We're taking the bed, right? Is there anything else?" Ben scanned the living room.

"It's up to you, but I don't think so. We'd have to store everything for four months and may not need it, but we can think about it."

"I agree. We'd have to rent an air-conditioned storage facility and haul it to the next place; if we don't have any use for it at the new place, we'd have more storage costs for something we didn't need the past several moves. As long as we have a bed to sleep on, we can always get a card table, a couple of chairs, and a sofa, except new furniture is crazy expensive, so we might want to take the sofa because it's in good shape."

"We've got until Friday to decide which will feel like an eternity, won't it? Isn't it interesting that you're going to be the new guy at GBI, and I'll be Doc Seth's new vet tech?"

Ben smiled. "I hadn't thought about it that way. I'll remind the sheriff that the new guys have valuable experience that hasn't been tapped yet, and they're just new to the department."

"Good insight. I'll share that with Doc Julie Rae. I'm not sure I told you we have two new vet techs starting today. Whitney has two years of experience, but Doc Julie Rae's philosophy is foreign to her, and Norm is a bright, eager new grad. They're nothing alike, but both of them are willing to learn."

"That describes the new deputies. One has experience, and the other has none, but both are smart. The sheriff made good choices. Your lunch is in the refrigerator, babe. See you after work." He stopped for a quick kiss and then left.

Riley loaded the dishwasher and then put her manila envelope with the papers into her backpack. "Ready to go, Toby?"

After Riley and Toby reached the clinic, Toby rushed to the kennel while Riley went to the receptionist's desk to check the overnight messages.

Only three messages. Riley took notes as she listened, then wrote at the top of the sheet, 'Nothing Urgent."

She left her note on the desk before she joined George and Toby in the kennel.

George smiled when Riley and Toby joined him in the kennel. "Archie had a good night and is doing much better this morning," George said. "I expected the antibiotic to affect his appetite, but he ate all of his breakfast."

Archie purred, and Riley giggled.

George glared at Archie. "You weren't supposed to brag about the double portion."

Riley lightly stroked Archie. "How's your foot?"

Archie purred again.

"George, Archie thinks the swelling's gone down."

"I wouldn't be a bit surprised."

When Doc Thad, Zach, and Hector came to the kennel, Doc Thad said, "Zach's going to help me with Archie's dressing; after I examine the wound, Zach will let you know whether we'll be tied up for a while."

"We'll be in room three, Riley, if you want to assign someone new to work with us," Zach said.

She nodded and left to check in with Claire at her desk.

Claire put down the phone. "No new messages. Doc Julie Rae told me to pass the word that Pia let her know we'd be having Italian cream cake for dessert today, so she'll bring in Charlie's surprise tomorrow."

"Thanks. I had a fleeting thought that I might have to order a salad at lunch today."

"Fleeting?" Claire snickered. "You ignored it, right?"

"Of course." Riley smiled.

Whitney joined them at the desk. "Norm's putting his lunch into the refrigerator; he'll be here in a second."

"Zach and Doc Thad are moving Archie to room three; Doc Thad will examine Archie's foot and maybe put in stitches," Riley said. "Whitney, you can go to the kennel to work with them."

When Norm hurried to the desk, Claire said, "Our first patient will be here in ten minutes; while you read over the file, I'll let Doc Julie Rae know she's up first."

"I glanced at the file earlier, Norm. Take your time," Riley said.

After Norm read the file, he said, "We have a new patient that was a patient of Dr. Witmer. I didn't know there was another vet in Barton."

"After Dr. Witmer died, many of his local clients eventually shifted to Doc Julie Rae, and Pia adopted Dr. Witmer's Jordy."

"Our new patient is a four-year-old Great Dane named Iris. According to Dr. Witmer's records, she doesn't have any history of any medical problems, but the latest date was two years ago."

"What do you expect Doc Julie Rae will do?"

"A thorough physical, to start."

Riley nodded. "She will review Iris's immunization dates and order routine bloodwork unless she finds something that warrants additional bloodwork and tests."

When the client and the Great Dane came into the clinic, Norm smiled. "Hello, Iris. I'm Norm, and this is Riley. Let's stop at the scale for your weight, then we'll go to the exam room."

The client smiled at Claire. "You told me that Iris would be treated like a special guest at the clinic."

Iris and the client followed Norm to the scale. Norm coaxed Iris onto the scale, recorded her weight, and then led the way to room three.

"I have to take your temperature, Iris, but I'm fast," Norm said as they went into the exam room.

When Doc Julie Rae came into the exam room, Riley slipped out and strolled to the receptionist's desk.

Pia glanced up from the file she was reading. "Did you abandon Norm?"

"More or less," Riley said. "I didn't see any reason to hover while Doc Julie Rae examined the patient. Doc will take advantage of any teachable moments if I'm not there because she won't be worried about stepping on my toes. After Doc leaves, I'll go back and assist Norm."

When Norm and Riley returned to the desk, Zach was waiting. "The next patient is ours, Norm."

Before the sheriff arrived to pick up Riley for lunch, Riley frowned as she glanced at the stack of files for patients with appointments.

Claire asked, "Are you worried we're overwhelming Whitney and Norm?"

"Not really, because I know Whitney and Norm will be fine, but it doesn't seem right for me to walk out when we have such a busy schedule. This is going to be a hard week for me, isn't it?" Riley asked.

"I'll miss you, Riley; we all will."

"Ready to go, Riley?" the sheriff asked. "Brian Johnson will meet us at the restaurant north of town near the interstate."

As they left town, the sheriff said, "Brian Johnson called me a few years before your dad died. He told me he and his wife were from Atlanta and were visiting her family. He had promised Frank he'd give me a call when he was in Georgia. I only heard from him that one time until he called me and told me he had accepted a position in Atlanta to be near the families, and they were house hunting this week. I told him you were here, and he wanted to meet you."

When they went into the restaurant, a tall, heavyset man with gray hair sat near the host stand. He grinned as he hurried to Riley. "Riley Erin, I'd know you anywhere! You look like your mother when she was your age, except her hair was what she called chestnut brown. I was surprised when Sam told me you were in Barton."

"Your table's ready, sir. Come this way." The host led them to a table near a window. Riley chose the chair facing the front door and next to the window. The sheriff sat next to her, and Brian Johnson sat across from Riley.

Riley smiled. "I've never been here; I love the atmosphere, don't you? My social media's going to light up when I post these pictures." She snapped a photo of the menu and snapped several photos of their surroundings.

Sheriff chuckled. "We never thought about posting pictures on the internet to impress our friends. What about you, Brian?"

Brian shook his head. "It's beyond me."

After they ordered, Brian said, "Tell me about you and your husband." He pointed to Riley's ring on her left hand. "I have a story about my wife, Lynn, and your mother that I'm sure you'll enjoy."

"I'm a vet tech, and my husband, Ben, is a deputy sheriff. He was hired by the GBI and begins his training next week. I'll work with a veterinarian as a vet tech on farm visits."

"A vet tech? Your mother told Lynn that her mother-in-law had a way with animals; Erin called Mrs. Malloy a 'whisperer.'"

Sheriff smiled. "Riley's a whisperer."

"That makes total sense. Lynn will be so excited to meet you. We're staying with her mother until we can move into our own house near Atlanta, and I start my new position next week, too. Would you like to hear about the first time Lynn and Erin pulled a prank on your dad and me not long after your dad and I began working together?"

Sheriff nodded, and Riley smiled. "I'd love to."

"Lynn and Erin became close friends, and Erin invited us to have dinner at their apartment. Lynn told me that Erin confessed that she wasn't much of a cook, but she had a new recipe that she wanted to try. After work, I picked up Lynn; when we arrived, the Malloy apartment was filled with a cloud of acrid smoke from something in the oven that smelled like burnt old shoe leather. Frank had opened all the windows, turned on a fan, and stood in the doorway waving a kitchen towel while he coughed. My heart sank for Erin when I saw her red-rimmed eyes and sad expression."

Riley's eyes widened. "So much for the new recipe. What went wrong?"

The corner of Brian's mouth quivered, and his eyes twinkled. "She didn't say, and I certainly didn't ask. Erin told us she heard there was a great restaurant within walking distance of their apartment. It was a nice evening, and their house was still filled with smoke, so we walked to the restaurant. I was shocked when I realized she thought we could eat at one of the most exclusive restaurants in the district of expensive restaurants. Reservations were almost impossible to get, and I knew there was no way we could walk in and expect to be seated. I started to suggest another restaurant that was four blocks away and out of the fancy district, but Lynn whispered that Erin had a magical way of making things happen. Against my better judgment, I kept my mouth shut."

Sheriff shook his head. "There was not much else you could have done."

Riley narrowed her eyes and examined Brian's face. *Sheriff's as much into the story as I am. There's a catch because Brian said it was a prank. How did Mama set up Dad and Brian?*

"Erin was a beautiful young woman, just like Riley is now, and had a remarkable aura of charm, just like Riley. She smiled at the snooty host, and he beamed; I almost passed out when he bowed."

"The host said," Brian cleared his throat, then spoke in a melodious, snooty tone. "'Mrs. Malloy, how lovely to see you. Do you have four for dinner this evening? Give us just a moment.'"

Riley giggled. *I love my mama.*

Riley jumped when their server brought their food, refilled their sweet tea from a large pitcher, and then disappeared. *I forgot we were here, not at a posh restaurant in a big city.* She snapped photos of their plates of food and then took a selfie.

"Lean close to me, Sheriff, so I can have a snapshot with you," Riley said. The sheriff sat close to her, and Riley tilted her head. "Got it."

Brian continued, "Dinner was extraordinary; Lynn told me later that the first day Erin and Frank moved into the apartment, Erin walked to the restaurant shortly after they opened their door for customers and chatted with the owner, the host, and the chef. She continued visiting the restaurant every day; Lynn went with her a few times, and Lynn told me that Erin told them fantastic stories about a woman who chatted with animals."

"I wish I could have heard the stories." Riley sighed. "So, what was in the oven? Old shoe leather?"

Brian laughed. "Exactly. Lynn told me that Erin found a tattered single shoe with a leather sole in the street. She washed the sole and then broiled it in the oven. Lynn wrote down as many of Erin's stories as she could remember after Erin died. I'm sure she'll be happy to send them to you."

"Frank always told me that Erin was one of a kind." The sheriff winked at Riley. "He was almost right."

"Did you know Vivian Echols?" Riley asked.

Brian scowled. "Yes. Lynn isn't exactly what you'd call a fan of Vivian Echols. Vivian convinced your dad that you needed a mother; your dad relented after he talked to his sister. When we heard that Vivian had adopted you, Lynn hired a lawyer who could not find any records of an adoption in Georgia. Vivian Echols discovered someone was investigating her and left your dad. No big loss, as far as we were concerned."

Sheriff narrowed his eyes. "Why did Lynn hire someone to investigate Riley's adoption?"

"I should have known you'd catch that. Frank told Lynn he was concerned about Riley's future if anything ever happened to him. They had a long discussion, and then Lynn found a lawyer to coordinate an investigation into the adoption; Frank paid the lawyer. Ask Lynn about the lawyer's findings, Riley."

"I will."

After they finished eating, Brian snatched up the check, pulled a business card, and wrote on it. "My treat. Riley, here's my card. I wrote Lynn's email address on the back; she works from home as an editor. I'll let her know you're interested in Erin's stories. If you email her, she'll send you the stories and probably lots of questions because I never get enough details for her, and I forget the ones I do get."

Before they left, Riley said, "Selfie-time, Brian."

He shook his head. "Oh no, I'm camera shy."

Before he finished speaking, she jumped up and stooped close to him, snapped a photo, and then stopped the server and took a selfie with him.

On the way back to the clinic, the sheriff asked, "What was all the photo shoot stuff all about?"

"I don't know why I went overboard, but I wanted a picture of my dad's friend and knew he'd balk. As a bonus, I also got a picture of my dad's best friend."

The sheriff laughed. "I thought you'd lost your mind until I realized I could watch a genius in action. Send me the picture of you and me and the one of you and Brian."

Riley sent the pictures.

"Did you ever meet my mama?"

"Only once, and Brian was right; she was an attractive, engaging young woman. It's hard to believe she was the same age as you are right now. In retrospect, her death affected Frank more than I realized, not that I blame him; they were young and had their entire lives together ahead of them." Sheriff shook his head. "Tragic."

"Thanks for arranging the lunch; I never imagined how much it would mean to me."

"I do know that Erin was always thinking, just like you."

After Sheriff parked in the clinic back lot, he chuckled. "I had a long talk with Ben about you when I realized he was getting serious; now I think I should have had the long talk with you about Ben instead. Enjoy your afternoon, magical girl."

Riley went inside and then hurried to the receptionist's desk.

"How was lunch?" Claire asked.

"It was great; where do you need me?"

"Right here. I'm taking a break so you and Toby can watch my desk and phone."

She slipped her feet out from under Toby, who was sleeping. Toby opened one eye and then went back to sleep.

After Claire left, Riley reviewed the day's remaining appointments. When the phone rang, she answered.

"Riley Malloy, please," a man said.

"Sorry, you have the wrong number. This is a veterinarian hospital." She hung up.

When Claire returned, Riley asked, "Are you still getting calls for Riley Malloy?"

"Yes," she said.

"I just got one, too; I have an idea. Next time, make it obvious that you're trying to keep the caller on the phone. Everybody who watches TV knows it takes like thirty seconds or a minute to trace a call."

Claire giggled. "I like it."

"Thanks; seems like if someone's going to be nervous, it needs to be the caller."

Doc Thad joined them at the desk. "I'm glad you're back, Riley. Archie has stitches in his paw, and I put the cone on him so he can't bite or lick his bandage. I'd like to ask Archie's family to pick him up; would you tell him that keeping his wound dry is important?"

"Sure, doc."

Hector was outstretched on the cool floor near Archie's crate; he grinned as Riley hurried into the kennel.

"Archie, did Doc Thad tell you keeping your bandage dry is important? The cone will help you to keep from licking or biting your bandage because we don't want you to get an infection. He's calling your family to take you home."

Archie purred.

"It is good news. You're doing great."

As Riley headed back to the desk, she met Pia in the hallway.

"Zach's taking the next patient so I can have a break," Pia said. "Come join me."

Pia pulled her water bottle out of the refrigerator before she sat at the table. "I'm trying to break myself from snacking on every break, so I thought I'd try water." She took a big gulp. "I'm not sure it's quite the substitute I hoped it would be. How was your lunch?"

"It was great; I've never heard any stories about my family before from anyone except Grandma. How are you doing?"

"I'm obsessing over snacks when I'm not wishing I could take a nap, and I'm a little snappish, but overall, I'm fine." Pia smiled. "Tom and I decided to talk to Jackson this evening before eating supper. We decided against telling him last night because he would have been too excited to sleep. I am glad you have the cabin, so you'll be visiting us occasionally."

Claire said at the end of the day, "I'll plan on seeing you at six, but I can adjust if Ben's not home yet; just let me know."

After Riley and Toby were home, Riley let Toby out back while she showered. While she dressed, Ben came home, and she quickly texted Claire to let her know they'd be at her house by six.

She kissed Ben when he came into the house, and he hugged her and nuzzled her neck.

"You smell good; do I have time for a shower? I like that shirt." He gave her low neckline a slight tug and wiggled his eyebrows as he leered. "Nice chest."

Riley giggled. "You're so funny; Claire doesn't expect us until six, so you have plenty of time for a shower."

While Ben showered, Riley called Toby in and fed him. "We're going to Claire's tonight; are you going with us?"

Toby yipped, then nosed the back door, and Riley went out back with him. "You deserve a little quiet time. It's been a busy week already, hasn't it?"

When Ben swaggered out the back door and joined Riley on the porch, she jumped up from her rocking chair and hugged him. "You look nice in your jeans and cowboy shirt and smell good too."

"I've been looking forward all day to getting home and taking a break from being on call, so I'm celebrating," he said.

After they went inside, Toby jumped up on the sofa and stretched out.

"If we weren't going to have dinner with Claire and Thad, I'd be right there with you, Toby," Ben said.

Riley picked up her backpack. "I'm ready."

On the way to the Faradays, Riley's phone buzzed with a text from Pia. She read it and laughed before she read it to Ben: "Jackson already knew. Jordy can't keep a secret."

"I've wondered a few times about Jackson and Jordy, probably because of you."

Before Ben turned off the main road, he asked, "How was lunch?"

"It was great; I have a lot to tell you after we get home this evening."

"Anything bad?" he asked.

"No, nothing bad."

Ben smiled. "Good; we can enjoy the evening and relax."

Ben inhaled deeply when Doc Thad opened the door to let them in. "Cherry pie?"

"Tart cherry pie is one of my favorites in addition to any other pie that Claire bakes." Thad smiled. "We can stay out of the way on the back porch with drinks. What would you like? Wine, beer, sweet tea?"

"Sweet tea," Ben said.

"Come join me in the kitchen, Riley. I've already poured our wine," Claire called out.

After Thad and Ben went outside, Claire said, "We're having broiled lobster tails, coleslaw, and rolls. I'll show you how I prepare the lobster tails for the broiler. You'll only need to learn how to make a tender pie crust, which isn't hard, but I'll bet Ben's mother could teach you or not; that's your choice."

Riley sipped her wine and stared at the lobster tails. "I'm not sure I'll be able to tackle lobster tails."

"You'll be fine because it's logical."

While Riley set the table, Claire said, "Whitney and Norm survived both the day and Pia; I had a few moments of doubt, but any day that nobody walks out in a snit or tears is a good day. Archie was excited to be going home with the Hartway family. Mrs. Hartway's daughter told me her mother was initially agitated in her new surroundings but settled down when she found her favorite shawl on her old rocking chair in her room. The doctor told her that familiar, beloved items would comfort Mrs. Hartway."

"Pia said she was feeling snappish," Riley said.

"She didn't seem any different to me." Claire pulled out the lobster from the refrigerator and a pair of kitchen shears from a drawer. "Watch closely. The trick is to cut the shell all the way to the tail, then stop before you cut the tail."

Riley watched as Claire cut the shell. "You make it look easy."

As Claire spread open the shell, the meat separated from the sides. "I'll push the meat above the shell by pushing underneath the shell to push up the meat."

Claire handed Riley the bowl of melted butter with herbs and spices. "Brush the meat with about a tablespoon of our butter mixture."

"Now what?" Riley asked.

"I'll insert the wooden skewers lengthwise to keep the lobster tails from curling. When we're ten minutes away from being ready to eat, I'll pull out the pie from the oven, turn on the broiler, and then pop the lobster tails under the broiler."

"That's it?" Riley stared at the lobster tails.

"That's it. I made the coleslaw earlier, but that was just adding the dressing to the shredded cabbage and carrot mix and giving all the ingredients time to mingle. Speaking of mingling, want to join our husbands on the back porch for a few minutes?" Before they went out the door, Claire slid the pan of rolls into the oven and placed the butter on the table.

Chapter Eight

When Riley and Claire stepped outside, Thad said, "You're just in time; we've been discussing Doc Julie Rae's offer of a partnership in the clinic. What do you think, Riley?"

"I think it sounds wonderful, but it depends on where you want to be in fifteen or twenty years."

"We're happy in Barton and plan to be here for a long time," Claire said.

Thad nodded. "If we bring in a third veterinarian, we could definitely expand the practice. Doc Julie Rae wants to broaden our services to include large animals and have a regular rotation of the local farms. She and I talked about both of us having clinic time and farm visits so that we can back up each other."

"What about the vet techs for the farm visits?" Riley asked.

"We talked about hiring another vet tech but didn't think about a vet tech for the farms. Is that something we need to do?" Thad asked.

"I think so, but I'm prejudiced; that may be a good topic for you and Doc Julie Rae to discuss because she has the experience of going to Lindsey's farm with and without a vet tech."

"I'm announcing a ten-minute warning for our elegant dinner." Claire rose from her camp chair and headed to the door, and Riley followed her.

While Claire pulled out the pie and the rolls and then changed the oven to broil, she asked, "What would you do in our place?"

Riley placed the hot rolls into a basket covered with a cloth napkin and then covered them with another napkin. "Exactly what you're doing: look at all sides and consider the options, but I do think you're past the first step of deciding whether you want to stay in Barton long term."

"What we didn't mention," Claire added, "is that Charlie wants me to take over the business side because he wants to open a fine dining restaurant. It would mean enrolling Kenny and Freddy in public school, but Charlie thinks that's where they should be anyway when school starts up this next year. The partnership would have to hire a third veterinarian for Charlie to be able to focus on his restaurant business, so Doc Julie Rae would be available to take over more of the parenting responsibilities."

Riley shook her head. "There's a lot for everyone to think about, isn't there?"

Claire slipped the pan of lobster tails under the broiler. "Nothing's simple except on paper."

"Isn't that the truth; who said that?" Riley asked.

"I did; weren't you listening?" Claire smirked.

Riley giggled. "I knew you'd catch that, but it was already out of my mouth before I could stop. Should I pour sweet tea for us?"

"Go right ahead, then tell our men it's time to come in."

Riley opened the back door. "Time to come in."

Claire removed the skewers and then plated the lobster tails while Riley pulled out the coleslaw from the refrigerator and set the bowl and a serving spoon on the table. Claire set two plates on placemats, and Riley picked up the other two plates and put them on placemats, too.

Ben added ice to Thad's glass, then his while Thad refilled the glasses with sweet tea.

Claire and Riley sat at the table, and then Thad and Ben joined them.

Ben raised his eyebrows. "I feel like I should have worn a tie to this fancy restaurant."

"You've outdone yourself, honey," Thad said. "It's been a while since we've had a special occasion that we could celebrate. The lobster was an excellent choice."

"It's always been your favorite." Claire passed the coleslaw to Ben.

As they ate, Ben explained their housing dilemma. "While I'm still not excited about staying at the training center from Monday through Friday, it was our best alternative. Rent prices are steeper than we can manage on our budget, and I still wouldn't be home much because of the training demands."

Riley nodded. "I'm looking forward to working with Doc Seth. If you didn't already have an offer that you were considering, I'd tell you that Doc Seth is looking for someone to take over his practice so he can slow down and then retire."

"Uncle Seth works only on farms. He hired another veterinarian to take the clinic patients." Ben slathered his roll with butter.

Thad took another bite of lobster. "Mmm. This is really good, honey. I had several job offers around Atlanta, but we decided we weren't city people. I like Doc Julie Rae's plan of splitting our time between the farms and the office. I'm not quite ready to drive around the county every day, regardless of the weather. I won't mind being brave for an emergency call, but I like to have the option to be warm when it's cold and cool when it's hot."

"Working with Doc Seth is a great opportunity for me to find out what I like," Riley said.

Claire nodded. "Amanda told me she wouldn't mind working half days in the morning. Doc Julie Rae and I discussed the possibility of arranging the work so that Amanda could work from home. We've been so focused on getting Norm and Whitney up to speed that we haven't worked out the details for transition. Are you bored this week?"

"Not at all. I'm available this week for questions; I won't be next week, so it would be a disservice to them if I hovered all week."

Claire picked up her plate and Riley's. "Did everyone save room for pie?"

"I paced myself," Ben said.

Thad cleared the rest of the table. "I'll dish up the ice cream."

Claire sliced the pie. When she used the pie server to pick up a slice, most of the cherries slid out of the crust and onto the pie pan. She grabbed a spoon, scooped up the cherries, and dumped them on the broken crust.

"We'll call this cherry crash pie." She giggled as Thad dropped a scoop of ice cream on the hot pie filling and then handed it to Riley.

"I want a piece exactly like Riley's," Ben said.

"I think that might be easy for me." Claire carefully picked up a slice with the pie server, but before she could lift it away from the pie pan, the cherries slid out of both sides of the crust. She scooped up cherries and dropped them onto the crust in one swoop.

Claire sighed. "At least I'm consistent."

While the four of them ate pie, Thad's phone rang. He glanced at it and frowned. "I have to take this," he mumbled as he hurried outside.

"I've never seen him do that before." Claire headed to the back door. "I'm going to check on him."

"Riley, we need to hurry to the clinic; we've got four dogs from your neighborhood that appear to have been victims of a hit and run."

"Tell the caller to call nine-one-one. I'll bring Riley in my truck," Ben said.

Thad looked at his phone. "They already hung up."

"I'm riding with you, honey," Claire beat Thad to the front door. Ben and Riley dashed past them, then Thad locked the door, and the two men raced to the clinic.

On the way, Ben said, "I'm going to the sheriff's department and put myself on duty."

Riley nodded. When Ben stopped by the clinic's back door, she jumped out of his truck, and he sped away.

George unlocked the door as Riley, Doc Thad, and Claire rushed to the clinic, and Doc Julie Rae and Zach pulled into the employee lot.

Claire unlocked the front door, and Thad and Riley raced to the trauma room. Zach beat Riley to the x-ray and turned on the machine.

"Hector's with me, Zach," George said, then he and Hector left for the kennel.

Riley pushed their transport cart to the front door as Whitney and Norm ran to Claire's desk.

Riley scanned the room. "Whitney, grab the first patient and go to the trauma room. Norm, find another transport cart or steal the utility cart in the breakroom."

Riley frowned as she stepped to the front door and peered at the empty front parking lot. "Claire, I'll be right back."

She ran to the breakroom and called Ben. "Something funny's going on. I think someone is trying to get the entire team here because we haven't seen one patient."

"Get everyone away from the windows."

Riley breathed in, then exhaled before she stepped into the hallway. "Doc Thad, can I talk to you for a minute?"

Doc Thad hurried to join her.

"Who called you?" Riley asked.

"I'm not sure; it sounded like a frantic neighbor." He narrowed his eyes. "Why?"

"No patients and our entire team is here. Ben said to get everyone away from the reception area. I'll call the sheriff to see what he wants us to do."

Riley stood in the hallway out of sight from the front door to call the sheriff while Doc Thad sent Claire, Whitney, and Norm to the kennel and then locked the front door.

"Zach, make sure the back door is locked. Doc Julie Rae's in the trauma room; I'll check on her," Doc Thad said.

When the sheriff answered, Riley said, "We've all backed away from the front windows. Doc Thad said he thought it was a frantic neighbor who called him and told him four dogs had been injured by a hit-and-run car. We haven't seen one patient."

After Riley hung up, the office phone rang; she called out, "I'll answer the phone in Doc Julie Rae's office."

Riley took a cleansing breath and then answered the phone in the most bored tone she could manage. "Vet clinic. Do you have an emergency?"

She recognized the man's voice. *Same man.* "I need to talk to Riley Malloy."

"May I ask who is calling?"

"Doesn't matter. I need to talk to Riley Malloy."

"She's not, um..."

Riley sent another text to Ben and the sheriff. "Man asking for Riley M on work phone again, and phone display says out of the area."

She tapped the record app on her phone and then turned up the volume on the office phone.

"Can I take a message?" she asked.

The man sighed. "I just need to talk to Riley Malloy."

Riley frowned. "Fine. Go ahead."

"You're Riley Malloy?" he asked.

"You said you needed to talk to Riley Malloy. Why?"

"You're Riley Malloy? Can you prove it?"

"Sure. Can you prove you need to talk to Riley Malloy?"

The man snorted. "Give her a message. Tell her Vivian is poison, but there is someone more deadly."

"That sounds strange. Will she know what that means?" Riley asked.

"She's smart; you'll figure it out. Nice talking to you."

The man hung up; Riley stared at the office phone, then stopped recording. *Interesting choice of words.*

"Are you okay, Riley?" Doc Julie Rae stood in the doorway.

"Do you know about the man who has repeatedly called here and asked to speak to Riley Malloy?"

"Claire told me." Doc Julie Rae narrowed her eyes. "Was that him? What did he say?"

"Before he hung up, he said, 'Nice talking to you.'"

"What?" Doc Julie Rae sat down on the visitor's chair. "I don't get it. Is that code for something?"

"I don't know, but I don't think he's the man who called Doc Thad."

Riley headed to the hallway. "I have to find Doc Thad."

Doc Thad stood at the intersection of the hallway, where he could see the front and back doors. "Do you carry, Riley?" he asked quietly.

When she nodded, he said, "Good."

"I'd like to see your phone. I'm interested in seeing the phone number from the caller who reported the dogs being hit."

Doc Thad pulled out his phone and then handed it to her.

Riley sighed. "Not a surprise: Restricted number. I think we can send everyone home, but I'll check with Ben first."

She sent Ben a text: "Nothing. Can we send people home?"

Ben replied, "Yes, but ask Thad to stay until I get there."

Riley showed the text to Doc Thad.

Doc Thad nodded. "I'll release Whitney and Norm; will you talk to Doc Julie Rae? I'd like for her to leave at the same time as Zach and Hector, and I'll ask Zach to follow her home."

"First, I'd like for you to listen to a call that I recorded earlier; tell me if this is the same voice as the frantic neighbor that called you." Riley played the first part of the recording.

Doc Thad shook his head. "Not the same at all; your caller didn't call me."

While Doc Thad headed to the kennel, Riley returned to Doc Julie Rae's office.

"Anything new?" Doc Julie Rae asked.

"Ben said everyone can go home. Doc Thad is sending Whitney and Norm now; he'd like for you and Zach to leave together, and Zach will follow you home."

"Was it a prank call?" she asked.

"We don't know, but we don't have a number to call back, so we can't check. If any of us ever get another call like that, we should refer them to nine-one-one."

"I probably would have been caught up with a surge of adrenalin, too; we'll have a staff meeting and debrief in the morning."

"Doc Thad will probably want to lead the meeting," Riley said.

"You're right; I'll suggest it to him before Zach and I leave."

Not long after Doc Julie Rae and Zach left, Ben arrived. "One of the deputies is canvassing homes in our neighborhood. We didn't want to start a panic, so he's asking about a lost medium-sized brown dog."

Riley giggled. "That's pretty generic: it describes half the dogs in town."

"I'll bet he gets a few leads on that poor dog," Claire smiled.

"Everybody ready?" Ben asked.

George accompanied them to the back door. "I'll lock the door."

On the way home, Ben asked, "What did the guy who called say this time? Did he escalate to threats?"

"I recorded him so you could hear for yourself," Riley said. "That's okay, isn't it?"

"It's okay in Georgia because one of the parties on the call was aware the call was being recorded, but sometimes I worry about where you get some of your ideas. Play it after we get home so I can concentrate. Before I forget, out of area means your phone couldn't resolve the area code; it's typical for international calls and new area codes that haven't been updated yet across all the systems."

Riley frowned. "An international call? He said he couldn't find Barton on a map, so it was obvious he wasn't in town if he was telling the truth."

When they climbed out of the truck, Riley said, "That's odd. I don't hear Toby."

"He's probably sleeping," Ben said as they strolled to the porch.

"No, that's not it." Riley rushed to the door, but Ben dashed in front of her.

"No, Riley, step back and stay out here. I'll check," Ben growled.

Riley crossed her arms and glowered as he unlocked the door and went inside.

Ben called out, "He's not here, and the back door is open."

Riley rushed into the house. "My private box was on the table; it's gone."

"It's on the back porch. I think the lid might be broken." Ben reached inside and flipped the back porch light switch. "Babe, there's blood on the box and on the porch."

"Oh, no! Toby's hurt!" Tears streamed down Riley's face. "We need to find him."

"Come look, babe; why would the box have blood on it if Toby was hurt?"

Riley stared at the box. "We still need to find him."

While Ben called the sheriff, Riley listened to the neighborhood dogs.

"I think Toby might be okay," she said. "I'm going to check."

"Wait," Ben called out as Riley ran toward the barking dogs through the open back gate and down the alley.

Ben caught up with Riley at the end of the block, where she had stopped to catch her breath.

"Which way?" he asked as the neighborhood dogs continued to bark.

"I don't know; the dogs are irritated that Toby is running free, and they aren't. Just a second." Riley whistled a loud, piercing whistle, and the dogs stopped barking.

"Where's Toby?" she shouted, and her answer was a single bark.

"Come on, Toby, good boy! Let's go home," she called out.

Ben exhaled. "I recognized Toby's voice. He's about a block away, right?"

Toby dashed full speed to Riley with a big grin on his face and his tongue hanging out.

Ben called the sheriff. "We found Toby, but someone broke into the house. Toby must have chased them because we found blood on a small box of Riley's that was dropped on the back porch."

"Good boy," Riley said. "Did you bite the burglar?"

Toby yipped, then whined.

"It's okay; Ben won't be mad that you bit a bad man. We saw some blood on my box on the porch; we're glad it wasn't your blood."

When they went into the house, Ben rubbed Toby's ears and told him what a good boy he was before he fed him while Riley refilled Toby's water bowl.

One of the new deputies came to the house in a cruiser. He took pictures of the box and the porch, and Ben gave the young deputy a statement. Ben hovered while the deputy filled out his report.

"I have to take the box, Mrs. Carter," the deputy said.

"I understand," Riley said. "I'll eventually want it back because it's a family memory."

The deputy nodded. "I'll let the sheriff know."

After the deputy left, Ben locked the deadbolt on the back door. "I must not have checked the deadbolt before we left, but I have a feeling the burglar would have broken a window to get in if it hadn't been so easy to get into the house. I'd sure like to go off duty; do you suppose that's possible?"

"Yes, can I get you a beer? I'll have one with you."

Ben hugged her and chuckled. "A beer, my babe, listening to an anonymous caller and sifting through clues sounds like a normal, quiet evening for us."

After they sat on the sofa, they clinked their bottles.

Ben took a big first gulp. "Okay, I'm ready to listen to the caller."

Riley turned on the phone, and they listened.

At the end of the recording, Ben shook his head. "I have the strangest feeling that this guy was determined to warn you because he's concerned about your safety and not that he was threatening you. Am I just tired?"

"It was obvious he realized that he was talking to me; did you catch that?"

"Right; when he said, 'She's smart,' then followed it up with 'You'll figure it out.'"

Toby nosed the back door. "I'll go out with Toby. I need some fresh air to clear my head," Ben said.

"I'll go too; I'll tell you about lunch."

While Toby prowled the yard, Riley told Ben about Brian Johnson and his wife.

Ben chuckled. "Do you think the fantastic stories were about your grandma?"

"I'm sure they were. Do you think the Johnsons think a whisperer is someone who can calm animals?"

"That must be it. How did you keep from laughing when the sheriff told them you were a whisperer, too?"

Riley giggled. "It was awfully hard not to laugh when he winked at me." She smacked at a mosquito on her arm.

"Time to go in, Toby; the mosquitoes have found Riley," Ben said.

After Toby rushed to join them at the door, Ben asked, "Shall we look at the papers from your private box?"

"I'd like that." Riley pulled out the manila envelope from her backpack and handed it to Ben as they sat on the sofa.

"We can read together." Riley snuggled against Ben.

Ben reread the letter from Riley's grandma. "Does keep dancing mean something?"

"It was Grandma's way of encouraging me. I truly hated Vivian because of the way she treated me, and then I felt guilty because I assumed it was my fault. One time, I begged Grandma to let me stay with her, and she told me I was brave, smart, and a beautiful girl." Riley smiled. "Grandma told me to study Vivian to learn her mannerisms and what made her tick, then after that, I could watch out for Vivian, stay on my toes, and protect myself: keep dancing."

"So, keep dancing meant to watch for Vivian and protect yourself. Your grandma tried her best to give you good skills to help you cope, didn't she?"

Ben scanned the next document and then handed it to Riley. "This is your original birth certificate. You might want to read it closely."

Riley narrowed her eyes. "The original says I was born in Barton. Does that mean Mama lived with Grandma for a while?"

"She must have." Ben frowned. "I wonder what the Vivian birth certificate says."

He searched through the papers, found the more recent birth certificate, and frowned. "This one says you were born in Atlanta, and your name is Riley Echols Malloy. Did you ever see this birth certificate?"

"No, and that's not my name. The summer that I was seventeen, Grandma enrolled me in driving school; when I applied for my driver's license, Grandma drove me there, and she had all the documentation they needed. That was the same summer we applied for my social security card. Grandma opened a bank account with both of our names on it."

"Was that before or after Vivian Echols left your dad?"

"It was two years after she left."

"My untrained eye says this Riley Echols birth certificate isn't valid. What do you want to do? Should I give it to the sheriff?"

"I'd rather wait until I get to Carson. That will give me some time to think about it, and maybe Mom would have some ideas."

"I saw adoption papers; I'd like to look at them next," Ben said.

Riley nodded, and Ben held the document where both of them could read it.

"I want to take a closer look, then I'll give it to you." Ben flipped to the last sheet. "The signature sheet has only Vivian Echols listed; your dad didn't sign it, and the document isn't notarized; this must be a draft."

"I'll email Lynn Johnson right now; maybe I can talk to her tomorrow and ask her if Mother ever mentioned adopting me."

"Here's another interesting document. It's a marriage license from Cobb County, which is about twenty-five miles northwest of Atlanta, that was signed by your dad and Vivian but not by a judge or pastor, so this isn't a copy of the license submitted to the county, and it isn't a marriage certificate, which is the official county record of a marriage. That's a fine line, I know. We don't have our marriage certificate yet because it takes up to thirty days to get it from the county."

Riley's eyes widened. "Does that mean we're not married?"

Ben kissed her. "We're married, babe. There's nothing anyone can do to halt a legal marriage after the officiant delivers the marriage license to the county. If it's okay with you, I'm turning this piece of the puzzle over to Mom because it's exactly what she likes to do, and both of us will be too busy for any follow-up."

"You'll be too busy, honey, but I'll be looking for something to do after supper every evening. I'll see what I can find; it looks like they were married in Cobb County, so I can request a copy of the certificate. If it's not there, I can ask Mom if she has time to search for a marriage certificate; she'll turn the state upside down until she finds the right county."

"Here's a picture of your mama."

Riley stared at the photo of the young woman who was spraying flowers in front of the cabin with a water hose and was laughing as she looked over her shoulder at the photographer. "Grandma tried to get a candid shot, but Mama caught her."

Riley smiled as a tear slipped down her cheeks. "Mama was pretty, wasn't she? I love her brown hair and dark eyes."

"You look exactly like her, Babe," Ben said quietly. "I've seen you look at me like that. Your grandma didn't take the picture; your dad did."

Riley lightly brushed the photo with her fingertips. "I'll bet she sprayed him right after he took the picture."

Her eyes welled up, then overflowed, and her voice cracked. "She loved Dad."

"Very much. I understand why your dad's heart was broken." Ben swallowed hard and tried to sniff back any tears, but one slipped down his cheek.

He brushed it away as he hugged Riley and audibly exhaled. "Here's a newspaper clipping; it's your mama's obituary."

Riley blinked away her tears and read. "Mama had a younger brother; his name is Connor Larson. I didn't know that."

"What?" Ben read over Riley's shoulder. "He was sixteen years old. I wonder where he lived because there's no mention of any other relatives besides Erin's parents who predeceased her."

"I never heard anything about him; Dad never mentioned him."

"It might have been because Vivian may have insisted that you needed to bond with her, but to your credit, you didn't. It's a little surprising that Vivian didn't try to interfere between you and your grandma."

"Not really; Mother made it quite clear that she didn't like children at all, and me in particular, so she was probably happy that Grandma would take me off her hands until she realized Grandma and I would be happy if I stayed with Grandma permanently." Riley sighed. "She was 'Mother' to me for my entire life; it's hard to think of her as 'Vivian.'"

"She would have lost your hold on your dad," Ben said.

Riley frowned. "Right. I wonder if Dad asked Aunt Millie for her opinion, and she agreed that every girl needs a mother; she may have felt guilty because she was always traveling and was frequently not available, even by phone, but what was it about Dad that motivated Mother to push him to marry her?"

"That's a hard one to answer; we may never know," Ben said.

"Everything we've learned has helped me to put Vivian and her impact on my self-esteem into perspective. I had always felt it was my fault that she left Dad, but now, I'm proud of myself if I did have any part in it."

"You are awesome, babe. I can't imagine why anyone would want any of these documents. Other than the photo of your mama and the obituary, everything else we've seen is incomplete information that can be replaced with official records."

'What else do we have?" Riley peered at the envelope.

Ben frowned as he read. "Your dad's obituary. Vivian obviously wrote it or provided the information. I'm surprised your grandma kept it. I would have burned it."

"Dad died two years after Vivian left. I'm not sure why she would have been involved."

Riley read the obituary. "Ben, I've never seen this obituary for Dad; I'm not even mentioned. I have a copy of the one that Grandma and I wrote for the Barton and Atlanta papers. It's nothing like this."

Chapter Nine

Riley pointed to the first paragraph in the obituary. "Loving wife, Vivian? That's a flat-out lie, and what about this? Dad's brother-in-law, Ronald Echols, is listed as a close relative? I've never heard of him. There must be something significant that Grandma wants me to know."

"My suspicious side wonders if he's Vivian's brother or a husband, but wouldn't that be too blatant to have printed in an obituary?" Ben asked.

"It was blatant enough that she called herself his wife, but I'm not objective when it comes to Vivian Echols because my first thought is that she would have been happy to flaunt an ex-husband because she was always so mean to me."

Ben peered into the envelope. "There's one more piece of paper in here."

He pulled it out and grinned. "I love your grandma. There's a short note attached with a paper clip."

Ben read the note aloud. "You were five; this is one of my favorite drawings you did for me. Love you, Grandma."

Ben handed the hand-drawn picture to Riley. "It appears to be a family picture."

Riley smiled as she gazed at her drawing . "There's Grandma and Dad, and that's me in the middle, holding hands with both of them. Don't you love my wild, red hair? I think the dog next to Grandma was Old Dog."

She squinted as she searched the drawing, then laughed. "See the tiny black squiggles in the bottom left corner? That's Vivian."

Ben laughed as he hugged her. "Ole Vivian couldn't totally squash your spirit, could she?"

"I guess not. I think Grandma wanted me to remember that I was tougher than I realized."

"She got that right." Ben rose to let Toby outside.

When he returned, he said, "The last document is the trust company's address and phone number and a contact name; that's it."

Riley asked, "What if the thief was not interested in the papers but in the few pieces of jewelry that were in the bottom of the box?"

"I suppose, but it was a pretty elaborate scheme to get us away from the house for a random thief to use," Ben said.

After Toby came back inside, Riley yawned.

"My feelings, exactly." Ben swooped her up from the sofa and carried her into the bedroom.

The next morning, Riley woke with a heavy weight across her chest. She stifled her giggle. *Wonder if I can slip out from under his arm without waking Ben.* She shifted slightly toward the edge of the bed.

"Where are you going?" Ben mumbled.

Riley climbed out of bed. "You were supposed to stay asleep because I'm so stealthy. I'll start the coffee if you want to shower first."

Riley grabbed her robe from the closet while Ben grumbled, "It's too early for it to be morning."

He stumbled into the bathroom and turned on the shower to warm the water.

Toby waited for her in the kitchen, then nosed the back door.

"I'm not going out with you, Toby. It's too cold for me." Riley started a pot of coffee, gathered the papers from her grandma, and returned them to her backpack.

After Ben dressed, he came into the kitchen, and Riley poured him a cup of coffee.

"Eggs, bacon, and toast?" he asked.

"If that's what you're having," Riley took her cup to the bedroom to select her clothes for the day before she took her shower. When she returned to the kitchen, Ben had already fed Toby, and she and Ben sat down to breakfast.

"I forgot to tell you that you got an email while you were in the shower." Ben dipped his toast into his egg and smiled when the yoke broke, and his toast soaked up the silky richness of the bright orange egg. "Mmm; the best way to start the morning."

Ben had cooked Riley's egg yolk a little firmer. *Exactly the way I like it.*

She ate her egg and then her toast. "I'll check my phone after breakfast. It's not from you, so it isn't urgent."

After she cleared the table, she picked up her phone. "I have an email from Lynn Johnson. She invited me to have lunch with her, but there's no attachment." Riley responded to Lynn's email.

"Good timing," Ben said. "I haven't made your lunch yet."

"I'll make your lunch for you, or do you have a lunch date?"

Ben smiled. "I'm having lunch with the sergeant. I'll run pick up something for both of us, and we'll eat at his desk. Neither one of us wants to be in a diner and have to dash out. I'll drop you off at the clinic when you're ready to leave."

"There's no reason for you to chauffeur; I'll take my car. Toby and I will be fine."

Ben rolled his eyes. "I'm not so sure about that, but I don't have a decent argument." He hugged her tightly, and then she kissed him.

As Ben headed to the front door, Riley said, "Be safe."

"That's my line, babe." Ben smiled. "Call me if you need me."

"Always. I'll always need you."

Ben strode back to Riley, kissed her with longing, and then dashed out to his truck.

Riley glanced at the back door. "Deadbolt is locked; let's go to work, Toby."

When she and Toby went into the building, Doc Julie Rae met them in the hallway. "Will dinner at six work for you? We'll want you there at five-thirty, and the boys want to pick out the yellow flowers after school." Doc Julie Rae smiled. "I think that's everything I'm supposed to tell you from the ranch hands. Can we take an early morning break? I'm afraid we won't have any time to talk when the patients start rolling in."

Riley poured their coffee while Doc Julie Rae pulled out a white sack from the refrigerator. "Charlie made the Danish dough last night, then made the cheese danishes for us this morning as a treat. I can't imagine not being married to a chef who also runs my business." Doc Julie Rae pulled out two dessert plates from the sack. "Charlie didn't want us to put our pastries on a paper towel."

Riley smiled. "He's definitely a keeper."

Doc Julie Rae sipped her coffee. "The smartest thing I've ever done in my life was to let him propose. I can still hear my Mom: 'You're a doctor, and you want to marry this man who has to go to people's houses to cook because he isn't even good enough to cook in a diner?'"

Riley giggled. "She evidently didn't understand what a personal chef did."

"Now she absolutely loves Charlie and brags about him all the time. 'My daughter is married to a big-time chef.'" Doc Julie Rae bit into her Danish. "Mmm; good as ever. So what's up with you? Where are we with the investigation into why Thad got that phony call?"

We? Riley rolled her eyes and bit into her Danish. "We really don't know any more than we did last night, except for the reminder not to rush to the clinic for an off-hours emergency unless we hear about it from the sheriff's office."

"That was actually a very timely lesson, wasn't it? You kept us from stewing about our missing patients with your instinct to check with the sheriff. So, what are your plans between now and Friday? Are you leaving on Saturday?"

"I'm having lunch with the wife of one of my dad's closest coworkers. She knew my mama and had stories. I can't wait to hear what she has to say. She and her husband came to see the sheriff because they knew he was Dad's best friend."

"How wonderful that you were here to meet them. Enjoy your lunch, and don't rush on our account unless you get bored. Then you better cut it short because we need all the help we can get," Doc said.

"It's good to have options, thanks. Before we come to your house this evening, we'll load what we want to take to the cabin in Ben's truck. After we leave your house, we'll go to the cabin and unload. It won't take long because we really don't have very much. We'll pack up everything else on Thursday night and load my car and Ben's truck after we get home on Friday. I suspect Mom will want us to have supper with them, so we'll leave as soon as we have everything loaded. Helen told us not to try to clean the house after we leave because she has a crew coming in on Monday that will deep clean."

"I'm sure Ben will follow you because he doesn't trust you to stay behind him without wandering away and catching a bad guy on the way to Carson." Doc Julie Rae wiggled her eyebrows before she ate her last bite.

Riley chuckled. "If I tried to convince him that I wouldn't go off on a tangent, he'd tell me I couldn't help it because that's how I roll."

"You'll have to admit that's true."

Riley shrugged. "What about you and the clinic? What are your plans?"

"Our first step is to get Whitney and Norm settled in, but from what I've seen, that won't take very long; I'd like to start the process of finding a third veterinarian. Thad and I have been talking about a hiring process. We realize it might be hard to find anyone willing to come to a small town, but we can't afford to bring in anyone who is mediocre or has a big ego. I don't want anyone here who would upset our balance and culture. Although, our crew would have no qualms at all in setting them straight or setting their hair on fire."

Riley smiled. "That's the truth."

"Claire, Amanda, and I are talking about a job share, and I think it's an excellent idea. We're working on the logistics, which means Claire and Amanda will tell me what they decide we're going to do, and Charlie will pay the bills. Speaking of which, you have a job here anytime you want. Charlie wanted me to remind you that he has a special Riley fund set aside, except the boys said you have to bring Ben, too. Your biggest fans live at my house, so if you ever need a little lift, come visit, and you'll be fed and bombarded with Old West trivia."

"The boys and yellow flowers reminded me that I need to drop by the grocery store before we leave town. Maybe Toby and I can do that on our way home."

"Mrs. Smythe will enjoy that; Sheriff is coming to our house for dinner, too. I thought he'd like to spend some time with you."

"Thank you; he was my dad's best friend and has been representing Dad when I needed him."

Doc Julie Rae sighed. "Sadly, Charlie gave us only one Danish each and laughed when I asked for extras to share with the office. Am I that transparent? Don't answer; I have paperwork to finish for that stingy chef."

Riley drained her cup and then hurried to the receptionist's desk to listen to the messages and take notes for Claire. When she listened to the last message, she hung up the phone, and Toby trotted to the kennel to check in with George to get his morning treat.

The phone rang, and the display showed 'Out of Area.' Riley shrugged and answered.

The man with the familiar voice said, "I have one last message for Riley Malloy. Are you ready?"

"Go ahead," Riley said.

"Tell her she will get a text with a number. Anytime she is in trouble, tell her to send a text to that number. It doesn't matter what she says in her text; she'll get help. Got it?"

"She'll get a text with a number, and if she needs help, she's to send a text that says anything to that number. Is that right?"

"Yes. I won't call again. It was nice chatting with you." The man chuckled as he hung up.

Riley shook her head. *My prank caller and I have a code phrase.*

Her phone buzzed with a text from a national bank. *Good spoofing.*

She sent herself an email with "kitchen mixer product number" as the subject and the number to text in the body of the email. *This secret code stuff is contagious.*

Claire joined her at the desk. "Anything interesting?"

"Just two messages, but neither one is urgent. I wrote down the callers' phone numbers and the patients' names so you can follow up." Riley pointed to her notes. "The first one is a question that Pia can answer; the second one will need an appointment when you can slide them into the schedule."

Claire looked at the notes. "Is this a question that Norm or Whitney could answer?"

"Actually, yes, I wasn't thinking. Either one can answer the question."

"Good. Send me the first vet tech you see, and we'll call our client right back. There's no sense in dragging it out. Then I can call the appointment client."

On her way to the kennel, Riley met Whitney, who was coming in the back door. "After you put your lunch away, see Claire. She needs you to answer a client's question."

Whitney grinned and muttered, "Oh boy, oh boy," as she hurried to the breakroom.

"Excited about finally getting your own assignment?" Riley asked when Whitney raced past her to go to Claire's desk.

"You got it," Whitney said.

That Claire is really smart.

When Riley went to the kennel, George was packing his lunch bag and thermos. "When do you leave, Riley?"

"We'll leave Friday afternoon," she said.

"I never fraternize with coworkers, but I'm making an exception. I would like a farewell hug on Friday morning if you won't go all teary on me."

Riley raised her eyebrows. "No promises, but I'll try my best."

"Good, that's all I can ask." George saluted her before he left.

"I'm getting all teary just thinking about it, Toby. This will always be our hometown, won't it?"

When Riley joined Whitney and Claire at the receptionist's desk, Claire said, "The first patient is yours and Whitney's, Riley. The original appointment was this afternoon, but the client just called to ask if they could come in earlier. They'll be here in fifteen minutes. Here's the folder."

"We'll do a quick morning check of the trauma room, and then you can decide which room we'll use for our patient, Whitney; have you already reviewed the file?" Riley asked as they strolled to check the trauma room first.

"Sure did. Collette is an eight-year-old French bulldog. You probably know her because I saw your notes in the file."

Riley nodded. "She's a sweet girl."

"She hasn't been eating very well for the past three days and shaking her head frequently."

"What do you think?"

"I think she most likely has an ear infection. After we weigh her and take her temperature, I'll ask the client if she's drinking less water and whether there has been any change in her bowel habits." Whitney smiled. "Claire warned me about saying poop around the younger set, so I thought I'd try different ways to ask. I'm sure Doc Thad will want to look at her ears."

"So why are both of us seeing Collette? Not that I mind," Riley said.

Whitney bit her lip. "Riley, Pia doesn't intimidate me at all with her blustery ways because my sister is a perfectionist just like Pia, so I'm used to it. I can't explain why you intimidate me, but I'd like to understand so I won't be nervous around you. I know that it must sound strange to you, but what if we get an extremely talented vet? I told Claire I was really worried that my performance would suffer, and she told me not to worry because she'd take care of it."

Whitney side-glanced at Riley. "I thought Pia was tough, but when Claire told me you and I had the first patient this morning, I almost passed out."

"The only thing I think you may have missed is that Claire said Collette had an appointment this afternoon, but the client called this morning and asked to bring her in earlier. Your instincts were right about asking whether she's drinking less."

"Thanks, but I did miss the point that Collette's condition may have worsened."

"How can I help?" Riley asked.

"Claire told me you'd ask me that; she suggested that I ask you to come after me and push me back into the exam room if I start crying and run out of the room." Whitney snorted.

"That Claire's all heart, isn't she?" Riley asked.

"I guess you have to watch out for the quiet ones." Whitney sighed.

"I'm sorry I intimidate you; I put on my superhero cape every morning before I leave the house just like you do," Riley said.

Whitney smiled. "I'll remember that. Knowing that Collette's condition deteriorated gave her visit a completely different perspective, didn't it? The first step before anything is to assess her condition to see if she's in danger."

"Absolutely; let's see if Collette is here."

When the client carried Collette inside, she was limp, and her eyes were listless.

"Oh, dear, Collette, you look like you don't feel well at all," Riley said. "Whitney and I will help you. She'll get the transport cart, so you won't have to walk to the exam room then while you and I go to your exam room, she'll get Doc Thad for us."

The client sighed in relief. "Thank you, Riley. She hasn't felt well for a couple of days, but she couldn't even make it to her water bowl this morning."

When Whitney brought the rolling transport cart, Riley helped the client put Collette on the cart.

Claire asked, "Would you like to have a cup of coffee with me while Doc Thad examines Collette?"

"Thank you, Claire. I was so worried I hadn't had any coffee this morning."

"I'll take care of that," she said.

When Riley rolled Collette into room three, Doc Thad came into the room from the back hallway.

"We'll get some fluids in her," Doc Thad said. "Whitney's getting the IV fluids set up."

Riley took Collette's temperature. "Her temp is elevated: one hundred four."

Doc Thad looked at her ears, listened to her heart, and checked her gums. "Both of her ears are infected, but her heart's good, and her gums are gray. George will have company this evening. While Whitney and I treat Collette, would you talk to the client, Riley?"

Riley nodded. "Claire took him to the breakroom for coffee."

"Perfect, I'll join you there after Collette is settled in the kennel."

"Ask Whitney to find me after she's been released so we can clean the room and replenish supplies together," Riley said before she went to the breakroom.

Claire slipped out while Riley sat at the table with the client.

"Both of Collette's ears are infected, and she has a high fever. She wasn't drinking water because she didn't feel good, then she became dehydrated from not drinking and became too weak to drink, and her fever rose higher because her ears were infected, and she was dehydrated. It is a really vicious cycle. That's why she was so sick this morning. You were smart to call and tell Claire you needed to come in immediately."

Whitney quietly stepped into the breakroom and stood near the doorway while Riley and the client talked.

"I was?" the client asked. "I thought she was sick because I'd done something wrong."

"Not at all. We'll keep her here until she's feeling better, but Doc Thad will talk to you more about that. Do you know George, the retired animal control officer? He stays here at night and takes care of our overnight patients."

"I've known George for years. He never had what you'd call people skills, but he always had a way with animals." The man chuckled. "The city council decided they needed to get rid of George long ago because he told one of them to get out of his office. I never heard why, but we all knew it had to be justified."

"Did someone stop the city council?"

"Sure did; those pompous hyenas forgot the following month was an election. Did you know your grandmother was instrumental in getting the recall vote on the ballot? They were lucky she didn't decide they needed jail time for harassing a city employee."

Riley giggled. "I didn't know about that, but I'm not a bit surprised. Grandma didn't have much use for people either."

"She certainly was good with animals, just like you, Riley."

Doc Thad joined them. "Are you ready to see Collette? She's sleeping, but it's like I've heard my friends who are people doctors say, go ahead and talk to her; she may not respond, but your voice will comfort her."

After Doc Thad and the client left for the kennel, Riley asked, "We really made a mess in the room, didn't we? I am usually more organized, but sometimes, being fast is more important than being pretty."

On the way to the exam room, Riley asked, "How was the intimidation factor? How did you do?"

"I was too busy with Collette to worry about myself; that was huge." Whitney raised one arm to her side and swung it. "The biggest boost was my cape."

Riley giggled. "What color is it?"

"Deep purple, for royalty." Whitney fluttered her eyelashes.

Riley burst out laughing; Whitney grinned, flourished her arm, and curtseyed. When Riley applauded, Claire hurried from her desk.

"What's going on in here?" Claire asked. "I think I just missed out on something fun."

"Whitney was showing off her royal purple superhero cape." Riley laughed, and Whitney snort-laughed.

Claire flipped her hair and minced away with a princess wave.

"We're out of control," Whitney said when she caught her breath.

"Nothing new about that." Doc Julie Rae came out of an exam room with a patient and a client, and Riley and Whitney hurried back into their exam room and finished cleaning and replenishing supplies.

"Are we going to stay here for the rest of the day?" Whitney asked.

"There's no way a little embarrassment and intimidation would keep me from a meal." Riley wiggled her eyebrows.

Whitney nodded. "I like how you think."

When they reached the desk, Claire said, "Riley, you're going to have a visitor this afternoon. Tamara called to make sure you'd be here after school because Mini-me wants to see you before you leave Barton."

Whitney cocked her head. "You have a mini-me? Is she like a cousin or something?"

"Maddie Price is five years old and Riley's absolutely precious doppelganger. You'll see when she gets here."

"How did she become a mini-me?" Whitney asked.

Claire chuckled. "She and her dad were at the gas station not long after they moved here, and she told everyone that Ms. Riley saved her baby sister, and she had a surprise for her. One woman told her that she was Ms. Riley's Mini-me, and she insisted that everyone, even her parents, call her Mini-me. I accidentally called her by name, and the temperature in the reception area dropped twenty degrees." Claire shivered. "I never made that mistake again."

"What? Saved her baby sister?" Whitney's eyes were wide.

"That's a story for another time," Claire said. "Don't let me forget, and before you ask, wait until after lunch."

"Shoot. I was going to ask how soon I could ask again." Whitney rolled her eyes. "You've definitely taught middle school."

Zach and Norm joined them at the desk. "Is this a meeting? Who's next?" Zach asked.

"Norm is." Claire handed him the file.

"Doc Thad told me to give you a break, Claire, so I'll take the desk," Zach said.

"Thanks, Zach. I don't get a chance to take a break with my husband very often." Riley walked with Claire toward the breakroom and then continued to the kennel.

"I thought I'd find you here, Toby. How's Collette doing?"

Toby whimpered.

"Sorry," Riley whispered. "She does need the rest. I'm going out to lunch soon."

When Lynn pulled up in front of the clinic, Zach peered at the car. "I heard Brian Johnson was in town. Who is the woman in the car with him?"

"That's his wife; we're going to lunch together. Do you know Brian and Lynn Johnson?" Riley asked.

Zach strolled with Riley to the door while Claire was on the phone. "My mother does," he said quietly. "I'm going to call her; just be careful what you say. We'll talk after you get back."

Zach put his hand on Riley's arm; when she turned to look at him, she was startled by the seriousness of his face. "Riley, be very careful."

She nodded. *That was a little unsettling.*

As Riley climbed into the car, Lynn said, "Our real estate agent called; she has a house that she said won't be on the market long. It sounds ideal, so I'm driving back to Atlanta after lunch."

"That's exciting; have you been staying in a hotel?" Riley asked.

"Sure gets old." Lynn shook her head.

Brian said they were staying with Lynn's mother. This is going to be an interesting lunch.

"What about you? I understand you're leaving Barton at the end of the week because your husband's going to work for the State Police. Do I have that right?"

Riley smiled. *Testing me?* "He will be working for the Georgia Bureau of Investigation. We'll be in Macon for a while."

"Macon? That's wonderful because it's close to Atlanta, except isn't the cost of housing a little steep for you?"

"It has been tricky trying to find something we can afford that is move-in ready, but we have a great agent here in Barton, and she knows everyone."

"Who is that? Oh, I'll bet it's Helen. My real estate agent wanted me to drop by Helen's office, but she wasn't there."

"Helen is always busy. The best way to contact her is by phone; her business number is on her door."

"I saw that and wrote it down; I'll give her a call after I drop you off to see if I can swing by her office before I have to leave town."

After they were seated and had ordered in the small diner, Riley stopped the server and took a selfie with her. Then, she snapped photos of the diner's décor and menu. *I have to maintain my reputation as a social media freak.*

The owner came out of the kitchen. "Take a selfie with me, too, Riley. I'll post it on the restaurant's social page. Send me the best of the others that you took, too; you did what I've been thinking about doing for three years in three minutes."

When he chuckled, Riley got a good candid shot of him and then took the selfie he had requested before she sat down.

"Did you ever meet my dad's sister?" Riley asked.

"Mildred? She and I were very close. What do you remember about her?"

"She traveled a lot. I seem to remember mostly internationally, but I'm not sure. She called me when she could after Grandma died."

Lynn nodded. "That was Mildred. She'd pop in from time to time when we were in Germany. She was really close to Erin but didn't care much for Vivian. Did you get along with Vivian?"

"Hey, Riley," a man in the corner booth waved. "I need a selfie with you."

Riley rushed to stand near the man.

The server giggled as she rushed past them. "You're short like me, Riley, and don't even have to lean over."

Chapter Ten

After Riley took selfies with the man and his boothmate, she returned to sit with Lynn and snapped a quick selfie with Lynn before Lynn could cover her face.

"Don't do that again," Lynn hissed. "Delete it immediately."

"Sorry." Riley deleted a random photo and then put her phone in her back pocket. "Deleted. Mother wanted the best for me and taught me life skills that I wouldn't have learned anywhere else. I know a lot about nutrition, finances, and physical health; I was surprised that my friends at school didn't know how to balance a checkbook or plan a budget." Riley giggled. "Mother had impeccable taste in fashion; I'm not sure I inherited that."

Lynn smiled. "Vivian could be a little harsh, and sometimes she got under my skin, but it sounds like she did a great job of raising you."

Riley nodded. "That's what Grandma thought, too. Brian said my dad asked you to look into my adoption because the papers weren't complete or something like that, and you had a report from a lawyer. Do I have that right?"

"Almost," Lynn chortled. "I don't know where Frank got the idea that the papers hadn't been filed correctly, but the lawyer charged me an exorbitant fee to tell me that everything was in order. When I gave Frank the lawyer's report, he was obviously pleased; I didn't keep a copy of the report the lawyer prepared because it belonged to Frank, not me."

"That makes sense."

"Mildred once told me she was jealous of Vivian's wardrobe, and I completely understood because Vivian really was a fashionista. I don't hear much from Mildred anymore, but Vivian and I still touch base from time to time. I'll catch her up on your news the next time I talk to her."

While they ate, Lynn asked, "Didn't you say your husband's new job begins on Monday? Where are you going to stay until you find a place to live?"

"We have several possibilities that sound very promising, but we have friends who live in the area, so we'll be fine."

"You young people are so flexible; I'd be a wreck from worrying about going to a town and not having anywhere to live."

"We have options, so we'll be fine. Brian mentioned that you have a record of some of Erin's stories and might send them to me. I'd be interested in reading them."

"I'd love to. They're packed in a box somewhere, but I'll mail them to you as soon as I find them. Just send me your address after you move."

Brian said you could email them to me. My head hurts. "I will do that," Riley said.

When the server stopped by to drop off their check, Riley said, "I'll take that."

"I invited you, so I should pay for our lunch," Lynn said.

"You're a visitor, and I enjoyed hearing about Mother and my aunt; you can pay when I visit Atlanta." Riley smiled.

"That's a deal. I know a really nice place that's halfway between Atlanta and Macon where we can meet for lunch," Lynn said. "Did Mildred leave any papers with your grandma for safekeeping? I wonder if she might have some pictures of Vivian."

"No, my aunt cleared Grandma's house of any personal items while I was attending college to become a veterinary technician because she rented the cabin to vacationers."

As Lynn pulled into the clinic parking lot, she asked, "You wouldn't happen to have Mildred's phone number, would you? I've lost touch with her since I got my new phone six months ago, and my contact list didn't transfer correctly."

"I don't have her phone number. As long as I can remember, she always bought local phones; she told me it was much cheaper than the extra taxes and fees she would have to pay if she used a US carrier."

"I knew that; I had just forgotten. I always thought that was really smart of her. Do you hear from her very often?"

Riley smiled as she opened the door. "Sometimes every week, and sometimes less frequently; it all depends on where she is."

"If you hear from her, let me know. I'd love to catch up with her."

Riley nodded and then closed the car door.

When she went into the clinic, Claire asked, "How was lunch?"

"Not as much fun as eating here, but I might be prejudiced."

"Next patient is Pia's; Whitney's finishing up her patient, and Zach, Hector, Jordy, and Toby are with Collette," Claire said.

"I'll check on Collette," Riley said, and Claire nodded as she answered the phone.

When Riley joined Zach in the kennel, Collette, Toby, Jordy, and Hector were asleep.

"How was lunch?" Zach asked.

"Brutal; I'm glad you warned me because it was a cat and mouse game the entire time, and I'm pretty sure I was the mouse. I did snap pictures of both of the Johnsons. So, what do you know about Lynn Johnson?"

Zach chuckled. "I doubt you were the mouse. Lynn Johnson was a friend of my mother's when my parents lived in Atlanta. What's the one thing you know about my mother?"

Riley frowned, and then her eyes widened. "Any of her friends would be Vietnamese."

"Right. L-i-n-h Johnson."

"Wow. You didn't have time for a complete explanation because there were other people around, and I was halfway out the door; telling me to watch what I said was brilliant."

"Thanks. At first, I was worried that I was being too obscure, but then I realized you'd get it."

"That means that Brian Johnson is not who he said, either. I need to tell the sheriff." Riley picked up her phone to send a text and then exhaled. "My text has to be casual, or the sheriff and Ben will race to the clinic with a SWAT team."

"You could always tell him you're back from lunch with additional information. Send me the pictures; maybe Mom's friend knows the people."

"You're on a streak of genius ideas, Zach." Riley grinned, then sent the text to the sheriff and the two photos to Zach.

As she strolled to the reception area, her phone buzzed with a text from the sheriff. "Meet me at the back door."

She about-faced and hurried to the back door as the sheriff pulled into the employee parking lot.

He climbed out of his cruiser. "Whatcha got?"

Riley told him about Zach's mother and Linh Johnson and concluded with her conversation with the imposter, Mrs. Johnson.

"You got a selfie with her too, didn't you?" the sheriff smiled.

"Of course, I had to keep up my reputation of being obsessed with social media. I'll send it to you."

While Riley scrolled to the photo then sent it, Sheriff said, "I'd forgotten what Millie's given name was, and I have never heard anyone call Millie 'Mildred'. How did you keep from slipping?"

"I just called her my aunt. I don't think I gave the imposter Brian Johnson any information either that he couldn't have gotten from the gas station, and I didn't even think of him as an imposter."

"You must have had some inkling, though, because I caught the mood from you. After you left yesterday morning, he asked me more pointed questions about you and Ben, so I texted one of the new deputies to take a photo of the man when he left the building, then told Brian an emergency had come up and apologized for having to end our conversation so abruptly. I walked him to the front door so the deputy would be sure to get a picture of the right person."

"You mean both of us got photos of him?" Riley giggled. "You could have saved me from all my embarrassing antics if you'd told me."

"And missed that show? Not hardly." Sheriff grinned.

"I'm not sure I could have gotten the picture of Mrs. Imposter if I hadn't practiced earlier."

"It's interesting that she insisted that you delete it." Sheriff narrowed his eyes. "I'll get it out right away unless you have something else."

"Just one more thing: do you think Brian's story about Erin was true?"

"Normally, I would say no, except knowing you, I think it is, and there was too much detail for it to be something someone had fabricated. Our imposter might have worked with your dad and Brian Johnson and heard the story from them."

"That's an interesting perspective; if I think of anything else, I'll let you know."

Sheriff nodded. "I'm going to miss you, Riley Malloy Carter, but I'll always be here for you and Ben."

Riley brushed away a tear as she hurried inside, and Zach met her in the hallway. "Did everything go okay?"

"It did; thanks for your help. When do I get to meet Kayla?"

Zach groaned. "She asked me the same thing. She doesn't work tomorrow. We could bring fried chicken and potato salad to your house, help pack and load, or just loaf around and be in the way. I'm highly trained at all of the above. I could pick up the fried chicken at the grocery store; Kayla's potato salad is the best in the world."

"I'm sold. You and Ben could run a load out to the cabin after we eat while Kayla and I finish packing."

"What about dessert?" Zach asked.

"I'll take care of that."

Zach smirked. "I'd forgotten you were going to Doc Julie Rae's tonight. I relinquish dessert to you in deference to the leftover dessert from Charlie's kitchen."

"You're up, Ms. Riley. Mini-me is dancing toward the front door," Claire called out.

Riley hurried to the reception area with Toby, Hector, Jordy, and Zach on her heels.

"Your Mini-me is here, Ms. Riley," Maddie squealed as she twirled into the reception area from outside. After she performed a deep, low curtsey, Mini-me gracefully waved her arms in an arc. Claire led the applause.

Mini-me bowed and grinned. "I can touch the floor with my forehead sometimes."

The intrepid five-year-old leaped across the room, smoothing her red tutu over her pink jeans, as her mother came into the clinic and grinned at Riley.

"Mommy, may I have Ms. Riley's surprise?"

Tamara handed Mini-me a gift box with a red bow, and Mini-me marched stiff-legged, ballerina-style, to Riley. She then held out the box with two hands as she solemnly bowed her head.

Riley bowed as she accepted the box with two hands. "Thank you, Mini-me. The box and the ribbon are beautiful."

Mini-me beamed. "I wrapped it myself, except I let Mommy help a little bit."

Riley set the box on the counter, then slipped off the bow and handed it to Doc Julie Rae, who accepted it with two hands as she bowed to Riley.

Riley removed the lid, and then Pia took it with two hands and the ceremonial bow.

Riley's eyes widened. "For me, really? This is beautiful, Mini-me."

"I know. I picked it out myself after Mommy said you probably already have a tutu."

"Mommy was right." Riley smiled, and Pia snickered.

Riley lifted out the red felt western hat with a feather in the band.

"It's a real chicken feather, Ms. Riley. Me and Mommy visited Ms. Lindsey, and she said it would be perfect for your western hat."

Riley tried on the western hat and assumed a modeling pose. Holding her head high, she sashayed to the front door and returned to the desk amid cheers and whistles; Toby, Hector, and Jordy howled.

Riley carefully returned it to the box. "This is positively the most breathtaking present I have ever received. It's better than Santa Claus."

Mini-me nodded. "Yes, it is, but don't say that too loud because you still want Santa Claus presents."

"Thank you so much. Please ask your mommy to send me pictures of you at Christmas and on your birthday."

Tamara nodded. "Good idea."

Claire wrote on a clinic business card and then formally presented it to Tamara. "This is Ms. Riley's email address."

Tamara winked as she bowed and accepted the card. "Catching, isn't it?" she whispered, and Claire giggled.

"Ms. Riley, I will always be your Mini-me." Mini-me pirouetted in her charming five-year-old style.

Riley nodded. "I count on it."

After Tamara and Mini-me left, Whitney sighed. "I need a Mini-me."

Doc Thad nodded. "Don't we all."

"Doc Julie Rae got all teary," Pia said.

"Only after you did, you old softie," Doc grumbled as she headed to her office.

"She definitely is your Mini-me, Riley," Norm said.

"She's only five; watch out, world; there's two of them." Zach chuckled as he followed Toby, Jordy, and Hector back to the kennel.

"The Next patient's yours, Pia." Claire handed her the folder, and the reception area cleared.

As Riley and Norm walked to the breakroom, Norm said, "I snapped a lot of pictures. Shall I send them to you?"

"I'm so glad you thought of it, thank you. I'd love to have them."

"I'll download them to a flash drive and bring it in tomorrow for you."

"Riley," Doc Julie Rae called out, and Riley hurried to Doc's office.

Doc Julie Rae smiled. "You'll have to wear your western hat tonight. Wasn't that a surprise? I know you planned to pack tomorrow night, so why don't you leave a little early today so you can go by the grocery store? Charlie and the boys decided you needed to bring the yellow flowers tonight because when they went to the store, Mrs. Smythe was stalking the aisles, watching for you. Charlie said the manager told him that some of the customers were worried about Mrs. Smythe, and he dared the manager to tell Mrs. Smythe about the nosy customers."

Riley's eyes widened. "What did the manager say?"

"He laughed, thanked Charlie, and said he may sell popcorn for the show."

"I guess I better go to the grocery store so I don't miss out on the popcorn and show."

"Good choice. Take pictures or take Norm to take pictures."

"I'll snap photos; I'm not sure Norm is ready for Mrs. Smythe yet."

"Good point. See you at five thirty?" Doc Julie Rae asked.

"Absolutely; if Ben gets caught up on a call, Toby and I will be there without him."

"Tell him the boys will round up their posse to rescue him, so he better tell them bad guys to vamoose."

"I will pass on the message verbatim."

When Riley approached the back door, Pia called, "One second there, Ms. Riley."

Riley stopped and smiled as she waited for Pia.

"Tom has Friday off, and there's no school on Friday, so we're going to descend on you and bring lunch. You have to eat, you know, so plan on it. We're willing to help load if you want us there in the morning. Jackson said he'd play with Jordy and Toby in the backyard."

"That's a great idea. We'll have to wait until Friday to load the heavy boxes that are mostly books into the back of Ben's truck; I'll check with Ben and let you know what time he plans to load up. I'll go to the clinic at my usual time for one last good-bye to everyone, then I'll have to leave because I would be all mopey. Helen told me not to bother cleaning the house before we left because she has a deep-cleaning crew scheduled next week, but Grandma taught me to leave a house broom clean."

Pia nodded. "Mine said the same. When I told her that other people didn't do that anymore, she told me I wasn't other people."

"She was right; neither one of us is other people." Riley giggled. "Grandma had two rules: her number one rule was to pay attention to the animals and birds, and the second rule was to leave a place cleaner than you found it."

After Riley dropped off Toby at the house, she went to the grocery store. When she went inside, she inhaled the aroma of freshly popped popcorn and realized the buzzing noise was the sound of excited customers who jockeyed for a place in the line near the exit door.

She stared in disbelief at the produce cart with a red and white striped cloth draped over it. The store manager wore a white apron as he scooped up hot popcorn from the retro popcorn maker with a gleaming garden trowel to pour servings of popcorn into small, brown paper sacks.

Riley smiled as a cashier hurried to give the manager another bundle of sacks that they normally used to protect greeting cards purchased by customers. One of the stockers stood next to the cart and handed out the popcorn, as quickly as he could, to the growing line of folks. The manager waved and grinned as Riley pulled out her phone and snapped a picture for Charlie and the boys.

Riley strolled past the customer service desk and gaped at the usually modest, small flower section that had invaded the produce and bakery departments with a tsunami of bouquets of yellow flowers artfully arranged in their vases.

Wow. Sunflowers, lilies, roses, zinnias, daisies. The grocery store smells like a perfume factory.

While Riley took pictures of the flowers, a customer stopped next to her and stared at the sea of yellow.

"What an excellent idea!" The customer surveyed the flowers, picked up two vases arranged with sunflowers, and put them into her cart. "I need to invite our neighbors over for dinner tonight; I'll make peanut butter and jelly pinwheels. Is there another appetizer I'm supposed to serve with spaghetti?"

"I'm certain that peanut butter and jelly appetizers go with everything."

"You're right: they're the universal appetizer."

Riley hurried back to the entrance, grabbed a cart, and then returned to the flowers. *I'll buy two bouquets: one for Doc and Charlie and one for us.*

As Riley browsed the tables, Mrs. Smythe said, "I heard your young husband has a new job. Isn't yellow a cheerful color? Yellow roses symbolize joy and friendship; did you know during the Victorian era, yellow roses signified jealousy? Too often, joy and friendship turn to jealousy, don't you think? Which flowers call to you?"

Riley pointed to the flowers where she had stopped. "I don't know what kind of flowers these are, but I'm really drawn to their pure yellow color and delicate petals." Riley picked up the vase and set it in her cart.

"I'm not surprised. Dahlias are a symbol of strength and commitment."

"Really?"

Mrs. Smythe smiled. "Mr. Smythe planted dahlias for me on the day we bought our home." Mrs. Smythe bowed her head in respect when she mentioned her husband, and Riley reflexively did the same.

"Doc Julie Rae asked me to take pictures of me with the flowers. Would you mind posing with me?" Riley asked.

Mrs. Smythe twittered. "This will be my first selfie. Snap away, dahlia girl."

Riley leaned close to Mrs. Smythe and then took their selfie. When she showed it to Mrs. Smythe, the older woman asked, "Does this make us BFFs? One of the ladies where I stay told us that BFFs take selfies together. I'll have to ask her what a BFF is."

Riley smiled. "A BFF is a best friend forever, and taking selfies together is what BFFs do."

"Good. I'll be the first one there to have a BFF. Is it rude to mention I have a BFF during dinner, or is it more appropriate to wait until evening cocktails so I can tell them to eat their hearts out? I'm not quite up to date on BFF etiquette. Can you send our house manager a copy of our picture?"

Mrs. Smythe pulled out a business card. "I carry a supply of her cards, which reminds me of an envelope with a key in it that your grandmother gave me. Do you remember helping her lift up the floorboards in her closet? You were only three or four, but your grandmother said you were always eager to help."

Riley smiled at the memory. "I'd forgotten about our cabin mouse. It was a rainy day, and Grandma told me a story about a house mouse who told wonderful stories of adventure and lived under an old woman's floor in the closet. After we made cookies, we looked to see if we could find our cabin mouse, but she wasn't there. Grandma put a box with a lock under the floor for the cabin mouse to use as a cabin, just like the old woman did in the story. Grandma told me the box was locked to people but not to a cabin mouse."

Riley giggled. "It took us all afternoon; Grandma wasn't in a hurry and let me do everything. When Mother arrived to take me home, she scolded me for not having packed before she got there, but Grandma told her we'd been busy cleaning the house, then talked Mother into letting me stay another week. Now I wonder if the mouse found her cabin in the cabin. I'll have to check sometime."

"There are people who don't deserve yellow flowers because they live in a world of poisonous, black roses." Mrs. Smythe solemnly gazed at Riley and lowered her voice as Riley met her gaze. "Never let the black roses close; their thorns are deadly."

Mrs. Smythe hugged Riley. "You have always been a yellow dahlia and will flourish wherever you're planted."

Riley continued to gaze at Mrs. Smythe as the words *Be Safe, Dahlia* floated through her thoughts.

Riley blinked, and Mrs. Smythe was gone. The chatter and laughter at the popcorn line broke Riley's deep concentration.

Riley hurried to the customer service desk and then rushed to her car with her much-loved flowers.

When she reached home, she went inside, let Toby out back, and then poured a tall glass of tea. She downed half her glass of tea. *I understood Mrs. Smythe's warning, but I'm not likely to ever run across Mother; it's not like I'd even want to find her.*

She opened the back door. "Are you ready to come inside?"

Toby shook his head and continued stalking the yard for any lizards or moles.

Riley sat at the kitchen table and started her packing list with three columns: Wednesday, Thursday, and Friday. She looked in the pantry with her paper in her hand. *I've got thirty minutes before Ben will be home; I can take a quick shower and then pack everything in the pantry except for the bread, so I don't have to write everything down.*

She wrote 'pantry' under her Wednesday column, then called Toby inside and fed him before she jumped into the shower.

After she dressed, she opened an empty medium-sized box and began packing. She was almost finished when Ben rushed inside.

"I need a shower." He gave her a quick smooch, then pulled off his shirt as he rushed to the bathroom.

"I'll bet I can pack the pantry before he gets out of the shower," Riley said as Ben turned on the water.

"You're on, babe," he called out as he closed the door.

Riley quickly finished packing as Ben came out of the shower.

She raised her hands in triumph, and Ben dropped his towel when he copied her.

"Ooo-la-la." Riley wiggled her eyebrows as he rushed to the bedroom to dress.

"Not fair; we're expected to be at the Sorensens' in twenty minutes," he growled from the bedroom as he dressed. "I saw the flowers; they're beautiful. I assume you ran into Mrs. Smythe."

When he came into the living room, Riley said, "There's a story behind that."

Ben chuckled. "There always is. Where'd you get the red Western hat?"

"It was a Mini-me present, graced with a chicken feather from Lindsey's farm."

"I'm jealous; now I need a beat-up old Western hat. Are you ready to go? Are we taking both bouquets?"

"One is for us."

Ben asked when they were in the truck, "Is it a long story?"

"Yes, but here's the short version." Riley told him about Mrs. Smythe, the cabin mouse, and the dahlias, then finished by telling him about the black rose and the warning that she heard from Mrs. Smythe.

After he parked in front of the Sorensens', Ben frowned as he walked slowly around the front of the truck. He opened Toby's door, then Riley's, and cocked his head as he peered at her. "Have you ever heard anyone speak to you like Mrs. Smythe did?"

"Kind of. When I was six or seven, I realized that Grandma sometimes said things when she was extra worried that no one else seemed to hear. I thought that was normal for people and animals who were close because Old Dog heard her too."

"That's really interesting. Was Toby with you at the grocery store?"

"No, he waited in the car for me."

"I'd ask if you've ever heard me, but the only times I've been extra worried were when I couldn't find you or when I was trying to get to you because you were in danger."

Kenny and Freddy wore their cowboy bandanas and cowboy hats as they ran out the door and whooped; their German Shepherd-Airedale Terrier mix, Chuck, followed them, and then he and Toby pranced into the house.

"Howdy, Cowgirl Riley and Ranger Ben; welcome to our bunkhouse." Kenny saluted Ben.

Ben returned the salute. "Howdy, yerself, pardner." Ben put his thumbs in his belt, so Kenny did too as they swaggered into the house.

"They brought yellow flowers," Kenny shouted.

"I like your red hat, Cowgirl Riley." Freddy took Riley's hand as they walked into the house.

When Riley and Freddy strolled into the kitchen, Doc Julie Rae said, "Charlie told me the grocery store manager and Mrs. Smythe planned a big surprise for you today. Looks like they went all out."

"They sure did," Riley said.

Charlie grinned. "Now that's a real cowgirl hat. What kind of feather is that?"

Doc Julie Rae smiled. "A rare chicken feather from Lindsey's farm, and I need a fancy cowgirl hat, y'all."

Ben sniffed. "Something smells good."

"We're having pulled wild boar sandwiches. It took me two days to wrassle that big fella to the ground, and I've been turnin' that ole boar for two days on an old spit." Charlie's eyes twinkled as he pointed to the bowl of chips on the bar. "Help yourself to the store-bought version of pork skins."

"It's getting a trifle deep in here, Riley." Doc Julie Rae raised an eyebrow. "Shall we disengage ourselves from the prevaricator and meander to the veranda with our wine for some privacy and a more suitable ambiance?"

"We shalt." Riley smirked.

"Lawdy, y'all talk fancy," Ben drawled.

"I got yer sweet muddy water right here in the fancy ice box, Range Rider," Charlie said. "I'll pour you a big glass."

When Riley and Doc Julie Rae went out back, Toby and Chuck followed them.

"It's going to be a long evening; Charlie has been talking like that since I got home, and the boys are picking it up. He was calling me Doc Holliday until I told him to cut it out before I called my Earp gang. He told me he was impressed and is planning a trip to Tombstone, Arizona."

Riley giggled. "You know your Old West history."

"It's self-preservation. Our wild boar is actually a nice pork butt that Charlie bought at the pig farm outside of town, but Charlie told the boys that city folks had pulled pork, so we'd have wild boar. He smoked it all day yesterday, and the neighbors hate us. I'm actually grateful he didn't tell the boys we're having pig butt."

Riley giggled. "I'm not telling Range Rider about the pork either, and don't you think that's a great name for him?"

Toby and Chuck raced to the door and whined to be let in.

"Sheriff's here," Riley said as Doc Julie Rae opened the back door for the dogs; Riley and Doc followed Toby and Chuck inside.

"It's the town marshal," Kenny shouted when he opened the door.

Freddy yelled, "Marshal's here."

Doc Julie Rae glowered, and Charlie chuckled. "One of these days, we'll look back and wish they would announce our guests with a bellow for old times' sake."

"I doubt it," Doc Julie Rae grumbled as she hurried to the front door.

When the boys raced into the kitchen, the sheriff and Doc Julie Rae came in behind them.

Sheriff grinned. "Howdy, folks. Did I get a promotion, or am I now the target of bank robbers and cattle rustlers?"

"Might be both." Charlie chuckled as he weaved his way past the boys and the dogs so the two men could shake hands. "Good to see you, Sam."

"You too, Charlie. I heard you were looking at one of the vacant storefronts downtown."

When Charlie raised his eyebrows, the sheriff smiled. "You ought to know nothing's secret in our small town."

"Would you care for coffee, sweet tea, beer, wine, or cold water?" Doc Julie Rae asked.

"A glass of sweet tea sounds good." Sheriff sat at the bar, and Charlie gave him his sweet tea.

"We're talking about it. I'm not homeschooling because we decided it was time for the boys to go to public school, so I'm not tied to the house during the day. I'd like to open a café and start serving only lunch to see how that works for us. I'll need adequate parking to provide take-out because not everyone has time at lunch to go into a café and sit at a table, and I want a large room for groups. If the boys go to aftercare, I could drop them off at school in the mornings and pick them up before Julie Rae got home."

Charlie set a plate of hot hush puppies on the bar next to the chips, and Ben popped one in his mouth and then added two hush puppies to his plate of chips.

"I'm not sure Main Street is the location that would work for me. I'm at the stage right now of looking around to see what's available, and Julie Rae and I are still trying to decide whether I need to be open for lunch on Saturdays, too; I want to work only five days a week, but that means I'd be closed maybe on Monday."

Sheriff nodded. "There are a lot of angles to consider."

"Sure are. Zach is helping me with my business plan and told me I need to decide who my target customers are, so Julie Rae and

I are trying to do that. I'm glad I asked Zach for the help because I'd be floundering later."

The boys tore out of the house to the backyard, and Chuck dashed out with them. Toby ambled out the open door, and Doc Julie Rae rolled her eyes and closed the door.

"I heard you're going to be doing farm visits, Rowdy Cowgirl," Charlie said.

Ben smirked, and Riley sighed. *I'll hear that again.*

"I went with Doc Seth on an emergency call last weekend. It was a great opportunity for us to see how we could work together." Riley told them about the calf being in the wrong position to be delivered and what Doc Seth did.

Ben added, "Uncle Seth told Dad that Riley calmed the heifer and the farmer in addition to assisting him with the delivery of the calf. Uncle Seth said she made the entire process much smoother and less stressful for everyone."

"I was nervous about being an additional burden for Doc Seth, but I loved it and learned a lot on that one farm visit," Riley said.

"What about you, Ben?" Doc Julie Rae asked. "You spent your summers working with your uncle. Why did you decide against a veterinary career?"

"Riley came home from her farm visit energized by the entire experience and ready to go to another farm; I always came home completely drained," Ben said. "I didn't realize the difference until Mom pointed it out, but I knew all along veterinary medicine wasn't right for me; I just didn't know why."

Sheriff nodded. "Your heart is definitely in law enforcement."

Chapter Eleven

Millie

Millie's phone rang while she was in the elevator, and the other occupants glared at her. She glanced at her phone and then quickly silenced the ring before she returned it to her purse. "*Mi scusi.*"

One of the women glared at Millie and hissed at her friend; Millie turned and raised an eyebrow at the woman, who pursed her lips and stared at the floor.

Millie sneered. *I understood every word you said about me, and now you know it, don't you?*

When the women exited the elevator, Millie shifted slightly and bumped the disapproving woman, who hurried to get away.

The lone man in the elevator chuckled and winked at Millie when she glanced at him, and she shrugged.

She found a seat in the lobby and checked her phone. *No message.*

The phone showed the caller ID as *Unknown,* but Millie recognized the number and returned the call.

The phone rang four times before he picked up. *Smart man; decided against playing any games after all.*

"Why didn't you answer, Mildred?" he asked.

If I react, he'll know how much he irritates me by calling me Mildred.

Millie assumed a bored tone. "The elevator was crowded."

"You're still in Paris at that hotel with the slow, creaky elevator? I'd thought you'd have moved on by now."

Millie narrowed her eyes. *Why do you care where I am?* She shrugged off her suspicions so she could maintain her calm tone. "It's comfortable and convenient to the airport, and I have a great view; I really don't have any reason to leave a prestigious, luxury hotel because of a few annoying inconveniences; it's all part of the charm of its old-world elegance. What did you learn? What does Riley know about the explosion?"

"Nothing, and neither does Sheriff Sam Dunn. Dunn might be a backwoods sheriff, but he's pretty sharp, and you were right: he thinks a lot of Riley. I decided right away to stay low. I entertained him and Riley with stories about Frank Malloy. As far as Riley's concerned, she's very social, just like the rest of the younger crowd, but she doesn't miss much at all. I'm glad you warned me, or I would have been fooled and not played it cool."

"Good, because you're right about Sheriff Dunn."

"Mrs. Johnson went to lunch with Riley and reported to me that Riley is an airhead, typical of her generation. Riley was snapping photos of her food, the diner, the other patrons, and Mrs. Johnson."

Millie raised her eyebrows. *You're on a fact-finding tour of your own now, aren't you? I'll take the bait.*

Millie chuckled. "Riley started doing that her first year of vet tech school. I thought it was just another one of her fads because she told me everyone else in class took pictures of each other, their books, food, and who-knows-what, but she kept it up; most of her pictures are pretty fuzzy because she doesn't take her time to frame a shot at all, which drives me crazy. She snaps pictures of everything imaginable, then does a mass delete every evening without reviewing any of them so she can take more the next day. I don't understand her age group and their fascination with taking pictures of everything under the sun. My family was always cheap, and Riley's no exception, so there's no way she would pay for extra storage of the throw-away snapshots she took all day. Did she offer to send Mrs. Johnson a copy?"

"No, she didn't, or Mrs. Johnson would have bragged she had the only copy. Mrs. Johnson said she was extremely irritated with the way Riley caught her off guard and took a picture of her without her permission; she told me she was quite firm in her insistence that Riley delete the picture immediately. I thought she may have blown the incident out of proportion."

"She shouldn't have called attention to herself like that. What did you report to Vivian?"

"I reported exactly what I told you, including the entire report from Mrs. Johnson, who is now the recently deceased by suicide Mrs. Johnson."

"She's been cruising that line for a while because she couldn't keep her temper in check. You do excellent work, by the way. There will be a bonus tacked onto our usual arrangement. Keep up the good work."

"You're the best, Mildred; I do have one thing that will give you a chuckle: Vivian told me she wasn't a bit surprised that Riley turned out to be an airhead. She wanted to know if Riley had finally slimmed down. Riley's an attractive girl, but definitely not slim."

Millie smiled. "What did you tell Vivian?"

The man chuckled. "Riley was an overweight airhead."

Millie laughed as she hung up.

Millie poured a glass of wine and then gazed out the window of her suite at the too-familiar haze that covered Florence like a shroud.

You left out one important detail, Bucko. Millie toasted the former Mr. Johnson, then sat in her comfortable chair and propped up her feet.

Riley snapped a photo of you, too, didn't she? You obviously didn't react to it, but that explains why you needed to know about Riley's picture-taking habits when we talked about photos and Mrs. Johnson; when it comes to Vivian, you're smart to keep it to yourself.

Millie glanced outside and wrinkled her nose at the pollution. She sipped her wine and leaned back, and then her eyes widened, and she dropped her wine glass. *I'm in Vivian's way; I need to disappear fast.*

Chapter Twelve

Charlie pulled out a pizza from the oven. "This is the boys' wild boar pizza. It needs a little time to cool."

"Has Toby eaten, Riley?" Doc Julie Rae asked.

"He did, but he might want a snack with Chuck to be sociable."

"I'll bring the boys inside; they can feed Chuck and give Toby a bite to eat, too," Doc said.

"While they wash their hands, I'll put their pizza and carrot sticks on pie pans and pour milk into their cowboy cups," Charlie said.

After Kenny and Freddy returned to the kitchen, Riley and Doc Julie Rae carried out their pie pans and milk and set their food and drinks on the table.

"We'll eat at our campfire," Kenny said, and they carried their pie tins to sit next to the sticks they'd arranged to be their campfire in the middle of the yard.

After Riley and Doc went inside, Charlie said, "We're ready to eat. Range Rider poured iced tea and put our condiments and sides on the table while I made everyone's first pulled pork sandwich. We can sit and chow down."

While they ate, Charlie peered at the sheriff. "How are them new deputies of yours coming along, Marshal?"

Sheriff smiled. "Better than I expected. The smartest thing I did was to ask Range Rider here to develop a training plan for them. The deputies will be ready to operate independently next week. This is the first time I've seen deputies come up to speed so quickly."

Charlie nodded. "I'm not surprised; that Range Rider does good work."

When Ben's cheeks turned bright pink, Doc Julie Rae said, "Don't mind them, Range Rider; they're just jealous."

After they ate, Charlie asked, "Did everyone save room for dessert?"

Charlie pulled out a lemon chiffon cake from the refrigerator. "Riley, Mrs. Smythe gave me the recipe today and asked me to make it for you because she wanted to do her part in making your day special. I won't send you the recipe because she wanted the lemon chiffon cake to be a bribe for you to return to Barton."

Tears rolled down Riley's cheeks, and Ben put his arm around her shoulders. "That is so sweet, Charlie; thank you so much."

Charlie smiled. "I told her you would love it and invited her to join us, but she declined."

"She thrives on being at the grocery store where she can help brighten the day for new people who need a lift in spirits," Riley said. "I'm not sure she goes anywhere else except home."

After dessert, the boys, Toby, and Chuck, went outside to play a game that involved running and shouting. Ben stood at the window and watched, then put his arm around Riley when she joined him.

"I've played that game," he said.

"What's it called?" Doc Julie Rae asked.

"Let's go outside and run around, and maybe they'll forget it's past our bedtime," Ben said, and Doc Julie Rae laughed.

"I was at the top of my class for that game," Charlie said. "I think I have a trophy and my participation award around here somewhere."

Doc Julie Rae snort-laughed. "I almost feel guilty about calling them inside for their bath."

"Come on, Ben," Charlie said, "Let's mix it up."

"Sheriff, are you coming?" Ben asked.

"Y'all go on; I'll stay here with the smart people."

Charlie stuck his thumbs into his belt as he swaggered toward the door. "You can't argue with that, Range Rider; Marshall Sam definitely has a good point, so let's mosey on out because this ain't the place for us."

After Ben and Charlie went outside, the sheriff chuckled. "Those two crack me up."

Doc Julie Rae rolled her eyes. "I'll be glad when Charlie and the boys go to their next phase, but I'm almost afraid of what it will be. Were you able to take any pictures at the grocery store, Riley?"

"I'm glad you asked. Let me show you, and then I'll send them to you."

As Riley scrolled through the grocery store photos, Sheriff and Doc Julie Rae stood on either side of her, chuckled at the popcorn venture, and were in awe of the beautiful yellow field of flowers.

"This is absolutely amazing. Charlie and the boys will love seeing them. Send them to my email; Charlie has the TV hooked up as a computer screen. These are the perfect bedtime story. You'll provide the pictures, and Charlie will provide the narrative."

"Send them to me too," Sheriff said.

"We're going to have to go home to pack; I'm sorry I'll miss the story." Riley selected all the photos from the grocery store and sent them to Doc Julie Rae and to the sheriff.

"Can you stay, Sheriff?" Doc Julie Rae asked.

"Thank you for the invitation because I was about to beg to sit in on the show." Sheriff grinned.

"I'll call in the cowpokes so everyone can say goodbye, Riley. Can you take the lemon chiffon cake home with you? Charlie told me to ask you if he didn't."

"I'd love to. Zach and Kayla are going to help us pack and load boxes. Some of the boxes will go to the cabin, and the rest will go in my car until it's full. Zach was hoping we'd have leftover dessert from Charlie."

"Did you want any of the cake to take home, Sheriff?" Riley asked.

Sheriff shook his head. "No, thank you; my waistline tells me I have to pass."

When everyone came in from the backyard, Freddy said, "Mama said we needed to tell you to come back to see us; Daddy said it's okay to hug."

Riley swallowed and then smiled. "Yes, it's definitely okay to hug."

The boys rushed to Riley, hugged her, and then clung to her.

"We'll miss you, Rowdy Cowgirl. You have to wear your red Western hat when you come to visit," Kenny said.

Freddy added, "And bring Range Rider."

"Absolutely," Riley said.

"Do ranch hands hug?" Freddy asked.

Ben nodded. "It's part of the ranch hand code."

Freddy and Kenny released Riley and then hugged Ben, who patted their backs.

"Okay, cowpokes, it's time for baths," Doc Julie Rae said. "You have to come by the clinic before y'all leave, Ben."

Charlie gazed at Riley and Ben. "You'll always be in our hearts and will always have a place at my table; the good news is that we aren't saying goodbye; it's see you later."

"Thanks, Charlie," Ben said.

After Charlie hugged both of them, the sheriff said, "What the heck," and hugged both of them too.

"Be safe," the sheriff said as they left.

On the way home, Ben said, "I've never had such a hard time leaving a place as it is to move on from Barton."

Riley sighed. "I like what Charlie said; it really is see you later, but everything will be different."

"That's not all bad, but it still seems sad in a way, doesn't it?"

"It does." Riley blindly stared out her window as they drove through the familiar streets, then smiled. "My favorite memory of Barton is the first time I saw you when you carried in Carlie and brought in Mr. P. I thought you had a cute smile and nice eyes."

Ben chuckled. "That was one cranky cat." Ben put his hand on her shoulder and gently massaged her with his fingertips. "I thought you were the prettiest girl I'd ever seen, and I drove the sheriffs in two counties crazy because I kept coming up with reasons to be close to you."

After Ben parked in their driveway, Riley said, "While we pack, I'll tell you about my cabin mouse."

As they packed their clothes, Riley told Ben about her grandma, the floorboards, the cabin mouse, and the key that Mrs. Smythe gave her.

"I'd be amazed about the key, except Barton is a typical small town, and just about everyone has been here their entire lives; it makes total sense that your grandmother and Mrs. Smythe were close friends."

"Do we need to get a clothes bar to put in my car to hang up your uniforms?"

Ben frowned. "I'm not sure why I'm taking them. I'll talk to the sheriff; maybe one of the new deputies could use an extra uniform or two."

"I packed the pantry earlier; if you pack the rest of the kitchen, I'll take care of the bathroom," Riley said.

After Riley finished packing, she joined Ben in the kitchen. "I'm officially exhausted."

"You're in good company; Toby has been outside for his bedtime break and is already asleep."

On the way to the bedroom, Ben said, "We took dishes, pans, and utensils from the kitchen at the cabin. I packed them separately, so they'll be there when we come to Barton. We may have to buy a few replacements after I finish my training, but we'll have enough of the basics until we do."

"Good, I did the same with the bathroom and the linens." Riley yawned.

The next morning, Riley listened to the water running in the shower, stretched, and hurried to the kitchen for a cup of coffee. Toby rose from the floor, yawned, and stretched before he padded to the back door.

After Riley opened the door, she sipped her coffee and checked inside the cabinets and drawers for a mental list of what was left to pack in the kitchen. While Ben dressed, Riley hurried to take her shower and dress.

When they sat down to breakfast, Riley picked up her breakfast taco of scrambled eggs, their favorite blend of four grated cheeses, and diced deli ham. She spooned cold salsa over the hot taco and took a bite; salsa liquid drizzled down her chin, then down her hand, and onto her plate as she quickly leaned forward.

She stared down at her chest. "I didn't get any salsa on my shirt for a change; that's different. There must be a way I could eat my taco without having to change shirts before I go to work."

Ben tugged at the top of her shirt and leaned close to ogle her chest, then suggestively raised one eyebrow and spoke in a husky voice. "If you don't wear a top to the table, you'll be fine."

Riley laughed. "I'd be late for work, though."

"It's a trade-off." Ben leered and wiggled his eyebrows as he twirled his imaginary moustache and then refilled their coffee cups.

"We're going to be at your parents for four months. Do you think you can behave and not embarrass me for that long?"

Ben downed his coffee and then pulled out his lunch from the refrigerator before he kissed Riley's neck. "Nope. Gotta run." His chuckle was evil as he left.

Riley exhaled, then strode to the back door and let Toby inside. "It's going to be a long four months."

Riley sent a text to Melissa. "I apologize in advance for my husband's embarrassing behavior."

Melissa replied, "Apologize for your father-in-law's behavior while you're at it."

Riley laughed, loaded the dishwasher, and pulled out her lunch. "Let's go, Toby."

Doc Julie Rae met Riley when she went to the breakroom; Toby trotted to the kennel.

"Ready for your day's challenge, Riley?" Doc Julie Rae asked.

Riley put her lunch into the refrigerator and smiled. "Ready."

"I don't want you to see any patients or assist with any patients. Read the files, then ask Whitney and Norm about their assessments of their assigned patients and share any points that you saw but they didn't. I think we can train them to see their patients through your eyes."

"That's really devious, Doc." Riley stared at her.

"I know; Charlie told me that was the most underhanded sidewinder scheme I've ever had. I'm really proud of myself." Doc Julie Rae beamed.

"I do have one request: if a critical patient comes in, I can jump in."

Doc Julie Rae nodded. "As long as you pull in Whitney or Norm so they can see how you manage the patient, I'm fine with that."

"You're tough. I'll check in with George to see how Collette's doing, then I'll check the phone for messages."

Doc Julie Rae shook her head. "Nope. Let Whitney or Norm, whoever comes in first, check the messages. Claire will manage if no one writes up a summary before she and Thad arrive. If any of them have any questions, you'll be available if they want to ask; otherwise, you can relax and think mentor thoughts."

Riley bit her lip. "I wouldn't have thought of it, and as much as I hate it, you're right. Your entire stinky plan goes against my instincts to jump in. You're telling me that I have to stop interjecting myself into the day-to-day processes." Riley glared at Doc.

"That's exactly what a mentor does." Doc Julie Rae headed toward her office.

Riley called out, "For the record, I agree with Charlie."

Doc Julie Rae cackled a wicked laugh, and Riley giggled in spite of her irritation at Doc's plan.

When Riley strolled into the kennel, George smiled. "Collette had a restful night. Doc Thad will be pleased. How are you doing?"

"I'm not sure; Doc Julie Rae gave me an attitude adjustment about stepping in to help, so I'm a mentor today and tomorrow."

"You can do it, Riley. You've got a lot to share, and the folks around here are smart enough to ask good questions," George said.

"Thank you, I'll remember that."

At noon, Pia joined Riley in the hallway. "Are you lurking or moping? Jordy and Toby spent the morning with Collette, so I took them outside for a short walk. Let's eat lunch; Claire made brownies and put them on the counter in the breakroom five minutes ago. I announced we had seniority and were eating lunch first; Doc Julie Rae was in her office and didn't hear me, so we're safe."

After examining the brownie plate, Pia said, "We really need a food scale in here; I'm having a hard time deciding which one is the largest. Do you suppose Claire measures the brownies before she comes in?"

"I'm certain she must; she'll always be a teacher at heart." Riley selected a brownie and then pointed to another one. "That one's the biggest."

While they ate, Pia asked, "What time are you leaving today? Zach's all fidgety because he's worried you might leave to go home to pack, and he won't know, so you'll end up doing all that hard work by yourself."

"I'll talk to him."

Pia finished her sandwich and her brownie, then licked her fingers as she frowned. "Don't do that because he'll know I told you, and you'll blow my cover as the unapproachable, cranky vet tech, and people will think I'm nice and will start talking to me or something." Pia shuddered. "You know how Zach is; he'll kind of show up in the kennel and ask you if he needs to clean anything or something inane like that."

Doc Thad came into the breakroom. "Is this a private meeting?"

Pia glared. "It's lunch, Doc, and there's no such thing as a private meeting around here; where'd you come up with an idea like that? Don't eat all the brownies because I want to take two home for Jackson and Tom."

Doc Thad shrugged. "You better sack them up now because you know how long it takes for this crowd to clean a plate of pastries or desserts."

Pia strolled to the drawer with the sacks. She dropped three brownies into a sack and sniffed as she raised her nose into the air. "My family won't eat dessert if we're short one. I'll put this in my car, so I won't forget it. I made that mistake once around here, never again."

After Pia left, Doc Thad unwrapped his sandwich. "Did I chase her off?"

"No, you gave her an excuse to take her three brownies with a clear conscience."

"Doc Julie Rae told me her mentor plan. How are you holding up?" Doc Thad ate half his sandwich and his chips.

"Terrible. If nothing else, I've realized I would have been an awful veterinarian because I'd want to jump in right away. All the vet techs who worked with me would hate me. Did you have that problem?"

"I sure did. Part of it came from my training and being graded on the diagnosis, treatment, and results of each case that was assigned to me. After I graduated, it took me a while to understand that while I was responsible for the overall management of a patient, it was my job to identify and communicate the diagnosis and treatment plan to the vet tech, not just do it. It was a big step, and I have a lot of classmates that still haven't crossed that threshold. What's your moving plan for today and tomorrow?"

Riley smiled. "Zach and Kayla will come to our house later and bring grocery store fried chicken and homemade potato salad. I have part of a cake from Charlie; otherwise, I'd be arm-wrestling Pia for brownies. Ben and Zach will take the cabin boxes we've already packed to the cabin, and I suspect Ben will unpack and put away everything before they return, but that shouldn't take too long. While they're doing that, Kayla and I can finish packing everything else except what we'll need tonight and in the morning. On Friday, Pia, Jackson, Tom, and Jordy will come to help us. Ben and Tom can break down our bed and load it and the other heavy pieces into my car or the truck while I do laundry. Pia is providing lunch, so we'll leave sometime in the afternoon."

"I like that schedule, except for the work part." Doc Thad chuckled as he finished off his lunch and picked a brownie. "If Ben and Tom need any lifting help, call me; I'm sure I can take off an hour or two to help. I told Ben the same thing, but he wouldn't think of it until they were done. If you call me, and I show up, Ben will be glad for the help."

Riley nodded. "I'll remember. Will Collette be going home today?"

"I'd like to keep her until tomorrow morning; French bulldogs worry me when they get sick, and Collette has the added disadvantage of being a senior. She's doing fine, but I'm being extra cautious with her. She'd be more comfortable over the weekend at home than here, so that's my goal: to make sure she's strong enough to go home tomorrow. Are you going to be here tomorrow?" Doc Thad asked.

"I have to because George told me he wanted to hug me on Friday before I left. He said hugs go against his fraternizing with the enemy rule or something like that, but he'd make an exception in my case."

Doc Thad laughed. "That sounds like George."

He ate his brownie then picked up another and tossed his trash into the can before he strolled out of the breakroom. "See you in the morning."

When Riley went to the kennel, Toby, Jordy, Hector, and Zach were keeping Collette company. "You have quite the entourage of admirers, Collette."

Collette grinned and gave a short yip, and Riley smiled.

"She's definitely feeling better," Zach said.

Riley's phone buzzed a text from Ben: "When can you leave?"

Riley said, "I just got a text from Ben asking when I can leave."

"I asked Doc Julie Rae if I could leave at three, and she said, "Yes, please." Zach grinned. "The time's really dragging today, isn't it?"

"I'll be back." Riley hurried to Doc Julie Rae's office, but it was empty, so she carefully listened at each exam room door for Doc Julie Rae's voice. When she leaned against the second exam room door to hear better, the door abruptly opened, and Riley fell into the exam room. The client stared at Riley and Norm, who had caught her before she landed on the floor.

"Sorry, Riley," Norm said. "I didn't realize I'd pulled the door open so quickly."

Doc Julie Rae cleared her throat. "I'm glad you got my message, Riley. I have a question about our next patient. Norm, we'll finish up here while you get the medicine, and meet us at Claire's desk."

Norm winked as he passed Riley and handed her a flash drive. She exhaled while Doc Julie Rae walked the patient to Claire's desk.

When Doc Julie Rae returned to the exam room, she said, "You can leave anytime you want. I'll tell the staff they can call you today and tomorrow, but after that, you're a dear friend but no longer on our clock."

"Thank you; I'll feel more comfortable knowing they'll call if they have any questions."

"Don't be hurt if they don't. They can't be dog whisperers any more than I can, but they quickly learned to understand the chart and pay attention to the patient, thanks to you. Will you be here tomorrow?"

"I'd like to come in at my usual time and then leave after I say goodbye."

Doc Julie Rae hugged her. "That's an excellent plan. I'm sorry this is so hard for you, but I understand how you feel about this team because I feel the same way."

Riley returned her hug. "Thank you."

On her way to the kennel, Riley sent Ben a text. "Anytime."

Ben replied, "Will be home by four."

"What did Doc Julie Rae say?" Zach asked.

"Anytime, so I'm leaving now; Ben said he'll be home by four."

"That's good; then I won't have to stress if I have a patient around three," Zach said. What are you going to do?"

"I have some documents to read that I keep setting to the side; I'd love to take care of all those loose ends before we leave. This is perfect for me."

"We'll be there a little after four, then."

"Ready, Toby?" Riley asked.

After they were home, Riley poured a glass of sweet tea, and she and Toby went back out. While she rocked, the neighborhood mockingbird serenaded her, and Bob White called from a distance; she smiled. "Hello, Bob. I've missed you."

The quail moved closer and called, "Bob White."

Riley relaxed and sipped her tea. *It's nice to hear from old friends.*

She stared at her phone. *I'll bet Mom could help me with the jewelry.* She called Melissa.

Melissa was out of breath when she answered the phone on the third ring. "Are you okay, Riley? Have your plans changed?"

"I'm fine; I'm at home and taking a break outside. No change in plans; we'll be at your house tomorrow in plenty of time for supper."

"Well, good, then I'll plan to have supper on the table at three o'clock." Melissa chuckled. "So, what is bothering you? Something's obviously on your mind."

"I found some jewelry that Grandma left me, and I'd like to understand what it's worth. I don't care if it's costume jewelry; I'd like to know."

"That sounds like a good project for us. I'll check with my friends to see where we could get a fair appraisal. We can talk about what my friends say, and then I could take your jewelry to have it appraised next week while you're working."

"That would be great. How's everything there?"

"Nothing new. Mugsy wants you to come to her coffee shop in town when you can. She told me she has access to a genealogy database and would like to talk to you about a few things."

"Really? I've got some paperwork from Grandma that I don't understand, and I think a genealogy search might help, but I hadn't even considered it."

"I'll let her know. She really is uncanny sometimes; I have stories to tell you, but she'll probably tell you first."

After they hung up, Riley stretched and then headed to the back door. "I'm going inside; are you coming?"

Toby glanced at her and then continued patrolling the yard.

Riley folded clothes for her and Ben to have available to wear while they moved and put them into a duffel bag. She laid the remaining clothes on her bed so she and Kayla could pack them later. Before she left the bedroom, she double-checked the closet to be sure she hadn't left anything behind.

She frowned. *There aren't any uniforms. Ben must have taken them to work this morning.*

She examined the bathroom counters, drawers, and closet. *Everything stays until we leave.*

She emptied the kitchen cabinets onto the countertop, then placed the plates, bowls, silverware, and glasses that they would use before they left on the table. *There isn't much left to pack. Ben did a good job.* She did the same with the few pots and pans that remained in the lower cabinets.

She opened the back door, called Toby inside, and lay down on the sofa with a book. She woke with a start when Toby yipped as Ben's truck pulled into the driveway.

"Thanks, Toby; I must have fallen asleep." She hurried to open the door, but Ben opened it and lifted her off her feet in a big hug. "It's starting to feel real, babe."

"You're right, it is. I lost track of time; are you here early?"

"If five minutes until four is early, yes." He put her on feet, then kissed her with his open mouth, and she met his passion.

He stroked her lower back. Riley smiled as his hand drifted down past her waist.

She tapped his shoulder and whispered, "You left the front door open. The neighbors had to pull out their binoculars."

Ben laughed, turned, and waved as Zach and Kayla parked in front of the house.

"Dang good thing we're leaving town," Ben whispered, and Riley giggled.

Chapter Thirteen

Zach opened Hector's door, then brought in a large recycle tote, and Kayla carried a large, covered bowl. Kayla wore jeans and a dark green T-shirt. She was slender and the same height as Zach; she had pulled back her long, dark blond hair into a ponytail.

Toby greeted Hector and then trotted into the house. Hector followed him.

"We're bringing food and willing hands in peace, earthlings." Zach grinned.

Kayla smiled. "Hi, I'm Kayla. I'm a science fiction freak, so Zach is pretending to understand me."

"Can you imagine?" Ben side-glanced Riley, and Zach laughed.

"I'm Riley, and this is Ben. It's nice to meet you, Kayla."

Ben took Kayla's bowl and put it in the refrigerator, and Zach took out the box of chicken and put it in the refrigerator, too.

"What's the game plan?" Ben asked.

"You and Zach can take the boxes marked 'cabin' to the cabin while Kayla and I pack," Riley said. "We can eat after you get back, then we'll load my car."

"Where will Toby ride?" Zach asked.

"With me," Riley said.

"Good."

Ben and Zach loaded the cabin boxes, and then after they left, Kayla asked, "Where do I start?"

"The kitchen. Pack everything on the counter and mark the box. Unfortunately, I didn't do that at first, and I'm not sure why."

"Do you have any? Never mind. I see the bubble wrap for the dishes. Will we tape the boxes after they're full?"

"I knew there was something: Ben used the last of our tape. I'll send him a text."

"Don't bother; I brought some in my backpack."

"Wow, you came prepared." Riley smiled. "You've done this before."

"My dad was in the military. You wouldn't believe what all my mom had in her purse at any one time when I was growing up; when she discovered backpacks, she was in heaven. Being prepared is genetic, which is why I love post-apocalyptic science fiction."

"I'll be in the bedroom if you need me."

Kayla raised an eyebrow and surveyed the house. "Do you mind giving me a house tour?"

"Not at all." Riley opened the back door, and Toby and Hector dashed out. "Here's the back porch, and the backyard is fenced."

"This is really nice. You can let Toby out back without worrying whether he'll wander away."

"That's high on our list of requirements for anywhere we live."

"Mine too, but I didn't know it until I met Zach and Hector."

"I never knew how important a utility room was until I lived in an apartment." Riley stopped at the washer and dryer.

"Did you buy these?" Kayla asked.

"No, they came with the house."

"There's nothing special about the bathroom: sink and tub with a shower. There is a linen closet in the bathroom, which we like."

When they moved into the bedroom, Kayla said, "This room is huge. Is that a queen bed?"

"Yes, look in the closet."

Kayla stood in front of the closet with her mouth open. "Wow, do you have enough clothes to fill the closet?"

Riley laughed. "I had the left side, and Ben had the right side."

"This is so nice. Is it already rented? I'm not trying to kick you to the curb, but I'd love to rent this house. Is it furnished?"

"Only the bed is ours. Do you want me to call the owner for you?"

"I'd love it. I'll get busy in the kitchen; otherwise, I'd stand here in the closet, loving how much room there is."

Kayla left for the kitchen while Riley called Helen.

"How settled are you on selling our house? I have a good friend who would love to rent it."

"Are you serious? I was going to sell it because I've grown weary of screening renters. Is your friend there? Can I come by?"

"Sure, we're just packing up. Her name is Kayla, and she's an RN at the hospital."

"I know Kayla's mother. I'll be there in ten minutes."

Riley hurried to the kitchen. "Helen will be here in ten minutes to talk to you; she said she knows your mother."

Kayla smiled. "I don't know if that's a good or bad thing. I'll call Zach real quick."

Kayla picked up her phone, and Riley returned to the bedroom to pack. Before she finished, Kayla came into the bedroom.

"Zach is as excited as I am. My apartment has a little more room for the two of us, but it's on the second floor. His place is too small, and there's not much of a yard for Hector, so we take him for walks, which isn't bad, except we don't go outside enough to suit Hector."

Kayla cleared her throat and then peered at Riley. "We aren't exactly a couple; Zach told me Ben moved in with you when the house he was going to rent fell through, and he couldn't find anything else right away. Can I be nosy and ask about your sleeping arrangements before you were a couple?"

Riley smiled. "Ben's tall, and I'm not, so I won the argument. He slept in the bed, and I slept on the sofa."

Kayla nodded. "That makes sense."

"Tell Helen that you and Zach aren't really a couple yet. Don't you work nights occasionally? She might have some ideas."

"I'll do that. It'll feel awkward, though. Will you prompt me?"

"You don't want to ask me to do that because some people say I don't have a subtle bone in my body."

"Direct is all I know, so I get it; just don't abandon me."

Helen knocked on the door and then came into the house. "Yoo-hoo!"

Riley and Kayla hurried to greet her, and after introductions, Helen said, "I would have known who your mother was if I had seen you in the grocery store. You look just like her when she was your age, not that I'm old enough to remember that."

Kayla smiled. "Zach and I aren't a couple yet. This month I'm working nights, but some months I work the swing shift, which means I get home a little before midnight. It all depends on staffing and patient load. Do you have any ideas for us?"

Helen's eyes twinkled. "I sure do. You aren't the first to have asked for a place when one person worked shifts and the other one days. The other request I get even more often is an office because people aren't excited about having their work-from-home computer and desk in the living room. Come with me to the bedroom, and I'll show you what I have in mind that takes care of both requests."

Helen rushed to the bedroom, and Riley and Kayla stared at her back, then hurried to catch up.

Helen stood on the other side of the bed. "This bedroom has always bothered me because it's so big. Let's move this queen bed away from the middle of the room and a little closer to the door."

After the three of them moved the bed a foot closer to the door, Helen said, "Do you see how much room there still is all around the bed? I could easily put in a three-quarter height wall a little longer than the bed to turn this room into a suite for a queen bed on this side and a twin bed or a desk for an office on the other. What do you think?"

"I think you're a genius." Riley smiled.

"I call dibs on the queen bed side," Kayla said.

Helen chuckled. "Perfect. I'll have your contract ready for you or Zach to sign on Monday and will have the house ready for you to move in next weekend. Oh, and your rent will be the same as what Riley pays."

Before Helen left, she and Kayla exchanged phone numbers.

Kayla's eyes twinkled. "This is exciting; thank you so much. Let's get you out of here so I can move in."

Riley laughed. "On it."

After Riley finished packing the clothes, she joined Kayla in the kitchen. "You know Helen will build the wall herself. Did you see how her hand was twitching to grab a power tool and get to work?"

"I never would have thought to take that large bedroom and convert it to a suite that included an office. Zach and Hector are going to be so pleased."

When Riley opened the back door, Toby and Hector dashed inside and headed to the water bowl. Toby waited while Hector had his fill before he stepped up to the water.

Kayla refilled the bowl. "That was very nice of you, Toby, to let your guest have a drink first."

Toby grinned as he joined Hector under the dining room table. Riley moved back the chairs so they wouldn't be crowded, and both dogs stretched out.

"What about packing the utility room?" Kayla asked.

"I'm doing laundry in the morning, so that will be another last-minute thing."

Kayla nodded. "I do laundry under duress. I hate the germy community laundry room. I have to sanitize the washer and dryer before using them; I leave my laundry basket outside when I return to my apartment and carry in my clean clothes before I sanitize the bottom of the basket. It's the nurse's curse: I see germs everywhere. Your house doesn't creep me out."

Toby yipped but didn't move from the cool floor.

"They're back." Riley opened the door. "Ben's backing into the driveway."

Ben strode into the house, and Zach followed him. Ben kissed Riley, then hurried to the refrigerator, poured two glasses of sweet tea, and handed one to Zach.

"Thanks. I was parched," Zach said.

"So was I. What's next, babe?"

"All we have left to do is load up my car, then enjoy supper."

"Are all the boxes fair game for your car?" Ben scanned the kitchen and living room.

"Yes, including the boxes in the bedroom. I'll pack the books later, but they will be heavy, so they can go in the back of your truck tomorrow."

"We'll move all the boxes into the living room so we can see how many and what size boxes we have." Ben went to the bedroom, and Riley, Zach, and Kayla followed him.

Zach picked up a box. "Did Helen show up? What did she say?"

While Riley and Kayla picked up smaller boxes, Kayla said, "We can talk while we eat; let's get Riley's car loaded first, then we can relax."

After all the boxes were in the living room, Ben said, "I think we can fit all the small boxes into the car and still leave room for Toby in his usual spot in the back seat."

"Got it: small boxes first," Zach said.

"It won't take you two long; we'll pull together supper," Riley said.

After Ben and Zach went outside, Riley set the table while Kayla pulled out the chicken and potato salad from the refrigerator. Riley handed Kayla a large serving spoon for the potato salad and tongs for the chicken.

"Drinks are next. We have sweet tea, wine, beer, and water."

"Zach will want sweet tea because he's the driver tonight; we take turns being the designated driver. I'll have what you're having."

"Ben always has sweet tea if he's driving or on call, but I was thinking about a glass of wine."

"Sounds good to me, too."

Ben and Zach finished loading the small boxes and then came inside.

"Kayla and I are having wine. She said Zach would like sweet tea; what do you want to drink, Ben?" Riley asked.

"Sweet tea for me, too."

Riley peered at him while Kayla poured sweet tea into glasses with ice. "Are you on call?"

"Back up," he said. "I'll open the bottle of wine and pour two glasses."

Riley moved the chairs back into place, and Zach fed Toby and Hector. When they finished eating, Kayla let them out.

"Where do we sit?" Kayla asked, and Riley pointed.

After everyone served themselves cold fried chicken and potato salad, Zach said, "We're eating. What did Helen say?"

"The short, boring version is that we can sign the rental contract at her office tomorrow before we leave for your parents' house and then move in next weekend," Kayla said.

"That's great news." Zach frowned. "You and Riley did this together; I want to hear the long, exciting version."

Ben nodded. "So do I."

"Help me if I leave anything out, Riley," Kayla said. "I told Helen we weren't quite a couple yet, and sometimes I worked the night shift."

"What did she say about that?" Zach asked.

"She was very excited." Kayla took a bite of chicken and then glanced at Riley.

"Helen said she gets requests from people looking for an office, and she showed us how our big bedroom can be split into two bedrooms with a three-quarter wall separating the two rooms. The smaller room can be an office or a bedroom with a twin bed."

"I've always thought the bedroom was much larger than it needed to be; can you show us where the wall will go after we eat? Will it be like a separate room with a door?" Ben asked.

"No, she said the wall length will be longer than the queen-sized bed," Kayla said. "The smaller room will still be a part of the larger room, so there's no need for additional heating or air conditioning."

Zach raised his eyebrows. "She said she'd have it ready before next weekend? I guess I shouldn't be too surprised because my family here in Barton always said that Helen could have been a carpenter if she wanted. I'll bet she'll do the work herself."

After everyone ate, Riley said, "There's still a little chicken and potato salad left for you to take home for your lunch tomorrow, Kayla."

"What about you?" Kayla asked.

"Pia and her family will be here in the morning to help Ben load his truck; Pia is bringing lunch, then after we eat, we'll leave in the afternoon for the folks' house in Carson."

"We'll have it for lunch, then leave to see Zach's parents," Kayla said. "Honey, I love that you can tell them we're renting a two-bedroom house because you want Hector to have a fenced backyard."

Zach smiled. "It certainly will save us from having to deal with a lot of drama. One of my cousins, who is in medical school, rents a large house with four other male and female med students, and the family thinks it's great. I think we'll be able to stay under the radar, and Mother can brag about how smart we are to save money and how well we take care of Hector. She really likes Hector."

"We've got lemon chiffon cake courtesy of Mrs. Smythe, who provided the recipe, and Charlie, who prepared the cake."

"Mrs. Smythe is a legend. Is that why you have the yellow dahlias? Mom called me after I got off work yesterday and told me to go by the grocery store and pick up some ice cream. Of course, I thought she was nuts, but I went anyway. Mrs. Smythe told me I needed to tell my young man about yellow flowers. I bought a vase of tulips and picked up the ice cream."

Zach smiled. "I had heard Mrs. Smythe was eccentric, but I'd never heard the complete story and certainly didn't know the significance of the yellow flowers. Did Charlie make peanut butter pinwheels?"

Ben chuckled. "He certainly did, but their boys ate them."

Kayla took a bite of the cake. "Mmm. It's light and really lemony."

After they ate, Ben said, "There are two pieces of cake left; take them with you too."

Riley cleared the dishes and wrapped the cake, and Ben loaded the dishwasher while Kayla disinfected the table. Zach brought Toby and Hector inside.

When Zach, Kayla, and Hector were ready to leave, Kayla hugged Riley. "Thanks for everything, Riley."

Zach hugged Riley. "It was great working with you."

Zach and Ben shook hands, and then Zach, Kayla, and Hector left.

Riley dropped down onto the sofa and exhaled.

"Would you like a refill on your wine?" Ben asked as he headed to the kitchen.

"I'd like a cup of hot tea while I pack the books; that's all we've got left beside the laundry I do in the morning."

"I'll help; do you want all these books to go with us?" Ben asked.

"I might have gone overboard. Should we leave some books here? I hate to bring that up because I should have thought of it earlier, and you already made a trip to the cabin."

"Pick out the books you want to have on hand when we move from one place to another. We'll pack the rest of the books, and I'll take them to the cabin in the morning."

"That's smart. There are a few books that I enjoy rereading and a couple of reference books I like having around, but all the rest of them can stay."

"Start with the top shelf and pack all the books from each shelf that you want to take in a box. I'll pack any books from the ones that you left into a box, and then we'll pack the remaining to go to the cabin. Tom and I can take them first thing tomorrow and load everything else in the truck after we return."

After all the books were packed, Riley scanned the boxes of books to go to the cabin. "We're leaving a lot of books here."

"My back thanks us." Ben kissed Riley. "Ready to call it a night?"

During breakfast, Ben asked, "What time will you leave the clinic?"

"Pia and her family may be here by nine, so I'll plan to leave before the first patient arrives. I'd like to say goodbye to everyone and not skulk around while they're trying to work. George told me he wanted to give me a hug on Friday morning. I have the feeling he expected me to come in early as usual but didn't want any witnesses."

Ben chuckled. "I don't know when I'll be leaving; it's up to the sheriff, but I suspect I'll be here by ten at the latest."

After Ben left, Riley's phone rang. *Mugsy.*

"Is this too early to call? Cookie and I couldn't sleep. I have you on speakerphone because Cookie couldn't wait to hear your voice. Can you come have coffee tomorrow? Cookie can't wait until next week to see you."

Riley smiled. "Hello, Cookie."

Cookie answered Riley with a yip.

"I suspect Ben and Dad will come up with a project in the barn tomorrow, so I'll bet I can come into town and see you," Riley said. "I'll let you know in the morning when Toby and I will be there; Mom might want to come too. Mom said you had access to a genealogy database; I was going to ask you to look up a couple of people for me."

"I had a feeling you could use my help on something. Give me some names, and I'll get started on it."

"Erin Larson Malloy and Vivian Echols Malloy. Erin was my mother who died in a car crash when I was six months old, and Vivian Echols Malloy was my dad's second wife."

"What was your dad's name?" Mugsy asked.

"Franklin Malloy; I just realized I don't know his middle name."

"That's okay; I should be able to glean enough from the genealogy records to search census data and other public records. What's your full name?"

"Riley Erin Malloy Carter."

"Gotcha. See you tomorrow, Short-stuff."

Riley smiled. *I knew that would become Mugsy's permanent nickname for me.*

"Ready to go, Toby?"

When Riley and Toby stepped outside, she squinted to see the street in front of their house. "This fog is thick, and it certainly rolled in fast; Ben would have said something if it had been this foggy when he left."

She shivered as they hurried to the car. "The air isn't cold, but the dampness gives it that clingy feel. I'm guessing the fog will probably burn off by daylight." Riley opened the door for Toby, and he hopped in.

Riley dimmed her headlights and turned on her fog lights as she clutched the steering wheel and peered through the fog for the line in the center of the road so she could stay in her lane while she crept to the clinic. "This is awful."

As she neared the clinic, she said, "My nerves are shot; if some guy with a ripped shirt and blood on his clothes steps in front of my car, I'll have a heart attack."

After she parked, she exhaled. *What an ordeal.*

"I scared myself: now I'm afraid to get out of the car and afraid to stay here."

Toby growled.

"Fine; let's go in."

After Riley opened Toby's door and locked the car, she raced to the clinic door; the muscle memory in her hand took over, and she unlocked the door. Toby darted inside with her as she slammed the door and leaned against it.

"You okay, Riley?" George asked.

"The fog is super thick and gave me a panic attack." She slowed her breathing. "I'm okay."

"I made fresh coffee in the breakroom. Get yourself a cup and come to the kennel."

George headed toward the kennel, and Riley hurried to the breakroom.

As Riley poured her coffee, Doc Julie Rae came into the breakroom. "I'm glad you're here. After you get your George hug, come to my office so we can have some private time before you leave."

When Riley reached the kennel, George smiled at her. "Collette is excited about going home today. I told her Claire would call her family the second Doc Thad said she was ready to leave. I have something for you, Riley."

George reached into his bag and handed her a wood-carved dog that was an inch and a half long and remarkably resembled Toby.

"My granddad taught me to carve, and I've always carved dogs because that's where my heart is." George pulled out a smooth carving with almost indistinguishable features from his pocket. "This is the first dog that my granddad made for me, and I've always carried it. It isn't a good luck charm or anything like that; it's a reminder of my talent. I'm not quite the dog whisperer you are, Riley, but close. I hope your carved dog brings you hope the same way mine brought me."

He hugged Riley and walked out of the clinic; Riley watched him with tears streaming down her cheeks. She stared at the carving and then stuck it deep into her jeans pocket.

"I hope I'm not going to be sappy all morning." She sniffled, and Toby leaned against her while Collette whined.

"Thanks, Toby and Collette; I thought it was a wonderful gift, too."

Riley sighed as she refilled her coffee before she went to Doc Julie Rae's office with Toby at her side.

Doc Julie Rae smiled when Riley came in and motioned to her small conference table. "Let's sit. How are you doing?"

Riley sat down and put her coffee cup on a coaster. "Great and awful."

"Like what?" Doc asked as she sipped her coffee.

"I'm excited about our new jobs but hate leaving Barton."

Doc nodded. "I understand Zach and Kayla helped you pack yesterday, and they will be renting your house, or they aren't if Zach and Kayla are supposed to be a secret. I ran into Kayla's mother in the grocery store, and she was very excited about Helen's plan for your house. She told me she likes Zach because he's so smart and kind. She thinks Kayla and Zach are a perfect match. I never knew how much she liked to talk before yesterday; I guess she had things to say."

Riley smiled. "I hit it off right away with Kayla. I really like her; she's genuinely fond of Zach and Hector."

Doc Julie Rae frowned. "Kayla's mother told me something else that mildly troubled me because I didn't know if you knew this or if it was my place to tell you, but I'd want to know if I were you."

Doc Julie Rae stared into her cup.

"Do you want more coffee?" Riley asked.

"No, I've had my quota for the day. Kayla's mother told me she was excited for you and Ben and your new job opportunities, but she asked me if I knew about Vivian Malloy, which I didn't. She told me Vivian Malloy was in the final stages of adopting you and getting full custody when Mrs. Smythe dug up some dirt and went to the sheriff. The sheriff stepped in, and the adoption was canceled."

"What was the dirt?"

"I don't think she knew, but she hinted at criminal activity," Doc said.

"Grandma had an incomplete copy of the adoption paperwork but not the final, so I knew Vivian Malloy had started the process. If Kayla's mother didn't know what Mrs. Smythe found, then nobody else in town would either except the sheriff, and he's not likely to tell me, is he?" Riley frowned.

"Probably not."

"I need to go by the grocery store before I go home. We need snacks for our trip."

Doc Julie Rae smiled. "You know where I am if you need me or want to talk or kick around an idea; don't forget that Charlie, the boys, and Chuck are always up for a road trip."

"Thanks, Doc."

When Riley rose to leave the office, Doc Julie Rae hugged her. "Be safe, Riley, and take care of Ben and Toby. I'm going to hide until you leave because it's not professional to blubber at work."

"Thanks, Doc."

Chapter Fourteen

After Riley made a fresh pot of coffee, Claire and Thad came into the breakroom; Claire carried a plate of cinnamon rolls.

"I brought cinnamon rolls for your last day on the job," Claire said.

"Where's Doc Julie Rae?" Doc Thad asked.

"In her office," Riley said.

"She told me she was going to hide after she told you goodbye today. I'll take her a cinnamon roll." Doc Thad pulled out a paper plate, added two paper towels to serve as napkins, then picked up three cinnamon rolls and put them on the plate.

"Riley, the good news besides your new jobs is that we'll keep in touch." Doc Thad hugged her and then picked up the plate.

"Wait a minute there," Claire said, "You have three; I thought you were taking a cinnamon roll to Doc Julie Rae."

"I'm being sociable by making sure she doesn't eat her cinnamon roll alone." Doc Thad strode to the door. "One for me, one for her, and one for me. She eats slow." He chuckled as he left.

"Will you miss my husband's childish sense of humor?" Claire rolled her eyes as she placed cinnamon rolls on plates for Riley and herself.

"Not at all; my husband has the same sense of humor." Riley bit into her cinnamon roll. "These are good, Claire."

Claire giggled. "They should be; it's your recipe, Riley."

Norm hurried into the breakroom and smiled. "I was afraid I was too late. Thanks for everything, Riley." He strode to her with his hand outstretched, and they shook hands.

"You'll do great, Norm. I'm proud of how quickly you've caught on," Riley said.

"Me too?" Whitney grinned as she stood in the doorway.

"You too." Riley smiled, and they shook hands.

"I'll walk with you to your car, Riley," Claire said.

Riley opened the back door, and Toby jumped in.

"I'd be all sad that you're leaving, but you're like my sister, except you didn't put gum in my hair." Claire's eyes crinkled as she smiled.

Riley hugged her. "See you later."

Tears rolled down Riley's cheeks as she drove away. "This was harder than I expected, Toby. I'll drop you off at the house before I go to the grocery store."

Toby whined.

Riley shrugged. "You're right; it's cool enough that you can wait for me by the door. I won't be long."

After Riley parked, she strolled to the store, and Toby followed her. Toby waited in the shade as she went inside. Riley strolled through the chips aisle and looked for likely snacks. She picked up a sack and headed to the produce department. She smiled at the table of yellow flowers. *I'll bet this is all that's left after the big flower sale.*

While she examined apples, Mrs. Smythe stood next to her. "You came to see me before you left and have a reason."

"You stopped Vivian Echols from adopting me. How?"

Mrs. Smythe picked up an apple and then handed it to Riley. Riley took it but didn't break her gaze.

"Vivian Echols was still married to Ron Echols when your father married her. The marriage was not legal. You can find the Echols marriage records in Lancaster County, Pennsylvania. They were married two years before your father married your mother. There must have been a reason why she wanted to adopt you. I think it was tied to your father's death, but that's purely speculation on my part."

"How did you know?"

"Old people are invisible; I'm always here, but no one ever sees me unless I speak to them. Have you noticed? People talk about their private business when they're in public and think no one is around; Vivian Echols was a prime example."

Mrs. Smythe turned to Riley and stroked her face. "You're a precious child."

The old woman wandered to the vegetables, selected a smooth, shiny eggplant, carefully placed it in a cart, and winked at Riley before she disappeared around the corner.

Riley smiled as she stood in the cashier's line to pay for the bag of chips. *I wonder if that customer knows how to cook eggplant.*

After they were home, Riley stripped the bed, gathered the rest of the dirty clothes, and then started a laundry load.

She carried a glass of sweet tea to the back porch and called Mugsy.

"Big Mug Coffee Shop. May I put you on hold while I finish serving my favorite customer?"

"Of course."

"My customer left the shop. Whatcha got, Short-stuff?"

"Vivian Echols married Ronald Echols in Lancaster County, Pennsylvania, two years before my parents married."

"When were they divorced?"

"I don't have any idea."

"Let me know if you run across any other twists. This is turning into an old-fashioned, one-thousand-piece puzzle of three polar bears in the snow, isn't it?"

"Sure is; I'll see you tomorrow." After they hung up, Riley took the wet clothes out of the washer and tossed them into the dryer.

When a car pulled in front of the house, Riley said, "We have company, Toby."

Riley opened the door, and Jordy bounded into the house; Jackson raced inside to catch up with him. "Can we go out back, Aunt Riley?"

"Go right ahead."

Tom hurried around the car to open Pia's door. When he reached in to help her out, she glared at him. "There will be plenty of time for that later."

Tom chuckled. "I'm practicing."

"Is Ben home? I need Tom to have another hobby besides hovering." Pia held onto Tom's hand and climbed out of their car as Ben backed into the driveway.

"Good; you all can load while Riley and I inspect the house."

Tom carried a large sack into the kitchen and set it on the table; Pia put most of the items in the refrigerator.

"We have a slight change in plans, Tom," Ben said. "We're going to take a majority of the books to the cabin, then we can come back to the house and pack my truck."

"One-time move for the boxes you'll never open until you're finally settled? That's probably violating the standard moving rules because it's sensible, but I like it," Tom said.

After Ben and Tom loaded the heavy boxes, they left.

Pia pointed to the cast iron skillet she had placed on the counter. "We're having slow-roasted pork sandwiches, fried sweet plantains, and cookies for dessert. I brought my skillet to fry the sweet plantains because it's my favorite. I brought milk for Jackson and extra sweet tea; I didn't know how much you might have left. It depends on how much Tom and Ben drink after they get back from the cabin, right? Were you okay with the fog this morning?"

"It scared me because I couldn't see where I was going, and I kept thinking something was going to jump out at me." Riley shuddered.

"I am not crazy about driving in thick fog or heavy rain either. Give me a tour so we can decide what we need to clean."

"Helen reminded me that she has a crew coming in on Monday to do a deep cleaning, but she might reschedule them because she has a construction project in mind; I'll show you. I think all we need to do is sweep the floors."

"Literal broom clean. Show me."

When they went into the bedroom, Pia's eyes widened. "This room is huge."

"That was my first thought when I saw it, too. I really stressed over where to place my bed; can you tell it's been moved closer to the door about a foot?" Riley explained Helen's plan while Pia examined the room and then the closet.

"I can understand why someone who couldn't afford a two-bedroom house would love to have a desk and an office they didn't have to straighten up when someone came into their house, and that closet is definitely rare for an older, small house like this one. After Helen builds the wall, this room will look like the office space was part of the original design."

Pia checked the bathroom. "Sweep and run."

When they returned to the kitchen, Pia said, "I can dust the washer and dryer tops and wipe down the vent hood over the stove. Pitiful, isn't it? I couldn't find anything else to do. What about cobwebs?"

"I don't really see any, but I can swipe at the corners before we sweep."

"Won't hurt, and we'll feel like we cleaned. We can't sweep until Tom and Ben have loaded Ben's truck. I'd like to peek at your backyard, then bring in Jackson, Toby, and Jordy for a little cool down and a drink."

"Go ahead, and I'll run around and swing my broom at the ceiling."

After Riley put the broom back, she unloaded the dryer, folded the clothes, and put them into a spare backpack before putting the backpack in her car's passenger seat.

When Ben and Tom returned, Ben said, "We stacked the boxes in the bedroom closet so we can unpack them at our leisure." He poured two glasses of tea and handed one to Tom. "I'll show you the bed; it goes on first, then we'll load everything else, starting with the large boxes."

They downed their tea before carrying out the bed frame, mattress, and box springs, which they then lashed to the truck with Ben's ratchet tie-down straps.

Ben surveyed the large boxes. "If you'll climb in the truck bed, Tom, I'll bring out the large boxes. Push them against the cab."

After loading the large boxes, Ben said, "We'll fill the truck bed with boxes, then load what we have left into my truck."

"I can help carry out to the truck," Riley said. "You've already loaded the heavy boxes."

"Aren't you taking any of your furniture?" Pia asked.

"The house came furnished; Helen offered us any furniture we might want, but we wouldn't have room to take it. I can't believe how much stuff we have as it is." Riley scanned the boxes still left to load and shook her head.

"While Ben's in training, you might want to go through your boxes and cull a little more," Pia said.

Ben and Riley carried boxes out until Tom filled the truck bed. Then, Tom and Riley carried the four boxes left out to Ben, who put them in the back seat of his truck. Tom returned to the house, and Ben said, "Wait a second, Riley. We've got a box here of things we don't need."

Riley hurried to check the box. "Pia told me I'd need to get rid of a few things before we move again. What is it?"

She read the top of the box and then glared at him. "R's shirts?"

He chuckled. "It's the first thing I'd get rid of."

"Hush, Jackson might hear you," she whispered.

"Hey, Jackson," Ben called out, and Riley elbowed him as Jackson hurried to the front porch.

"Is it time for lunch yet?" Ben winked at Riley.

"Mom says two minutes, and we oughta wash our hands first," Jackson said.

While Ben and Jackson poured drinks, Riley and Tom placed paper plates of sandwiches with generous servings of sweet plantains on the table.

After everyone sat where Riley had indicated, Jackson said, "I set the table; I always set the table at home. You can have extra mustard on your sandwich if you wanna."

Ben took a big bite. "Mmm."

"The pork is tender and tasty, Pia. Where did you buy it?" Riley asked.

"At the hog farm outside of town." Pia said.

Tom grinned. "She slow-roasts a lean pork roast and uses her secret recipe of spices; I can't even order pork when we go out to eat because nobody can cook it like Pia."

"I think I'm ruined, too," Ben said.

"Mom's a good cook," Jackson said.

"She certainly is," Riley said as she ate a bite of sweet plantain. "I think I've found my new favorite side dish. I'm glad you brought your favorite skillet."

"There's a little rendered pork fat in the oil for flavor," Pia said.

At the end of their meal, all the plantains were gone, and everyone had eaten their sandwiches.

"We have cookies for dessert," Pia said, "but I know everyone's full, so we'll split them with you, Riley."

"Just leave us four and take the rest home with you."

"Make that five," Ben said.

While Tom placed Pia's skillet and tongs into a sack, Pia divided the cookies. She placed her family's cookies in the tin she had used to bring them and Riley's share into a freezer storage bag. "The cookies freeze really well," she said.

Pia and Jackson hugged Riley while Tom and Ben shook hands, then Riley hugged Tom while Pia hugged Ben, and Jackson shook hands with Ben.

Jackson called Jordy inside, and Jordy trotted to Riley. She hugged him, and when he whimpered, she said, "I'll never forget you either."

After they left, Toby whined, and Riley brushed away a tear. "Jordy has been a great friend to both of us. I'm glad we'll see him again, too."

Ben picked up the cookies from the counter. "Ready?"

"One last walk-through of the house, then I'll be ready."

After Riley walked from room to room with Toby by her side, she picked up her backpack and stood at the front door. "Goodbye, house; thanks for everything."

"I'll follow you," Ben said. "I wish we were traveling together. I should have rented a trailer for your car; my truck could have pulled it."

"It's only an hour."

Toby stood at his car door and whined. Ben opened the door for Toby while Riley climbed into the driver's seat. She lowered her window, and he leaned in and kissed her, then handed her a cookie before he strode to his truck.

Riley backed out of the driveway and headed to the highway that led to Carson while she ate her cookie.

"This has been such a busy day; I haven't had a chance to tell Ben about what Mrs. Smythe told me, and after we get to Mom and Dad's, we'll be busy unloading all the boxes. Where's everything going to go? I'd stress about it, but I'll bet Mom's got something in mind. I meant to check the weather, so I don't know whether it's going to rain; I'm worried about the boxes in Ben's truck."

After a half hour, Riley tapped her fingers on the steering wheel. "Do you suppose Aunt Millie would know why Vivian Echols tried to adopt me?" Riley sighed. "She's stopped calling me, so I can't ask her. Maybe my mama's brother knows; I hadn't thought about him, but I wonder why he hasn't tried to get in touch with me."

Riley smiled when she turned onto the road that led to the Carters' farm. "I've really gotten used to talking things over with Ben; we're almost home, Toby."

Toby yipped.

"Mom, Dad, Duffy, Finn, and Princess will be excited to see us too."

She turned at the driveway. "I'll bet Duffy and Finn have grown since the last time we saw them."

When she parked at the end of the driveway, Duffy and Finn rushed to her car while Ben parked near the house. Melissa beamed as she hurried to hug Ben; Jake strode from the barn, and Princess pranced along behind him. Jake stopped and opened Toby's door while Riley climbed out of her car. Toby, Duffy, and Finn rushed to the field in the back of the house, and Jake hugged Riley. "I'm so glad you're here. None of us could have waited much longer."

Melissa met Riley halfway between the car and truck and hugged her. "We're so happy you're here. We may get some rain, so we'll need to unload Ben's truck before much longer."

"Where are we going to put our bed and all these boxes for the next four months, or are we renting a storage unit in town? I should have thought of that earlier," Riley said as they walked to the truck.

"We'll put all your things in the downstairs guest bedroom, except we still call it Riley's bedroom." Melissa chuckled. "We call the bedroom upstairs Ben and Riley's bedroom."

Ben and his dad strode to the house and went inside.

"They're going to scope out Riley's bedroom to see where they want to put everything. Ben's just like Jake: both of them have a good eye for efficient packing and storage."

After they returned, Ben said, "We'll put the smaller boxes in the hallway and stack the large boxes on the outside wall of the bedroom. The box springs and mattress can go on top of the bed, and the bedframe will fit under the bed. We'll stack the small boxes on top of the large ones. There should be plenty of room to walk around, and we won't block the window."

Jake nodded. "If we end up needing to use that bed for some reason, we can move the box springs upstairs because it's light and lean the mattress against the inside wall."

Ben lowered the tailgate. "Riley, if you'll climb into the truck and slide the boxes to the edge, Dad and I will load his utility wagon and take them to the house; we'll carry them in from there."

"Do you need me for anything?" Melissa asked.

"As far as unloading the truck, no; I do need dessert, though." Jake's eyes twinkled.

Melissa smiled and went inside.

After the large boxes were unloaded, Riley hopped down from the truck and went inside to stack the small boxes.

"This is an efficient operation," Riley said as she and Melissa stacked boxes. The back door opened as they finished, and Ben called out, "We're bringing in the box springs."

After they brought in the mattress and the bed frame, Ben said, "Your car's next, Riley. Is there anything that needs to go to our room?"

"All the boxes marked 'bedroom,' will, but the rest of the boxes are marked 'kitchen' except for the books."

"Where do you want the books?"

"You can put them in the living room; I cleared a shelf for you," Melissa said.

After all the boxes from the car were taken to the appropriate rooms, Melissa said, "I have a pitcher of fresh lemonade and snacks in the kitchen."

"I haven't had fresh lemonade in ages," Riley said.

"Take your snacks to the living room and put your feet up. You've had a busy week," Melissa said.

Riley and Ben took their lemonade and homemade trail mix to the living room as the sky darkened and the wind picked up.

"After I eat my trail mix, I have a lot to tell you," Riley said.

"Tell me while you're eating."

Riley nodded. "George hugged me, as promised, and gave me a dog that he carved." Riley pulled the dog out of her pocket.

Ben examined it and then gave it back to her. "That's just for starters, isn't it?" Ben popped a handful of trail mix into his mouth.

She rolled her eyes. "I thought it was an indication of how the day would be, but I was wrong."

Riley told him that Doc Julie Rae talked to her privately in her office after she left the kennel. "Kayla's mother told Doc Julie Rae that Mrs. Smythe had information about Vivian Echols, and after Mrs. Smythe told the sheriff, he stopped the adoption process."

"Really? What was the information?"

"I went to the grocery store and talked to Mrs. Smythe, who said Vivian Echols was still married to Ronald Echols when she supposedly married Dad."

Ben gazed at her and then put his arm around her. "So they were never married. If something happened to him, everything would have come to you. That's why she wanted to adopt you, but how much could he have been worth for her to push him into marriage?"

"I don't have any idea because Grandma and I were always happy with what we had, but we weren't dripping with gobs of money or anything like that."

Riley ate more trail mix and sipped her lemonade before she continued, "Mrs. Smythe also told me she suspected that Vivian's motive for adopting me was tied with Dad's death, but she didn't know how."

Ben exhaled. "Vivian pushed your dad into marrying her, she tried to adopt you, your dad dies in an explosion, a phony Brian and Lynn Johnson show up in town and ask you questions, so it's obvious you're tied into this somehow. I can't believe I'm saying this, but you know what bothers me? Nobody has shot at you, tried to kidnap you, or threatened you. Why are you at the center of the storm? What is protecting you from whatever is going on? Do we know what caused the explosion that killed your dad?"

"I don't; I'm certain there must have been an investigation, but I never heard of any investigation or any results. How do I find out what the cause was? He was at a plant in Germany."

"Why don't you let me take that on? The library at the training center probably has access to records that may not necessarily be readily available on the internet. This will be a good research project for me."

Ben grabbed Riley when she jumped at a loud clap of thunder and a sudden crack of a nearby lightning strike and held her. When the lights went out, he kissed her. "Your nerves are fried, aren't they, babe?"

"The fog this morning scared me."

He pushed away her hair from her face. "I wish I could hum your calming tune. I didn't even know about the fog until I came out of a long meeting, and someone mentioned the fog had been thicker than they've ever seen before."

The rain pounded the roof and the windows, the thunder boomed, and the wind roared as the storm continued; Riley leaned against Ben's chest and relaxed as she listened to his heartbeat.

Melissa came into the living room with two candles. "I lit the kerosene lantern in the kitchen and thought you might like some ambiance in here." She placed the candles on the fireplace hearth and then returned to the kitchen.

Riley listened to the raging storm and to the muffled conversations in the kitchen and snuggled closer to Ben. "This is nice."

Ben chuckled as he held her close. "I think so, too."

She sat up and gazed at the flickering candles when he loosened his hold. "I love to watch the dancing shadows."

Ben nodded. "What could be protecting you from Vivian?"

Riley shrugged. "It's not you, and it's not the sheriff; it must be Aunt Millie."

"What? How could Millie protect you from Vivian?"

"I don't know why she popped into my head or what she could do to protect me."

Ben rose and paced. "Sorry, but I think better on my feet sometimes, and it's too wet to go running."

Riley kicked off her boots and sat with her legs crisscrossed while she watched him.

"Maybe she isn't actually protecting you; maybe she's just in the way." Ben stopped pacing and gazed out the window.

"Are you thinking that Aunt Millie is more interesting to Vivian than I am right now?" Riley asked. "Of course, we're assuming that Vivian is the bad guy; it could be someone else."

"Maybe, but if I'm right, as soon as Millie is out of the way, there's nothing left between you and Vivian or whoever."

"So Vivian can claim something of Dad's as the sole heir?"

"It's pretty far-fetched, isn't it?"

"I guess so. Mugsy's checking genealogy records for me; I'll see her tomorrow."

"Why is Mugsy checking genealogy records?"

"She has access to a genealogy database."

"That's not what I meant." Ben sighed. "You'll tell me what she finds, right?"

"Of course."

Jake came into the living room and joined Ben at the window. "We've needed a good, soaking rain; looks like we got it. Is it slowing down?"

"Seems like it," Ben said.

Melissa stood in the doorway. "I'm giving you all a twenty-minute warning for supper."

"You okay, babe?" Ben asked after Jake left for the kitchen.

"I'm fine now, thank you."

Ben blew out the candles before they joined Melissa and Jake in the kitchen.

"We're having comfort food tonight: chicken and dumplings with carrots, celery, and peas. I'll be dishing it up in five minutes," Melissa said.

"We'll take care of drinks, Mom, what do you want?"

"Hot tea."

"I'll take care of the hot tea and have some, too," Riley said.

"Sweet tea and I'm the closest to the refrigerator, so I'll get it," Jake said.

"I'll feed the dogs, then see if I can entice them to go outside for a break." Ben strode to the utility room and the dogs' bowls.

After the dogs ate, Ben and Riley and the dogs went outside. Duffy and Finn raced around the yard, and Toby trotted to the middle of the yard and watched them.

Riley held out her hand. "I thought we'd be getting wetter; it's just light sprinkles now."

When Riley and Ben headed toward the house, Duffy and Finn dashed past them and waited at the door while Toby followed Riley and Ben.

"Your tea got cold, Riley; shall I warm it up on the stove?" Melissa asked.

"It's probably exactly the way I like it," Riley said.

"If you're sure." Melissa rolled her eyes and then pulled out an apple pie from the oven. "In keeping with tonight's theme of comfort food, we're having warm apple pie with ice cream for dessert."

"The ice cream is to cool down the pie, in case you were worried about the pie being too warm, babe," Ben said, and Riley wrinkled her nose at him.

"I'll dish up your pie, and Jake will scoop the ice cream. Large slice or small, Riley?" Melissa asked.

"Medium," Ben leaned over and whispered.

"Medium."

Melissa nodded and handed Riley's plate to Jake as the lights came on; Melissa lowered the wick to extinguish the kerosene lantern.

"That's too bad," Jake said. "I was planning to finish off the ice cream so it wouldn't melt in the freezer. One scoop or two, Riley?"

"One."

"If you don't keep looking in the freezer to see what the temperature is, the ice cream won't melt, Jake; I tell you that every time our power goes out," Melissa grumbled. "What about you, Ben?"

"Large."

After Jake dropped two scoops of ice cream on Ben's pie, he raised his eyebrows.

"Two's good, Dad."

"Is this slice mine?" Jake asked after Melissa handed him a plate with an extra-large slice of pie.

She laughed. "It would take me two days to eat that much pie, and you know it. Take as much ice cream as you can eat. Here's my plate." Melissa handed him a slice of pie that was comparable to Riley's, and he gave her a small scoop of ice cream and then scooped up a double for himself.

Jake took a big bite of his pie and ice cream. "Mmm. Nobody can bake a pie like yours; it's excellent as usual."

Melissa smiled. "When I was a kid, my dad always had a slice of cheddar cheese with his apple pie. I always thought that was strange until we didn't have ice cream one time, and I tried it. It was actually pretty good, but I always stuck with ice cream."

"He must have come from a line of dairy farmers," Jake said. "Before there was ice cream, families served cheese with apple pie."

Melissa's eyes twinkled as she waved her fork.

Ben elbowed Riley as he whispered, "Get ready for a story."

"Actually, he did. He and Mother came over on the Mayflower and brought a dairy cow with them. I had an English milking stool, which goes on the cow's right side, not the left like the American ones. My brother always fell off the milking stool because he tried to sit on it like an American."

Ben and Riley laughed.

Jake shook his head and chuckled. "Darlin', how do you come up with these stories off a random word?"

"I have no idea; I suppose talking about apples and cheese evoked that long-forgotten memory," she said.

"Applies and cheese reminds me of Grandma, who gave me apple slices and cheese snacks," Riley said. "I really enjoyed it, but I never thought about cheese on apple pie, even when we didn't have ice cream."

After everyone finished what was on their plates, Melissa said, "Help yourself if you want more." She rose and then put the ice cream in the freezer.

"Go put up your feet in the living room, Melissa; we'll take care of the dishes. Shall I bring you a glass of wine when we're through?"

"Sounds good." Melissa headed to the living room, and Duffy and Finn trailed along behind her.

After the dishes were done, Ben asked, "Would you like a beer or a glass of wine?"

"Yes, later; I'd like to unpack our boxes in our bedroom."

"Let's go; it shouldn't take long."

While they unpacked, Riley said, "I'd forgotten Mom's cousin is a lawyer. Is he the type of lawyer who could review Grandma's updated will?"

"We can ask. Speaking of wills, how do you suppose you can get a copy of your father's will?"

"I don't know; Grandma said that her will was on file with the probate judge. Do you suppose Dad's would be too? I don't know anything about wills."

"My uncle should if he's a will-type lawyer. Let's talk to Mom."

"Grandma always told me not to worry about Mother because I'd always have family who loved me; she was right."

Ben hugged her, then they went downstairs. Ben poured Riley a glass of wine, then pulled out a beer from the refrigerator, and they walked to the living room with their arms around each other. Riley giggled as she tried to match Ben's stride.

After they relaxed on the sofa, Riley said, "Mom, I have a copy of my grandma's will and a note from her about a trust fund that I didn't know about. I've also realized I never saw a copy of my father's will."

"I realized I don't know what kind of law Uncle Grayson practices. Could he review her grandma's will and contact the trust company for her? Could he help Riley find her father's will?"

"I think he could, but I'm not sure; I'll ask. If he can't, he'll refer us to someone who can. I'll send him a text as soon as I find my phone." Melissa left the living room to find her phone.

Jake frowned. "What's going on?"

"We'll tell you the whole story, at least what we know when Mom gets back," Ben said.

"Grayson said that was right up his alley. He wants us to meet him at my brother's house on Sunday because he's been meaning to see all the family again; he told me I could arrange it, then laughed." Melissa snorted.

"Want a refill?" Jake asked.

"No," Melissa grumbled as she left the living room. "I'll call Hank."

Riley peered at Ben. "I missed something, didn't I?"

"Mom has always gotten the best of Uncle Grayson; he just turned the tables on her." Ben chuckled. "Sunday is going to be exciting."

Melissa returned to the living room and glowered as she sat on her chair. "We're set."

"Good; Ben and Riley will tell us what this is all about now," Jake said.

Riley told them about all the documents in her private magical box and what she had learned from Mrs. Smythe.

"I think it's great news that you've learned so much about yourself. Is Mugsy searching the genealogy records for Erin Malloy?"

"That's right," Riley said. "I'll see her tomorrow."

"You know she'll have Erin Malloy traced back at least ten generations by then," Melissa smiled.

Chapter Fifteen

Millie

Millie tapped the window, and the pigeon perched on the ledge stared at her before flying to the building below her hotel. *There was only one solution.*

She glanced at the clock. *One in the morning here, so it's seven pm in New York and four pm or something like that in California.*

She picked up her phone; when a man answered, she said, "It's me."

"Yes, ma'am, I believe we do; I'll check and call you back. Is this number good?"

"Sure is," Millie said, and the man hung up.

She refilled her wine glass and examined the bottle. I've gotten lazy and lost my discipline. She poured all the wine into the sink and rinsed it before she opened her closet to pack. *My clothes scream 'typical rich American.'*

When her phone rang, she answered.

"Haven't heard from you in quite a while, Millie," the man said. "Must be critical if you're calling me."

"It is: I need to be dead."

The man chuckled. "I can give you a list of names that would be happy to accommodate you at no cost."

"You and your jokes." She smiled. "I'll bet you could, but I need to disappear and not be found."

"My specialty. Where is this death supposed to take place, and when?"

"Paris, any time after 11:00 pm on Sunday, Paris time."

"Very sudden death, then? That's much cleaner than natural causes of death; you always make things easy for me. I'll need your current passport and ID right away so we can drop it near the scene of death for the crack Parisian investigating team to find. I'll text you the location in Paris where my courier will pick up your passport; another operator will hand it off for the final drop. Put your passport inside an envelope or a leather holder so no one accidentally sees your name. We need this to be a clean operation."

"It's what you do; that's exactly why I called you."

"When are you going to ditch this phone?"

"No later than 5:00 pm, today, that's Saturday, Paris time."

The man repeated the times in Paris time; after Millie agreed he was correct, he said, "Perfect; just text me before you ditch your phone, then corrupt the data and dump it. Let me know if your timeline changes so I can adjust it on my end. It's been nice working with you over the years. I know you wouldn't be doing this unless you had no other choice."

"You always told me to have an exit plan. I'll send your usual plus a bonus."

"I'll take the bonus to offset the team, but my time is gratis on this one. Take care, Millie. I'll post a status and any messages on my website just like the old days on the products page."

After they hung up, Millie picked up the house phone and spoke in Italian. "I just received a call about an emergency in Paris that I must handle immediately. How quickly can I get there?"

After the desk clerk put her on hold, Millie received a text from her trusted contact with the Paris address before the clerk returned to the phone with the information for an early morning flight.

"Perfect. Book that for me, please, and I'll be ready to leave for the airport in three hours."

She stripped to her underwear, pulled out a nice bright pink suit to wear, and tossed two suits, three dressy blouses, two pairs of slacks, and her underwear into her suitcase. Millie tossed the rest of her suits, dressy clothes, and laundry bag for the local dry cleaners from the closet into a large shopping sack from a prestigious boutique. After she set her alarm and lay down on the bed, she closed her eyes and willed herself to fall asleep.

When her alarm sounded, Millie hurriedly dressed and put her laptop and purse into her backpack but was interrupted by the ringing house phone. "We're sorry you have the sudden emergency in Paris, madame," the clerk said in Italian. "Shall I book a room for your return, or would you like to keep your room?"

Shift in plans, but what a good idea. "My room is lovely; I'd love to keep it. Thank you, now I won't have to take all my things with me. I expect to be back on Wednesday, but I might be late. I'll be here the rest of the month, but I'll let you know if anything changes."

Millie hung up the clothes from her large shopping sack and returned most of her underwear to the shelf in the large closet. After she neatly lined up her shoes on the closet floor, she packed the plastic laundry bag, the boutique shopping sack, and clothes for four days in her suitcase.

Millie examined the bathroom, her closet, and her room. *Perfect; neat but not overly.*

She rushed to the elevator and tapped her foot as she waited for it to creep to her floor. *If I keep my heart rate up, I'll look appropriately frantic.*

After the taxi dropped her off at the airport, she checked her suitcase and then strolled to security and customs.

She quickly cleared customs and found her gate. While she waited for the plane to board, she sat at a table near a window and called her favorite hotel in Paris to make her reservation through Wednesday. She checked the time and then strolled to the nearest shop to browse. She found a rack with passport holders and felt the leather on one that caught her eye. *It's appropriately expensive for a rich American businesswoman.*

"How much is this?" she asked in English.

The two clerks side-glanced each other, and then one of them quoted a price in US dollars that was three times the cost posted in euros.

Millie beamed as she put her credit card on the counter. *I'm officially a rich American woman.*

"Broken." The clerk pointed to the card reader.

The other clerk added, "Cash only."

Millie paid in cash in US dollars. One clerk gave Millie a handwritten receipt and her change in euros while the other clerk placed the holder in a sack.

She stopped outside the shop, counted her change, and chuckled. *Those little thieves had short-changed me on top of collecting a week's worth of their combined salaries in cash.*

When the plane cleared the airport, she smiled. *I'm ready for my short stay in Paris.* She closed her eyes, leaned her head against the window, and feigned sleep before her seatmate could strike up a conversation.

I'll need to make arrangements to wipe my computer of any sensitive information without looking like it was wiped so I can leave it in my room.

After the plane landed, Millie breezed through customs and then picked up her checked suitcase.

When she was in her hotel room, Millie kicked off her high heels and made her next call.

A bored female voice answered in French.

It's handy to be multilingual. Thanks, Mom, for recognizing my linguistic talents when I was so young.

Millie spoke in broken French with her German accent. "This is Lena Fischer. I'd like to pick up my artwork today."

The woman spoke in French. "We'll be open until two."

"Thank you," Millie responded in German.

I have a busy day ahead. Time to get moving.

Chapter Sixteen

The aroma of bacon and coffee drifted up the stairs, and Riley elbowed Ben, who was still sleeping.

He yawned. "You can shower first so I can sleep longer."

Riley grinned and dashed to the bathroom; when she stepped out of the shower, Ben glowered as he stood in the doorway. "You forgot to tell me about the bacon."

"I didn't mention it?" Riley giggled as he turned on the water, and she rushed to their room to dress. She was hurrying to the stairs when he came out of the bathroom.

"Save some bacon for me," Ben said.

"Shhh, you'll wake Dad," Riley whispered, then raced down the stairs.

"You all were making a lot of racket up there," Jake said when Riley bounded into the kitchen.

"I told Ben not to wake you before I came downstairs; he's the noisy one."

Jake nodded. "I guess he's developed a new skill: mimicking your voice."

Melissa chuckled. "The disadvantage of being upstairs is that it takes longer for the bacon aroma to reach you. Ben used to complain about that all the time."

Melissa poured two cups of coffee: one for Riley and one for Ben as he thundered down the staircase.

"We'll have bacon, eggs, grits, and biscuits for breakfast unless y'all eat all the bacon before I can get the rest of your food on the table."

Toby whined.

"I don't think so," Riley said. "Mom, Toby wanted to know if he could have more bacon. Does that mean he's already had some?"

Melissa flipped her hair. "I play favorites. Toby, Duffy, and Finn were up when I got up."

"Have they eaten?" Ben asked. "I mean besides bacon."

"Not yet; I think they were waiting for you," Jake said.

Toby yipped, and Ben said, "Will do."

After Ben fed the dogs, he opened the back door for them.

Riley rose and frowned. "I planned to go outside with you, but it might be too cold for me without a coat."

"Sorry, babe. It is a little chilly for you right now, but it will warm up in an hour or so. Stay inside and drink your lukewarm coffee." Ben winked and then went out with the dogs.

"Are you feeling okay, Riley?" Melissa asked.

"I'm still easily chilled, but Ben understands and doesn't push me. He told me I'd adjust to the cooler weather over time, and he's probably right."

"Is your room too cold for you to sleep? We can adjust the house temperature," Melissa said.

"I'm doing fine. I've folded the cotton blanket over me that was in our closet, so it keeps me warm but doesn't overheat Ben."

Melissa peered at Riley. "Let me know when you're ready to go into town. What kind of pie is your favorite? I'll bake this afternoon."

"Your peach, apple, and pumpkin pies are my favorites."

Melissa chuckled. "I think those are the only pies I've made while you were here. Jake and Ben are partial to peach; we'll save the pumpkin pie for hunting season. We still have leftover apple pie, so that wouldn't be anything special for us. I haven't made a bourbon pecan pie in a while, except when my stuffy cousin's around, I call it a pecan pie. I'll make a coconut custard pie. It's easy, and it's been ages since I made one. I'll put some pecans in some bourbon to soak, check my recipes to be sure I have everything on hand, and start a load of laundry, and then I'll be ready to go to Mugsy's."

"What can I do to help?" Riley asked.

"Rough chop two cups of pecans," Melissa said.

Riley washed her hands before she pulled out the pecans from the freezer and measured two cups. While she chopped, she said, "I told Toby about Cookie, and he will want to go along; should I tell him to stay here with Duffy and Finn?"

Melissa put the large canisters of flour and sugar on the counter then pulled out the binder marked 'Pies'. "Not on my account; I'd enjoy having Toby go with us. I'll gather the rest of the ingredients when we return."

Riley finished chopping the pecans, raced upstairs, and returned with her sweatshirt. "Ready."

While they headed to Melissa's car, Melissa called out, "Going into town."

"Smackeroos," Jake called out in return.

Ben ran out of the barn, kissed Riley, and then rushed back.

"Smooch and run," Melissa smiled. "Ben learned that from watching his dad when he was growing up. Jake can't run as fast as he could at one time, so smackeroos has become our code for a mushy kiss, and I know the sentiment's still there."

"Ben is romantic and sentimental; I'm learning from him," Riley said.

After Melissa parked in front of the Big Mug, Toby whined.

"Yes, this is where Cookie works." Riley hopped out of the car.

Riley opened the back door for Toby, who pranced to the coffee shop door. "Toby's much more outgoing than I am; he manages our social life."

Melissa smiled as she waited for Riley on the sidewalk. "He's good at it, isn't he?"

When they went into the coffee shop, Cookie yipped from the back of the store, and Toby trotted to join her.

A man with dark-brown hair and graying temples sat at the counter; Mugsy smiled, and her dimples deepened. She wore her white apron with dancing coffee cups on the bib over a red T-shirt. Mugsy was tall, well-padded, and in her forties; the silver streaks in her black hair gave the illusion of a glittering frame around her face.

Mugsy rushed to hug Riley and Melissa, then filled two large mugs with coffee from a pot after it had finished brewing. She cleared her throat as she refilled the man's cup.

When the man turned to face them, his dark brown eyes twinkled as he smiled.

"This is the famous Riley Malloy Carter, and I'm sure you remember Melissa."

"Sure do." The man rose; after he and Melissa hugged, he held out his hand and smiled. "I'm Ryan Cruz."

Riley returned his smile as they shook hands.

"Are you visiting, or are you coming back to Carson?" Melissa asked.

"Visiting with an eye on coming back." He chuckled. "How's that for a straight answer? My brother wanted to retire, so I told him to sell his business. I was there only to support him, so here I am." He drained his cup. "Good coffee, just like always, Mugsy. I'll let you know how it goes."

Ryan kissed Mugsy on the cheek before he left, and red spots appeared on her cheeks.

She fanned herself with a napkin. "Ooo must be getting warm in here; I'll check the thermostat. Meet me at the listening table in the back."

Mugsy rushed to the back; when she joined them at the table, she set her laptop on a table.

"Short-stuff, I have the appropriate genealogy sites marked, so you can browse them; I can print any that you want to take with you after you've read through them. If you tire of watching our girl read, join me up front, Melissa."

Melissa watched Riley read and take notes for half an hour before leaving to join Mugsy in the front. Melissa whispered, "Is there anywhere we can talk so we won't annoy Riley?"

"Nope, but I can fix that; I'll be right back."

Mugsy joined Riley in the back and handed her a headset. "Here's some classical music so you can concentrate without any interference from conversations at the counter and tables up front."

Riley put on the headset and adjusted the volume. "Thanks."

After another two hours, Riley leaned back in her seat, rose, and stretched before she took off her headset.

She strolled up front and glanced around the shop while Mugsy waited on a customer. *Where's Mom?*

After the customer left, Mugsy said, "Melissa left for the grocery store a half hour ago; she'll be back soon." She pointed to the notebook in Riley's hand. "Did you wear out or finish?"

Riley smiled. "I'm finished and not worn out at all; I was surprised at how useful the information is. I can't thank you enough for searching the genealogy records for me. Here is my list of the records I'd like you to print for me." She placed the list on the counter.

"I started on census records this morning but haven't gotten very far yet; the traceability isn't quite as clearcut when people move around. Do you have a priority for people you'd like to see first?" Mugsy asked.

"I hadn't thought about that, but from what we have with the genealogy records, I'd say Erin's brother, Aunt Millie, and Vivian Nichols."

Mugsy nodded as she looked over the list. "Why your aunt?"

"I'm a little worried that she might be in danger, and there are big gaps in my memory of her."

Melissa hurried into the shop with Toby following her. "I hope you haven't been waiting long, Riley."

"Not at all; I've done all I could do in one sitting. I'm ready to go home and make pies or stay out of the way, whichever is more helpful."

"Toby went grocery shopping with me; it was nice to have the company. You were right about how social he is. There were two young women talking to him when I came out of the store. They may have exchanged cell phone numbers." Melissa grinned when Toby yipped, and Riley giggled.

"I'll give you a call with a status report of my progress on Tuesday or Wednesday, Short-stuff. The census might take a little more digging than the genealogy records did."

On their way home, Melissa asked, "Was your genealogy session productive or tedious?"

"Very productive. I couldn't have managed it without Mugsy."

Melissa glanced in the back of her car at the sleeping Toby. "What did Toby say when I told you they'd exchanged cell phone numbers?"

"He said he'd wished you'd mentioned that earlier. He's such a goofball sometimes."

Riley's phone buzzed a text; the caller ID was blank. "I just got a text from a blank caller ID. I don't think I've seen that before," she said.

"I think that means a telemarketer," Melissa said, "but I'm not sure."

Riley tapped the text and stared at her phone. "This is a little strange."

"What?"

"It says, 'Keep dancing! Your favorite guardian angel.'"

"Who is your guardian angel?"

"The only person who could have sent that is Aunt Millie. We used to have a running joke; she has always traveled a lot and called me frequently. Before Aunt Millie hung up, she told me she loved me, and I was her favorite niece, and I'd say she was my favorite aunt."

Melissa chuckled. "I get it: you were her only niece, and she was your only aunt. Was she ever your favorite guardian angel?"

Riley frowned. "We never talked about a guardian angel."

"It's too bad you can't call her or return her text and ask her," Melissa said.

"I've never been able to call her because she changed phones every time she went to a new country; she always said it was cheaper to buy a new phone than to pay the excessive fees for international calls." Riley rubbed her forehead. "I'm getting a headache."

"After we get home, it will be getting close to lunchtime. I'll pull together sandwiches; you can relax because Ben will probably want to spend the afternoon with you."

Riley sighed. "You might be right. I can't believe he has to leave tomorrow for training. He may want to leave from your brother's house."

Melissa's face paled. "I didn't think about that; I suppose I thought he'd leave late Sunday night or early Monday, but he'll want to get situated in his living quarters, and don't schools begin their year with a Sunday evening get-together for the new students? Should I ask my brother to reschedule?"

"I don't think we should reschedule because we'd come up with another conflict; it's what we do." Riley smiled. "I need a lawyer to review the papers I have, and I just realized I might need a will, too, so Ben will be protected."

"You've got a good point; Ben might want to draw up a will at the same time. Jake and I have relatively simple wills and haven't made any changes in years, but we have them because my mother insisted we have wills when Ben was born, and I'm glad she did."

After Melissa parked at home, she said, "If you'd like to talk to Ben, I'll have lunch ready fairly quickly."

"Thanks." Riley strolled to the barn while Toby trotted ahead of her.

When Riley went into the barn, Ben and Jake were putting away tools. "Mom's gone inside to start lunch; she'll be baking pies this afternoon for lunch at Hank's house tomorrow."

"She might need a pie consultant." Jake wiped his hands on an old rag and tossed it onto his workbench before he hurried to the house.

Ben kissed Riley and then put away the rest of the tools. "How did it go at Mugsy's?"

"Great; I've got a ton of stuff to tell you after we eat, but first, I wanted to talk to you about lunch tomorrow. I just realized you may want to leave from there for the GBI training center."

Ben put his arms around her. "I hadn't thought about it until I got a text not long after you and Mom left. There's going to be a get-acquainted social tomorrow at six o'clock with food and drinks. The GBI training center is under two hours from Uncle Hank's house, so I could leave as late as two thirty or three, have plenty of time to check in after I got there, and then go to the get-together. I guess I'd have to pack this afternoon, but I don't have that much to pack since I'll be gone only a week. Won't you feel abandoned?"

"Never by you." Riley hugged him. "I could ride there with you and back home with Mom and Dad. I'll help you pack this afternoon."

Ben exhaled. "I must be more stressed about the training than I realized. I hit a short-circuit in my brain for a minute there."

When they went into the house, Melissa smiled. "You're just in time for lunch."

While Ben hurried to wash off the dirt and grime, Melissa's eyes twinkled as she said, "Riley, you'll be happy to know my pie consultant came up with three pies for me to make tomorrow: peach, pecan, and coconut custard pies."

Jake beamed.

"That sounds great to me." Riley smiled. "Shall I pour drinks?"

While they ate lunch, Ben said, "I've decided to pack today so I can leave tomorrow for the training center from Uncle Hank's house."

"Sounds smart, and Riley can come home with us, so they won't be rushed if she needs extra time with Grayson. You'd spend double the time on the road and burn more gas if you returned home and then left for training from here." Jake peered at Riley. "Are you okay with that?"

"I think it's a great idea; otherwise, Ben would barely have time to eat lunch there before it was time for him to leave."

"Sounds like we've got our plans laid out for the weekend." Melissa finished up her sandwich. "If you'll excuse me, I'd like to get the custard pie in the oven."

"I offered to cook supper tonight," Jake said. "Are hot dogs with chili okay?"

Ben nodded, and Riley said, "Sounds great to me."

After they went upstairs, Riley sat on her chair, and Ben sat on the bed.

"It won't take me long to pack. What did Mugsy find?"

"The database showed the date that Dad and Mama were married and that I was born two years later. I've been so confused by Vivian that I was starting to wonder who I was. It was great to see the proof for myself. Dad was never married to Vivian, according to the genealogy records or any of the records in Cobb County, which is where Vivian claimed they were married. Mugsy checked because I told her Vivian was a priority, and the genealogy records must have waved a huge red flag for her."

"Do you think your dad thought they were married?"

"More than likely because he signed the license; he must have assumed everything was okay from there."

Ben rose. "You can keep talking, but what should I pack?"

"Underwear and socks, five T-shirts, a pair of jeans, a towel, shampoo, soap, and your shaving kit."

"They provide towels," Ben said.

"I'm sure all of them are the same color, probably white. You'll need one that you know is yours. I just remembered Mom would want to send snacks with you. Will you have a refrigerator in your room?"

"I don't remember. I'll have to tell her I don't want to take anything that has to be refrigerated until I scope it out."

"There's more about Vivian."

Ben stared at his T-shirts and then picked out five. "Why five?"

"One for each day that you're there."

He nodded as he packed. "What else about Vivian?"

"Mrs. Smythe told me that Vivian married Ronald Echols, and Mugsy's database showed it was thirty or so years ago, just like Mrs. Smythe said."

Ben tilted his head. "But no record of a divorce?"

"Not that Mugsy could find; she searched the county records around Atlanta and Lancaster County, Pennsylvania, and the internet, just in case there was a notice of some type. She even checked Ron Echols; he didn't show any marriages after Vivian or a divorce. They didn't have any children, which is good news, as far as I'm concerned."

"I would think it's safe to say that they never divorced."

"I'll tell Mugsy I'm satisfied with the genealogy records that show them as still married. I have more information about Mama. Her parents did predecease her, but her grandmother died when I was seven, so Mama's brother, Connor Larson, would have been about twenty-three. I'll bet his grandmother raised him after his parents died. The genealogy database showed him as still single, but I don't know how often the records are updated. I can ask Mugsy."

Ben finished packing except for his toiletries. "Were you surprised by how much information the genealogy database had?"

"It was a jolt to see everything laid out for anyone to find, but I needed time to process all of it; talking to you helped."

"That's my job, babe."

Riley kissed him and smiled. "I love you."

Ben shook his head. "I know, but I'll never understand why you do."

Riley opened her mouth in feigned surprise. "How can you say that, sexy cowboy?"

She sashayed to the door, but Ben got there first. He leered as he blocked the door. "Do that there walk again while I lock this door."

Riley giggled as she swayed her hips as she strolled to her chair and back. When she stopped in front of Ben with her hand on a hip, she said, "Whatcha gonna do about it?"

Ben tugged at the neck of her T-shirt, then grumbled, "This was a much smoother move in my mind."

They raced to undress.

When they went down the stairs, Ben whispered, "That walk of yours gets me every time."

Riley giggled. "Who knew? Besides me and, quite possibly, you."

"What's funny?" Jake asked.

Riley and Ben side-glanced each other, and Riley giggled as Ben's cheeks reddened.

"I need to check on the chickens." Ben strode out of the house.

"We don't have chickens yet, or did you get some and not tell me?" Melissa asked.

"I'll go help Ben," Jake said. "It's getting warm in here."

"What on earth are they talking about? Do you know?" Melissa asked.

Riley shook her head. "How can I help?"

"I just put the pecan pie in the oven. Jake poured in the whiskey, so we'll have to warn Ben not to eat any. The cooking process for the filling is supposed to burn off the alcohol, but I'm not positive that much whiskey will burn off; the taste should be great, though. You and I can share a sliver of a slice. Next up is peeling peaches. Jake wanted to soak the peaches in whiskey too, just to get under my stuffy cousin's skin, so I'm glad Ben lured Jake outside. I'll show you my process. I have a pot of water that is boiling on the stove and a bowl with a little water in it that is filled with ice cubes in the sink."

Melissa slipped the peaches into the boiling water, then, twenty seconds later, immersed them into the ice water and added more ice cubes. She picked up a peach and made a small slit in the skin with her paring knife, then peeled back the skin.

"That's it?" Riley asked.

"That's it. Here's a knife. You can help me peel."

While Riley peeled a peach, she said, "I didn't mention the text to Ben because he's stressed enough about his training."

Melissa nodded. "It was such a vague text, too."

After Riley peeled her third peach, she picked up a fourth one. "This is really slick. I think Grandma must have peeled peaches something like this, but I was always outside if I wasn't reading, and sometimes I was reading outside."

Melissa chuckled as she put more peaches into the ice bath. "That was me as a kid, too. When Jake and I married, my mom cried because she said he'd starve before we were married a year. Jake's mom told her it wouldn't hurt Jake to lose a few pounds. Neither one of them was the typical mother-in-law." Melissa grinned. "Still aren't. My mom worries about Jake all the time."

Riley raised her eyebrows.

"What? You think I worry about you all the time?" Melissa grinned. "It's genetic."

After the peaches were peeled, Melissa said, "I'll remove the pits, and you can cut up the peaches for a pie. We'll have more than we need, so shall we can some peach jam?"

"That would be terrific. I love peach jam, and I've never canned before."

Melissa pulled out the large canning pot. "Did you notice the two-burner propane cooker near the back door? That's what I use to can because otherwise, the kitchen would get too hot. I fill it with the hose because it's too heavy for me to carry when it's filled with water. Take the pot outside and fill it about three-quarters, then turn on the burner. It takes a while for the water to get to a good boil, but it will be ready when we have the jars ready to process."

After Melissa put the peaches, sugar, and lemon juice into a cooking pot, Riley stirred until Melissa declared the jam was ready to put in the sterilized jars.

Riley carried the filled jars outside; Melissa put them on the canner's rack and lowered the rack into the boiling water bath.

"I'll set the timer for fifteen minutes, then we'll bring the jars inside."

Melissa loaded the dishwasher while Riley washed the pot they used to make the jam.

"Wow, the house smells like peaches," Ben said as he came inside.

"We made peach jam," Riley said.

"Your dad's grilling hot dogs for supper, and I'll make the hot dog chili you like. What else would you like with your hot dogs?" Melissa asked.

"Homemade steak fries," Ben said.

Melissa smiled. "I'm not a bit surprised; I'll warm the pie in the oven for dessert."

The timer dinged, and Ben said, "Is that for the peach jam? I'll bring in the jars, then after the water cools, I'll pour it out."

After Ben went outside, Melissa asked, "Have you noticed how helpful Ben's being? Jake does that when he wants to speed up something I'm doing so he can pull me away to see or do something he's interested in. Watch."

Ben came back inside with the rack of jars. "Where do you want them, Mom?"

Melissa placed a towel on the counter. "Right here's good."

After he set down the jars, Ben said, "Come check the coop. Dad and I built an addition."

Riley smiled at Melissa's smirk as Ben ushered the two of them outside.

Jake grinned when Melissa stopped and stared at the addition on the coop. "What is that?"

"It's for baby chicks," Jake said. "Come check inside. It can also be used for sick bay if we have a sick or injured chicken. We built two sick bays for isolation."

"This is great. I assume that small area is for the chicks when they're small, and they have their own small run that isn't part of the run for the full-grown chickens. Duffy and Finn will have time to adjust to the baby chicks, and I won't worry about the dogs accidentally hurting the babies. The sick bays have roosts, and you've left room inside them for food and water. Well done, honey; this is a fantastic design. You must have been working on this for a while, and I didn't notice." Melissa smiled. "Very sneaky and one of your best surprises."

Jake beamed. "How many chickens do you want?"

"Eight," Melissa said.

"Whatever you want, sweetheart," Jake said. "We can go into town on Monday after Riley leaves for work, and you can take your time at the farm store to look around and decide. While you're picking out chicks at the farm store, I'll wander next door to browse at the sporting goods store; they're having their big pre-hunting season sale."

Melissa winked at Riley, who nodded and walked away before she giggled.

Ben joined her. "Was Dad too transparent?" he whispered.

"Mom predicted something was going on, but she's happy with the surprise and knows that was Dad's goal. A new rifle will be his bonus."

"Did Mom tell you that?" Ben asked as they strolled to the house.

"She saw it coming and won't blow his cover, and neither will I."

Ben kissed her. "Good to know, babe."

Thanks to Mom, I've just set myself up for a lifetime of wonderful surprises.

When they reached the house, Ben said, "I'll get the wagon from the barn, then empty the canning water in the garden."

"I'll help," Riley said.

When they reached the garden, Riley said, "I didn't want to stress you, but I have one more thing to tell you."

Ben put his arms around her. "Okay, I'm ready; bring it on."

She pulled out her phone and showed him the text.

He narrowed his eyes as he read the text. "We know what keep dancing means. Didn't you tell me once that you and your Aunt Millie have always had a running joke that you are her favorite niece?"

"Right, and she is my favorite aunt."

"This is from Millie, and she's telling you to protect yourself from Vivian."

"Yes, because I'm sure Aunt Millie knew what keep dancing meant, but I'm not sure she knew that I became an expert when it came to Vivian Echols after years of studying her."

"Wow, babe, I didn't even think about that either."

"Neither did I at first, but talking with you helped me to put the pieces together."

Ben nuzzled her neck. "You can tell me later how awesome I am."

Riley giggled and pointed to the garden. "The jalapenos and tomatoes look like they're ready to be picked."

"Mom will probably pick them up on Monday and make salsa. I love her salsa; if I have a refrigerator, I'll take a jar back with me next weekend."

I am going to learn so much here.

When they returned to the house, Melissa asked, "Ready for your hot dog chili lesson? Ben knows how to make hot dog chili, but he told me he doesn't have the patience to make it when he can buy a can of hot dog chili at the grocery store. I was going to disinherit him for that remark, but we forgot to have a second child in case Ben was ornery."

Riley smiled. "I'm ready and not all that great with a can opener."

"I'll open the book to the recipe, and you can get busy on it as long as you don't remind Ben that I start with a can of tomato sauce."

After Riley browned the hamburger and onion and then added the tomato sauce and spices, she stirred the mixture, and Melissa peeked into the pot.

"Stir in a little water and put on the lid so the sauce can stay warm on the stove. After Jake puts the hotdogs on the grill, turn the heat up a bit and stir it until it's the thickness we want. We'll get to work on Ben's steak fries."

The steak fries were seasoned and ready to be cooked when Jake opened the back door and called inside, "I'm heating the grill."

"He gives me a warning so I can roast the steak fries." Melissa spread the potatoes on a wire roasting rack on a small baking sheet before she slid the baking sheet into her large air fryer.

After Ben and Jake came inside and washed their hands, Jake carried out the hot dogs and the buns; Melissa put the apple pie into the oven, Riley stirred the sauce, and Ben set the table.

When they all sat down at the table, Riley took a bite of her hot dog. "This is exactly how Grandma made her hot dogs; I've tried, but I haven't been able to eat a hot dog for years, and now I know why. This is really delicious: perfect char and perfect hot dog chili. It's all I ever wanted: perfection."

Ben's mouth was full, so he nodded in agreement.

"It's how you cook, honey, and I appreciate it," Jake said.

"Thank you; I love to feed people who enjoy how I cook, and Riley's right about the perfect char. You are the grill master."

After dessert, Ben fed Toby, Duffy, and Finn, and then he and Riley went outside with the dogs.

When they strolled past the chicken coop, Riley asked, "How long were you and Dad working on the addition?"

"Dad started on it this week and put in the posts, then buried the wire and built the frames for the floor and walls. We added the floors, walls, and roof yesterday then did everything else today. Mom never comes outside to check on Dad when I'm here, and he was hoping that today was no exception."

While they walked to the garden, Ben asked, "Do you think your 'nice talking to you' guy is your mama's brother?"

Riley stopped and gazed at Ben's worried face. "I'm willing to believe his intentions were to warn me about Vivian and a second person. I'm not sure it matters if I know who he is."

"You have a different perspective; you always have, so I guess I shouldn't be surprised, but I always am."

Riley smiled. "What's the best way to get Mom started on a story?"

Ben chuckled. "Finally, something I can teach you. Watch the master."

Jake met them at the back door before they went inside.

"Dad, we were thinking the best send-off for me tonight would be snacks, drinks, and some of Mom's stories," Ben said.

Jake grinned. "Good idea; ask for snacks with our drinks, and make mine a beer. I'll take care of the rest."

When Riley and Ben went into the house, she elbowed him as she whispered, "Watch the master?"

He nodded.

Riley said, "Mom, since this is Ben's last night before his training begins, we'd enjoy it if the four of us could relax with snacks and drinks."

"That sounds wonderful, but are you sure? Wouldn't you rather have a quiet evening of the two of you alone?"

Ben smiled as he hugged Riley. "We're sure; we have a lifetime of evenings together ahead of us."

"I'll pull together the snacks," Melissa said. "Are you drinking wine, Riley?"

"Sure am; shall we pour a glass for you too?"

"That will be great; pick a bottle, and Ben can open it."

"Which wine, babe?"

"The one on the left," Riley said.

Melissa glanced at the wine. "Good choice; that's my favorite. I bought grapes and chocolate today in case we decided to snack this evening; we also have crackers, cheese, and jalapeno cheddar sausage."

"It's party time," Riley said as Jake came into the house.

"Did I hear party?" He smiled.

"You're just in time to help me pull together snacks, honey," Melissa said.

Ben opened the refrigerator. "Beer, Dad?"

"Sounds good to me."

"Riley and I will take the drinks to the living room," Ben said.

"We'll be right behind you in one minute," Melissa said.

On the way to the living room, Ben asked, "Where's your cell phone, babe?"

Riley tilted her head. "It's in my backpack in the kitchen."

"Good; can you ignore it this evening, or should you turn it off?"

Riley laughed. "I can ignore it."

After Melissa and Jake carried in the snacks and everyone had selected their first round of snacks, Jake asked, "Do you think anyone will try to pull a prank on Ben or Riley, or have they all outgrown that?"

"I didn't even think about that. Riley, I'll give you some hints of what to look for and how to retaliate," Melissa said.

Jake winked at Riley as Melissa launched into her first story.

Chapter Seventeen

Riley woke the next morning and kissed her sleeping, naked husband, then dashed for the shower before he realized she was still naked, too.

When she stepped out of the shower, Ben came into the bathroom.

"I let you get away on purpose," he grumbled, and she smirked.

When she tried to slip past him, he tugged on her towel, and it dropped on the floor.

He kissed her. "Now, we're even."

He leered as he picked up the towel and handed it to her. "You dropped something."

Riley giggled.

After he climbed into the shower, she said, "You told me to watch the master. I think Dad loves Mom's stories as much as I do."

When Ben mumbled his reply while he washed his face, Riley smiled as she hurried to their bedroom, dressed, and made their bed. She sat by the window and combed out the tangles in her wet hair while she listened to the morning songbirds. *The birds said there would be no rain today.*

Ben came into the bedroom, and Riley said, "I smell bacon."

"I'm hurrying."

After Ben dressed, they headed to the stairs.

On the way down, Ben asked, "Are you ready to take on the world, or do you want coffee first?"

While they strolled to the kitchen, Riley asked, "Is that what you think of me?"

"What? That every morning you wake up wondering if the world's villains can wait long enough for you to drink your tepid coffee?" Ben nodded. "Yep, that pretty much sums it up."

Jake grumbled as he followed them into the kitchen. "I hate coming in at the end of a movie or an argument because I miss so much."

"Don't even joke about Riley's tepid coffee." Melissa waved her spatula at Ben. "Your coffee's on the table, Riley. I poured it while you were taking your shower."

Ben elbowed Riley and laughed.

"I have cinnamon rolls in the oven, and I'm scrambling a mess of eggs. Does anyone feel like bacon?"

"It's what got me out of bed," Riley said.

"I thought..." Jake's voice trailed off when Melissa glared at him, and he sipped his hot coffee while Ben covered his smile by holding his cup in front of his mouth and then taking a sip.

Riley's eyes twinkled. "Would you check outside for me, honey? I need to know if I have time for another cup."

Ben sputtered his coffee, then snort-laughed, and Riley giggled.

"You two are an even match," Jake laughed.

Melissa smiled as she put the plate of cinnamon rolls, the plate of bacon, and the bowl of scrambled eggs on the table.

After breakfast, Melissa relaxed at the table with a cup of coffee at Jake's insistence while he and Riley took care of the dishes. Ben fed Toby, Duffy, and Finn and took them outside.

"We'll need to leave in an hour," Melissa said.

"Is there anything we can take in Ben's truck for you?" Riley asked.

Melissa frowned. "I just realized I have a logistics problem. I don't think Duffy and Finn can stay in their crates for the entire day without a break, and I'm uncomfortable with leaving them outside, even if Toby supervises them. I'd worry that a thunderstorm might pop up, and Duffy and Finn might panic and run off. We can't take them with us because the truck's backseat would be too crowded for Riley with three dogs, and my car's not big enough. I could drive my car, then Riley and Toby could ride with me, and Duffy and Finn could ride with you, Jake."

"I'll be fine coming back in the truck's backseat with Toby next to me, and he'll tell Duffy and Finn where to sit. Will they be okay at your brother's?" Riley asked.

"There will be all kinds of dogs running around there. It will be a good chance for Duffy and Finn to start socializing, especially with Toby there to keep them in line," Ben said.

"Does that help, hon?" Jake asked.

"It helps a lot; sometimes I get wound up over the what-ifs in my head," Melissa said. "Back to your question, Riley. I can put the cream pie in an ice cooler, and it will be protected from Duffy and Finn, but if the pecan and peach pies could ride with you, I'd appreciate it. I have pie carriers for them, so they can ride on the floor in the backseat if they don't bother Toby."

"He'll be fine."

"Get all your stuff pulled together for Grayson, and then we'll be ready to leave," Melissa said.

Riley made sure all the papers were in the manila envelope, including the handwritten note from her grandma. She put a lightweight long-sleeved shirt and a sweatshirt into her backpack and brushed her hair while Ben carried down his duffel bag.

When she went into the kitchen, Melissa said, "Your skin is so fair; we'll put sunscreen on you and me when we get there, and I have sunhats for us. Which one do you want? Pink or camo?"

"I'll take camo." Riley pulled on the hat. "It's comfortable, and I love the wide brim. I wear a lightweight long-sleeved shirt in the sun, but sunscreen is a good idea if it's too hot to wear."

"I can't imagine your long-sleeved shirt ever being too hot for you, but it's good to have options," Ben said. "Let's go. I need pie."

After everyone was loaded, Ben said, "You lead, Dad."

Before they reached the end of the driveway, Riley's phone rang.

"I hope now's a good time for you," Helen said. "I won't keep you very long. I wanted you to know that I received a small box of jewelry: a necklace with a small turquoise pendant, diamond earrings, and a beautiful pearl ring. I took the jewelry to Mary Ruth at the pawn shop, and she told me the pieces were lovely fakes. They aren't completely worthless because they are pretty, but they aren't precious stones by any means. If you like, I'll hang onto them, or I can talk to Mary Ruth about putting them on consignment."

"I don't wear jewelry and don't really know anyone who does, so see what Mary Ruth says."

After she hung up, Riley said, "Tell me about GBI and what you'll be learning."

Riley relaxed and listened to Ben as he explained his upcoming classes, some of the instructors and their reputations, a few of his classmates that he already knew, what he expected housing to be like, and his class schedule.

Riley smiled and gazed at him while he talked. *I need to give him more opportunities to talk about what he loves.*

Ben glanced at her. "I haven't given you a chance to say anything."

"I'm really interested in what you're saying. Do you know anything about any of the field exercises?"

"Not really, because they'll be actual cases from previous years." Ben continued with an example of a murder investigation that he expected would be one of their case studies before they went into the field for hands-on practice and talked about the expected pitfalls that he already saw.

"The gotchas will getcha," Riley said.

Ben chuckled, "Can I steal that without being charged with plagiarism? Who said that?"

Riley grinned. "I'm sure somebody, but I did just now."

Ben laughed. "I set myself up for that, didn't I?"

Toby yipped, and Riley laughed.

Ben exhaled. "Toby said you got me, didn't he?"

Riley laughed harder, and Ben joined her when Toby howled.

When Ben turned behind Jake at the driveway, Riley's eyes widened at the expansive, well-kept lawn, flower gardens, and magnolia trees. "This is beautiful."

"Would you like something like this?" Ben asked.

Riley frowned. "Never; it's not our style."

"Every time I come to Uncle Hank's, all I see is the amount of maintenance the yard must require to look like this. I need to step back and enjoy its beauty because I don't have to take care of it."

Riley nodded.

After Ben parked, Riley grinned at the five elementary school-aged children who ran from the front to the back of the house, followed by a determined two-year-old and a laughing young man who was trailing the toddler.

"There will be a lot of people here, and they know your name; you don't have to learn theirs, though. Uncle Hank's wife is Alondra. Her name is Spanish and translates as lark in English; we call her Tia Alondra in respect of her Puerto Rican roots. It's perfectly acceptable for you to hide out with Mom if you don't feel like mingling because everyone knows how overwhelming it can be. I'll check in with some of the cousins, then join you."

"You don't have to do that. I'll venture out if I'm feeling brave, but I'm sure Mom won't mind hovering over me."

"That's for sure; let's take the pies to the kitchen."

Riley smiled. "Mom's waiting for us to follow her and Dad. Does she think I'm going to bolt?"

Ben chuckled, then opened Toby's door, and Toby hopped out. Ben opened Riley's door, and she giggled at the gasps as she climbed out. *I wonder how many folks are comparing me to Pamela Suzanne?"*

"Sweetheart," she whispered, "you owe me a dollar every time someone tells me I'm short and two dollars for each time someone slips and calls me Pamela Suzanne."

"You're on; I'll collect three dollars from them."

When they reached the kitchen, Melissa introduced Riley to Alondra, who was round like Riley and only a little taller.

Alondra hugged Riley. "You call me Tia Alondra, and I'll call you what?"

Melissa chuckled. "Call her Riley."

"Okay, you're Riley for now, but that will change after I get to know you. What have we got, Missy?"

Ben whispered to Jake, who grinned. The two men fist-bumped. Ben glanced at Riley and raised three fingers, then five.

She giggled. "Three and five?"

Ben winked at her as he and his dad left.

"The coconut cream pie goes into the refrigerator; the other two pies are peach and pecan," Melissa said.

Alondra removed the lids and inhaled. "Mmm. Fresh peaches and a healthy dose of Tennessee whiskey. We'll put our pecan pie on the counter next to the toaster; it will be for nondriver adults only. We have over twenty-five dozen cookies, so the children will be appropriately wired when they go home. Hank was roasting a pig all night, so we'll have plenty of meat. We have a ton of potato and pasta salad and, for the diet-conscious, one tiny plate of fruit."

The toddler came into the kitchen, and his red-faced dad followed him. Alondra handed the young man a tall glass of iced tea, and the dad snatched a strawberry from the diet plate and gave it to the toddler.

The toddler popped the entire strawberry into his mouth, and red juice drizzled down his chin as he chewed. He stared up at Riley. "I like your dog."

"I'm sure Toby likes you too."

The toddler repeated, "Toby."

"What did he say?" Melissa asked.

Riley cocked her head. "The strawberry did muffle him, didn't it? He said he liked my dog."

"Of course, I should have guessed from your reply."

When the toddler sped to the back door and outside, his dad downed his glass of tea, placed the glass on the counter, and rushed out to catch up with his son.

"Your Riley understands babies, Missy?"

Melissa shrugged with her palms up. "I guess."

Alondra shifted her gaze to Riley, and Riley copied Melissa's shrug. "He talked about Toby, so I answered him."

"I like this one, Missy. You did well."

"Thank you. I think so, too." Melissa winked at Riley.

Ben strode into the kitchen, "Babe, Uncle Grayson's here. Want to get your backpack out of my truck?"

He took her hand, and they strolled outside together and headed to his truck.

"What have you learned so far?"

"Tia Alondra has a remarkable sense of smell. She sniffed the pecan pie and knew Dad had put in Tennessee whiskey, not Kentucky bourbon. She set it aside for non-drivers."

Ben chuckled. "I heard you understand the babbling of a toddler. My cousin's husband was the baby chaser."

"He told me he liked my dog; I'm a softie when it comes to a dog lover, you know that."

Ben grinned. "Is that how I won your heart?"

"That, along with your cute smile and your hazel-green eyes."

Ben looked down and grimaced as he tried to see his own smile. "I didn't know I had a cute smile."

Riley laughed and kissed his contorted mouth.

He hugged her and whispered, "Go with me; I'll smuggle you into my room in my duffel bag."

She studied his face and then exhaled. "Only sixteen weeks: we can do this."

I'll ask Mugsy to help me find a place that will accept Toby and is as close to the school as possible.

She pulled out her backpack, and they strolled to the playground. A gray-haired man in gray slacks and a white long-sleeved shirt with a dark blue tie sat at one of the tables while he watched the children.

The man smiled as they neared him, then rose and held out his hand. "Hello, Riley; I'm Grayson."

After they shook hands, he said, "I'm on playground duty, but here comes my replacement. She's a school teacher, so she's imminently more qualified than I am."

The teacher waved, then smiled as she neared the picnic table. "Hello, Riley; you're as pretty as they say and probably twice as smart."

The teacher kissed Grayson. "You're off duty now, hon. Thanks for the break. Y'all can use the office to meet; I cleared it with Alondra."

After they went into the office, Ben closed the door.

"Anybody mind if I sit behind the desk?" Grayson asked.

"Not at all," Riley said.

"I'll probably just pace anyway." Ben smiled.

"Give me a quick intro, then I'll read these papers."

Ben said, "Riley's dad was an engineer and was killed in an industrial explosion in Germany six years ago. Riley's mother died when she was six months old. Riley's dad thought he married a woman when Riley was around a year old, but we've discovered the woman was married at the time and still is."

Riley continued, "The will that's with these papers belongs to my grandma; I've never seen a will for my dad. Grandma set up a bank account for me; the contact information is in the documents. We found the documents at my Grandma's cabin a week ago but haven't had time to follow up on the bank account because we've been busy packing so Ben can attend his training."

"Got it. Do I start with this handwritten letter?"

Riley nodded, and Ben paced while Grayson read and took notes.

After he read the last page, Grayson rose from the chair. "Put away the papers, Riley, and let's eat lunch, then get back together before Ben has to leave. I have a few questions."

Riley put the document into her backpack; Ben slung her backpack's strap across his shoulder and carried it while they filled their plates. Riley carried their plates outside while Ben searched for drinks.

Jake sat at a picnic table with a full plate in front of him and a second plate with less food on it next to him.

He rose and waved. "Saved you a spot with the in-laws, Riley."

She giggled as she hurried to join him.

"Melissa's on a search for drinks. I'm guarding the food and the table. There are only four picnic tables, and Hank never puts out the folding tables because the young guys will take care of them. It's become a tradition that when the last child graduates from college, the parents are elevated to the elderly ranks and have priority over the picnic tables. Unfortunately, the picnic tables go fast because there are so many of us now; Melissa and I split duties. I saw that you and Ben went into the house with Grayson. How did it go?"

"He read through the papers and then said we should take a break. We'll get back together after lunch; he said he had some questions."

Ben showed up at the table with a pitcher of sweet tea and four glasses. "Mom's getting dessert for us; I'll be right back."

"I guess you can tell this isn't our first family picnic. Most people wait until after they eat to get dessert, but there may not be much pie left by the time we finish eating."

Ben and Melissa came to the table with five dessert plates, each containing two slices of pie: three of the plates had coconut cream and peach pie, and the other two had coconut cream and half a slice of pecan pie.

"Alondra had these put back for us," Millie smiled. "The fifth plate is for Ben and Jake to share because they don't get any Tennessee pecan pie, as Alondra has renamed it."

Riley tasted the roasted pig first. "I'm not sure if I've ever had pork roasted like this before. This is awesome."

"Do not tell my brother, but I can't eat roasted pork anywhere but here," Melissa said.

"Mom, I've noticed Dad calls you Melissa, but everyone here calls you Missy," Riley said. "Is it because Alondra likes nicknames?"

"It's my brother. When we were kids, he called me Miss Smarty Pants. Those were the days before I learned not to react to him, so I got really mad and beat him up."

"She was younger and smaller, but she was meaner," Jake added, and Melissa glared at him. "Sorry for interrupting."

"When Mom asked me why I fought with my brother, I told her he called me names. My brother called me Missy in front of the folks, but I knew what Missy stood for. Mom told me Missy was a lovely nickname for Melissa, and Hank laughed, so I waited until he came outside and ambushed him, and I spent my entire childhood being teased by my older brother and giving him black eyes."

While they ate their pie, Jake glanced around. "Speaking of your mom, where is she?"

Melissa smiled. "She's on a cruise. Hank's going to be in big trouble when she finds out about the big send-off for Ben and his new job."

"If I were him, I'd turn it over to Alondra for my cover story," Ben said.

Jake nodded. "It's the only solution."

When Riley ate her last bite of pie, Ben asked, "Ready for Grayson's questions? I just saw him go into the house."

As they headed back to the house, Riley asked, "Did you really see Grayson go into the house?"

Ben shrugged. "It might have been him. Mom's going to explain to Dad why he'd ruin everything if he told Hank to turn over his big problem with Grandma to Alondra. It will be more relaxing in the office, and I can't get into trouble for laughing at the wrong time at something that is totally hilarious."

A man who was helping a three-year-old on a toddler-sized climbing tower waved. "Hey, Ben!"

"Do you mind, babe? I haven't had a chance to talk to him. I'll just be a few minutes."

"Go right ahead. I'll be fine."

Ben loped to the playground, and Riley stepped inside the cool house and found a bathroom. She pulled out her phone. *Helen tried to find something affordable for us that was halfway between UGA and Ben's training. I hate to bother her again.*

She sent a text to Mugsy. "I'm at Mom's brother's house at a party. Can you call? I've got five minutes alone."

Riley's phone rang.

"What's up, Short-stuff?"

"I need to find a place to live within twenty minutes of the GBI training center. I don't have any contacts that far away from Barton and hoped you might."

"You'll want to have Toby with you, so you'll need a bit of a yard for him. What's your price limit?" Mugsy asked.

"No limit on price at all; I'll take care of it. I'll get a loan if I have to, but Toby and I have to be with Ben; it's the only way Ben will be able to get through his ten or twelve weeks of training."

"I hadn't thought about it from that angle, but you are most likely right, Short-stuff, because everyone knows how smitten that GBI guy is with you. I'm on it." Mugsy hung up.

Riley exhaled. *If anybody can find us a place to be together, Mugsy can.*

She hurried to the office and waited for Ben and Grayson.

It wasn't long until Ben sauntered into the office. He kissed Riley. "Thanks, babe. Are you okay?"

"I came inside where it's cool and have been sitting alone in a quiet room. It's been glorious."

Ben shook his head. "It's amazing how different we are."

Riley fluttered her eyelashes. "Imagine that."

Ben laughed as Grayson came into the office.

Grayson stared at Ben. "Glad you're enjoying your afternoon. Riley, I'll need a retainer to serve as your lawyer."

Riley opened her backpack, and Grayson said, "Ten dollars will do."

"I have ten dollars in cash." Ben rose to pull out his wallet.

"No offense, Ben, but in this case, my retainer fee has to come from my client."

Riley nodded. "Is a check okay?"

"A check is fine. I'll prepare your receipt and an agreement between you and me for you to sign tomorrow. I'll need your email address."

Riley wrote the check and then carefully printed her email address on the notebook he had handed to her.

Grayson endorsed the back of the check that she gave him. "This is binding. Next, priorities. I assume contacting the bank is a priority, along with an in-depth review of your grandmother's will. The next priority is finding your dad's will. Correct?"

Riley nodded.

"That's great because I have two new, impatient lawyers in my practice who are bored but not licensed to practice law in Georgia, and they are driving me crazy in their insistence they need to be doing work that isn't what they consider administrative or mundane. I hate to break it to them, but administrative and mundane is the job description for any lawyer, even the hotshots." Grayson smiled.

"That's my problem," Grayson continued, "but I'll solve it by having them first find your father's will and provide a client summary for you, then find the results of the investigation of the explosion in Germany that killed your father and determine whether you have a case for wrongful death. I expect them to provide a briefing and a recommendation for the partners of the firm. I'll give them your email address and tell them they can contact you via email for any questions. I won't give them your cell number because I won't have a record of the client contact at the office, but I need your cell phone number and yours too, Ben. Do you have a will, Riley?"

"No."

"I don't either," Ben said.

"Perfect. Give me ten dollars, Ben."

After Ben gave him ten dollars, Grayson said, "I'll assign someone in my practice, not an intern, to be your lawyer, Ben. I have a form with me that you can sign for a simple will just to protect Riley. Now that I think of it, Riley, you should also have a simple will to protect Ben until we unravel all this to see if you need something more complicated."

Grayson pulled out the forms for them. "Read the forms, but don't sign them. I need to get witnesses in here. I'll be right back."

"What do you think, babe?" Ben asked.

"I feel like we've found someone who will take over. I've been floundering and didn't realize it, and I think that it's smart for both of us to have wills."

"I agree with everything you said." Ben sighed. "It's going to be a long week."

"We'll just take each day as it comes, honey. We can do this," Riley said.

Ben frowned. "It will be hard."

"Is it worth it?" Riley peered at his face.

He stroked her face. "Yes."

"So, hang on to that: it's worth it."

"You're worth it, babe." He leaned close and kissed her as Grayson opened the door and cleared his throat, and a woman giggled.

"We're your local neighborhood kill-joy committee," the woman said.

Grayson chuckled. "Now that introductions are over, did you have a chance to look over the forms?"

"Yes," Ben replied.

Riley nodded. *We aren't in a court or under an oath, and we won't go to jail for lying.*

Ben signed his form, and the two witnesses signed. Riley signed her form, and the witnesses signed and then left the office as they giggled and whispered.

Grayson sighed. "Hopefully, they'll get it out of their systems before they enter the general populace of nosy family members, but I doubt it. Consider it common knowledge in the family that you two have wills, leaving everything you have to each other."

"I'm not surprised; we'll survive the family gossip. What else do we need to do?" Ben asked.

"Cell phone numbers." Grayson tapped his notebook.

Riley wrote down both of their numbers.

"Riley, I'll text or call you only if I need to; otherwise, any communication from my practice will come by email from my company domain."

He pulled out two business cards and wrote on the back of the cards before he gave one to Riley and the second one to Ben. "My cell phone is on the back. Call or text me if you have any questions or changes or if you have any discomfort with the questions the team is asking, Riley. Remember, I'm your lawyer. I'm involved with and coordinating all of your legal and financial business until you decide you need a financial manager."

Grayson's serious face suddenly brightened, and he chuckled. "Ben, you're my first cousin's son, but you're on your own."

Ben grinned. "I expect nothing more from my family."

Grayson rose to his feet and shook Ben's hand. "I rarely hug clients, Riley, but in your case, I'm making an exception because you're family, unlike that interloper, your husband."

Ben laughed as Grayson hugged Riley and then left.

Riley stared in awe at the door after Grayson left.

"Do you see why you fit into this family so well, babe?"

"Surprises in a good way along every twist and turn. I think I love being part of a large family."

Ben frowned as he glanced at the clock on the office wall. "I need to leave."

Riley hugged him and then pulled him into a sweet kiss that became an intensely passionate kiss of longing. When she broke away, she said, "I love you, Benjamin Jacob Carter."

"I love you more, Riley Erin Malloy Carter." Ben pulled her close and held her tightly, and tears slipped down her face.

He held her where he could gaze at her face. "I need to leave, but I'll be home Friday night after class."

She smiled. "I know."

They slowly walked outside to the picnic table, where his parents waited for them.

"I have to leave," Ben said.

Melissa rose and hugged him. "Have a great week."

"We'll take care of Riley," Jake said, then he hugged Ben.

As Riley walked Ben to his truck, Toby joined them. Toby yipped when they reached the truck.

"I'll miss you too, Toby," Ben said.

Ben scratched Toby's ears, kissed Riley, and whispered, "Keep dancing, babe."

Riley smiled.

Ben lightly traced her lips with two fingers. "I live for that smile."

He hopped into his truck and left.

Riley and Toby stood in the driveway while she waved until Ben's truck was out of sight. Riley listened as Ben drove away from her on the country road until she couldn't hear the hum of his tires anymore.

"Are you okay?" Melissa stood next to Riley.

"No, can we go home now?"

"Yes, we can." Jake unlocked his truck and whistled for Duffy and Finn.

Chapter Eighteen

Millie

Millie dropped off her laptop in her room at the hotel in Paris after five o'clock on Saturday and waved at the desk clerk as she left. Before she approached the ticket counter at the train station, she hurried into the restroom and changed into one of her thrift store outfits that she had carried in the boutique sack. She rolled up her Paris suit and put it into the laundry sack, then put all her thrift store clothes into the travel bag she had bought at the thrift store. After she folded her boutique sack, she added it to the sack with her suit. She donned her black wig and then checked for any strays of her hair. *Lena Fischer is officially ready to travel.*

On her way to the ticket counter, she placed her plastic laundry sack with its contents into a large, half-full trash can. She bought her ticket with euros from a disinterested agent, breezed through customs, and found the right track for her train.

While the night train raced through the countryside, Millie stared out the window. *Was it a mistake sending that text to Riley?*

She exhaled and leaned back. *Riley will be Vivian's target as soon as the news of Millie Malloy's death is out. I was right to warn Riley.*

When her seatmate made noises to start a conversation, Millie, now Lena Fischer, pulled out the crime novel written in German that she bought at the train station and began reading.

"What are you reading?" her seatmate asked in French.

Lena peered at her seatmate as she shrugged and replied in German. "Sorry, but I don't understand what you said. Excuse me, I'm reading."

When the train pulled into the Frankfurt station, Lena marked her place in the book with her ticket. She stopped at the ticket counter and bought a ticket to Augsburg, Germany, for the morning.

Lena had selected a modest, nearby hotel for her first night. She called them on one of the courtesy phones and reserved her room.

She stepped outside and hailed a taxi. Three passed her by, and she smiled. *They're cruising for a rich or inebriated foreigner they can take the long way to their hotel, not a local woman who would berate them and probably knows their mother.*

An ancient taxi stopped, and a wizened man yelled in German. "Get in, woman; standing out here after dark is not safe."

When Lena climbed into the cab, the driver and the interior reeked of beer. She told him her destination, and he drove the three blocks and then quoted her a fair price. She paid him and added a reasonable tip. He waited until she was inside the hotel, then drove away.

After Lena checked in and found her room, she inspected the bed and then strolled down the hallway to examine the shared bath. *Everything is clean.*

She locked her room door, stripped off her clothes, and removed the wig then brushed her hair. *I'll get my hair cut and colored in Ausburg next week.*

Lena slipped under the bed covers and fluffed the pillows to prop her up. She read until her eyes drooped, then turned off her bedside lamp and closed her eyes. *I can finally sleep.*

The next morning, Lena put on her wig and another one of her thrift store outfits. *It's a little tight, but it will fit in a month.*

She went into the small bakery in front of the nearest bus stop and selected a pastry to go with her coffee. Lena carried her breakfast outside and sat on a bench. After she polished off her breakfast, she dropped her crumpled napkin and cup into the trash as she stretched so she could surreptitiously scan her surroundings. *No one is stalking me; so far, so good.*

She smiled as she boarded the bus to the train station. *Next stop, Augsburg.*

Chapter Nineteen

After Riley and the three dogs crowded into the backseat, Toby growled a low, short growl at Duffy and Finn, and the puppies squeezed together on the seat next to the window.

Riley smiled and hugged Toby as she whispered, "Thanks, I have plenty of room now."

While Melissa and Jake discussed the party, Riley leaned back and gazed out the window. *I've done everything I can. Nothing to do except wait.*

As they traveled toward Carson, Riley's phone rang. *Doc Seth.*

"You ready for tomorrow, Vet Tech Riley?"

"Sure am, Doc Seth."

"Meet me at the office at eight thirty and bring your lunch and drinks. I have an ice cooler in my work truck that will have plenty of room. Dress for farm visits. I ordered two butcher aprons for you and light jackets for both of us with our names embroidered on them. They can serve as rain jackets in all but the heaviest rain. I've been wanting a professional-looking jacket for my farm visits, and you were my perfect excuse to order them. All of our visits tomorrow are routine except for our first one. We have a young horse that the new owner says has an attitude problem, which is a huge red flag as far as I'm concerned."

"I understand; we'll rule out any physical problems first."

"Exactly. In my experience, too many times, the problem is the human's attitude, not the animal's, but I might be prejudiced.

I know the man who sold the horse. I might give him a call to get an insight into the horse's personality. See you in the morning."

Riley smiled as he hung up.

"You smiled but didn't glow like it was Ben; it must have been Seth," Melissa said.

Riley nodded. "I'll meet him at the office in town at eight thirty. He told me to bring my lunch and drinks. He has a cooler big enough, so I don't have to take one."

"What about Toby?" Jake asked. "Is he going?"

"Doc Seth mentioned earlier that we might consider taking him occasionally, but Toby and I haven't really talked about it; it's different than going to the clinic with me because there's nowhere he can relax, and we'd be gone all day," Riley said.

Toby whined, and Riley nodded.

"Toby thinks riding around all day sounds boring. He'd rather be here with Duffy and Finn while I work. He can always change his mind, and we already agreed he'd go with me on any emergency calls at night."

As they drove through Carson on the way to the Carters' house, Riley's phone buzzed a text, and she squealed. "Ben's in the parking lot. He arrived safely."

"Are you going to scare me half to death every time you get a text from Ben?" Jake asked.

"Sure; why did you ask?" Riley's eyes twinkled, and Melissa laughed.

Jake mumbled, "I walked into that one."

Riley replied to Ben, and then her phone rang.

"It's Ben!" she squealed, and Jake flinched.

"We're almost home," Riley said. "Dad gets nervous when you text or call me because I squeal."

Ben chuckled. "Be easy on the old guy. I love you, babe. I have to find my room. See you soon."

"I love you too, sweetheart," Riley said.

"Is everything okay with Ben? What did he say?" Melissa asked.

"He has to find his room."

"Good to know he's there," Jake said.

When Jake turned off the road and headed down their driveway, Duffy and Finn whined, and Toby leaned on Riley to peer out her window.

"You're not a lap dog." Riley pushed on Toby and then giggled when he kissed her.

"I think we're all ready to be home," Melissa said.

Jake parked and then opened the passenger's door, and the dogs leaped out and raced to the garden and back before they dashed into the barn. Princess yowled, and Duffy and Finn raced out.

Riley picked up her backpack. "Princess was napping in a sunbeam, and Duffy and Finn disturbed her."

"Let's go inside, boys, and get you a drink." Melissa carried in the three pie tins while Jake lifted out the ice cooler.

While Riley washed the dogs' water bowl and fed them, Melissa asked, "What are your plans for this evening?"

"Tom gave me his completed 'Phantom Cattle' novel. I plan to put up my feet and read."

"You have 'Phantom Cattle'? Can I read it after you're finished?" Melissa asked.

"I have it on a flash drive. You can copy it onto your laptop, if you like."

"I'd love it; we could read together. Do you need reading snacks or a glass of wine?"

"I hadn't thought about it, but a cup of hot tea would be great; I should probably have said a cup of campfire coffee, but I can't drink coffee at night."

"I'll make you a cup of campfire tea," Melissa smiled. "Are you going to change your clothes?"

"After I take the dogs out for a walk, I'd love to change into my flannel pants." Riley smiled.

Riley strolled up to the driveway; Duffy and Finn followed her halfway up, then became distracted halfway to the road by a hole dug next to the fence by some type of critter, but Toby stayed with Riley.

When Riley reached the road, she listened to the faraway traffic on the state road and sighed. "I just realized I was listening for Ben's truck."

Toby trotted ahead of her as they returned to the house, and Duffy and Finn joined them when they went inside.

"Your campfire tea will be waiting for you in the living room after you change into your soft pants," Melissa said.

"I'll bring my flash drive and copy 'Phantom Cattle' to your laptop, so you can read it now or whenever you like."

"I'll have everything ready before you're back."

Riley changed and then carried the flash drive and her laptop to the living room. After she copied the story to Melissa's laptop, she sat on the sofa next to the end table with her hot tea and propped up her feet. Riley smiled at the plate of cookies on the table. She opened her laptop, grabbed a cookie, and read.

Three hours later, Riley's phone buzzed with a text from Ben. "Good night, babe."

She replied, "Love you."

Two hours after Ben's text, Jake cleared his throat as he stood in the doorway. After he came into the living room, he sat next to Melissa. "I just got a call from Seth."

"Is something wrong? Is Seth okay?" Melissa asked.

"He's on his way here; he'll stay with us tonight."

Melissa's face paled. "What happened?"

"He got a call from someone who claimed they bought the old, abandoned farm that's supposed to go up for auction. They said they had a horse that was breathing funny, and they needed help. They said the house was dark because their electricity wouldn't be turned on until tomorrow, and their generator quit working. Seth was at the diner, and Ryan offered to go with him. A couple of guys at the diner tried to talk them into calling the sheriff to send a deputy with them, but Seth said that was a waste of county resources and that he and Ryan would be fine. Ryan removed his deer rifle from his truck and took it with him."

Jake exhaled. "They were ambushed outside of town. A man threw a fifty-five gallon drum in front of Seth's truck, and Seth went into a ditch. The assailant shot Seth and then Ryan. Ryan immediately shot and killed the assailant, but Ryan had been hit in the femoral artery. Ryan was lucky he was in the truck with the best vet in the county because Seth saved his life. The bullet grazed Seth's left arm, but the ER doc cleaned the wound and stitched it up; he'll be fine. The paramedics on the scene called for a helicopter, and they flew Ryan to the trauma hospital in Atlanta; a sheriff's deputy is taking Mugsy to the hospital. The sheriff is bringing Seth here. Everybody knows the guy who shot them has hated Ryan since high school. Some say this guy was obsessed with Mugsy and thought he would have had a chance with Mugsy if it weren't for Ryan, but that wasn't true."

"That explains the note," Melissa said.

Jake furrowed his brow. "Note?"

Riley ran to her room and then returned with the note and the envelope. "Mugsy found this on the floor in her coffee shop. She thought RC was me."

Jake shook his head. "That's exactly what that guy has said about Ryan since high school. I'll give this to the sheriff."

When Seth and the sheriff arrived, Melissa and Riley helped Seth to the spare bedroom while Jake and the sheriff had a quiet discussion in the kitchen.

After Seth was settled and the sheriff left, Melissa and Riley resumed reading the 'Phantom Cattle."

An hour later, Jake stood near Melissa and cleared his throat.

"What?" Melissa asked without looking up from her laptop.

"I woke up the dogs and took them outside. It's pretty late; you'd say it was past bedtime, Melissa," he said.

"One more chapter," she said; Riley giggled when Jake snorted.

"I'll see you in the morning," he grumbled.

A half-hour later, Riley said, "I have to stop. I've read this page three times, and I have no clue what it says."

"Good. I couldn't have stayed up much longer, either. We'll pay for this in the morning, but I love Tom's story. He's a really talented author, isn't he?"

Toby left the kitchen and followed Riley upstairs. Riley set her alarm and climbed into bed without changing. *My new rule is that soft pants count as pajamas when I stay up too late.*

When her alarm went off, Riley took a quick shower, dressed, and smoothed her bed before she hurried down the stairs.

Before she reached the kitchen, Melissa said, "Your coffee's on the table; how about biscuits and gravy with a fried egg?"

"That's perfect. I had planned to leave before eight; how's Doc Seth doing?"

Melissa rolled her eyes and pointed to the table where Doc Seth was drinking a cup of coffee. "The ER doctor told me he put in the stitches so I could call in sick this morning. An old friend is dropping off a truck at my office for us to use, but you'll have to drive us into town and then drive the truck today. Are you okay with that?"

"Sure," Riley said.

"Are you sure you're up to working today?" Melissa asked.

"I'd go stir crazy if I didn't work; you know that," Seth said.

While Riley sipped her coffee, she texted Ben. "Good morning, sweetie. Have a great day!"

He immediately responded. "On my way to breakfast. Wish you were here. Love you, babe."

Riley sighed. "This is hard on Ben. Maybe he'll be less lonesome after he's immersed in his studies."

Melissa pursed her lips and then nodded her head. She set a plate with a biscuit and an egg in front of Riley. "I'm sure you're right."

Riley split open her biscuit and poured gravy over it and her egg. "We're not very convincing, are we?"

Melissa smiled as she joined Riley at the table with her plate. "Not one bit."

While they ate, Melissa asked, "What would you like for lunch? We have some roasted pig that I planned to slice for sandwiches."

"That sounds great; I can make my sandwich."

"I'd like to pack your lunches; it's my way to feel like I'm helping you and Ben." Melissa tried to hide her smirk as she raised her eyebrows. "Do you think Jake would balk at driving up to Macon and taking Ben a sandwich?"

Seth chuckled. "Probably not if you made one for him and threw in an extra cookie."

Riley took another bite of her yolk-dipped biscuit and gravy. "Where is Dad? The dogs aren't here either."

"They went to the gas station to fill up Jake's truck, and then Jake texted me that he decided to get a haircut while he was in town. He likes to keep his tank full, and his barber keeps asking Jake to bring in his dogs."

"Duffy and Finn will whine every time a kid walks by. Does Dad know that?"

"As much as we laughed while Duffy and Finn were on the playground yesterday trying to play with all the children at once, I am guessing he does, but he'll warn his barber."

After they finished eating, Riley took over the dishes while Melissa prepared her lunch.

"I'll text you when we get back to Doc Seth's office from the farm visits, so you'll have an idea when I'll be home," Riley said as she and Seth headed to the door.

"Be safe," Melissa said.

As she drove to town, Riley sighed. *I wish I could call Ben and tell him about Doc Seth, Tom's story, and his dad's haircut. I'll make a list for tonight.*

When Riley arrived at Doc Seth's office, she parked on the side away from the door into the clinic.

"Let's put our lunches and drinks in the truck, then come inside with me. I'll show you our new gear."

After they were in his office, Doc Seth opened a large box. "There are our official Carter Animal Clinic jackets. The salesperson recommended a bright color, and I wanted camo, so we compromised on rusty brown. What do you think?"

"I love it. A bright color might have been fine if we were on a road crew, but the rusty brown seems more professional to me, and it's camo."

"Glad you agree. Our names are embroidered on removable name tags. We have alternate name tags that have only the word staff in case we're not interested in advertising our names, like at a café or something. Your butcher aprons came in, too. They say vet tech without your name, but they're yours. We'll put those in the back of the truck. Ready to go?"

"Ready. I brought my laptop in case we have any downtime. Is that okay?"

"It's absolutely okay; I always have mine."

On the way to their first visit, Doc Seth said, "I got a call from my friend, Bud, who sold the attitude problem horse. He told me he talked to the new owner and assured him that he would accept the horse for a full refund if the new owner wasn't satisfied with keeping the horse after my visit. Bud told me he always hated to hear about an unhappy horse, especially one that was so personable like the horse he sold, but we'll see what's going on."

Doc Seth's priority is the well-being of the young horse. No wonder Ben loved working with him.

After she turned at the farm gate, Riley's eyes widened as she scanned the property.

"The fence looks like it has been recently repaired, and the fields along the driveway look like professionally tended lawns," she said. "I've never seen anything like it outside of a city."

Doc said, "This new guy has already put in a lot of work here; I'm impressed. Maybe there's hope for him after all."

After she parked the truck, the man rushed out of the house to greet them. Riley examined the flourishing flower beds and a recently mowed and edged lawn. *It is unusual to see a yard as carefully manicured as this on a farm.*

As he strolled with them to the barn, the man said, "The seller called me earlier this morning and told me I could have a full refund, no questions asked, if I wanted to return the horse to him. I've had the horse for almost six months, so I appreciate his generous offer. I would have taken it yesterday, but today, I'm wondering if it's something simple and she'll be fine in a day or so. I don't really know much about horses, but my wife has always wanted a pony, so I got her one as a surprise for her birthday. I'm worried the horse might be going lame, and that's why she's developed such a contrary attitude about eating and the bridle when I put it on her; I haven't been able to take her to the field for exercise in over a week."

When they walked into the barn, the young horse whinnied. Doc Seth glanced at Riley, and she pointed to her mouth.

"We'll go through a physical exam, then we can talk," Doc Seth said. "Riley, check her legs while I check her mouth, gums, and teeth. This is the first time I've seen her since she was five months old, so you can take your time."

Riley hummed while she carefully palpated each leg and watched for any reaction that would indicate tenderness.

As Doc Seth palpated the young horse's abdomen, he asked, "What's her name?"

"Name? We haven't gotten around to that yet; should we make that a priority?" The young man said. "I'm a professional landscaper and have always lived in the city, so I don't know much about horses. My wife told me the horse doesn't like her, so she doesn't spend much time in the barn."

Doc Seth nodded as he moved to check her mouth. When he examined the horse's teeth, he said, "Here's the problem: she has retained caps."

The young man's eyes widened. "What does that mean? Is it life-threatening?"

"Maybe over time, if they become infected, and she's still not treated, and the infection leads to sepsis, but that's unusual for anyone to let a condition like this go that long without treatment. You might think of them as baby teeth that didn't fall out."

"I didn't know horses could have problems with their teeth. What do we do?" the young man asked.

"We'll extract them and put her on antibiotics for the swelling and inflammation."

"I don't know; will she need a special diet? Is that something I can buy, or do I have to cook her something special?" He rubbed his hand through his hair. "I'll have to talk to my wife."

"I'll be happy to go with you to explain the procedure and the necessary care to both of you at the same time."

"Thanks, but I'm not sure she'd be all that interested in the details. I'll just run in and be back in a few minutes."

"Go right ahead. We'll wait," Doc Seth said.

After the young man left, Doc Seth asked, "What do you think?"

"I think he feels overwhelmed because having a horse wasn't quite as simple as he expected; if his wife had really wanted a horse, she would have been out here unless she's not able to get to the barn."

"Do they need a dog?" Doc Seth asked.

"They'd be better off with a feral barn cat for a while."

The horse nodded her head, and Doc Seth chuckled. "I'll give Bud a quick call."

Riley stepped outside the barn and gazed at the gathering puffy, white clouds as the cicadas and tree frogs buzzed and chirped. *It's going to rain this afternoon; as long as it's not cold, I'll be okay.*

Doc Seth joined her. "I told Bud about the horse's condition; he expects a phone call as soon as we leave. If he does, he'll pick her up, and we'll go to his place tomorrow and take care of those teeth."

"The horse wins either way unless the folks here don't want her treated," Riley said.

"That's not an option because the county would step in," Doc Seth said. "I'd drop a dime on that one."

Riley nodded. *I'll have to ask Dad what 'drop a dime' means.*

The young man returned. "My wife agrees the horse would be better off with more experienced people. I'll call my seller."

Doc Seth nodded. "Let me know if there's anything else I can do for you folks."

The young man gave a quick nod and then hurried to his house.

As they strolled back to the truck, Doc shook his head. "Like you said, the horse wins. Have you ever known a horse with no name? I mean, besides the song."

Riley giggled. "No, all of the horses at Ms. Lindsey's had names."

After she turned onto the highway, Doc Seth said, "The horse's name is Spice. I never forget a horse's name, and I know Bud; he would have told them. They must have forgotten or didn't pay attention. That young man seems to be under a lot of stress, so he could have been distracted. I'm still not clear why he bought the horse, though. I'm glad Bud offered to take Spice back, or you and I would have been going to my house for the horse trailer, and my brother would have a new Spice."

As Riley slowed to turn at the next farm's driveway, Doc Seth's phone rang.

"Thanks; I'll drop off the antibiotics later this afternoon."

After he hung up, Doc said, "Bud will pick up the horse in an hour. Are you okay with taking the extra time to drop off the antibiotic? I'm sorry; I should have asked before I committed us. You can drop yourself off at the office first so you can go home on time. I'll be fine driving."

Riley frowned. "That won't work unless you want me to follow you there, but I'm okay with whatever you say."

Doc Seth chuckled. "You're everything Ben said; did you know that?"

The next two farm visits were routine, and Riley exhaled as she drove to a nearby park so they could sit at a picnic table.

"I'm glad our other two appointments were routine, but I'm glad Bud has Spice at his farm," Riley said as Doc Seth handed her their lunches to carry to the small picnic area while he pulled out drinks.

"Looks like we might get a shower or two," Doc said as they ate lunch. "How did this morning compare to your Monday mornings at the clinic?"

"We almost always started the day with an unscheduled client, then the rest of the morning was fairly routine."

"Sounds exactly like my Mondays, and today was no exception," Doc Seth said. "What did Melissa send us for dessert?"

Riley snickered, then opened the sack and peeked in. "We have a large slice of apple pie for you, a smaller slice for me, and slices of cheddar cheese. She told us her dad always ate a slice of cheddar cheese with his apple pie instead of ice cream. This must be her offering to assuage our sadness over no ice cream."

After they ate their pie and cheese, they headed to the next farm. Riley glanced in her rearview mirror and frowned at the black car behind them. *Why does a car behind us make me nervous?* She shook her head. *I wouldn't give an old truck a second glance.*

When the car turned at a farm driveway, Riley exhaled in relief.

"The cheese with the pie was surprisingly good. I'll have to tell Melissa she has another winner," Doc Seth said.

While they were at a farm for their second afternoon appointment, the rain caught them out in a field as they headed back to the truck. They ran back behind the farmer, who dashed for the barn. When they joined him, the farmer was soaked, but they were drenched. Riley shivered as the wind blew and the rain pounded the barn roof.

The farmer threw an old horse blanket over her. "Sorry about the smell. We haven't had anyone other than a horse to need a blanket out here."

"This is great," Riley said. "I chill easily."

"I need to carry a warm, dry blanket in my truck and have to see if I can find some old-fashioned slickers," Doc Seth said.

The farmer shook his head. "I have one, but I never remember to wear it; I should hang it on that peg near the door. It would be downright handy to have with these sudden showers we get that roll through."

After the rain slowed, Doc Seth asked, "Ready to go, Riley?"

"I have dry clothes in my backpack. Maybe I could change in a stall before we leave."

"No need to do that," the farmer said. "Let's go into the house. Mama will give you a towel so you can dry off before you put on your dry clothes."

Off in the distance, a quail whistled, "Bob White."

Riley smiled. "Hi, Bob."

Doc Seth peered at her.

Riley giggled. "Bob White's an old friend of mine."

The farmer laughed. "Mama will get a kick out of that. Let's get you dry."

The farmer's wife insisted that Riley have a cup of hot tea after she dried and changed and that the two men have coffee with their cookies straight from the oven. She laughed when the farmer told her about Bob White.

"Bob's an old friend of mine too, Riley. I'll tell him you said hey." The woman smiled.

"Thanks, I'd appreciate it." Riley returned her smile.

After the farmer's wife was satisfied that Riley was dry and warm, Doc Seth said, "Let's go see my new girlfriend."

"Not so fast, Seth. You owe me the story about your new girlfriend, or I'll tell my own faulty version," the woman said.

Seth laughed. "Her name is Spice, and she's a cute little filly with cap teeth. We'll start her on antibiotics today, and she'll be my first appointment in the morning to take them out."

The woman sighed. "My version was much more interesting, but I like her name. Be careful on the road, y'all."

As Riley drove to Bud's farm, Doc Seth said, "I'm sorry I forgot about your terrible episode with hypothermia. We need decent rain gear, dry towels, and warm quilts. It's still hot around here, but that cold wind that blows in our storms this time of year would chill anyone who was the least bit susceptible to hypothermia. Do your doctors think the severity of your reaction will lessen over time?"

"I don't think a doctor ever mentioned a subsequent reaction to the cold."

"It's very common, at least in my patients," Doc Seth chuckled. "You'll just have to be the poster child for layering. Be sure to include socks and boots."

Riley nodded. "I had my change of clothes but forgot footgear, and that's the most important thing, isn't it?" *Ben will love hearing that my best medical advisor is Doc Seth.*

When she turned on Bud's driveway, Riley said, "Bud's fields aren't mowed; they're planted. Is that peanuts?"

"Looks like they loved that rain, doesn't it?"

Riley parked near the barn, and a man rushed to greet them.

"It's nice to meet you finally, Riley." Bud shook hands with Riley and then Doc Seth.

As they walked to the barn, Bud said, "Spice is in the barn in her old stall. I never should have sold her and regretted it that same day, but the young man begged me and said Spice was exactly what his wife wanted. I'll always regret that I never got up the nerve to tell him I'd take Spice back anytime. Anyway, Spice is here permanently, and I told her so."

"I brought her antibiotics and a little something for pain. I never carry the stronger stuff because if word got out, I'd be robbed twice a day and beaten the second time because I let myself get robbed the first time. I carry, but I feel a lot safer with my sidekick here."

"Where's Toby?" Bud peered at the truck, and Riley raised her eyebrows.

Bud chuckled. "You didn't know Toby's a big celebrity around here? I might know Seth's nephew if I saw him, except he's probably grown, but everybody knows Toby; it's just like you know Spice, Riley."

Riley giggled. "I can remember the name of every dog, cat, or horse that I've known, but I have no clue what their humans' names are."

"Come say hello to Spice, and then feel free to head out. I appreciate that we can start Spice on her medicine right away, Seth, and she'll appreciate a little pain relief. She's bone tired and deserves a good night's sleep."

Riley cooed and whispered to Spice, and Spice nuzzled Riley.

"See you in the morning, Spice," Riley said, and Spice whinnied.

After leaving the farm, Doc Seth said, "Today was remarkable."

"I really enjoyed it."

"Meet me tomorrow morning at eight. I want to be able to take my time at Bud's with Spice."

After they reached the office, Riley put her backpack, the sack of wet clothes, and her laptop into her car, and Seth went into the office while she sent a text to Melissa to let her know she'd be home soon.

Before she pulled away from the parking lot, her phone rang. *Mugsy.*

"I won't keep you; I wanted to tell you that Ryan is fine and might be home by the end of next week. He'll stay with me for a while to recuperate. Is it possible for you to wait a week or two before you move into a place? I have a serious lead on an old house that's out in the country but close to the training center. A friend of a friend bought the house a year ago and has been doing major repairs to the electrical, plumbing, well, air conditioner, you name it. My friend gave me the house owner's number, so I called him."

Riley smiled. *Not a surprise.*

Mugsy continued, "The owner wants to refinish the old wooden floors and put in new appliances because the old ones don't work. He's open to you all moving in as soon as the house is barebones ready. He'll be able to sell the house for four times what he paid for it, but he needs to repair the detached garage roof and either repair or tear down the barn. He's leaning toward repair but needs to save up some money first. He likes the idea of having someone in the house, so it will be occupied, and he can collect a bit of rent, and he's not looking for much in the way of money. He'll let me know how much the rent will be tomorrow. He's not interested in advertising it because he doesn't want a long-term renter and will rent it only to someone recommended by a friend. You're a perfect match."

"Sounds like it definitely meets our criteria, so he'd be okay with Toby?"

"He told me he'd rather have Toby than a houseful of rowdies."

After they hung up, Riley shook her head. *Mugsy's got more than enough worries with Ryan, but she is still looking out for me. She's amazing.*

On her way home, Riley glanced at the plastic sack of wet clothes. *Can I sneak these wet clothes upstairs without Mom catching me?*

Riley giggled. *I don't have anybody to help me with that except Mom.*

As she neared the house, she caught herself speeding, slowed down, and sighed as she set her cruise control. *For a minute there, I had the idea that Ben was waiting for me to come home.*

Chapter Twenty

Toby was watching for her when she turned at the driveway. She jumped out and opened the back door, and he hopped in. She hugged him and cooed, then headed to the house. Toby laid his head over the back of the seat and leaned against her headrest. His soft whiskers tickled her neck, and she giggled.

After she parked, Duffy and Finn ran out of the barn, barked at Toby, and Riley laughed. "They're jealous."

She sent Ben a text: "I'm home."

Ben replied, "In class."

Riley frowned as she read the text. *I wonder if I shouldn't text him unless I know he's not in class. I'll have to ask him.*

Jake strode out of the barn and grinned as he joined her. "I wondered where Toby had gone. He was in the barn with us and then took off up the driveway. He must have heard your car."

"He was waiting for me at the driveway," Riley said.

As Riley and Jake headed toward the house, Toby stayed at Riley's side, and the puppies followed them.

Jake said, "I just got a call from Sheriff Sam Dunn. He's been in a meeting with our sheriff and would like to drop by. Before you ask, Ben's fine, which is the first question I asked. Melissa insisted that I invite him to dinner, but he said he had already eaten and couldn't stay long. Melissa will probably bribe him with dessert. Melissa is putting our supper on the table, so we'll have dessert with him. How was your day?"

"I have lots to tell, but I'll wait until after the sheriff leaves."

Before they went inside, Riley stopped at the door, sniffed, and inspected the bottom of her boots. "I've been on farm visits all day. I'll leave these out here."

Jake chuckled. "Melissa will appreciate that."

After they were in the house, Jake fed the dogs while Riley poured three glasses of sweet tea.

"I knew y'all would feed the dogs and pour tea as soon as you came inside." Melissa frowned as she stared at Riley's boot socks. "Where are your boots, Riley?"

"I caught a whiff of my boots and realized I'd brought my work home with me. I left them outside, and they can be my work boots. I've got a pair I can wear for home and going to town."

Melissa nodded. "Makes sense to me and saves me from chasing you around the house with a can of disinfectant in one hand and a room deodorizer in the other."

The dogs gobbled down their food, then Jake let them out before the family sat at the table.

After they ate and cleared the dishes, Jake said, "I've got something to show you in the barn, Riley."

Riley ran upstairs, put on her newer pair of boots, and then returned to the kitchen.

When they strolled together to the barn, Jake asked, "Seth called me while you were on your way home, and he told me about Spice. Bud's barn has become too crowded for all the horses to be comfortable; Bud thought he was doing the right thing for Spice but feels guilty about selling her in the first place. Seth asked if we'd be willing to foster a horse because Bud has two other horses he wants to have fostered rather than sell right away, so he could be picky about the buyers. Melissa and I are willing to foster a horse for him, and I've been working on a plan for the layout of a horse stall. I could use an expert eye to see if I need to make any adjustments."

"I'm definitely not an expert, but I can tell you what Lindsey and Bud did in their barns."

While Riley and Jake moved around the two-by-four lumber to indicate the placement of the stall, Toby barked.

"Sheriff's here!" Riley said.

When the sheriff climbed out of his cruiser, his face was expressionless. He averted his eyes and didn't meet Riley's gaze. After he strode to join them, he hugged Riley and kept his arm around her.

"Let's go inside." His tone was flat.

Riley glanced at Jake, who walked alongside them. The concern on his face heightened her dread.

When they went into the house, Melissa narrowed her eyes at the somber faces. "We'll go into the living room."

The sheriff sat with Riley on the sofa, and after Jake and Melissa sat in their chairs, he said. "Riley, I received word earlier that Millie died in a tragic accident in Paris."

Riley examined his face, and she saw his grief when he met her gaze. *They were close friends for a long time.*

"Do we know what happened?" Jake asked quietly.

"It was late Sunday night, and she was hurrying through a crowd to catch the Paris metro, their subway, that went to her hotel. She tripped, stumbled, and fell on the tracks as the train sped into the station. Two men tried to grab her but were unsuccessful, and the metro engineer never even saw her. There were a number of witnesses, and except for a few outliers, they all told the same story. The two men were not identified because so many men came forward and claimed to have tried to pull her back. That's normal in a tragedy like that."

Riley maintained her gaze. *There's more.*

"What else?" Riley asked.

Sheriff shook his head, and a slight smile passed his lips. "You never miss a thing. I asked if she'd had a stroke or if they had any idea what could have precipitated the fall. According to the coroner, her body was too mangled by the train for an autopsy, but some witnesses said her heel got caught by the edge of the platform, and she pitched forward. Her bag was recovered, and the police found her ID; the FBI called me because her ID still had your Grandma's cabin as her address. The coroner in Paris recommended the family allow them to cremate and bury her ashes in Paris and hold a memorial service for her in the US if that's what you want to do, and I agree with him."

"Sheriff, you know Aunt Millie much better than I do. Would she want a memorial service? I don't think Grandma had one. Aunt Millie told me she shook out the ashes on a windy day near the hunting stand that Grandma built because that was what Grandma would have wanted."

Sheriff nodded. "Millie loved Paris; she would have preferred for her ashes to be buried there; she always told me that she didn't like anyone to make a fuss over her."

Riley smiled. "Grandma was the same way."

"Her will is probably on file in Barton. Do you have a lawyer?" Riley nodded.

"Good; your lawyer can handle everything, but I doubt if Millie had much to leave; she told me she always traveled first class and stayed at the best hotels because she liked to be comfortable." The sheriff sighed. "I have to go. It's going to be a long night. Millie used to always laugh at me for working so much, but I've never known anyone who worked as hard as she did and told her so. It has been our running joke for years."

"Would you like to take along some coffee with you? I've got some large disposable cups, and the coffee's fresh," Melissa said.

"That sounds great."

Melissa hurried to the kitchen, and Jake followed her.

"I called the director at the GBI training center, and he'll talk to Ben after they have supper. He's worried Ben will bolt to get back here, but I told him to have Ben call you," the sheriff said. "I know you'll encourage him to stay focused on his studies, but let me know if I can help. Jake's a good resource for you, too." Sheriff peered at Riley's face. "Are you going to be okay?"

"I'll be fine; thank you so much for telling me."

"You're welcome. I knew you'd be okay, but Ben's protective side might overcome his good judgment. Take care of that cop for me, Riley."

Riley grinned. "Will do, Sheriff. That's my job."

The sheriff hugged her, and then they strolled together to the kitchen.

Melinda handed Sheriff Dunn the large coffee cup and a sack. "It's just a little snack for you."

The sheriff hefted the sack. "Feels like ten pounds of pie." He opened the sack and sniffed. "Peach pie?"

Melissa smiled. "You have a discerning sense of smell; you have a napkin and a fork that you may or may not use; it's your choice."

"Thank you, Melissa. I'm going to come back when we can visit and laugh with Riley and Ben. Those two are like my own."

"Are you sure you're okay?" Melissa asked after the sheriff left.

Riley nodded. "Aunt Millie and the sheriff have been friends for years. I think the news hit him hard."

"Ben will call as soon as he can find somewhere to have a private conversation," Jake said.

"I'll read 'Phantom Cattle' until he calls." Riley took her phone and laptop to the living room and put up her feet while she read. Melissa slipped in with her laptop and read, too.

When Riley's phone rang, Melissa quietly left the room as Riley answered.

"I'll be home late tonight, babe. Don't try to talk me out of it," Ben said.

"Did you just play your husband card?" Riley asked.

When Ben didn't say anything, she smiled. *I can't wait to hear his answer.*

"You shouldn't have to grieve alone," he growled. "Dad called me last night and told me about Uncle Seth and Ryan. It scared me because you might have gone if Ryan hadn't."

"I didn't, and Seth and Ryan are going to be fine. I'm not alone; I have Mom, Dad, Toby, and the puppies, but I would be inconsolable if you left your training. The sheriff is the one who is grieving because he and Aunt Millie were close friends for years. I'm glad he came here because he didn't have anyone else who could understand his feelings."

"I really hate it when you're logical and make sense," Ben sighed.

"Too bad." Riley giggled. "Tell me about your day."

Ben chuckled and then told Riley about his classes, new friends, and the instructors. Riley smiled as his voice became upbeat.

"You were sure right about the towel, babe; everyone is jealous because I know which towel is mine. What about you? How was your first day?"

Riley told him about Spice, the clueless man, and Bud's dilemma. "Your dad is going to foster a horse for Bud; he and I are working on a plan for a stall in the barn. I think he's hoping that you and I will go with him to pick up one of Bud's horses on Saturday."

"That sounds great," Ben said. "I'm looking forward to it, but not as much as I'm looking forward to seeing you."

Before they hung up, Ben said, "Thanks for setting me straight, babe. You're the best, and I love you more."

"Dang. Not fair: you beat me to it. I love you, Sexy Cowboy. Wrangle them there classes, and I'll see you Friday night."

Ben chuckled. "I finally won and didn't lose my husband card."

Riley laughed as she hung up.

"Well, that was a nice sound after what could have been quite a confrontational call." Melissa stood in the doorway.

Riley put the phone down. *Aunt Millie was always there for me and always called at the right time. She'll never call again.* A tear slipped down her face. *I'll miss her.*

"Did it just hit you that she's gone?" Melissa asked.

Riley nodded. "I think I was holding back for the sheriff's sake and to get past convincing Ben that he shouldn't leave his training."

Melissa sat next to Riley and hugged her. "It takes a lot to be strong for those we love, doesn't it?"

Riley nodded and let the tears flow until they subsided. "I haven't seen Aunt Millie in years, but she always knew when I needed her and stepped in."

"It's nice that she was able to do that for as long as she could," Melissa said. "I think you'll always miss her, but the grief heals over time."

Riley smiled. "Thank you. This is just between you and me, right?"

"Absolutely. Care for a glass of wine? I have a bottle of a special blend for reading."

"That sounds good; Ben won't be here until Friday night."

"Yay!" Jake called out from the kitchen. "I'll bring y'all a couple glasses of wine."

Riley whispered, "Kind of between just you and me."

Melissa covered her mouth to mute her snicker from Jake's ears. Jake arrived with their wine and poured two glasses with a flourish.

Riley took a sip of wine, set down her glass, and opened her book to where she'd left off.

She read:

Blair, the new editor and owner of the local newspaper, sauntered into Novalee's General Store. He leered at her pantaloons as she stood on a ladder to get down a bolt of fabric for the town's seamstress.

The seamstress smacked Blair's arm with her fan. "You mind your manners, young man."

Novalee glared at Blair from her perch, and he smiled at the fire in her eyes.

"What on tarnation do you want?" she asked.

"I'm looking for our local short, red-headed gunslinger. I got a job for her."

"She's over at the saloon," the seamstress said. "I just happened to peek in when I was on my way here to see what riff-raff go to the saloon so early in the morning."

Blair tipped his hat. "I'll see you later, Miss Novalee."

Blair pushed through the swinging double doors at the saloon and rushed to Rita's table.

She looked up from her eggs and bacon as she took a bite of her biscuit and then swigged it down with her beer. "I heard it was you that paid my bail," she said.

"I have a job for you. On behalf of the local ranchers, I'm authorized to offer you five hundred dollars to track down those thieving cattle rustlers."

Rita narrowed her eyes. "That's a month's wages when times are good. I'm a poker player, not a marshal."

"You're the only one the rustlers are scared of. You know about Ranger, right? He's in cahoots with them."

"That's what I heard. The ranchers can give the money to the banker to hold for me. If I don't make it back, give it to Deputy Joe."

"You'll be back." Blair grinned as she grabbed her biscuit and bacon and left.

"I suspect those varmints are hanging out at Dark Canyon." Rita stroked her horse, Stormy. "If they aren't there, we'll have some hard riding ahead of us to catch up with them."

Rita leaped onto Stormy and galloped out of town. She slowed as she neared the canyon, then left Stormy in the shade near a clear stream. "I won't be long."

Rita made her way through the rocks. When she found her best vantage point, she aimed her rifle and shot a campfire coffee mug out of a rustler's hand, then rose with her rifle aimed at Ranger.

"You boys with this no-good polecat Ranger will have safe passage if you skedaddle right now. I'll drop you if you even flinch like you're gonna touch a gun. Now git."

The rustlers scrambled to their horses and rode away.

Ranger sneered. "You have quite a way with the boys, don't you, Rita? I appreciate you coming all the way out here to save me from those cattle rustlers."

Ranger narrowed his eyes at a cloud of dust that was approaching them. His expression and his smile were evil. "I think one of them boys is coming back, after all."

He smirked at Rita. "Might even be a couple of them sneaking around back to surround you. Give yourself up, and I'll take you into the law and put in a good word for you. I'll tell the deputy how much you helped me by chasing off those rustlers."

"Drop your gun belt, Ranger." Rita kept her rifle aimed at him as the sound of a galloping horse neared.

"Of course. You got me dead to rights."

When the rider had almost reached them, Ranger glanced at a point to the left side of Rita and shouted, "Now!" as he drew his pistol and fired a split second after Riley squeezed the trigger. Her bullet hit him square in the forehead, and his bullet grazed a rock nowhere close to Rita as he dropped.

Deputy Joe jumped off his horse and raced to Rita. "Are you okay? Are you hit?"

She tilted her head and peered at him. "Of course not."

Joe glanced at the lifeless Ranger. "Dang it, Rita. I came here to save you."

He reached into his pocket, held out his hand, and grinned. "Want a piece of rock candy?"

The End.

Riley sighed and closed her laptop with a snap.

"Did you finish?" Melissa asked. "Don't say anything. I've got five more pages to go."

Jake looked up from his paperback and chuckled when Riley made a motion of zipped lips with her thumb and index finger.

After Melissa read the last line, she glanced at Riley, stared at her screen, and sighed. "Tom is an excellent writer, and I'm ready for his next book. I love Rita and Joe, don't you? Didn't you tell me Novalee is Pia's middle name and Blair is Tom's middle name? That Blair is going to get a black eye one of these days. Nobody messes with Novalee. Has Pia read this?"

"I don't think so, but I'm not asking her. Tom's going to publish his book next month. We need to get a copy for the bookshelf."

"Two paperbacks: one for you and one for me, and we'll get Tom to sign them," Melissa said.

Riley yawned. "I think I have to go to bed."

"Me too; I'm glad we finished the book, but I'm sorry I finished the book."

When Riley hurried into the kitchen the next morning, she smiled at her cup of coffee, and then Toby whined.

"Don't nag her first thing, Toby; I'll feed you," Melissa said. "Riley, enjoy your coffee, then you can take them outside and eat when you come back in; bring Jake with you. He hasn't eaten yet, either. Do you want pancakes or eggs this morning?"

"Eggs, and I love any way you cook them."

"Bacon, eggs, and a biscuit. Sound familiar?" Melissa smiled as she dished up the dogs' food.

After the dogs ate, Riley threw on her sweatshirt, and the four of them went outside. Duffy and Finn dashed to patrol the grounds for any critters that might have lingered as Riley and Toby strolled to the barn.

When Jake saw them, he grinned. "Good morning, Sunshine. Melissa had trouble going to sleep last night; she was really excited about Tom's novel, and I got a full synopsis of the story. How did our resident gunslinger sleep?"

Riley smiled. "I was exhausted. I was sleeping so hard this morning that my alarm startled me awake. I usually wake up before it goes off. As far as the novel's concerned, there are a few points that I'd like to argue with the author about his misrepresentation of Rita."

Jake laughed. "How well does the story follow what you learned about the GBI agent? His name was Marc, right?"

She nodded. "It's actually pretty close. I understood why Tom had to disappear; it was the only thing he could do to keep Pia and Jackson safe. What are you doing?"

"I was measuring the area that we laid out. I'll go into town today, and then maybe after you get home from work, we can finalize the location and our design. If I can get the stall built before Ben gets home, maybe the three of us could pick up one of Bud's horses."

"What's for breakfast?" Jake asked as they strolled to the house.

"Bacon, eggs, and biscuits," Riley said.

Jake chuckled. "Melissa told me about Rita's breakfast. I doubt if she'll let us have any beer, though."

Riley giggled. "Maybe we can have a beer breakfast to celebrate when Ben graduates. I have a question before we go in. What does drop a dime on it mean?"

"Give me the context."

"Doc Seth and I were talking about Spice and the young man, and I said something about the young man refusing treatment, and Doc Seth said that wouldn't happen; he'd drop a dime on it. Is that like a bet? Was he saying he'd bet that wouldn't happen?"

Jake smiled and shook his head. "In the old days, a phone call at a telephone booth cost a dime. You dropped a dime into the slot to get a dial tone, and then made your call. A snitch or rival could drop a dime and anonymously report a criminal to the cops from a phone number that couldn't be traced to anyone. I'm guessing Seth was saying he'd call the Animal Control officer if the young man refused to allow the medical treatment."

"Thank you."

"I'll start working on Ben's graduation breakfast celebration," Jake said before they went into the house.

"What does your schedule look like today, Riley?" Melissa asked as the three of them ate.

Riley smeared strawberry jam on top of the melted butter on her biscuit. "The first thing on our schedule is taking care of Spice's teeth. I think the rest of the day will be routine farm visits."

"You have a choice for your lunch: BLT or a ham and cheese. I can give you all the BLT sandwich components, and you can put your lunch together when you eat so it won't be soggy."

"If the BLT is not a big deal, I'd love that. I had a spare backpack, so I packed a change of clothes in case I get caught by another quick-moving rainstorm."

"Good," Melissa said.

Riley picked up her backpack, laptop bag, and emergency backpack. Before she left, Melissa and Jake hugged her.

"Be safe," Melissa said.

Toby whined at the door. "I'm taking Toby today so he can see whether it's something he'd like to do occasionally," Riley said.

Riley frowned at the blue car that had been trailing behind her for the past three miles. She dropped her speed by five miles an hour, and Toby woke from his nap and sat up. The car suddenly accelerated and then zipped past her on a curve. Riley focused on the road ahead. As the car passed her, she caught sight of the dark-tinted windows in her peripheral vision but didn't see the driver.

She fumed. *You had three miles to pass me, so you picked a curve. Do you have a death wish?*

When she neared the outskirts of Carson, she frowned. *The car passed me after Toby sat up. Was that a coincidence?*

As she neared Doc Seth's clinic, Riley squinted at the blue car facing nose out in an alley ahead. By the time she reached the alley, it was empty. *Must have been shadows.*

After she parked, she pulled out her laptop, two backpacks, lunch, and Toby's water bowl. While she and Toby walked toward the clinic's back door, she said, "Do I look like a bag lady? I feel like I'm carrying all my possessions in my bags, except aren't they supposed to be in black garbage bags?"

Toby yipped.

"I think you're right about only one black garbage bag."

As Doc Seth put their lunches into the cooler, he said, "I already have a water bowl for Toby. You can put yours back into your car."

After Doc Seth tossed Riley's emergency backpack into the back of the truck next to the cooler, the three of them got into the truck.

As they headed toward Bud's house, Doc said, "Thanks for not nagging me about driving. I'm glad we're taking care of Spice first thing this morning."

"I am, too. If we have enough time, I'd like to talk to Mr. Bud about the design Dad and I have planned for the stall in Dad's barn."

"We can make time."

Bud came out of his barn when Doc Seth parked. "I turned out all the horses to pasture except Spice. Normally, she would be giving me grief; I think she's looking forward to her mouth not hurting. She's in here."

When Riley and Doc Seth went into the barn, Spice blew out her nose with her ears pointed forward.

"We're happy you see you too, Spice," Riley said. "Doc Seth's going to take out those teeth that are hurting you."

Riley helped Doc Seth set up and then assisted as he carefully removed each tooth and tooth fragment. After they finished, Toby wandered outside, and Riley joined him while Doc Seth reviewed Spice's care with Bud.

Riley frowned as a blue car drove slowly past Bud's farm. She watched it until it was out of sight, then strolled into the barn. "Do you have any neighbors with a blue car?"

Chapter Twenty-One

Bud chuckled. "None of my neighbors own a car. We have new and old trucks and three or four minivans around here, but no cars. Where'd you come up with a question like that, Riley?"

"A blue car drove by real slow, and I thought it might be a neighbor who was looking to see whether you were home." Riley shrugged.

"Sounds more like somebody's lost and is looking for a place to turn around," Bud said.

Riley nodded. "Ben's dad is planning to build a stall in his barn so he can foster a horse."

Riley strolled to the stall in the back corner. "It will look something like this. Is there anything you would recommend doing differently?"

"Probably the biggest thing is that I would have made it a little bigger, but if it was the only one I had, I'd have my tack room next to it."

"How much bigger?" Riley asked. "Are you talking length or width?"

"Both bigger about a foot, but that's because this is my overflow stall, and I tend to put the skittish ones in here."

"Thanks, that was a lot of help."

"Tell Jake to call me if he has any questions," Bud said. "He's got my number."

When they stopped for lunch, Doc Seth asked, "Do you think Jake would be insulted if I offered to stop by and eyeball his plan for a stall?"

"I'm embarrassed that I didn't even think of that. I'll ask him, but I'll bet he'd appreciate the help. Just be warned that Mom will want you to stay for supper." Riley smiled.

"I guess I'll just suffer." Doc Seth's eyes twinkled.

Riley called Ben's dad.

"Are you okay?" Jake asked when he picked up the phone.

"You sound like your son; I'm fine. Doc Seth offered to come by after work to see if he had any suggestions for our stall design."

"I'm an idiot. Why didn't I think about my brother? Tell him to expect to stay for supper, but I'm sure he knows that."

Riley smiled as she hung up. "He's excited that you'll check our design. He said you knew you'd have to stay for supper."

"It's the advantage of having a knucklehead of a brother who marries a talented cook." Doc Seth chuckled.

After lunch, they visited two farms.

"We have time for one more," Doc said. "You game?"

"Sure; it's still early."

On the way to the farm, Doc Seth said, "This call came in around lunchtime, and my office took the message. It's a farm that has been abandoned for years, but the couple that bought it retired from active farming and sold their farm five years ago. They missed the country life and bought the old house and have been restoring it. I don't know them; that's what they told my office."

Riley frowned. "Can the sheriff send a deputy along with us?"

Doc Seth was quiet and then pulled into a driveway. "Is last night bothering you?"

"Yes, but I might be extra nervous."

Doc called the sheriff. "They'll let us know when the deputy is there. We'll wait until we get the all clear."

"Good."

"There's a park down the road that will be more comfortable. The farmer told my office that their barn had been overtaken by feral cats. They'd like us to capture as many cats as possible and take them to the county animal control to be sterilized; they'll pick them up in the morning and return them to their barn."

"That will not be easy," Riley said.

"I know, but I think Toby can help. Doc Julie Rae told me he has a way with animals, too."

"We'll give it a shot," Riley said.

The small park was a way from the road and hidden in the trees. Toby chased squirrels that dashed up nearby trees and then scolded Toby from their perches on a high branch.

After all the squirrels were treed, Toby trotted to Riley with a grin as the rude chatter continued.

"I don't think Toby's very popular here, and I don't even speak squirrel." Doc Seth chuckled.

Riley smiled.

Doc Seth's phone rang, and after a short conversation, he hung up. "It's all clear, and the county deputy welcomed the folks to their new home. The sheriff sends his thanks because his office didn't know the home was occupied."

When they reached the farm, Doc Seth stopped in the driveway between the house and the barn; they stayed in the truck and watched as cats ran into and out of the barn. Riley lowered her window to listen to the cats.

"They certainly are noisy," Doc Seth said. "What are they saying?"

Riley smiled. "They know why we're here, and the barn will be completely empty by the time we get out of the truck. There's no way we'll catch one of them."

Doc Seth chuckled. "Let's go look in the barn."

After Riley climbed out of the truck, she opened Toby's door, and he raised his head.

"You're not coming?"

Toby grinned, lay his head on the seat, and closed his eyes.

The farmer joined them as Riley and Doc Seth strolled to the barn. After Doc Seth introduced Riley, they went into the barn.

The farmer's eyes widened. "They're all gone. I swear this barn was overrun with cats five minutes ago."

"There must be a couple of old, savvy cats that warned them all to hide," Doc Seth said. "You'll need to hire a professional to set traps for them. I doubt if they'll catch any, but the cats may move on to friendlier territory."

"Friendlier territory?" The farmer narrowed his eyes. "I'll have a chat with my wife. Thanks for dropping by, Doc. Can I send you home with some blackberry jam?"

"It's my policy never to turn down a jar of homemade jam," Doc Seth said.

The farmer rushed into the house. While they waited, Riley frowned at a blue car that drove at a moderate rate of speed past the farm.

When the farmer returned with two jars of blackberry jam, he said, "They're still a little warm from their boiling water bath in our canner."

"Thank you; we'll enjoy it, I'm sure," Doc Seth said.

As he headed back to town, Doc chuckled. "You sure saved me at least an hour of roaming the property to find the elusive cats, and I'll never go on another call like that again unless I'm low on jam."

Riley smiled.

When they reached the clinic, Riley pointed at the blue car with dark-tinted windows that was parked across the street. "Do you know who owns that car?"

Doc Seth peered at the car as he pulled into his parking spot. "I don't know anyone around here with a blue car; it must be a rental."

Riley quickly glimpsed the license plate as the car pulled away. "I couldn't get the number, but I think it was an Ohio plate."

"Definitely a rental. I occasionally see cars rented at the airport, which almost always have out-of-state plates. Is everything okay?"

"It just caught my eye because it seemed out of place."

Doc Seth narrowed his eyes. "Like that blue car that went past Bud's place? You have good instincts: trust them and call me anytime."

Riley glanced at Doc Seth. *He knew I was lying, but he still offered his support.*

Doc Seth walked with Riley and Toby to her car. "I have a little paperwork to sign. I'll be about thirty minutes behind you."

He remained outside while she pulled away from the curb. She watched him in her rearview mirror as he headed into the clinic.

"This Carter family is really protective, aren't they? I know Doc Seth won't say anything to Ben, though, because Doc knows we couldn't stop Ben from coming here if Ben thought anything was wrong."

Toby yipped.

"Thanks. I've got my fingers crossed for the house Mugsy told us about, too."

Before Riley was a block away from the clinic, her phone rang. *Mugsy.* Riley smiled as she answered.

"Where are you, Short-stuff?"

"I'm still in town; I was on my way home."

"Good; since you're in town, call Melissa, tell her you'll be a few minutes late, and come by my shop."

"I'm half a block away; I'll be right there."

When Riley and Toby went into the Big Mug Coffee Shop, Mugsy was waiting for them near the door, and Cookie trotted to the front of the shop to greet them.

"I didn't see any reason for you to sit in your car half a block from me and talk to me on the phone when I could see your short self right here," Mugsy grinned as she waved at the tables. "Grab a seat; I have great news."

Riley hurried to the nearest table and sat on the one rickety chair in the shop.

Mugsy joined her at the table. "Why don't you move to a chair that isn't about to fall apart? I should have taken that chair to the dump ages ago."

"I'll be fine; talk," Riley growled.

Mugsy snorted. "Is that an example of your remarkable interrogation technique? The best news is that I can pick up Ryan from the hospital in two days. He told me he's been so pesky that the nurses have asked for permission to kick him out; isn't that awesome? I got a call back from the owner of the house that's close to the training center. He said you can rent it from him with one caveat. He ran out of money and hasn't been able to finish the updates for one of the upstairs bedrooms. If that's not a problem for you, you can look at the house and move in this weekend, if you like. If you can get the afternoon off tomorrow, you and I could go look at it, and you can decide. As far as the price is concerned, he's quoting a price that is well below the going rate for rentals of small apartments. The house has new appliances, but it's unfurnished. What do you think?"

Riley whooped, leapt out of her chair, and danced. Toby howled while Cookie danced with Riley, and Mugsy laughed as she applauded.

"Thought you'd be pleased, Short-stuff," Mugsy said as Riley hugged her.

"Very much so; I'll tell you when I can leave." Riley grinned. "Come on, Toby. We need to tell Mom and Dad."

"Are you going to wait until you're sure to tell Ben?" Mugsy asked as Riley hurried to the door.

"I don't know, but probably not."

After Toby hopped into the car, Riley headed to the Carters'. "I'm almost too excited to drive," she said.

When she caught up to a slow-moving gravel truck, she peered around it at the road ahead. "There's no good place to pass; I might as well slow down so flying gravel won't hit my windshield."

Another large truck came up behind Riley, stayed close, and finally backed off. "Sorry, buster. Both of us have been stuck here for a while, haven't we?"

The truck in front of her slowed even more as it continued up a hill, then it moved slightly to the left.

"There must be someone on the shoulder." Riley shifted left, too.

When they neared the crest of the hill, Riley saw the blue car on the shoulder with a man peering under the raised hood. As she approached the car, a rock from the truck in front of her flew at her, and she instinctively swerved to the left to avoid the rock hitting the windshield directly in front of her. The rock cracked her windshield in the middle, and then the sound of a second thwack startled her, and she saw the hole slightly above the crack. She crested the hill and exhaled as she left more room between her car and the gravel truck.

"At least we didn't catch that second rock after we had replaced the windshield from the first one."

Toby growled.

"What do you mean, not a rock? I'll check when we get home."

Riley exhaled when the gravel truck turned right at the next intersection after the hill. The truck behind her finally had a clear road ahead and passed her.

When they arrived home, she parked near the barn, and Jake frowned at her windshield. "What happened to your car?"

"Gravel truck. I left plenty of room between us until we came to a hill, and it suddenly slowed to a crawl."

"Sure got you good, didn't it?"

"No kidding. Doc Seth will be here in a few minutes," she said as they strolled to the house. "Mugsy called me, and I dropped by the coffee shop, which didn't take much time, but following the gravel truck for what seemed like miles really slowed me down."

"We'll take care of it in the morning. I'll follow you to work, then take your car to the shop so they can replace your windshield. It'll be ready in less than thirty minutes."

Riley stared at the back porch. "What's that?"

Jake chuckled. "It's a gift from Melissa for you and me: a boot scraper. Scrape off the bottom of your boots before you take them off. There's another surprise inside the house."

Riley scraped and removed her boots, then stepped inside. While Toby sniffed the large rubber tray on the floor, Riley asked, "What's that?"

"It's a boot tray for outside boots, so our boots won't be cold or have any critters inside of them when we're ready to put them on," Jake said.

Melissa asked, "What do you think?"

"This is wonderful." Riley set down her boots. "I worried about my boots getting cold but didn't think about critters."

"Run and change, then tell us the rest of your news," Melissa said.

Riley raised her eyebrows, and Melissa said, "Don't give me that look, Riley Erin. You always have news."

Riley smiled, dashed upstairs to change into a clean shirt and pair of jeans, and returned. "Doc Seth will be here in a few minutes, and Mugsy called me before I left town, so I stopped to see her. Ryan will be home in two days; she'll pick him up and take care of him at her house. The house near the training center is ours. If Doc Seth can spare me tomorrow afternoon, Mugsy and I will look at it to be sure it's safe and relatively clean, and then we can move in this Saturday."

"That's wonderful news. Is it furnished?" Melissa asked.

"No, but all the appliances are new, and we have our bed."

"We have spare furniture; Jake and I can load up his truck and help you move on Saturday," Melissa said.

Jake nodded, and Melissa turned back to the stove to stir the gravy.

"You don't have to do that," Riley said as she set the table.

"Yes, she does." Jake drained the potatoes and then added butter before he mashed them. "We want to see your house. Does Seth know you're moving this weekend?"

"Not yet; I wanted to tell him in person since he's going to be here soon."

Toby yipped as a truck rolled down the driveway.

Before Seth could knock, Jake opened the door, and the dogs scrambled outside.

"How do you like our early warning system?" Jake chuckled. "Come on in. The table is set, and Melissa will have the food on the table by the time we have our drinks. Iced tea for you?"

"Always," Seth said. "What happened to your car, Riley?"

Riley told him about the slow-moving gravel truck and the two rocks.

Seth narrowed his eyes. "Gravel truck? Did you see her windshield, Jake?"

Jake nodded. "She'll drive it into town tomorrow, and I'll follow her, then take it to the shop when they open."

Seth grunted. "Guess I better wash my hands."

While they ate, Riley glanced at Doc Seth. *Did he see something Dad and I didn't notice?*

"Doc, Mugsy found a house near the training center that Ben and I can afford," Riley said.

"That is the best news I've heard in ages, even though I hate to lose you. When are you moving?"

"If it's okay, I'd like to take tomorrow afternoon off. Mugsy will get the key, and she and I can inspect the house to see if it's habitable and safe. If the house is acceptable, Ben and I can move on Saturday. I plan to work on Thursday and Friday; otherwise, I'd go crazy waiting."

Doc Seth chuckled. "Whatever works best for you is fine with me." His eyes twinkled. "Does this mean you'll be late for work next Monday?"

Riley stared at him and then giggled. "I almost forgot what big teases are in this family."

"He definitely got you, honey, and me too, because I was about to snatch his plate away from him." Melissa raised an eyebrow at Seth.

"Glad we cleared that one up." Seth shuddered as Jake laughed.

"Tell Seth what you know about the house," Melissa said.

Riley told him about the appliances and the one bedroom upstairs that hadn't been updated.

"I admire the owner for postponing the work until he has the money to support it," Jake said. "Seth, Melissa and I are taking some furniture on Saturday, so Ben and Riley will have somewhere to sit in the evenings, and a kitchen table, and a couple of chairs, so they won't have to eat standing up. I'll let Bud know I'll pick up a horse on Monday."

"Melissa, you'll give me a full report, won't you?"

"Of course; do you have plans for dinner on Sunday?" She smiled.

"It wouldn't matter; I'd cancel them for dinner here."

After they had dessert, Jake asked, "Seth, are you ready to see what we have in mind for the stall?"

"Whenever you are."

"You two go on out to the barn. Riley and I will clear the table and take care of the dishes."

After the two men left, Melissa asked, "When will you tell Ben?"

Riley cleared the table. "I'm in a quandary. If I tell him now, will he be too excited to study, but if I tell him later, will he be hurt because I didn't tell him right away?"

"You're right about both." Melissa loaded the dishwasher and exhaled.

"I think I'd rather have him excited than hurt," Riley said, and Melissa nodded.

Riley texted Ben. "Call when you have a few minutes to talk. There's no rush."

Riley paced as she waited for Ben to call.

"If I bring you a cup of hot tea, if you sit'll in the living room. You're making me nervous." Melissa turned on the burner under the tea kettle.

"I'm making me nervous, too," Riley mumbled as she went to the living room.

When Melissa came into the living room with two cups, Riley's phone rang. Melissa set one cup of tea on the table and then left while Riley answered the phone.

"Thanks for telling me it wasn't a rush. I was on my way back from dinner and didn't knock anybody down to get to my room," Ben said. "What's up?"

"Mugsy found a house near the training center for us. She and I are going to look at it tomorrow; if it's okay, we can move on Saturday."

"Seriously? Saturday? You'll text me right after you've looked at it, won't you? What's the address?"

Riley told him the address, and he said, "Give me a second. I want to see if I can find a street view."

I wished I'd thought of that.

"It's creepy on the outside, babe, but as long as it's clean and safe, we don't care, right?"

"That's exactly what I told Mugsy: clean and safe. I'll text you more details after I see it."

"Of course, if it's not okay, we could rent it anyway and live in a camper trailer in the front yard," Ben said.

Riley snickered. "I like how you think, Sexy Cowboy. We'll make this work one way or another. How was today?"

"Rough until now. Classes are fine, and the homework is easy, but I miss you."

Jake, Seth, Toby, Duffy, and Finn came inside, and Riley said, "Doc Seth and Dad have been out at the barn discussing the stall and just came in. Call me back at bedtime, so I can tell you good night. I love you more."

"Will do, babe. I loved you first." Ben chuckled.

Riley giggled as they hung up. *I beat him to it, but I think he won.*

"Minor tweaks," Seth said when Riley came into the kitchen.

"Seth suggested a few things that will strengthen the stall and shorten my construction time," Jake said.

"It's time for me to go home. Our first appointment's at eight thirty, Riley, then we'll return to check on your car between eleven and eleven thirty. If your car isn't ready, someone from the shop will be there until you can pick it up later in the afternoon. They've always been good about that."

After Seth left, Riley said, "I need to check my emails. I've been carrying around my laptop while I've been at work but haven't checked my email."

Riley sat at the kitchen table with her laptop and tepid tea, reading a long, newsy email from Claire.

"How's everything in Barton?" Melissa asked.

"Everyone's fine, and there's no drama, which Claire says is terrible because it's boring. Charlie is training Claire to take over the finances for the clinic, and Zach's cousin Amanda is working at the desk in the mornings. Doc Julie Rae is looking for another vet tech so Pia can go to three-quarter time and spend more time with Jackson in the afternoon. Claire thinks Zach and Kayla are getting serious, but Doc Julie Rae won't let her start a pool."

After Riley responded with a long email to Claire, she checked the rest of her mail.

"Mom, I have an email from Uncle Grayson's staff."

"Really, what does it say?"

"It starts off, 'Dear Mrs. Carter,' do you suppose this is for you?"

Melissa laughed. "I'm sure it is, so I get to hear every word."

Riley's eyes widened as she read, and then she turned her laptop toward Melissa.

Melissa read and then pointed to a section of the email. "Riley, this is wonderful news, but what a surprise. Grayson's staff calls one annuity 'a sizeable sum' to allow you and your husband a 'comfortable lifestyle'. Did you know your aunt was sending money for you to the bank account that you and your grandmother shared, and the bank has been acting as the trustee? The bank seems to have managed your money wisely. The funds have been invested in stocks, bonds, and annuities. I wonder if your dad gave them instructions for the portfolio. If I'm reading this correctly, your dad sent money to your account twice a month, then when he died, your aunt continued the regular deposits."

"Not at all. Grandma told me to contact the bank, but I certainly didn't expect more than a modest savings."

Melissa peered at Riley. "Will this mean any changes for you and Ben?"

"I can't imagine what." Riley shrugged. "If the house works out, we'll have everything we want."

"The good news is that we don't have to worry about them being frivolous with Riley's money," Jake said.

"Are you going to be able to sleep tonight?" Melissa asked.

"I don't see why not. It's been a full day." Riley yawned.

"Is Ben going to call you before bed?" Melissa asked.

Riley nodded.

Melissa smiled. "Take a book upstairs with you, honey; he might get caught up in his studies and lose track of time."

Riley pulled out a book from the bookcase and moaned. "He knows what time I go to bed, but he does get heads-down when he's focused."

She trudged up the stairs. *It's been a long day.*

Riley quickly dressed for bed, plugged in her phone next to the bed, and turned off her overhead light.

After ten pages, she jerked her head at the sound of the book when it thudded on the floor. *I'm officially tired.*

Her phone rang, and she cleared her throat so she could sound perky. *Wonder what perky sounds like?* She giggled and answered.

"I'm so sorry I'm calling so late, babe. I've been researching the explosion that killed your dad. The official findings reported that it was an industrial accident in a high-risk industry, and the case was closed. One of the senior investigators didn't agree, and I found his notes. Your dad's company did research and development for nonnuclear weapons, and your dad was the senior engineer who led a project that wasn't defined in the report details I read. The investigator discovered that the company's officers had all disappeared a week before the explosion, and plant operations had been shut down the day before the explosion. The investigator didn't mention your dad by name, but the report said the evidence suggested that engineers were in the building, and the investigators proposed that the engineers may have been gathering some final documents to expose irregularities in the inventory of casings, explosives, and other key components in the manufacture of nonnuclear bombs. The report implied there was more detail to support the theory about inventory shortages, but that's all I had access to. I'm going to talk to one of my instructors tomorrow to see where I could find more detail or whether I have gone as deep as I can, given my trainee status. I also want to know whether I can share what I found with Sheriff Dunn."

Riley exhaled. "I always knew the explosion wasn't an accident. I knew Dad was a senior engineer and led a team at a research facility. I didn't know exactly what he did, and I don't think Grandma did either."

"You were a kid, babe."

"You're right; someone told me Dad's death was a terrible accident, and that was supposed to comfort me, I guess, but I knew it wasn't and wouldn't talk about it after that."

"Researching the report about the explosion gave me something to do because I've had trouble getting interested in my classes until you called me about the house, and that gave me the motivation to knuckle down and catch up on all my homework tonight. Were you asleep? How are you doing?"

"I'm tired and have been dozing off and on, but I'm glad you called. I knew hearing about the house would help you; I can't wait to see you Friday night and move into our house on Saturday."

"I have big plans to get ahead on my homework tomorrow to make the day go faster. Good night, my sweet wife. I loved you first."

Riley giggled. "Good night, my wonderful husband. I love you more."

After they hung up, Riley stared at her phone. *I forgot to tell him about the bank account.* She yawned and then turned off her bedside light as she closed her eyes. *I'll tell him tomorrow.*

While Riley was in the shower the next morning, her phone buzzed a text. She dripped on the floor as she stepped out of the shower and peered at the text from Ben. "Where are you?"

Riley smirked. *He knows my schedule; he knows exactly where I am.*

She called him. "I'm sunbathing with nothing on except the cucumber slices over my eyes."

When she heard him spew, she stifled a giggle. "Was that your coffee?"

"No," he growled, "it was my last beer."

She laughed, and he chuckled.

"You have officially been hanging around my family far too long. See you in two days, Fiery Sun Babe."

"Love your swagger, Cowboy."

After they hung up, Riley quickly finished her shower, dressed, and hurried downstairs.

"Your coffee is on the table," Melissa said. "It doesn't make time go any faster if you run."

"It might; I've never tried it before." Riley sipped her coffee.

"Our menu this morning is cinnamon rolls and eggs cooked to order," Melissa said.

"Scrambled for me," Riley said.

"I'll give your egg I just fried to the dogs."

"That was a trap," Riley said.

"Sure was," Jake said. "Doesn't matter what you said; she'd have been contrary. She gets like that sometimes, don't you, honey?"

"Never," Melissa growled as she fried eggs and then slammed three plates on the table. "I don't want Riley to leave, but I can't wait until she and Ben are together again because that's where they belong."

Riley sniffed to hide her snicker when Jake winked.

"What time are we leaving, Riley?" Jake refilled their cups.

A bit clunky with the change of subject, but it's early. Riley sipped her coffee before she answered.

Chapter Twenty-Two

"I'd like to be at the clinic at seven thirty but no later than seven forty-five. Doc Seth said our first appointment was at eight thirty, but he likes to arrive early so he can assess the setting before he steps into anything." Riley said. "Doc told me there have been several occasions when he backed out then called and told them he had a sudden emergency because he felt like something wasn't right."

Jake nodded. "I've always admired his radar for trouble. He kept us out of some bad situations when we were kids. When he said leave, I never hesitated."

"That's amazing; I thought it was just you. It must be a family trait." Melissa set the pan of cinnamon rolls on the table and then served Riley and Jake their fried eggs.

"I've always thought everyone else was just like me." Jake shrugged and put two large cinnamon rolls on his plate.

"They aren't," Melissa said.

"I don't think I'll take my laptop; it's too cumbersome to carry around." Riley polished off the rest of her cinnamon roll.

Jake frowned, and Melissa said, "It won't hurt if you take it along; it won't be in the way, and you'll be glad you have it if you need it."

Jake peered at Melissa, and she smiled. "I've learned to interpret."

"Dad?" Riley asked.

Jake shrugged. "Just a feeling."

"I made lunch for you and Mugsy; she won't be surprised. You'll have to pick up drinks somewhere." Melissa helped herself to a cinnamon roll. "Your sandwiches and dessert are in the insulated bag on the counter. I added an ice pack to keep everything cold."

"Thank you, Mom." Riley put her laptop inside her backpack, grabbed her sweatshirt, and put the lunch bag in before she changed into her work boots and headed out the door. Toby trotted alongside her as she hurried to her car with Jake behind her.

"I didn't think Toby would want to go," Jake said.

"He wants to see the house and check out the yard," Riley said.

Jake nodded. "Lead the way. I'll follow you. Duffy and Finn, you're going to stay."

The puppies bounded to the back door and whined, and Melissa let them in.

When Riley, Toby, and Jake arrived at the clinic at seven thirty, Jake asked, "Did you have any trouble seeing?"

"Straight ahead was fine, but when I glanced to the left, I thought I had faulty vision. The cracks grew overnight."

"I'm going to see who is at the truck stop; I haven't been there in ages. I'll come back around nine and take your car to the repair shop. Enjoy your morning."

Jake made a U-turn in the middle of the road and waved as he called out, "Don't tell my son, the cop."

He accelerated as he headed to the truck stop to meet up with old friends.

When Riley heard a vehicle headed her way, she said, "Toby, that's a car, not a truck. Let's find a spot that is less conspicuous."

Toby followed her to the small alcove at the back entrance to the clinic, where they stood in the shadows. Riley narrowed her eyes as a blue car stopped by her car for a few minutes before continuing toward downtown.

Her phone rang and startled her. She frowned as she peered at the display. *Why is Zach calling me?*

When she answered, Zach asked, "Am I calling too early?"

"Not at all. I'm waiting for Doc Seth to pick me up for our morning farm visits."

"Good. My mom visited Linh Johnson and took the two pictures I gave her of the phony Brian and Lynn Johnson. Mom called me last night, but Kayla and I decided it was too late to call you. Riley, Linh Johnson said the phony Brian Johnson was Ron Echols. Mrs. Johnson's husband, Brian, died in the explosion that killed your dad. Mrs. Johnson is still mourning him."

"What? The Brian Johnson I met is actually Ron Echols?"

"Yes. The real Brian Johnson took papers home from work in his briefcase two days before the explosion and then mailed them to Linh the day before he died. Linh gave the papers to Mom, and Mom is going to give them to us."

"I don't understand why Ron Echols would pose as Brian Johnson or make an appearance in Barton."

"I don't know either, but I think the answer is in the real Brian Johnson's papers. I'll scan the documents and then send them to you. I'm going to see the sheriff later this afternoon, and I'll tell him what I know and give him the papers. The only caveat is that Mrs. Johnson insisted that I don't tell anyone except you, who gave them to me. Kayla and I decided 'the extended family' would be vague enough and plenty of information as far as the sheriff's concerned. Kayla is off today, so she'll pick them up at Mom's.

Mom loves Kayla and told me I should marry her because she's smarter than a doctor."

Riley chuckled. "Your mom has a keen eye and great taste. I agree with her."

"Don't tell anybody, but I do too. We'll let you know when it's official. There's more. Linh Johnson also recognized the phony Lynn Johnson. The phony was Ron Echols' girlfriend before he married Vivian; her name is Rosalind Irwin, and Linh was certain their relationship continued after the marriage."

Irwin? Was Rosalind Vivian's sister? I'll have to look at the genealogy records again.

"What a jerk," Riley said. "All this definitely explains why the two glib phonies sounded so believable when they were in Barton."

"According to Mom, the real Mrs. Johnson had some colorful words for Ron Nichols and his girlfriend, but they weren't in English, and Mom refused to tell me because she said I didn't need any of those words in my vocabulary, and if they were, she didn't want to know."

Riley snickered. "Thanks, Zach. I wouldn't think I could interpret an engineer's files, but I'll definitely look."

"You might understand them. Mom told Linh Johnson that I was close friends with Frank Malloy's daughter. This is a direct quote: 'Erin's daughter will know what is here.'"

"She knew my mama?" A tear slipped down Riley's face.

"I think so, but she told Mom she never wanted to talk about those times again because the memories haunted her night and day. I'll talk to you later, Riley. I'll send the files as soon as I get them."

"Thanks, Zach," Riley said as he hung up.

When Doc Seth pulled into his parking spot, the blue car sped past the clinic and toward the interstate.

Riley scratched Toby's ear when he leaned against her. "I have no idea who that is or what's going on, but I don't like it."

Toby growled in agreement.

Riley strolled to Doc Seth's truck. She handed him the lunch sack, and he added it to his cooler.

"Are you two ready? We've got three routine visits this morning, and I have two this afternoon. I shifted one from the afternoon to the morning to soak up as much Riley time as possible."

"I'm sorry I'm leaving you like this," Riley said.

"Don't be; you'll still be in the family, and I'll bet you won't mind going on a routine call, which I shall declare an emergency, to get away from the circus called 'family time.' I know Ben will be happy to go with us."

Riley smiled. "I hadn't thought about that. Is there any way you could wrangle an invitation to Mom's family gatherings?"

"That's exactly the family I was talking about. Jake worked that out ages ago so we could get out before the fights erupted."

I hope he doesn't mean 'fights' literally.

"How's Ben?" Doc Seth asked.

"He's been struggling to focus on his studies, but he's managed to push himself to complete all his assignments."

"Ben's a good man, Riley; he has been crazy about you since the first day he met you, but I'm sure you knew that."

"Do you think we'll ever settle down from being so protective of each other?"

"Look at Melissa and Jake: there's your answer."

Riley smiled. *Mom and Dad tease each other constantly, but they are close.*

On their way back to the clinic after their third visit, Riley asked, "What time do we start tomorrow?"

"I have an eight o'clock appointment, but I'm sure you have a lot to do for your move on Saturday. You don't have to go with me."

"Oh yes, I do. There's nothing I can do until Ben arrives Friday night. We unpacked our clothes and toothbrushes but nothing else, and I could repack them in half an hour. It's up to you, but I'd drive Mom crazy by moping around the house all day, and she'd call you to come take me off her hands."

Doc Seth chuckled. "It makes no sense for me to get on the wrong side of Melissa if I can help it; we'll leave around seven."

Riley texted Mugsy. "Will be at the clinic in ten minutes."

Mugsy replied, "I'll be waiting."

"Mugsy will be waiting for us at the clinic," Riley said.

"I take it Toby's going too," Doc said.

Toby yipped.

Doc Seth nodded. "It's important to check the yard. Is it fenced, Riley?"

"We think so, but if it isn't, Toby will keep Duffy and Finn close when they visit. I'd invite Princess to visit or even stay with us, but she'd never leave Dad's barn because it's her barn." When Doc Seth pulled into the clinic parking lot, Mugsy stepped out of her car and waved.

After Riley and Toby climbed into her car, Mugsy said, "I brought drinks; I know a park with a picnic area halfway there that we can stop for our lunch break and stretch our legs."

"Sounds perfect. Where do we go to pick up the key to the house?"

"The owner told me he'd meet us there if I text him when we're thirty minutes away. My friend told me he was a good man; I'm looking forward to meeting him. How was your morning?"

Riley told her about the routine visits.

"Will you miss the farm visits? Are you going to find another vet tech position?"

"I'm not quite sure what I'll do. Doc Julie Rae spoiled clinics for me because she has assembled such a talented team, and I'll never find another clinic like hers. Doc Seth has spoiled farm visits for me because he is so brilliant, and I'll never find another veterinarian who is as talented and suited for farm visits as he is. I've always been in school or worked, so I can't imagine being satisfied to stay home all day."

Mugsy nodded. "You can't get chickens or goats because you don't know where you'll be in four months."

Riley nodded. "Maybe eventually, but now's not the right time."

When Mugsy pulled in at the picnic area, she said, "This is nicer than I remembered. The playground and restrooms are new."

While Toby relaxed in the shade, they ate their sandwiches, and then Riley pulled out their cookies. "Mom packed four."

While they ate their cookies, Riley said, "One of the vet techs from Barton sent me an email this morning after I left Mom and Dad's. Do you mind if I take a minute and read it?"

"Go ahead; I wouldn't mind a stroll."

Riley pulled out her laptop, opened Zach's email, and downloaded the documents. The first document was a copy of the company letterhead. *Bingo.* Riley smiled as she read the header. *The company's officers where Dad worked were Ron Echols, Virginia Echols, and Rosalind Irwin.*

A tear slipped onto her keyboard when she read an email string between Frank and Millie. The final words of the last email from her dad to Millie said, "Remind her to Keep Dancing." *Dad put the pieces together and wanted Millie to warn me.*

Riley closed her laptop as Mugsy returned.

"Are you okay?" Mugsy asked.

Riley nodded, and they strolled to Mugsy's car and left the picnic area.

On their way to the house, Mugsy handed her phone to Riley. "The owner is my most recent text. Send him our thirty minutes out warning."

Riley sent the text.

"What's your move-in plan?" Mugsy asked.

"Ben comes home Friday night. We'll pack, and then on Saturday morning, we'll load my car and his truck. Dad and Mom are going with us, so we'll load Dad's truck with spare furniture from Mom."

"You're lucky you're limited to Jake's truck for furniture. Melissa could probably furnish the entire house if she had the room to transport everything."

"I think you're right. All of us are excited about the house."

"Are you going to have a big open house?" Mugsy asked.

Riley's eyes were wide as she stared at her.

Mugsy chuckled. "I lost my mind for a minute there and forgot who I was talking to. Let me rephrase that. I'd like to tag along the next time Melissa and Jake visit."

Riley exhaled. "I'd like that."

When Mugsy turned at the driveway to the house, Riley smiled. "I'm glad this isn't one of those houses with the professionally landscaped yards. We couldn't keep it up; Ben would be too busy, and I'd be too incompetent."

"It's definitely in its natural state for animal habitat, isn't it?"

When Mugsy parked, she nodded at the middle-aged, slight man who stood on the porch. "There he is."

Riley examined the house. "Ben checked its street view on the internet and called it creepy on the outside. He got that right. Depending on the inside, I love it."

Toby trotted to the porch, and the man spoke quietly to him and then rubbed his ears. When they reached the porch, the man stuck out his hand. "Ralph."

"Mugsy." She shook his hand and then continued, "This is Riley Carter. Her husband is attending the GBI training."

Riley and Ralph shook hands.

"I brought you two keys, Mrs. Carter. The keys unlock all the exterior doors. The front door is unlocked. Take your time, look around, and then let me know your thoughts. I'll wait out here, but if you have any questions, holler. All the appliances are new, and the electrical system and plumbing have been upgraded. The water comes from a well, and it was inspected two weeks ago. There's no internet service worth paying for out here, but the cell phone coverage is excellent."

When they stepped inside, Riley stared at the gleaming wooden floors, fireplace, and high ceilings. "It's spacious and clean."

"Let's find the kitchen," Mugsy said.

After they entered the kitchen, Riley said, "I like it: a large, eat-in kitchen."

"How do you feel about a gas stove?"

"It's what I learned to cook on; Grandma had a gas stove at the cabin." Riley opened a door and peered inside. "This is a large pantry."

"I found the utility room and the new washer and dryer. Looks like you're set so far."

As they strolled down the hall to the main floor bedroom, Mugsy stopped and inspected the bathroom. "It's clean and has a tub with a shower."

"This must be the only bedroom on the main floor," Riley said. "It's clean and big enough for the two of us. The bathroom has a separate shower and tub but isn't huge, which is a bonus as far as I'm concerned."

"Big closet," Mugsy said. "What do you think?"

"I think it's great, let's find Toby."

"Let's check upstairs first."

The boards on the stairs creaked as they went upstairs. "Nobody can sneak up or downstairs here," Riley chuckled.

"This must be the one bedroom that's not finished," Mugsy said.

Riley peered into the room. "If the whole house looked like this, it would still be acceptable."

When they joined Ralph on the porch, he asked, "Did I tell you there's no cable out here? The air handler is in the attic and easy to get to, but I'll change the filter. The only bill you have is for electricity. You can go to the power company next week and transfer the bill to your name. If you want the house, I have a rental agreement for you to read and sign, so you'll have something to show to the electrical folks."

He handed a copy of the rental agreement to Riley.

"I love the house." After she read it, she signed it and the second copy.

"Do you want a check for the first and last months' rent or for the four months we'll be here? What about a security deposit?" she asked.

"Check for the first and last months' rent is perfect. I hadn't thought about a security deposit. Give me a second check for whatever you think, but don't tell my accountant. She'll refuse to give me any dessert tonight." He chuckled.

Mugsy smiled. "I like her style."

Riley gave him the two checks, and he stuck them in his shirt pocket before giving her the keys.

After he left, Toby rounded the corner and yipped.

Riley giggled. "Glad you liked it."

"Anything else you want to do while we're here?" Mugsy asked.

"Other than sneak up and see Ben at the training center? I guess not."

As they headed home, Mugsy said, "It was a shame that we couldn't just drop in on old Ben."

"I'll pretend I didn't know how close he was. I should send him a text to tell him that we have a place to live."

After she sent the text, Riley gazed out her window and occasionally glanced in the side mirror to see if the blue car followed them.

When they neared the picnic area, Mugsy pulled in and parked. "I don't understand how Ben can make that drive straight through without stopping for a stretch break."

While Toby romped, Riley watched the road and the parking lot for the blue car.

When her phone rang, she answered.

"Where are you, Riley?" Doc Seth asked.

"We're taking a break at a picnic area halfway between the training center and Carson. Why?"

"I got a call from the auto repair. They replaced your windshield, but that larger hole wasn't from a rock; it was a bullet hole, and they found the bullet embedded inside your car above the backseat window and close to the back window. They called the sheriff, and he'll be at my brother's place this evening to talk to you about where that happened and what you remember."

Riley frowned. "Really?"

"Afraid so; they'll drop off your car at my clinic for you in the next half hour and leave the keys with the receptionist in the clinic. Let me know if you need me."

"Thanks."

After Doc hung up, Mugsy asked, "Anything wrong?"

"Doc was letting me know my windshield was finally replaced and will be waiting for me at the clinic. My keys will be with the receptionist. He was disturbed because the second hole was a bullet hole. The sheriff wants to talk to me about where it happened. I think he might be worried that there's a careless hunter in the area."

"That's scary," Mugsy said. "I don't know any hunters who would shoot near a road, so it's either someone who is ignorant of gun safety or malicious."

Mugsy stopped in the street next to Riley's car. "I'm happy about your new house. Let me know what else I can do."

"Thanks for everything, Mugsy; the house is perfect, isn't it?"

Riley and Toby hurried into the clinic. The receptionist gave Riley her key. Toby visited with the receptionist, who giggled when he nuzzled her elbow and then gave him a treat.

The receptionist grinned as she gave Toby two more treats. "I'm a pushover for cute guys. Come back and see me anytime, big boy."

Riley snorted as Toby grinned, and the receptionist gave Toby another treat. "Your smile is so cute," the receptionist said in baby talk.

When they were outside, Riley said, "You are such a con artist."

Toby wagged his tail, and she giggled.

Riley slowed her pace when she saw the blue car in front of hers, and Toby stepped close to her and softly growled.

"Thanks for the warning; I'll keep my hand near my pistol."

When she approached her car door, a man got out of the driver's seat.

Ron Echols.

"I thought that was your car but certainly didn't expect to run into you in Carson. How have you been, Riley?"

I'll play.

Riley smiled. "Doing fine. What are you doing here?"

"Just a little wrap-up to my business."

When Echols stretched and casually moved his hand toward his right hip, Toby growled; Echols froze.

"What kind of business is that? I'd really like to know," Riley said.

"Is your dog dangerous?"

"Toby? Not often, Ron."

Ron Echols' face darkened. "How did you know? Did Mildred tell you? I thought your mother and your aunt were good friends, but evidently, your mother got greedy and got rid of your aunt before I could. As soon as Mildred was eliminated from the picture, your mother's usefulness to me was over. I guess that makes you an orphan now."

Ron's twitch of a smile gave his face the appearance of a leering cobra.

"You killed Vivian because she killed my aunt before you could?" Riley snorted. "You need to come up with a better story than that."

"Oh, I can. With Vivian out of the way, guess who the last person left is. Go ahead. Guess."

He slapped his hand on the butt of his gun and then ripped the gun from its holster, but Riley was ready and a split second faster. The two shots were almost simultaneous, and he dropped to the ground as the hole in the middle of his forehead grew red.

Riley quickly examined Toby and then hugged him. "Good. He didn't shoot you."

Toby whined, and Riley glanced at her left arm. Her vet tech jacket had a tear at her upper arm, and blood oozed onto her jacket. "Well dang, Ron. You got me."

She reholstered her gun and then held onto her left arm with her right hand for a minute. She released the pressure and examined the wound. *Good; it stopped bleeding; it's just a graze.*

She turned at the sound of the shriek of tires coming around the corner behind her.

Mugsy leaped out of her car. "I knew it was you when I heard the shots. I've already called the sheriff, the ambulance, the cavalry, and the national guard."

"It's just a graze. Do you have a bandage I could borrow?" Riley sighed. "Guess I better call Ben."

"Jake will take care of that. He and Melissa are the national guard I called."

When the sirens neared, Riley asked, "Who's the cavalry?"

Riley heard the familiar sound of Doc Seth's truck as it roared toward the clinic; she smiled. *Of course.*

Her phone rang. When she answered, Ben growled, "You better be okay. Who did you shoot?"

"I'm okay. Ron Echols, but he started it."

Ben's voice became louder. "I have two more days of homework, then you'll be twenty minutes from me. Where's Vivian?"

"Ron Echols told me he killed her, so I think that's it."

Ben's voice reached full volume, and Riley moved her phone away from her ear. "It better be, or I'm playing my husband card and telling Dad to bring you here. You can hang out in the library during the day and sleep in my room with me at night. Every man on my entire floor has agreed you're invisible. Note that I did not say invincible."

Two cruisers screeched to a stop. Doc Seth and Jake stopped their trucks in the street in front of Ron Echols' car, and Mugsy took Riley's arm and led her to the sidewalk. As the sound of a siren neared, all the occupants of the newly arrived vehicles jumped out and ran to Riley.

"Excuse me, Ben, but I have five irate people running toward me, so I guess I'd better go. I love you more, Angry Cowboy."

Ben's voice softened. "I loved you first, Gunslinger. Two days, babe. No bad guys for two days." Ben hung up.

"He's not leaving his training; that's good," Riley said, and Mugsy nodded.

"Does anybody have a bandage?" Riley asked as the group neared her.

What to read next?

DEADLY EQUITY, Book 5

Only Riley can stop the mastermind who murders farmers for their land; killer's plan: Riley dies.

Riley joins a rural veterinarian who visits farms to provide veterinary care for animals. Her dream job! Her dream turns into a nightmare when friends are left for dead. Riley's on the killer's list: next to die.

Find DEADLY EQUITY at Barrett Book Shop

BarrettBookShop.com

An independent online Book Shop owned by the author, Judith A. Barrett

Did you enjoy Riley and Toby's latest adventures?

Leave a review or a rating (ratings matter; reviews matter and are helpful) with Barrett Book Shop or your favorite book retailer.

A five-star rating means you're ready to read the next Riley book!

You keep reading; I'll keep writing!

More About the Author

SUBSCRIBE TO JUDITH A. BARRETT NEWSLETTER via the website

   judithabarrett.com/newsletter

www.ingramcontent.com/pod-product-compliance
Lightning Source LLC
Chambersburg PA
CBHW020840020726
47497CB00005B/1180